Norah

The Making of an Irish-American Woman
in 19th-Century New York

Cynthia G. Neale

Kestrel -
Hope dances!
Cynthia
6-19-11

Lucky
PRESS

Athens, Ohio

Norah

Lucky Press, LLC
PO Box 754, Athens, OH 45701-0754
Purchase order fax: 614-413-2820
Email: sales@luckypress.com   SAN: 850-9697
Visit the publisher's website at www.LuckyPress.com

First Edition
ISBN: 978-0-9846317-0-4   ISBN-10: 0-9846317-0-4 (hardcover)
ISBN: 978-0-9846317-1-1   ISBN-10: 0-9846317-1-2 (softcover)
Library of Congress Control Number: 2011921449

PRINTED IN THE UNITED STATES OF AMERICA

Cataloguing in Publication Data

Neale, Cynthia G., 1954-

Norah : the making of an Irish-American woman in 19th-century New York /
Cynthia G. Neale. -- 1st ed. -- Athens, Ohio : Lucky Press, c2011.

p. ; cm.

ISBN: 978-0-9846317-0-4 (cloth) ; 978-0-9846317-1-1 (pbk.)

1. Irish Americans--New York (State)--New York--Fiction.
2. Immigrants--New York (State)--New York--Fiction. 3. Journalists--
New York (State)--New York--Fiction. 4. New York (N.Y.)--History--
1775–1865--Fiction. 5. Five Points (New York, N.Y.)--History--1775–1865--
Fiction. 6. Ireland--History--Famine, 1845–1852--Fiction. 7. Ireland--
Politics and government--1837–1901--Fiction. 8. Return migration--
Ireland-- 1837–1901--Fiction. 9. Historical fiction. I. Title.

PS3614.E238 N67 2011   2011921449
[Fic]--dc22   1103

For Tim and Hannah, who welcomed
Norah into our home many years ago

Also by Cynthia G. Neale

The Irish Dresser
A Story of Hope during The Great Hunger
(An Gorta Mor, 1845–1850)

Hope in New York City
The Continuing Story of The Irish Dresser

Acknowledgments

Special thanks to my publisher, Janice Phelps Williams, who be-friended my Norah, believed in her, and wanted the best for her, even if it meant letting her go. Her professionalism, artistic vision, and warmth are a treasure.

Also, to fellow writer, Carole Auger-Richard, who listened to my raw, un-edited prose and envisioned a polished gem; to friend, writer, and spirit-sister, Mary Rose Glennon; to friend and writer, Nancy Kelley, for her keen editing eye; to friend and writer, Quincy Whitney; to Howard Winrow who made sure the *Diana* went in the right direction; to Julia Forbes who was inspired to compose *Norah's Dream Waltz,* and to my mother, Doris Force-Huston, who always believes in my dreams; to my Tim who is technical support, right word support, and who closes his ears to my giving-up times; to family and friends who rallied me on; and to my dancing friends who know how important it is to dance when rejection letters pile up.

I get up. I walk. I fall down.
Meanwhile, I keep dancing.
~Rabbi Hillel

Chapter 1

It was as if specters from the graveyards of Ireland had risen in Five Points, New York in the 1850s. The spud rot still clung to them and the fingers of death from the old sod they had labored in had kneaded them into something new. Norah and her family lived on the third floor of a lopsided gray tenement building with windows appearing from the outside like gouged-out eyes of a beast. The Mc-Cabes were restless, as were most immigrants in America, and sleeping in feather beds, when they could finally afford them, and stepping on creaking wood instead of the sureness of the earth, made them feel separated from the clay of themselves. It was a miracle to be free from toiling in fields and squatting in their cottages around the hearth. There wasn't nearly as much grime underneath their fingernails as there used to be and their bodies contoured to chairs and couches as if they had always possessed them. And yet they couldn't slough off their old skins so easily, for their memories contained not just the scent of decaying potatoes, but the familiar green and fecund land that had presented them with wild bouquets of heather and gorse, as well as potatoes in good times. They had been freed and unshackled from the potato fields, from British landlords and agents, as well as from starvation. But in this new liberty, they were not grounded. They stumbled and fell, only to get up repeatedly, something greater than themselves urging them on. All the while, the taproot of their mother country grew like the fingernails of the dead and clawed at them, forever pleading for them to return home.

The McCabes took comfort in one another, while their homesickness was replaced by novelty and their old exacting companion, survival. Many Irish families were ripped and torn asunder by the trauma of moving from rural poverty to urban poverty, but the McCabes tightened their seams and sustained one another in their early days in New York.

"There's gossip going around Five Points," Norah said to Mam, rotating her svelte figure before a large mirror. "Mrs. Riley down at the grocer's was whispering to Mrs. Donovan as Mary and I walked by. We heard them, alright, but Mary thinks the old bag was talking about her, but I saw them staring me down."

Norah stopped swaying before the mirror and faced her mother.

" 'Holy Joseph, will ye be looking at that one, now. She's a huckleberry above a persimmon,' Mrs. Riley said loud enough for us to hear."

Mam grunted, stared at her daughter and said nothing in response. Norah turned back to her image in the mirror, the corset surrounding her small waist was squeezing her insides and a fabric-covered button suddenly popped off just above her bodice.

"You don't need such a thing designed to be killin' a Protestant woman," Mam groused, reaching for her sewing basket and kneeling before her daughter. "Hold yourself still now so I can sew it back on strong enough for one of your deep breaths you're always taking."

Norah had found a clever way of relieving herself of panic, as well as impatience, by taking in a very deep breath and letting it out slowly. Her relief might include breathing in foul fumes from dead animals and unwashed bodies while walking down a street in New York City, but when she had learned to deeply inhale the air surrounding her rather than let it fill her unawares, she felt in control and consciously alive.

"I shouldn't be bothering with a darn corset. My waist is small enough already," she said, cocking her head to the side with a sliver-of-a-moon smile.

Norah stood stock still while her mother threaded the needle with trembling hands. Mam's knees were calloused and swollen with arthritis, but Norah knew better than to insist she would sew the button back on herself. After Mam muttered complaints about vanity and finished with needle and thread, Norah turned again to look into the full-length wardrobe mirror.

The mirror had been a gift from Da two years ago and caused her grief every time she stood before it. She twisted around to view her back, screwing up her face in disgust. Sighing loudly, she turned again towards the front image of herself. It was always this way, day after day, standing before the richly carved mahogany mirror, the shining glass exacting servitude. Norah understood what was required of her to gain the desired reflection. She no longer believed that if she rolled in the early morning dew, as the old women used to tell her as a child in Ireland, she'd become beautiful. Oh no, now she had to roll in the money to purchase the cloth and pay the dressmaker's fees to stand properly adorned before this demanding goddess of vanity.

"I've a mind to send you to your sister Meg to help her with her brood. Then you'd not have time to always be standing in front of yourself," Mam said, placing her needle and thread in the basket and struggling to stand. Norah quickly reached out to help her and Mam swung her arms at her like she was warding off an attack.

"You'd be too busy cleaning the spit up on your fancy clothes and then decide your money should be spent on other things," she said after she had gotten to her feet with much effort.

Norah ignored her mother's comments and engrossed herself in her reflection, humming a tune she had recently heard at a dance hall.

Mam pushed her sewing basket into a corner with her foot and placed her hands on her hips, smiling wryly at Norah. "You look as lovely and rich as a fancy lady in a magazine. No more homespun rags for the likes of Norah McCabe," she said. It was both high praise and biting criticism, something Norah was used to.

Mam worked nearly sixty hours a week cleaning and sewing for wealthy families in New York City, but took the time to embellish her daughter's clothing. The mimicries of Paris fashion, these fashionable duds, had been bought cheaply from high-society women and were quickly becoming the new skins of the young Irish women in New York. Exhaustion had seeped into Mam's bones, but she no longer expected to be free from its grip on her life. Overall, she had made peace with it, but this day she was weakened and trembling and wished to return to her bed, a thing unheard of for an Irish woman unless it was her death bed.

Climbing up the dangerously dark and rickety stairs of the tenement building in the morning after being out to purchase coal for their stove, she had nearly fainted. But she had made it, thinking about Norah who stood before her swathed in luxurious cloth she could never have imagined her half-starved daughter of the Famine ever wearing. Mam was displeased with Norah's self-absorption and vanity, but was convinced that her girl was more than flounces of petticoats and flowered bonnets. Didn't she know that every young girl in America who was to come to anything was required to hold her breath in corsets long enough to run through society's corridors of mirrors without having them break and bleed her to death? And especially for the Irish girls!

Mam likened Norah's time before her mirror to sitting before one of the itinerant painters who created portraits for wealthy families. Eventually, there would be a picture of who her Norah was, in all her worth and countenance. She would then go on to other things and maybe find herself a husband and have children, like her Meg. *But then, maybe not marriage,* she thought sadly. After Norah finished with this fashion show with herself, she would be ready for something really grand, but probably not marriage.

The more Mam thought about the prospect of marriage for Norah, the less probable it seemed, for her daughter wasn't the marrying kind. Many of the Irish girls who came to America weren't the marrying sort, she thought, and 'tis strange, but maybe they wanted their purses full, and in marriage, it wouldn't be so. And what kind of compliment was it to be compared to a huckleberry? She didn't understand the talk of the people in this country, but the tone and look of the eye said it all. Mam had no patience for these women who were born in America and felt superior and more important than the people who came from Ireland. Why, many of them had blood running through their proud veins that was just as Irish as hers! If she had been there when these women commented on her daughter, she would have known exactly what they meant by a huckleberry above a persimmon.

"I'll make us some tea before your da comes home," she said.

Mam didn't want to peer at herself in Norah's mirror because it frightened her to see mirrored back a ghost-like visage that was more spirit than flesh. Reflection often came to her alright, her memories staring back at her with vengeance, worse than what she would ever see in Norah's fancy mirror. She had done her own twisting and turning, before the images of her days of hunger that had gnawed on the soul when all they could do was suck the marrow out of soup bones for an evening meal. It was only now she remembered how pink the cornmeal had been when it was mixed with blood from a cow Norah had found in a field. Only now did she clearly remember the wailing and pleading to God that sounded like dying animals surrounding their cottage. The worst reflection of all was of her neighbors, who were barely recognizable, as their bodies thumped along the road in wagons to be taken to a mass grave, their grass-stained mouths the color of Ireland. She and her family had ridden still alive in a wagon and not dead with such mouths, clutching stale bread in their pockets, leaving for America. The guilt in being alive had sometimes been worse than the hunger pains. No, she did not need to look into Norah's mirror to know who she was.

Mam and Norah took their tea at the old wobbly pine table that sat in the corner of their apartment. The McCabes had purchased the precious piece of furniture after moving to their third apartment in the city. Norah was full of continuous chatter, mostly about her second-hand clothing shop, *A Bee in Your Bonnet,* "That is doing grand," she said, "and a fine gentleman from a newspaper is going to write an article about it."

"He's a bit of dandy, Mam, looking like a puffed-up bluebird in his blue velvet waistcoat and blue satin cravat." Norah laughed, hiccupping after taking a sip of tea. "He was wearing white French gloves and when he introduced himself to me after coming into my shop, he stuck out his right hand with his fingers limp and his glove still on!"

"Could he be one of those Nancy-boys?" Mam asked, her eyes going wide. "You know the talk of their feminine ways—"

"Holy Mother…he's not!" Norah said, laughing harder.

"Tell me then, Norah, don't ye be keeping things from me now!"

"He's a newspaper man who likes his fancy clothes. He's Irish, but born here, and he's the editor of the *Irish-American* paper. He came into the store hunting for a good story in Five Points. And don't we know there's plenty of stories around Five Points."

"Did he buy anything?" Mam asked, her curiosity growing.

"As sure as the sun rises, does a dandy purchase clothing."

"What did he buy then?" Mam's eyes widened as she leaned close to Norah's face, the need for silly talk and gossip taking over her weariness.

"Just some white stockings and a crescent-shaped bustle!" Norah exclaimed. Mam laughed and sprayed a little tea onto the table just as Da walked into the door carrying his fiddle.

"Eoin McCabe, you're late for tea," Mam said, wiping her mouth with the back of her hand. "It's a Sunday and ye shouldn't be playing your music in those foul watering holes."

She jumped up and quickly wiped the table with a rag and walked into their bedroom. There were only two rooms in their tenement apartment—the kitchen and living room used as one room and the other room serving as their bedroom. There was also a water closet one person could barely stand up in.

"May God be praised! Look at the likes of me own daughter sitting here, fit for a ball. I see with my own eyes that you're not wearing a worn-out rag from your store," Da said, his face creasing into a wide smile for Norah.

Norah paraded about the room, twirling and swishing her petticoats, smiling coyly and openly at Da. In the last year, she had made enough money to not only purchase cloth and pay dressmaker fees, but to visit a dentist. She was no longer ashamed of her teeth, for she had learned how to make them sparkle with baking soda, charcoal, and a good brush. Mam's front teeth had been broken, but between Norah and her da, they convinced her to go to the dentist, too. Mam had insisted she didn't want to pay the terrible fee to put some kind of cement in her mouth just so she could smile at the world. She would smile inwardly and through her eyes, she stated. But Norah knew how people talked about the rotten teeth of the immigrants, especially the Irish, and she was insistent that they all look proper. She told her mother, now that she had her own business, she would make sure they all kept up appearances. Norah remembered the sweltering summer afternoon when she approached Mam about going to the dentist.

"My business is a clothing store, Mam, and not just any clothing store. I have gowns worn by aristocratic ladies that don't look worn at all. I specialize in making Five Points women beautiful. So we McCabes can't be looking like we just got off the boat now, can we? We can't have our teeth rotting out of our heads!"

But that time seemed so long ago, and if rings signified the ages of trees, the McCabes also had their own rings. The year they arrived in America was one ring now surrounded by many others. Norah owning her own used-clothing store was quite an achievement, but just the family being alive was something to marvel over.

Norah sat down and looked up at her da, enormously pleased with the way her life was going. Da had walked in the apartment especially happy, but now she watched his face fall into sadness, the deep parentheses surrounding his mouth were elongated and more pronounced.

"What is it, Da?"

"I'm carrying a burden, God help me. It's Angus. And it's not just him I'm worried for," he said in a defeated and raspy voice, staring at his worn, laced-up working boots. He wore them all the time, whether he was playing fiddle at a saloon or working on the streets. Da's thick midnight-dark hair had nearly turned white in the last few years. When the silver started coming into his hair, Norah told him that he had a head touched with a few falling stars because he was a dreamer as much as he was practical. He never went to California to dig for gold as he had planned, but became quite well known as a fiddler in Five Points. The saloons were always competing with one another to get him in their establishments. His music caused people to dance wildly and freely, forgetting their harsh and impoverished lives.

"What's wrong with Angus?" Norah asked. Angus had been brought home to dinner many an evening. He was a piper Da played music with, and also being from Ireland, the two men had forged a close friendship. Da often said that Irish friendships were knit together like Celtic knots, and even if there were misunderstandings, the ancient circles and patterns formed the rib bones in Irish chests. He said that surgeons could open up the chests of Irish people and find the same Celtic designs.

"He's got the sickness. The consumption. And it's traveling throughout the city, mostly in Five Points. I'm worried for him and for all of us," Da said, sitting down at the table and running his hands through his hair.

"First I've heard of it. There's always some disease running its course through Five Points. I wouldn't worry. But for Angus, I wouldn't worry. Has a doctor taken a look at him?" Norah asked.

She had seen enough sickness and disease in Ireland and in this country and her vigor was still intact. She had been surprised by her buoyancy and strength to overcome such problems and now had the tendency to be flippant and brusque about other people's troubles.

"Angus has the fever. He couldn't play today. He's quarantined."

"Is his wife being kept from him, too? Who's caring for the poor man?" Mam asked, coming out of the bedroom and sitting at the table.

"I'm sorry to be interrupting, but me and Mary...I mean, Mary and I, will be taking our afternoon stroll. We don't want to miss any of the missionary women coming in with the society women's cast-offs," Norah said.

"Those Protestant ladies are trying to cover the half-naked ones selling their bodies on the streets. You shouldn't prevent the do-gooders from covering their poor arses with fine silk, Norah," Da said, slapping his knee and laughing.

"Eoin McCabe! Ye must not approve of Norah bribing the prostitutes."

"And do you think that putting fancy duds on these women will cure them of their sickness? Norah is helping them buy food."

"Our Norah is helping them buy the booze and whatever else it is they need to screw up their courage to be sellin' their skin, Eoin McCabe! And I don't approve.

"I thought you were meeting your newspaper man for an afternoon stroll, Norah. Not conniving with that Mary, your street urchin girl, now all grown and wandering the streets," Mam said, fear wrapping its fingers around her heart each time Norah walked out the door.

"Mary's a loyal friend all these years. She's stuck working at the orphanage, but she helps me with the shop. She's a hard worker and her heart's grand."

Norah was a clever and shrewd businesswoman on the cobbled, dank, and filthy streets of Five Points. As soon as the missionary ladies delivered clothing to the tenement apartments where known prostitutes lived with their snotty, half-naked children, Norah and Mary knocked on their doors and offered a handful of coins for the dresses.

Norah wrapped a shawl around her shoulders and prepared to leave, but suddenly there were repeated knocks on the door and a note was shoved underneath it. They all listened to the sound of someone leaving, struggling down the stairs, but Da didn't move. When he finally retrieved the note from the floor, he sat down and his face paled when he read it.

Mam and Norah begged him to tell them what the note said, when he crumpled it up and put it in his pocket. After a few moments, Eoin announced that Angus was dead.

"The fever killed both him and his wife. And it's likely to be killing all of us in Five Points."

Chapter Two

Norah hitched up her skirt just slightly to reveal her lace petticoat. A spring hoop widened the skirt only twelve feet in circumference, rather than the sixteen feet many women wore. She experienced discomfort wearing them distended to an enormous size and also disliked the crinoline in the hoop skirt she was presently wearing. It made her feel like a doll propped up for viewing, let alone the difficulty there was getting down the stairway of her tenement building and finding the required wide berth to sit at a table. It also took ridiculous measures to walk down the street and avoid getting caught in other people's clothing or snagged on a lamp post.

This afternoon Norah was hurrying down the street in her ballooning skirt, squeezing between people, when her petticoat became caught on the snaps of a man's ankle boot. Poor Norah had become attached to a very handsome gentleman wearing a velvet waistcoat, his hair arranged into earlocks.

"Excuse me, sir, but my dress is caught...," she cried out while being flung to the back of him as if he were dragging her to his cave.

She stumbled and tripped down the street, and when people noticed this amusing happenstance, they pointed and laughed. Norah was utterly humiliated, but the gentleman never felt the encumbrance of a charming and feisty Irish girl attached to him as if she were a bouquet of colorful balloons.

"Please sir, please…," her small cries were barely audible on the bustling and raucous street. Finally, she could no longer endure it. She grabbed her jeweled handbag off her right shoulder and flung it over her left arm, and with her right hand she reached for the petticoat. She clutched a handful of lace just below her knee, almost toppling over while trying to balance on her toes to keep up with the gentleman. Gripping the dear and precious red lace, she ripped it and freed herself from the man's boot. She backed up against a building, blushing and panting, and watched him continue down the street with the expensive lace adorning his polished boot. *Perhaps his wife would never trust her husband again,* Norah thought, for there could be no explanation he could come up with that would make sense.

Norah stood underneath the awning of a building away from the passing crowd and indulged in further imaginations regarding the handsome gentleman. After the man's wife would question his whereabouts and faithfulness, he would sit by the fire in his study, remove his boot and carefully untangle Norah's red lace. She pictured him bringing it up to his nose to take in the perfume of the lovely cursed material. Norah closed her eyes and imagined the gentleman closing his eyes and inhaling the scent of her lace. And then for the most delicious part of the scenario, she pictured his life now altered forever, all because he came into contact with her. His marriage would disintegrate and he would forever search the streets looking for the woman with the red lace, the scent of her forever in his memory.

Norah opened her eyes and giggled, feeling lighthearted and merry, for the story she concocted had made up for her embarrassment in stumbling down the street with her dress caught on a man's boot.

It was a shame that with all of Norah's scheming and preening to become presentable and acceptable within an oppressive social order, she still carried doubt regarding her appearance. She was always looking at her fingernails trying to rid them of invisible grime. Dirt from the west of Ireland, while imprinted on her mind, was nowhere to be seen on her body these days. She unconsciously hid her nails as she walked and talked in her fabulous used gowns.

Her wild and thick chestnut brown hair was tamed and coiled at the nape of her neck, held together with a comb adorned with faux rubies the color of her ripped petticoat. She felt confident her mam would sew on some extra lace where the torn piece was now missing. "Men," she uttered as a curse, "they have no perception!"

Norah continued standing against the building to regain her aplomb, feeling her embarrassment pass away. Surely, some people would be able to tell she was wearing ripped lace, but they would have to really give her a going over with critical eyes. And didn't she know that the streets were full of uppertons who would gaze at her and scrutinize what she was wearing. The men liked to look, but mostly they would set their lusty eyes on her bodice and not notice the torn skirt. But the women! They would be giving her a right going over, to be sure, and if there were any high-society ladies about, they would be sizing her up, trying to decipher if she was a real lady or one of the Irish domestics parading around the city in imitation of them. Those puffed up snoots and swellheads were threatened by the young Irish women like Norah, who was one of many fastidious Irish girls saving her money and able to dress like a Miss Astor of New York. It had been in the papers that the aristocratic ladies were incredulous that their employees, the Irish domestics who scrubbed their floors on hands and knees, were now promenading on Madison Avenue alongside them! It took just a few words for the domestics to be found out, however. Although their finery was as brocaded and richly textured as any high-society woman, if the Irish girls uttered a thick and ignorant speech, the ladies would breathe a sigh of relief. Mam said she heard a woman say no-one could cover up the "real filth of the Irish swine and rabble who carried on with their hysterical popery."

Norah had scrutinized the various classes of people on the streets of New York and worked exceedingly hard at ridding herself of Irish ways and speech. To her chagrin, she found it very difficult and could only leave off saying a few Irish words here and there. She encouraged her mam and da to overcome the use of their heavy brogue, but they stubbornly clung to it. It was deeply ingrained in their minds and ways, and she was oftentimes ashamed to be with them in public. They knew this and reprimanded her, for uppity and high-minded attitudes were a mortal sin in their household and Irish neighborhood. Her family reminded her that in Ireland there would be no tolerating such shameful attitudes towards one's own people.

Norah pulled out a handkerchief from her handbag to wipe the sweat that was beaded on her forehead. She was late in meeting Mary and felt disheveled and irritated over her recent circumstances. Her hair had started to come undone, and the humidity was causing it to frizz and curl. She dropped her handkerchief as she quickly tried to push her hair back in place with the comb that had suddenly come loose.

"'Scuse me, Miss, you dropped your kerchief," a woman with a bloated and pock-marked face, said. She was dressed in a black skirt and a torn gray blouse that was covered with splatters of mud. The woman picked up the handkerchief and handed it to Norah, who quickly put it inside her handbag.

"Could you spare a few coins for a wretch and her chillum?" she asked.

Two chubby faced boys, as dirty as their mother, hung on to her skirts. Norah tightened her grip on her bag. She had a few things stolen right off her body on the mean streets of New York over the years. She hurriedly hitched up her skirts and pushed past the woman and her children, determined to get on her way to meet Mary.

"Did you hear me, Miss? Me babies are hungering for bread…," the woman pleaded, getting in step with Norah. Norah was nonplussed, and detected an English accent on the woman. There were plenty of these English types who destroyed proper language and begged for bread on the streets. Norah thought that if it wasn't for novelists such as Mr. Dickens, the English would have the whole world thinking they were superior to anyone else. She quickened her steps determined to leave this hag with her crying children who scrambled after her.

"Go on now with your wee ones," Norah said, without turning to look at the woman.

"I'll be leaving them, Miss, if you don't give me some help. I'll be leaving them this very moment so they'll have more to eat in the poor-house—"

"Don't think you can fool me with your conniving ways!"

"You're Irish, Miss, I hear it in your speech. You should have the shame on you for ignoring my pleas…you of all people…you should know about being hungry."

Norah elbowed her way through the crowd trying to get away from the persistent woman. She passed another beggar who caught a piece of her petticoat and pulled at it, but Norah pushed her away.

"You know nothing of my hunger!" Norah shouted back at the woman whose children were following and crying loudly. Finally, she stopped in the midst of the crowded street to confront the woman. The other beggar woman came to her side and reached for her petticoat again, holding a piece of lace in her hand. People were shoving them and cursing at them to get out of the street.

"You've become so high and mighty, Miss, ye don't see that the blood in you and me is the same—"

"I may have worn your rags and been as hungry as you, but I've never begged—"

"A proud one ye are. I've seen you around, Miss," the woman said, her steel gray eyes squinting at Norah.

"I've lost nothing but my hunger, and don't I know there are floors to be scrubbed if you want to work for your food in this country. Your lot has no shame! A lazy bunch who'd rather beg on the streets!"

"My lot! I told you, Miss, ye and I carry the same blood—"

"We are as different as fire and ice. I know the ice flowing through your veins as you drag your poor children through the streets."

"Ye know not what you're saying!" The woman's children had

caught up with their mother and hid under her dirty skirts whimpering and glad to escape from the impervious noisy crowd.

"An Irish woman wouldn't leave her babies on the street!"

The woman stood on her toes, her red-rimmed, crusty eyes in line with Norah's face,

"An Irish woman would pretend to leave her babies on the street if she knew it'd get her some food for them."

"But you are not an Irish woman—"

"The same as you I am, Miss, the very same. The hunger sent us to Liverpool and I lived there for years. I come here with me husband five years ago and he was killed building up America. He was killed, Miss, he was killed just a month ago and we have no wages...so don't ye be pushing yourself through these streets thinking you are more important and grand."

The woman turned from Norah and yanked her children out from under her skirts, marching away with a trace of dignity in her straightened back.

Norah watched the woman and her children finally leave, and the soda bread and tea she had eaten in the morning churned and turned into bile in her throat. The beggar woman holding her petticoat lace yanked and ripped a piece, and before she ran away, Norah recognized Bridie, one of her neighbors in Five Points. Norah smoothed out her skirts and pushed some straying hair back into her comb and walked down the street to meet her friend, Mary.

Chapter Three

"Norah McCabe, aren't you all fancied up on a Sunday afternoon! 'Tis fine fashion for cajoling the adventuresses of Five Points," Mary called to Norah, sauntering proudly down the street, adorned and feathered as a peacock.

Norah smiled broadly at her most treasured friend, forgetting the opprobrium the street scene had caused her. Her only thoughts were of the afternoon's promising intentions. Her dear Mary was now with her and although they both were disappointed that Mary's address was still St. Paul's Children's Home of Mercy, they were the best of friends and always euphoric when together. Mary had resided in the home for impoverished imps and urchins for years, but in the past year she had been earning her keep cleaning and minding the younger ones. Norah watched her friend grow into a young lady who loved to stroll with the best of men, the worst of men, and all sorts of men on the streets of New York. Mary did it with great finesse, but the outcome would always be the same—entertainment, but not entanglement. Her friend was an artiste of street theater, donning the costumes of the fashion conscious of the city. She embellished herself with every style of dress available in New York, and mimicked the high-brow society women who wore European inspired garments. She wore just about everything, that is, but Levi's, soap locks, and turbans.

Mary was much like a caterpillar who molted into new brocaded skin almost weekly, and all for one sole purpose. She paraded and parodied the rich so as to entice the bewildered man of means who couldn't resist her flaming ginger hair and erotic chest. Mary pranced about the city to remove herself from the orphanage and its acrid carbolic spray used to disinfect the limbs and souls of the children who resided there. Both girls adored imitating high brow fashion, but Norah's garb was more conservative than Mary's, whose clothing, although costly, tended to be garish and flamboyant. Norah favored the subtlety of rich textures and fine lace, although this particular morning she had worn the red petticoat, the brightest finery she possessed. She often wore this when she was with Mary, feeling hopeful she wouldn't fade into the background.

The girls bartered for perfumes with their hard-earned wages in the boutiques they shopped in. The exotic perfumes could never cover the rancid scent of potatoes that Mary insisted she still smelled even after all the years since the Famine. She repeatedly reminded Norah that she once had to eat nettles and steal food out of starving children's mouths in the workhouse in Dublin.

"I convinced myself that I was helping them into heaven by relieving them of the hell they lived in at the work house."

When they first met years ago as young girls come from Ireland, Mary whispered to Norah in a confessional booth tone that she once had demon strength to survive when she boarded a steamship to Liverpool. From Liverpool, Mary traveled on a cattle ship to New York and was saved by St Pierre's Mission who possessed a holy desire to minister to the destitute children of Ireland by bringing them to New York. Norah watched this strength double in her friend while she lived at the orphanage, but in spite of her profligate effort to cover herself in fineries, Mary had been unable to secure herself the new station for which she hungered. Norah thought it ludicrous that her friend was only able to stay a caterpillar. Mary struggled to re-invent herself, as Norah also tried to do. However, each time Mary curled her delicate petite puffed-sleeved arm through a gentleman's black-suited one, Norah assumed it would be for the last time. It just had to be the last time so Mary could molt into a woman married to a wealthy gentleman of New York! Not so for Norah, although molting into someone other than what she had been was paramount in her motivation, albeit nebulous. When Norah would find her friend weeping bitterly at the end of a short-lived romantic promenade, she worried Mary would never fly the orphanage and morph into a butterfly. Norah was a loyal friend and would always be there each time the girleen was found bereft at the end of another ardent and promising excursion, ready to grow new wings again. She would stand ready with a new costume for Mary to gussy up in, taken from *A Bee in Your Bonnet*.

Norah's smile immediately retreated into the memory of her recent encounter on the street.

"I'm pissin' mad as a March hare, Mary, but seeing you in all your finery, so bird-like and rapturous, does my soul well. I'll soon forget what's just happened as we pull the wool, or preferably silk, over the seductive eyes of the unknowing ladies of the street."

Norah and Mary often mingled idioms and dialects, tossing in curse words to try for a shocking affect. Mary laughed and unfurled her silk shawl from around her shoulders and wrapped it around Norah's neck. When it had gone around her neck once, she knotted it, and there was a foot of material left. She pulled Norah to the right and then to the left, dancing a two-step. Norah went along with her friend, giggling and forgetting her day's recent disasters.

"As bold and bawdy as they come underneath all that lace and petticoat!" Norah heard a lady declare. She turned toward the old powdered bag and yelled, "You and yours go to the devil! Look at ye! All dressed up and sour-pussed without a pussy—"

"Norah dear, don't be wasting your fine words on the likes of them. And look smart for here is the constable, our loyal keeper of the peace for the privileged. He's talking to your woman…just follow me quietly," Mary whispered.

Mary let go of the shawl and as it dangled down the front of Norah's dress, the girls skipped down a narrow alley and away from the policeman and menacing woman.

Sometime later in the day, when the narrow path of the sky that hung between buildings turned such a light pink rose that Norah could nearly smell the scent of this flower, she and Mary unlocked the door of her clothing store in Chatham Square. They laid down the bundles of chiffon, silk, and lace clothing that they had absconded with for just a few dollars. The pungent aromas and stark miens of the prostitutes always lingered in Norah's mind. The thin ones with sharp shoulder blades looked like crows ready to unfold their wings; these women were pocked-marked and scantily clad, and peered at the world with whiskey eyes that tried to burn holes in her; their teeth were pointed from filing them to gnaw on a client who might turn mean. In a titillating tone to her voice, Mary had told Norah how these ladies of the night gnawed rather than sucked.

The prostitutes valued not the fancy clothing of the church ladies, for it was the dollar they coveted. They preferred a five-dollar bill rather than a dress they would only pawn later. For it was the grog and opium they hungered to fill themselves with, more so than covering their sick bodies in swaths of rich fabric bestowed upon them by the mission ladies. But with all Norah's recently learned street-wise ways, she still couldn't fathom what these ladies were about. She would walk away with their fine clothing, watching them smile and clutching the coins she had placed in their claw-like hands. If she had known that the money given to them could cause hideous groans and blood-filled gutters just a few streets away from where she sat sewing, she would have demanded her coins be returned and she would have given the dresses back. Maybe she would have gone to her favorite bakery to buy sweets to give to the women, as well. But she didn't know really, not really, what these prostitutes did with her money.

After sewing late into the night, Norah would lie on the sofa in the apartment she shared with her mam and da and be tormented by the plights of human-kind, especially the befallen women of the streets. Oftentimes, she would lie on her stomach and feel the beat of her heart in the lower half of her body and fear something was wrong. Why would her heart leave her chest in such a fashion, reside between her legs and cause her to sleep fitfully? Never had her heart and body linked itself to the filthy narrow alley ways and tenements where prostitutes lit scarlet light in the darkness of Five Points. But this singular night there had been an enormously good haul from the prostitutes; and what these women might possibly do with her money was not on her mind. She and Mary worked contentedly and quietly into the night and then stealthily and quickly walked home, listening to muddled, sometimes sharp, and odd sounds of a city needing sleep, but not resting.

A few weeks later, Norah and Mary were finishing up their work on another day of profitable business, but something was altering in Norah's feelings about her interactions with the prostitutes in Five Points. This day, she had conducted herself with more determination and vigor, her full skirts swirling as if in a dance before the scantily clad women. The guilt over their depraved lives dissipated as she convinced herself that their pathetic state of moral depravity wasn't her concern. *Let the church ladies awaken their dark souls to grace and redemption,* she thought. She was finally feeling free from her mother's criticisms and her own inner voice of doubt, but by the time she and Mary walked into her shop in the early evening, she felt depleted, exhausted, and was carrying a sense of uncertain, un-named doom. She didn't want to spend the night patching and sewing dresses. So Norah had bid Mary an early goodnight and made her way home.

Norah was unable to sleep and was lying on the lavish Victorian circular sofa in the living room of the tenement apartment. It didn't have a fireplace or hearth. She had seen the ornate brick fireplaces with gilded mantles in boardinghouses in Five Points and longed to have one. Each time she walked into a building that had a fireplace, she stood before it a long time trying to remember, but mostly trying to feel something she missed. Lurking in the memory of her childhood, there was the small, dirt-floor cottage in Ireland that contained the warmth of the hearth that had gathered the family together in the evenings to make sense of their plight and struggles. The rough-hewn, earthy hearth was where they had eaten their meals sitting on stools. It was where her da played fiddle, and other musicians and friends came for stories and a cup of tea. The fire had emitted ancient warmth that rose from the bowels of the earth, but the coal stove that sat in front of the sofa in New York was dirty and possessed an un-Ireland fire. It tried to burn its way into Norah's heart, determined to brand her an Irish immigrant forever, its flames small and limiting.

She looked fondly at the charming weathered dresser adorned with morning glories and sunburst designs that sat near the stove. It was practically an extension of her limbs, her heart, and her head. Inhaling the sea air when she opened its doors had memorialized her adventure as a child when she traveled inside of it on a coffin ship from Ireland to America. It cleansed her soul to open the doors and breathe in her past and become a child again, one who believed in fairies and hoped for a better life. It had been seven years since Norah's arrival in America, seven years away from her homeland. Seven, she knew, was the number of completion and, therefore, it had to be soon, very soon, she would be preparing to return. She had left her footprint in Cobh Harbor before embarking for America, the pieces of her skin buried there, waiting for her to return and graft them on to her new life.

Norah closed her eyes to sleep, but her mind bustled to gather the past and present together for some kind of coherency. She marveled that this place they lived in, that was so far from her childhood home, had become home just the same. Mam and Da had their own room with an amply stuffed feather bed, and covered in a quilt that Norah, Mary, and Mam sewed together one winter. Norah was much too impatient for sewing, but when she was called upon to spruce up a few of the garments she had bought for her store, she was more than able for the task. When she had made enough money to get rid of her parents' straw mattress and replace it with a feather bed, she wanted to embroider an intricate Celtic design on the quilt. She sketched out the design on a large piece of butcher paper and throughout the winter months as they sat by the stove with stiff fingers from lack of warmth, the three women created the circular designs that revealed their hearts were forever knotted to Ireland.

Before finding the sofa, Norah had slept on straw before the stove, covering herself with a horse blanket she had bought at a pawn shop. She and Mam scrubbed it so hard with lye soap that they created tiny holes in it. Then they sewed on patches of tapestry from her used-clothing store, and Norah covered her legs with the blanket in the wintertime whenever she was privileged to ride in a carriage. She still smelled the scent of the sweaty and muscular beast, but it was a welcomed earthy smell she relished, unlike all the other effusive odors from garbage and dung that piled up on the streets of the city. And then Da had surprised her with the elaborately designed mirror for her eighteenth birthday, a gift beyond his means but one that came serendipitously through the death of a saloon-keeper's wife. It had been given to her around the same time Norah found the ornately carved rosewood sofa sitting on the street. No doubt the sofa had been cast off by someone of means outside of Five Points and dumped on the corner of Mott and Baxter Streets. The rich paisley designed upholstery was torn and stained, and rats had made nests in it for the winter. Norah had immediately seen beyond the torn and dirty fabric and envisioned herself sleeping on it in front of the stove. When she ran her hands over the fine designs in the dark wood, she was sure it belonged in the old tenement apartment. She flagged down a business buggy and bribed the driver with a secondhand gown for his wife, a warm loaf of soda bread, and a dollar to collapse the top and rear storage areas of his buggy in order to fit the old sofa in. When she got home, he was so taken with Norah that he never complained about hauling it upstairs to their third floor apartment. Norah soon re-upholstered the sofa with the pieces of tapestry she had neatly shelved away in her store.

The past and present soon danced happily together in Norah's mind, bringing needed consolation. She pulled the blanket over her head, curled herself into a ball above the curve of the sofa, and finally, slept. As the night pushed her deeper into rest, she dreamed she was a passenger on a steamship sitting at a table covered with stiffly starched white linen. In her dream, she looked down into an empty delicate English bone china teacup with a violet pattern and then raised her head to gaze at a candle with flames flickering before a man's unfamiliar face, whose eyes were as green as hers. Mermaid eyes, Da always called them. But the eyes in her dream knew her differently than her da knew her, and they burned into hers. Or was it the candle, the flame too high and the wind causing it to dance hotly before their faces?

Much later, Norah was wrapped up in the blanket and snoring loudly. Mam grasped both of her shoulders and shook her hard enough to bring her out of dream and sleep. She sat up and stared into the stove at the small fire burning, for the door to the stove was open.

"Norah, wake yourself now! A police officer's here. I'll give him a cup of tea, but he's after speaking with you," Mam whispered, bending over the sofa.

Norah looked toward the kitchen table, thinking she might see the man in her dream. Instead, a policeman was sitting at the old pine table on the far side of the room. She felt embarrassed to be seen sleeping in her petticoat on the sofa, and when he glanced at her, she tossed her head and looked away.

"Tell him to wait on the stoop."

"He's a policeman for God's sake, you can't be asking him to wait outside," Mam whispered.

"He's not the grand landlord of the big house, is he now! He can wait for me to dress!"

Mam clucked her tongue and went timidly to the officer who was fidgeting with his club while sitting at the table. Norah listened to her mother apologize in an obsequious manner and was irritated. Sure, they were mostly Irishmen, these police officers, but in her mother's eyes these men were as important as Lord Trevelyan himself. As soon as the policeman left the apartment and she heard him amble down the dark stairway, Norah got up from the sofa and slowly walked into the small water closet to wash and dress.

She put on a modest dress and didn't take the usual time to make herself presentable. Walking by her mother, who was nervously strumming her fingers on the grooved and nicked table, Norah said in a staccato voice, "You'll be giving yourself slivers, Mam."

She walked down the stairs and out to the stoop to meet the officer who had awakened her from a most sensational dream. The feeling of the dream was all over her, but she couldn't recall the face behind the candle. She tried to remember as she looked at the broad back of the officer sitting on the stoop.

"I'm Norah McCabe."

The officer at once stood, smiled, and stared down at her skirts. She followed his eyes and saw that her skirt was caught up to her waist on one side. Her face warmed and she quickly re-arranged her clothing and looked into his face, waiting for him to announce himself. With his hands in his pockets, he glanced at her and then at the street, and back at her again, all the while moving about anxiously on the stoop.

She assured herself that she hadn't done anything wrong. She abided by the law, always stoically abided by the law. Da had taught her that living with purity and a clean conscience was far better than having the riches of the world. Often, she had bitterly thought that a good conscience had never gotten the Irish people very far.

Norah's hair was pulled back in a chignon, but sweaty strands corkscrewed around her head. Dark amber freckles circled and spiraled in patterns on her pale oval face and over the puffy shadows below her eyes. She tried to tuck her loose hair behind her ears, for she felt uncomfortable in front of the clean shaven officer who was wearing a starched uniform. She squinted at him in the morning sun and detected that, beneath his tidy appearance, he had recently come from the ole country. She reached up to unbutton the top button of her blouse, for she was suffocating not only from the heat, but in the sudden recognition that most of the people who came into her shop were similar to this officer— they were mostly Irish! And these people, her people, thought and lived in narrow ways—the rebel way, the slavish way, the gang way, the old-fashioned and stifling way! She looked at the officer and imagined him altered from his uniform into the rag tag clothes of a farmer from Ireland. She pictured him standing with a hoe and bending over to till the fields, but in a flash he was transformed back into the clothing of authority he was now wearing. *He must have thought he had found heaven on earth coming to America and scaling off his peasant farmer clothes to put on the stiffly pressed officer's uniform,* she thought smugly.

"And what might you, an important officer of the law, be doing on a fine summer morning visiting the likes of me and scaring the wits out of me poor mother?" she asked him.

She sized him up—he was medium-built, but muscular, with a face red from scrubbing it too hard. He had small brown eyes that were red rimmed, just like a piglet's. But then she thought that pigs have blue eyes. She nearly laughed aloud. His left hand fondled the large club hanging from a belt around his waist. Now why would he feel threatened by her, she wondered.

"You're Norah McCabe, is this right, Miss?" he asked, his face reddening even further.

Norah stifled a giggle and nodded affirmatively.

"I'm here to tell you, Miss…if you are she…if you are that one called Norah McCabe and are the proprietor of *A Bee in Your Bonnet Used-Clothing Store,* you're being summoned now for questioning in the murder of…"

The officer reached inside his pants pocket to retrieve a wadded up piece of paper. He tried to smooth it out and read slowly, "A woman…her name is Bridget McEnnis, also known as…uh, let's see here now, it being hard to read, Miss… Brazen Bridie of Mott Street Motleys."

Stuffing the paper back into his pocket, he shuffled on the stoop and didn't look at Norah. He turned to watch the kids on the street coming around to see why a policeman was out so early in the morning. The tenement was a crumbling, dirty building like most others in Five Points, but it wasn't one where anyone of real vice and crime lived. The renters were just a desperate covey of Irish and German families who had scraped and saved enough money to move into a slightly better tenement building on a slightly better street in Five Points.

"Go on now, go on back to your own!" he shouted at the kids and turned to look up at a window behind Norah. Norah turned, too, and saw her mother's face full of worry peering down from the dirty window that had a crack in it. The crack made her mother appear as a deformed creature, and Norah wished the landlord had fixed it as he had promised months ago.

Her first reaction to the officer's fumbling pronouncement was that it had to be an obvious mistake, or even a joke of some kind that her crazy friend, Mary, was playing on her. Certainly she felt there was no need to be alarmed, but the weight of the accusation began to worm its way into her mind. She suddenly felt chilled, although sweat dribbled down her back and into her undergarments. Dizzy and nauseous, she sat down on the stoop right next to the officer's legs and stared at his perfectly creased pants, inhaling the starch in them. Then she put her head in her hands, but abruptly stood, for she feared she might appear guilty.

"I'm here to take you to the station, Miss McCabe…it's only an investigation. Ye haven't been charged with anything yet."

"Oh sure…and that should put my mind at ease, now, shouldn't it?" she said, and quickly scanned the street to see who might be watching and listening. A few people had stopped to stare, and humiliation welled up within her.

"I think it might be time for you to be having your cup of tea now, Officer. It's mighty good of you to be coming over so early in the morning to give us the grand news," she said loudly for all to hear. "And you didn't give me your name…"

"Officer Leary, Miss."

"Officer O'Leary, pleased to meet you."

Officer Leary followed Norah up the stairs, embarrassed for the young woman, knowing well why she had suddenly invited him into her home so eagerly and warmly.

After Mam ordered Officer Leary to sit down at the table to take some tea, he poured numerous teaspoonfuls of sugar into his cup, added a dash of milk, and stirred slowly and vigorously before saying anything further to Norah and her mother.

"Thanks be to God, and you for the cup of tea, Mrs. McCabe. I sorely needed a bit of sustenance." He took a few gulps, wiped his mouth, and looked at Mam.

"I've come to inform your daughter, here, that she needs to be at the station before the end of the day."

"And why is she to go to the station? She owns her own shop, mind you, and she doesn't have time for all the shenanigans that go on in the neighborhood. And don't we know what goes on during the nights in the alleyways and saloons, Officer O'Leary. There's been many an officer like yourself who frequent the dens of iniquity and turn a blind eye to the vices and dirty dealings—"

"No, Ma'am, I'm not the drinking sort."

"And so tell me now, Officer O'Leary—"

"It's Leary, Ma'am…and your daughter is only being summoned to answer a few questions about her whereabouts last night—"

"My daughter was asleep before midnight, right here on this sofa. Her da and I were here and we can speak for her."

"I'll speak for myself," Norah said, standing up from the table. She had overcome her embarrassment and felt assured this officer was nothing but a greenhorn, fresh off the boat from Ireland. Young and strong he was, so he had been hired to patrol the worst place in New York—Five Points. He had to have been hired because of his fawning servitude so well refined from living as a peasant in the shadow of a big house in Ireland. Surely, he had first worked as a short man, a thug, to make sure people had cast their votes a certain way at the voting booths. She was certain the only work the lad had ever done prior to coming to America was digging for the spuds in Ireland.

Officer Leary gulped down the rest of his tea and also stood up, his teacup clanging on the saucer, nearly toppling to the floor.

"Sorry, Mrs. McCabe," he said, wiping up the drops of milky tea with his large calloused hand.

He looked fully into Norah's face and felt weak and nervous. Her lovely penetrating green eyes looked into his own that he knew were only the plain color of cow dung. His father had told him this when the two of them had been plowing a field when he was a boy. He had made his father angry that day when he asked why his Mam and Da had eyes the color of the sky, but his were so dark. And why, he had asked, were his siblings' hair dark and he had light hair. His father had stopped plowing and grabbed him by the collar of his shirt, jerking him up to look into his face, his sour breath smelling of pipe tobacco and poiteen, "Don't you believe that ye are one of us, lad? Don't you now? Ask the Almighty Himself why you possess eyes the color of cow shit!"

Leary's thoughts returned to the present while he adjusted the club hanging from his waist and looked at Norah who watched him intensely. He recognized the mockery in her eyes and feared she saw his weakness. He briskly turned toward the door and hoped she would follow him.

N orah had sharply stated she could handle this entire matter herself, thus Mam anxiously busied herself tidying up the small apartment while listening with trepidation to learn what might befall her daughter. Her Eoin should be present to handle this terrible event, not her, not even Norah herself. Eoin could put the whole affair in order, her Eoin could. She felt that Norah was being disrespectful to the officer, an officer of the law in America! She walked over to her daughter and touched her arm as the officer turned to go.

"Go on now, go with him, Norah," she whispered.

Norah brushed off her mother's hand and took a few steps behind Officer Leary. He stopped and turned around to face her.

"You'll be speaking for yourself, Miss McCabe, down at the station."

"I don't need a farm boy from the bogs of Ireland escorting me anywhere, especially to a police station," she responded, her temper as uncontrolled as her hair that curled in the sweltering heat. As soon as these words came rolling out of her mouth, she felt the acrid taste of loathing. Loathing the streets of New York, in particular Five Points, loathing having to live with her mam and da, loathing the tenement they were cramped into as if they were caged wild animals on display at a circus. *Barnum would love to put us Irish apes on display, wouldn't he now!* she thought. Norah felt revulsion toward an Irish boy dressed as an authority figure on the streets of New York.

Officer Leary's face changed from the light pink of a tender blush to the deep reddish brown that came from an indignant affront. He reached into his pockets for his handcuffs and moved close to Norah.

"I'll have to take you in wearing these, Miss, if you don't come willingly…and respectfully."

Norah brusquely walked by Officer Leary and opened the door, turning around and glancing at her mother.

"You'll not be needing those, now, Mr. O'Leary. Put them back in your pocket and stop gawking at me. Time is wasting and time is money in my line of business. Let's go to the station and be done with this nonsense."

Norah haughtily walked out the door and Officer Leary followed her. On the crowded street, she put her arm through his, "'Tis a fine day for a stroll to my shop, Mr. O'Leary. Thanks be to God for coming by to escort me."

Officer Leary gently took Norah's arm, and while they ambled down the street, he nearly forgot that he had come to take a suspect into the station. Wasn't he now living the grand life, dressed in the uniform of police prestige escorting a lovely girleen down the street; no matter that she was being questioned for murder.

Chapter Four

"Bridget McEnnis, aka Brazen Bridie of Mott Street, proprietor of *Mott Street Fashions,* a used-clothing boutique, a business conducted at her 23 Mott Street apartment, was found stabbed with a black lacquered hair ornament believed to have been worn in the deceased's hair," stated the pugilistic commissioner, from behind his desk. Norah sat before him, her hands knotted tightly on her lap. Her mind floated in and out of yesterday's and today's events while she barely listened to the commissioner's barking voice. Officer Leary and another officer were standing outside the open door of the commissioner's office. She noted Officer Leary's countenance displayed smug satisfaction because he had brought in a possible murder suspect. His chin was lifted too high and his mouth slightly curled on his young face. Their walk through the cacophonous streets swarming with the diverse tapestry of humanity had been uneventful, although she had kept up a constant flow of trivial conversation. She was fully aware that she had become the prey he wanted to hunt down for the almighty commissioner. She glanced at her hands and saw that she had forgotten her ring. She hoped that her most prized gold ring was somewhere under the cushion of her sofa, having perhaps fallen off in her troubled sleep. She clasped her hands together to stabilize her feelings of being ungrounded and unsure without her jewelry. The small jeweled ring had been a luxurious gift that had become a symbol of her right of passage from extreme immigrant poverty to just immigrant poverty, with all the signs of upward mobility. Norah was gossiped about and laughed at in her neighborhood, but no one disbelieved she would climb out of the black hole that was Five Points and away from them someday. They resented her for it, perhaps as much as they hoped it for her. Her hands were cold and slightly trembled while she sat in a silent daze. She felt certain that the whole ordeal couldn't really have anything to do with her! She looked at the commissioner's face; it was downright repulsive and ugly. He was quite portly; the brass buttons on his starched blue jacket were unable to lie flat on his chest, and shocking coarse gray hairs peeked out between them. The thick gray hair on his cannonball head was greasy and uncombed, his face unshaven. He fidgeted nervously with papers on his desk.

Norah didn't know this Bridie of Mott Street, a competitor in the used-clothing business in Five Points. Why should she? There were at least twenty such stores in her neighborhood. The old clothes men who wore layers of clothing, to entice people on the street to buy them, were now becoming extinct. They were climbing up in their world; at least whatever it meant to climb up in the world of Five Points. She was impressed by these uninhibited entrepreneurs who had accumulated so many duds over the years that they began opening their own storefronts, giving other street vendors the idea to do the same. So what if they had clandestinely confiscated a few gold watches that had helped them procure their businesses. Not her! She wouldn't just have a store in Five Points the rest of her life. She was going to travel first class to and fro across the sea to sell her clothing, and someday it wouldn't be used-clothing, either.

Norah was pleased with herself that she had been able to purchase her clothing store with the savings she had accrued since arriving in America. She had sold newspapers, hot corn, and apples and had handcrafted flowers for hats. She had also worked as a domestic at the Stewart mansion with her mam. Her store had been bought and established with honest hard labor, not with stolen goods.

Norah felt herself drifting further into the past in the airless and close room that didn't have any windows. Why wasn't she feeling anything more than the trembling in her cold hands?

"Miss McCabe, have you heard a word I've said? I'm waiting for you to give me any information you possess on the deceased, being that you are in the same line of business—"

"I have my own store in Chatham Square, Commissioner, not a home business in my apartment."

"Miss McCabe, you were seen with the deceased yesterday—"

"It's a lie!" The fingernails of her right hand dug into her left as she held it down on her lap. She feared both hands would begin flailing about her uncontrollably.

The commissioner looked down at his desk and straightened it as he spoke, his raspy breath carrying his words hoarsely out into the room. Norah stared at his heaving, noisy chest and swallowed with difficulty, closing her eyes. She tried to turn her active mind off, but couldn't. She suddenly imagined his brass buttons flying off his jacket and his ugly gray hair that covered his chest in her face. She breathed in deeply and looked at the commissioner's frightening face. She was ready to explain her whereabouts with Mary on the day before, but the commissioner had come out from behind his desk to stand directly over her. She smelled him now, a mixture of sweat, fried oysters, and tobacco.

"Miss McCabe, you could be charged with the murder even if you didn't do it. You could be charged as an accomplice."

His face was red as a tomato and bloated, and his eyes were bulging like a bull frog's she had once seen sitting on the bank of the Collect Pond in Five Points. She cringed, but didn't move as she listened to him wholeheartedly now.

"You could also be charged, Miss McCabe, for wasting my time sitting there all pretty and unconcerned, deliberately ignoring me. You could be charged....!" He stopped in mid-sentence and Norah smiled at him.

"I'm listening now, Commissioner. And you can rest assured that no charges need come my way, and I'll do what I can to help."

Commissioner Reilly folded his arms in front of his big belly and looked down at his chest, noticing that his buttons were about to come undone.

"I'm listening. You go right ahead now and tell me about yesterday."

"I awoke at six, went off to Mass with Mam...and then we walked over to Chelsea Street to visit my sister, Meg, and her brood. We had tea..." Norah hesitated and asked, "Would you be wanting me to tell you everything we ate, or just what I ate?"

"Do ya take me for a fool Miss McCabe? Do you really think it important for me to know what you et and all?"

"I believe not, sir, but details in an investigation can be telling. I know this from all the newspaper and book reading I do."

"Go on then, but without the descriptions of what you ate or wore."

Norah told about her day and didn't fail to include minute descriptions of the city. Eventually, she told the commissioner how she and Mary had gone to purchase the dresses from the prostitutes.

"Miss McCabe...," he said, releasing a husky sigh, sitting back down behind his desk. "You were purported to have bought a dress that had been stolen from a guest at the Astor House hotel that was worth hundreds of dollars. And this dress...," he hesitated, picking up some papers from his desk and reading from them. " 'The dress was a French make, yellow silk and embossed with brown velvet in an elaborate design. It was robe length, the waist a simple cut and buttons down the front.' " He put the papers down and continued, " 'Said dress contained an expensive bracelet in the under sleeve. And this same dress was bought off the deceased Miss Bridget McEnnis.' "

"I've never seen such a dress...Sure now, there've been a couple in the last few years that were that expensive and dear, but never did I purchase such a dress yesterday."

"You lie, Miss McCabe! Your friend, Mary Leavey, has already testified this morning. She claimed that she saw you hand the deceased five dollars for the dress at exactly six P.M. on Sunday, August twentieth."

Norah shifted her weight in the straight-back chair with the hard seat. Her clothes felt too tight and she couldn't breathe. Loud thudding filled her head and it took a moment for her to realize it was her own heart making the sound. Why would Mary tell the commissioner that she, Norah, had bought an expensive dress that would cause her to be questioned for murder? She leaned forward, but the back of her dress was stuck to the chair. As much as Norah relished wearing chic and elegant fashions of the day, she occasionally longed to throw herself on an early morning patch of grass in the summer clad only in her petticoat. How she wished for this now! To be unencumbered and a child again, running wild in Ireland! She gathered her skirts about her, leaned far enough forward so as to become unstuck from the back of the chair, and unabashedly looked at the commissioner.

"Ye can't be accusing me of something I didn't do!" She lifted her right arm and made a fist, but brought it down to her lap. "I would like my da to be here. Can you send that one out to get him?" she asked, turning and pointing to Officer Leary, her delicate, slender fingers trembling in mid-air. "And where is my friend, Mary? Where is she?"

She stood up, holding onto the sides of the chair, but quickly sat back down because a faint had crawled up her legs and into her chest where her corset was squeezing the life out of her. She had slept in it on the sofa, as she usually did, although Mam was always reminding her to take it off.

"Excuse me."

Norah got up and walked to a closet door on the other side of the room. She went inside, leaving it slightly ajar, and quickly reached under her skirts and deftly pulled the corset ties apart. The corset fell down to her feet and she let out a moan of relief. She picked it up to hide it somewhere, but didn't know where to put it. Officer Leary thought she was in distress and in a flash rushed to the door and opened it wide, exposing Norah holding her corset. In her surprise, she cried out and covered her mouth with the corset in her hand; and then dropped it and kicked it behind her. She looked at Officer Leary and then at the other officer who was still standing in the doorway.

They blushed and looked down when her eyes met theirs. The commissioner's swollen face turned purplish pink and he flailed his arms at her.

"I've never in my days! Miss McCabe! Sit down now!" he yelled.

She had to act quickly to gain the upper hand in all of this, and now that her corset was off, she could breathe and think straight. What was there for her to be worried about? She was innocent and only needed to tell the truth, because truth eventually prevailed in all matters. Her mam and da had drilled this into her as a child growing up in Ireland. Could they possibly believe this now since coming to America? Did she? She sat down in front of the desk, smoothed her skirts, and checked to be sure all her buttons were in place. She looked up at the commissioner and gave him a pleasant and confident smile.

The commissioner couldn't help himself in being taken with the spirited young woman sitting before him. Norah McCabe had boldly removed her corset in his office. It had been an affront for her to ignore his questioning and walk away from him, but how alluring she was! The girl was certainly just another laced mutton, another Irish commoner, but those eyes on her were making him fumble in his interrogation. He wanted to wrap this up quickly, but she was affecting his old heart. God, she wasn't so bad to set his eyes on, he thought, although her hair was wild and her face too freckled for his liking in a woman. He had hoped that the case of another prostitute being murdered in Five Points would be over and done with, like most. He didn't like to spend much time on such cases, for they were a dime a dozen; but the goddamn newspapermen—the conniving, sleek, and oily wordsmiths who always came sniffing around for a story—were salivating for this one. They didn't care about the mab who had been struck down in the prime of her lewd career. They were after the story of the ruby bracelet in the sleeve of the dress that some high-society woman had been careless with. It had to be a maid at the hotel—or even the cat herself, this Brigit woman found murdered—who took off with the dress without realizing the bracelet could have dressed her in fine silks. She wouldn't have to work as a maid during the day and a mab at night!

He grunted in self-satisfaction and swiped at the extra saliva that had collected in the corners of his mouth. *What a shame,* he thought, *but it served her right! Stealing and spreading her legs for money!* Now that the rich Astor bitch was making such a stink of the ruby bracelet being gone, he had to make a show of trying to find the murderer. Christ, should he find the murderer or the bracelet? Someone on the street had said a woman who owned a used-clothing store had bought the dress from the woman who was killed. He had sent his men out and they found the dress in McCabe's shop early in the morning. Mary Leavey was in the shop and said she had been sewing all night long, but he figured it was an unlikely story. The dress was found in Mc-Cabe's store alright, but the ruby bracelet was gone.

The commissioner looked at Norah's puny arms and considered that a bracelet of any kind would never belong on them. *It was those damn Irish arms,* he thought with disgust. Those arms were still starved looking even after the years since the Famine. He exhaled another noisy breath that reeked and defiled the close air in the room. He had to find the murderer. *It would be good if it could be this Norah McCabe even if she hadn't committed the deed,* he thought. He wanted to get on with this matter. He had gang members to be after, for Christ's sake. What did these sons of bitches newspapermen want from him? He was the commissioner and couldn't spend time looking for the murderer of some dirty no-count cat! Just about every other man on the streets of Five Points was a goddamn murderer, and most of them were Irish. He had real work to do and this broad was keeping him from it. He looked at Norah's face and, as pretty as it was with her coquettish smile, he detested her.

"Now that you've nearly undressed yerself before all of us, tell me how the fine dress from the hotel ended up in your shop with the bracelet gone from it?" he yelled at her, his eyeballs bulging.

"I never saw such a dress!"

Norah's stomach tightened with sudden nausea. Maybe she shouldn't have taken off her corset, for now she felt as if everything inside of her was coming undone. She wrapped her arms around her waist tightly. She began to see clearly what she was up against as she watched the commissioner's countenance waver from admiration to disgust. She had to appeal to his manliness and not make him angry, but if she was overly coy and subservient, she would become too weak to survive this ordeal.

"You're not making this easy, Miss McCabe," he stated.

A distraught woman wearing a ripped and torn red velvet riding dress appeared in the doorway. It was Mary, and her pale china doll face appeared pathetic with rivulets of eye make-up trailing her cheeks where tears had fallen. Her slate blue eyes were red-rimmed and swollen, and they appeared ghostly and unnatural. Her ginger colored curly hair was loose and hanging past her waist, matted to one side of her head. Norah stood up when her friend walked into the office. Mary was handcuffed and another officer was pushing her into the room.

"Who told you to bring her in here now?" the commissioner bellowed at the officer.

Mary hung her head and whimpered and muttered to herself. Enraged at her friend, Norah looked away, a wisp of pity sighing through her lips. The discomfort in her stomach caused her to nearly double over, but it was her heart that felt worse now. It ached because her best friend stood before her, soiled and weak, appearing to be nothing but the molly after all. The dirty no-good Irish woman that everyone around Five Points believed Mary was destined to be; an orphan from Ireland, no less and no more. Norah had assumed her loyal friendship with Mary over the years had bestowed some dignity and purpose in her friend's life. Certainly the girl was always being held back from destroying herself because Norah had been there beside her. And how she had loved her friend, Mary Leavey! But now she couldn't continue having anything to do with her! Norah glanced at Mary who stood disheveled and reduced to a sniveling thief and liar. She wondered if it really had been her own hope and strength that had sustained Mary

all through the years. She had always felt a visceral need for the en-
livening and bold friendship; having forgiven her for any demoralizing
acts she had committed to stay alive in Ireland. She herself knew what
it had taken for them to survive. If it hadn't been for Norah's own family
who surrounded her with love and crusts of bread, she might have done
the same as her friend. She might have taken food from the mouths of
others who had been starving like her. But now this friend stood before
her a wretched betrayer of their friendship. How could Norah continue
to rein in her friend's dark soul or cover the sins of her past? Her love
for Mary was beginning to shut down.

"Mother of God! What have you done?" Norah questioned, and
heard the ferocity of Mam's voice echoing through her own words.

"Sit down, McCabe! Murphy, bring the woman here! My God,
what a morning…I need a drop about now. Bring her over here, god
damn it all."

The commissioner jumped up from his chair and walked around
his desk to stand before Norah who had sat back down. Murphy
placed Mary in a chair next to her, but Norah stared stoically behind
the commissioner's head where a couple of pictures hung unevenly
on the wall, neither of them interesting.

She listened to Mary's whimper turn into sobs, but she hardened
herself against her.

"I'm sorry Norah…I'm so sorry."

Norah looked at Mary, and anger and empathy swirled simultaneously within her.

"Quit your damn sniveling and tell the truth, Mary!" she screamed,
grabbing Mary's arm and squeezing it, as if to force the truth from her.

The sweaty grip of the commissioner's meaty hand was suddenly
upon her shoulder. He clutched her with his left hand and with his
right hand he clutched Mary's shoulder. Norah tried to shake him off,
but he pressed harder. Mary wept loudly and Norah winced in pain.

"Shut up! You dirty molls, don't speak until I say so!" She felt his
spit strike her cheek, and she wiped it off as he tightened his grip on
her shoulder before releasing her and Mary. He walked back to his
desk, his raucous breathing in time with Mary's whimpers.

Norah watched the brute place his bear-like hands flat on the desk and saw that the forefinger and middle finger of his right hand had long, pointed nails. She wiped at her cheek and felt the heat from where his spit had landed. She didn't move or make a sound, fearful he would come across the desk at her again. How had she dared to take off her corset behind his closet door and speak to him with irreverence just a few minutes ago? Her boldness had melted away when he placed his disgusting claws on her shoulder and spit on her face. She gripped the sides of the chair to try and keep herself from shaking.

The commissioner nodded to Leary, "Get me a drink, man, and let's get this over with."

Norah heard Leary leave, and the sound of his footsteps were soft and distant as he walked down the hall. "Leary, please don't leave us. Please, Leary!" The words formed in her head, but never came out of her mouth. The commissioner moved papers around on his desk; his breathing was labored and loud. Mary had stopped whimpering and was now silent, and Norah didn't look at her.

Long moments went by and Leary came back into the room and handed the commissioner a mug of coffee. The steam from the hot coffee drifted into the air as if all was right with the world. She wanted her tea. She would have given anything to be having tea with her mam right now! She watched the commissioner's hands close around the mug; she watched him blow into it, and then he gulped the coffee as if it had been water. He set the mug down, opened his drawer and took out a flask and poured, what had to be whiskey into his coffee.

"I took the bracelet! I took it!" Mary screeched, "but I had nothin' to do with the dead woman!"

Norah remembered Mary telling her that the only time she had ever been a thief was in Ireland. "Never again, Norah," she had said, "Christ Almighty will strike me dead if ever I steal again. It's a right miracle I'm alive now and I won't tempt the good Lord ever again!" Norah had believed her.

An urge to kick Mary like she would kick a wild dirty dog on the street came over her. She was surprised by the strength of her feelings toward her friend.

"And didn't I go and tattle on me best friend here that it was her who bought the dress, not me," she said, erupting into sobs. She regained some composure and continued, "I saw that dress when Norah and me did our purchasing yesterday, sir. I saw it with me own eyes, I did, right on a woman brazen and bold in her trade. And I knew it'd be a fine piece of silk to be wearing meself right on these streets. The mabs, sir, the mabs…they don't care for the silks and lace as much as they care for the coins to buy other things… I'm a weak one for lovely silk dresses, alright, but I wouldn't be killing anyone for them. 'Tis the truth!"

Mary broke down again, and it sounded like the keening Norah had heard as a child in Ireland. She looked at her friend and was ashamed for her: for her weakness, for the snot that dripped between the fingers of her hands as she held them over her face. Norah looked at the lovely hair she had once brushed and put into combs, now matted and tangled. She felt shame for being Mary's friend. Hadn't she ever really seen who this girleen was? How could she not have known?

"I went back to her," Mary said after she dropped her hands from her face, staring into her lap, "I went back after you'd gone home, Norah. I took the money from the shop and bought the dress. It was like finding a pearl of great price, that one. I just had to have it. Me duds are all wearing thin…I was going to make it up to you…and I never wanted to lie, but when they accused me of murder, I didn't know what to say. I was so afraid. They said they were going to put me in prison, Norah. And I remembered the workhouse in Ireland. I couldn't take it…I'd even betray a friend so I'd not ever go to a place like that again!"

Norah stared at Mary, feeling nothing but revulsion.

"They asked if it was you who bought the dress. They asked before I knew what they were even asking me. I said that you bought it, for I didn't know it was about murder right off, I didn't. I'd never say you bought it if I knew they were going to accuse you of murder. Will you forgive me? It's me pride. You know that, don't you? I don't want to stay at the orphanage the rest of my life. I'm living like an orphan, but I'm a grown woman. The only hope I've got is the dresses…and you… Norah, you're my hope, too—"

"Enough of the drama...ye should be in a Blood-and-Thunder play! Stop carrying on and tell us where the bracelet is you found in the dress. And then you can tell us how you murdered the mab!" the commissioner interrupted.

Norah listened to Mary go on about how she made a wrong decision to purchase the dress, a costly one at that, especially if she had killed a woman for a mere dress. *Killed a woman!* And here she thought she couldn't remain her friend if she had been stealing and lying! Norah stared at the pictures on the wall and they began to blur and alter as she saw Mary transposed in one of them.

She imagined Mary in the picture draped in a fancy white silk dress, with horizontally striped bands of powder blue alternately with bands of exquisite yellow and blue flowers. Her bodice was trimmed with a fringed blue passé-menterie, and had collars with embroidered mull. Her bright and beautiful hair was not tightly knotted behind the nape of her neck, but flowing down her back. She was a fairy queen, alright. Maybe Mary had to eat nettles and steal bread, but she survived the workhouse. And everyone knew if you walked out of a workhouse in Ireland, you had to possess something special. The magic of the Sidhe, the touch of the fairy, pneumbral, earthy, was her Mary. These revelations danced in her head, pounding out the understanding that just like Mary, she too had survived a similar workhouse-type experience — the coffin ship. And she had emerged, perhaps stronger than Mary. Ireland and New York had wed themselves inside Norah's head and given her freedom to move with clarity and understanding as she worked harder than she ever thought she could possibly work, saving her money, dreaming of home, dreaming of living in both places. Seven years of looking at the sky between the tenement buildings and walking on garbage-strewn streets while she sought to place her feet on a patch of grass here and there, remembering the fecundity, beauty, and then the unyielding and stubborn earth of home. Yes, she needed the stars, too, not just the ground with its firm foundation that she had felt most at home on. But Mary hadn't learned about looking up at all. She was stuck in the past and deeply mired in the present. Why not just let Mary go now? She looked away from the vision of

Mary in the picture on the wall, this ridiculous fairy queen. She cocked her head to the side and glanced at her friend. She was surprised at the sudden feelings of forgiveness that shot through her dark thoughts about Mary. How could she go on without her friend in this city? And now here they were together in this shameful jailhouse, this place of interrogating truth, perhaps at the end of all their quests.

"I can't forgive the likes of someone who calls me her best friend and then blames the murder she committed on me!" Norah shouted and turned back to the picture on the wall, but Mary was no longer in it.

"I don't give a rat's ass about your bloody friendship," the commissioner yelled. "I want to know who committed the murder, and more importantly, who stole the bracelet. And even more importantly than the murder or the theft, where's the goddamn bracelet now?" His jacket buttons were straining and ready to pop because he was breathing so hard.

Norah's strong resolve to rid herself of Mary's friendship collapsed. She touched Mary's arm and looked into her eyes, nodding her head toward the commissioner to indicate she wanted Mary to tell him the truth so they could get the hell out of there. Mary could not have killed the prostitute. No, not her Mary! Mary wiped her dirty face with the back of her hand and her eyes grew large and mischievous. Her chin flicked upward and she smiled triumphantly at Norah. Then she reached down the front of the low bodice of her dress and pulled out the beautiful ornate ruby bracelet.

"I'll be damned! I don't know how it got inside this dress and stuck on me tit!" she exclaimed.

She tossed the bracelet onto the desk before the raging commissioner. Norah, surprised at the bawdy behavior of her friend, laughed aloud. She turned back to look at Officer Leary and although she wasn't able to ascertain if it was lust or admiration, or maybe both, something had come over him. She instinctively knew he was smitten with her friend. *He would be a cat in heat after her now,* Norah thought, as she saw him gazing at Mary's chest. In all the years Norah had known Mary, none of her friend's admirers had ever been able to fondle those lovelies, as Mary referred to them. "Not until the ring's on me finger!" she said to Norah many times. Officer Leary's eyes met hers and she knew he knew what she was thinking. He quickly turned from her, his jaw tightening and his eyes narrowing as he looked straight at the commissioner who clutched the bracelet with his bulky sweaty hand, his fingers wrapping around the rubies ensconced in fine silver, fingering them as he spoke.

"And how long were you planning on wearing this fine bracelet on your tit, Miss Leavey?" he asked. His face relaxed now, but his grip on the bracelet seemed desperate to Norah. His knuckles were white, and she thought how this lovely piece of jewelry would never be the same after having her friend's nipple wearing it and now the commissioner's foul dirty hands on it.

Mary stood up before the commissioner, keeping her eyes on Norah as she spoke. She was still begging for forgiveness. Norah returned a tight smile to her, hoping her friend would understand that she was forgiven only under strict circumstances. She sighed, unable to refrain herself from loving this girl! They were going to survive this ordeal and would soon be buying dresses and selling them in her shop again, but now they would always remember to look in the under sleeves and pockets and even in the hems to see if any gems were hidden.

"It was only yesterday I bought the dress off of the poor woman, Commissioner. I bought it, not Norah here," she said, her eyes still on Norah. "I had no idea the jewelry was hidden in it, sir. And I didn't know the dress had been stolen, either. And that the poor thing would be murdered after I bought the dress from her."

"Oh, you didn't, did you now?" The commissioner still clutched the bracelet, his eyes squinting at Mary, trying to figure her out. "So you're saying you bought the dress sometime in the evening, around five o'clock, you said, and then you went back to your friend's shop alone?"

"That's the truth of it, sir. I was keen on finding that dress after seeing the woman parading about the street in it looking as proud as if she was some rich high-society woman. I knew I shouldn't be doing business without me friend, here, but I had to have the dress. I just had to have it for myself. And so I—"

"I know your damn story… Who can vouch that you left the mab around the time you say and went to the store to work? The woman was murdered between nine and ten P.M. How do we know it wasn't you who done it?"

Mary begged Norah for help, "Norah, you know I wouldn't kill an insect or even one of those wild dogs running the streets even if it was baring its teeth and lunging at me throat!"

Norah didn't know what to say. "I don't know—"

"Leary," the commissioner said, "Put the cuffs on her and take her back to the clink."

Norah watched him open a drawer and lift out a safe deposit box, open it, and drop the bracelet in as if it were too hot to hold in his hand any longer. She stood up and watched Leary place the cuffs on Mary, who peered at her through her tangled mass of hair, surrendering to her plight. Leary walked Mary toward the door and looked back at Norah before leaving. She might be wrong, but was he trying to communicate to her that he didn't believe her friend had anything to do with the murder, and that he would help them? But if he did help them, he would be out of a job and maybe turned out of the country; and she knew he liked his new position in America, that she was certain.

After Leary and Mary left with the other officer, Norah turned back to the commissioner who was tidying up his desk. The door slammed shut and she felt frightened.

"I'll be going now, Commissioner," Norah said, and then her mind reverberated with an echo of a memory from long ago. She had been impotent in being able to help Mary, just as she had once been paralyzed with fear and overcome by the officers in Ireland when they had come to tumble and burn her friends' home because they hadn't paid their rent. She, a mere child, had stood with a pitchfork in her hand thinking she would strike the police officer.

Before her thoughts came back to the present, the commissioner walked around from behind his desk to stand near her, grasping her hands in his. She recoiled and tried to pull back, but he clutched them tightly. Pin pricks of light flashed around her vision and she felt herself giving way to a faint.

"If you'd like to keep yourself from a jail cell yourself, Miss...," the commissioner said, and then he hesitated to say anything more, realizing he must appear vulgar to Norah McCabe. Ah, but it had worked before for him, and why not now? He could break her in...like a wild colt, she was...she must be a virgin. He thought at first she was the typical prostitute from the streets, but he knew now she was quite innocent, this one. Unless they became mabs on the street, the Irish ones kept their cunts clean. The touch of her skin, as cold as it was, as well as her resistance and fear, aroused him. He'd get what he wanted. He usually did. He could tame her and show her that a man's prowess was in his genitals as well as in his position in this city. And although he knew he was repulsive to her, there had been others just as young who had salivated for more of what he had to offer. Sure, some trinkets they craved, but as ugly as he was certain he was, he was all the more certain of his cock and how he had learned he could pleasure the most resistant of women, young or old.

His breathing cadenced into a rhythm like one already engaged in the act of lovemaking. His eyes were half-closed in his excitement, his penis hardening with his thoughts and being so near her. When she began struggling to get away from him, he became aroused all the more. When her right hand slipped out of his, he was surprised. His eyes opened wide and he grabbed her around the waist when she turned and tried to run from him. He had Norah McCabe now...the god damn bitch...he had her now. The door was shut and if any officer had the gall to come near his office when the door was shut, they'd be out on the street without a job. *My God, her waist is so tiny,* he thought, pressing himself firmly against her.

"I can give you the bracelet and more," he whispered lustily. He held both of her arms behind her and slightly turned them to make sure it registered that he could break them if she tried to move. The fast beats of her heart against his chest felt soothing and comforting to him. He wanted to get his mouth on her, stick his tongue down her throat, and tame her. It was too late now to stop. He understood his body had gone too far and there was no will to turn back, even if this time, he might end up being caught. Her face was pressed onto his collarbone and he couldn't let go of her arms to force her mouth to his, but his hips were slightly moving against her, and he had to keep himself from thrusting violently and having it be over too soon. He wanted to get her to the floor so he could lift up her skirts and fully have his way with her.

He had become so excited he feared he would lose his grip on her arms. She had surprised him. It usually took time for him to woo someone like her, to be this hard so quickly. His body, not his mind, was now in control, and his desire for her had made him weak and at her mercy. He tried to tighten his hands around her arms, but his whole body felt shaky and weak, defeated with lust. He continued to move slowly against her and because she no longer tried to free herself from him, he was sure that she, too, was responding to him. Perhaps he had aroused her!

A couple of years ago, an Irishman from the gang, The Pug Uglies, had been brought in for questioning. The man had been handcuffed, but he had taken his handcuffed fists and thrust them into the commissioner's face. He would never forget the searing pain and how long it took for him to heal. He had never in his life experienced such agony in his body. Until the present, when Norah McCabe all at once brought up her right knee with such force onto his stiff penis that he backed away and fell to the floor.

Norah had felt the hardness of the man's groin against her, as well as the hardness of his collarbone pressing onto her face. Mostly, she felt the hardness of life rendering her too weak to fight. Her fear and disbelief that this could be happening to her, the very thing her parents, especially her da, had warned her about, caused her to become immobile against the commissioner's strength. Would he rape her? Kill her? Both? She couldn't adequately process what was happening to her and odd things came into her mind while he held her and moved his hips against hers. She thought about the mangy dog that had come upon her once and humped her leg. And then she imagined the commissioner's chest hairs against her breasts, and with this thought, bile came into her mouth that she swallowed. And she thought of her father and mother and wondered if they became like animals in their lust for one another. But she had never heard them breathe and moan the way this man was doing. Even with her nose and mouth pressed against his collarbone, she was glad for it, for she didn't have to inhale as much of his foul breath that now surrounded them both. And then she nearly laughed at the position she was in. She suddenly felt she was out of her body and hovering above them both. How comical they looked together, especially the commissioner!

But when he told her that he wanted to have all of her and then pushed harder against her, she came out of her dream-like place. She instinctively jolted her hips away from him and drove her right knee into his groin. And then she leapt from him, thinking how graceful she was in doing so. She never looked back to see if he had gotten up from the floor, but pulled open the door and ran out, slamming it shut when she left. And there was her man standing outside the door like a sentinel, a lowly sentinel, like the dirty Irishman that this Leary was.

"You knew! You knew what he was about! You filthy pig, you slime from a godforsaken cursed country!" she yelled back at Leary while running down the hall to get back on the streets of a city where she would never feel safe again. She had heard once that after you got married and lost your virginity, you would never be the same person. Her sister, Meg, had told her this. She felt it had already happened.

Chapter Five

By the time Norah escaped the lascivious grasp of the commissioner and ran out of the police headquarters, she had indeed been altered. Let out at the seams and sewn up differently, just like one of the dresses acquired for her shop that would be transformed to sit in the display window. She ran a few blocks, absorbing the curious expressions of people; kicked at a pig roaming the streets; and knocked down a wee lad hawking papers. Once, as a young girl, she sold newspapers on the street, too. His papers fell onto the road and were run over by a wagon and picked up by passersby who cared little about a child yelling and cursing. At another time, Norah would have helped him pick up the fallen papers, especially since she had caused him to tumble, but she fled from the boy and made her way down the street. Turning at the next corner, she encountered Mr. Harrigan, the editor of the *Irish-American* newspaper.

"What a lovely surprise, Miss McCabe!"

He was as meticulously groomed and colorful as when she first met him in her store. His hair was dark brown and curly, parted on the side, and oiled down to control its unruliness. Norah got a whiff of the perfumed Macassar oil and hoped it was strong enough to cover any odor of her unwashed condition. She glanced at his slightly bushy eyebrows and thought it odd that the rest of his face was free from facial hair and was baby smooth. He smiled at her and Norah stared at his pointed chin with an indentation prominently displayed. She didn't want to meet his gaze. His eyes, a slate color with flecks of robin egg blue were extraordinarily attractive.

She had liked Mr. Harrigan immediately when she first me him. He was articulate and intelligent, dispensing witticisms along with pertinent facts of city life; and he adored fashion as much as she did. This day he was wearing a black satin cravat, a waistcoat lined with blue velvet the color of his eyes, dark gray trousers, and a breast pin set in what looked like diamonds. Norah took notice right off that he wasn't wearing the French white gloves that he had been wearing at her store. She presented her hand to take his offered one and felt pain surge through her arm. The commissioner had held her arms tightly and at an unnatural angle. She stifled a moan. Her arm hurt, but she was also mortified to be seen in such disarray in body and spirit.

"I'm in a poor state now, sir," Norah said. Her hair was undone and in a mess of curls that frizzed around her pale face and dark circled eyes. And she could detect the commissioner's rancid cologne that still clung to her. Her stomach rumbled from a lack of food, and she felt nauseous and weak. She hiccupped and covered her mouth, further embarrassing herself.

"Miss McCabe, I'm sorry for your obvious unease," Mr. Harrigan responded, "but shall we take some refreshment?" he asked, smiling feebly, attempting to hide his surprise at her untidy appearance. He, indeed, was thrilled to have encountered Norah McCabe, for he thought she was a most interesting and lovely woman. Since meeting her in her shop, he had desired to make contact with her again. He was presently on his way to the police headquarters to investigate another murder of a depraved prostitute. It would be more sordid news to include in his paper, and he would soon enough be bored by it all. He recognized his lack of charity toward this human being, but was becoming more and more disgusted by the overwhelming number of prostitutes in New York who spread their legs with all sorts of diseases hidden between them. He, himself, had never visited a prostitute, not even a high priced one! Most of the newspapermen he knew visited Corlear's Hook at least once a year; the *Tribune* men especially boasted of their sexual exploits, barring they didn't have to prescribe to one of the potions advertised in their paper for syphilis. He possessed no desire for such sexual excursions; and except for the annoying urge that coursed through his loins in the early mornings, he ignored any reminders from his body that he should enjoy sex as well as his fellow men.

These days, he was more aroused by his work as a journalist that enabled him to view the parade of fashion on the streets of New York. He laughingly admitted to himself that he was an incorrigible dandy who postured as a newspaperman. He was also passionate about the rights of Irish Catholics in New York and thus started his newspaper to give the downtrodden paddies an intelligent voice. He felt his paper gave the Irish a voice of dissent and power, so they didn't have to flex the Tammany Hall muscle as much. Of late, he had been doing a series on Irish women who owned shops in Five Points. Hence, his meeting the singularly vivacious Norah McCabe at *A Bee in Your Bonnet.*

"My hair…'tis a mess…," she answered, looking over her shoulder to see if the commissioner might be coming after her. *What if he did? He wouldn't dare, would he?* She shuddered when she thought of him. She would scream to the world what he had attempted to do to her. Norah tried to smooth out her skirts as she faced Mr. Harrigan. Of course she would be safe, she thought, for Mr. Harrigan was an important newspaperman. He would write up what the commissioner had done to her; she was certain of it. He was dedicated to truth telling even if he was a bit too concerned with his fancy clothes. She smiled at him and played with her hair, suddenly forgetting her circumstances. Even in her terrible state, she became eager for him to escort her somewhere for tea, perhaps an eatery that accepted female patrons if accompanied by men. She desperately desired to shake off the nightmarish events of the morning. After all, what was there for her to be worried about? She was innocent and eventually all would be well. And for now she had someone accompanying her, a handsome newspaperman at that, who wanted to take her out for tea.

Norah didn't comprehend the devious political ties that existed between the commissioner, the police department, and the corrupt metropolitan government that controlled the city. The commissioner would be protected, not her, and there wouldn't be much Mr. Harrigan could do about it.

"You look fine, Miss McCabe," Mr. Harrigan said, forcing a smile she understood was to cover her embarrassment. He had already seen how chic and elegant she could dress. She had style and was capable of being one of the best dressed women in Five Points. He placed his hand on her elbow to escort her down the street, and she began to relax as they walked. *It was a fine life to be knowing a newspaperman like Mr. Harrigan,* she thought happily, her heart quickening. He moved his hand from her elbow to the small of her back to guide her more surely on the crowded street. He greeted people as they walked and she was honored to be with him, although conspicuously awkward.

A few minutes later, she abruptly stopped in the middle of the sidewalk and people behind them bumped into them. Apologies were made and Norah pulled away from Mr. Harrigan. Her face was hot with shame for acting abominably! What was she doing parading down the street on the arm of a gentleman when her friend, Mary, was sitting in a jail cell, and her poor mother was most likely sitting at home wringing her hands? How could she so readily forget that a woman had been murdered, an expensive bracelet stolen, and that she had been accused, attacked and had barely escaped being raped!

"Can we talk? Over here," she gestured toward a building where a few kids stood next to it hawking papers. There were also a few drunks lying close to the building whose bodies were curled up tightly, reminding Norah of cats sleeping peacefully in a ray of sunlight.

"Surely," Mr. Harrigan said, surprised by her behavior. They walked to an empty space next to the building, and he held his hand over his eyes to shield the sharp gaze of the afternoon sun that was beating down on them.

"I can't take time for tea as if I'm a lady of leisure. I've a business to tend to," Norah moved her hands nervously as she talked. Pride and fear rose from the pit of her stomach to her head, both vying for recognition. Which would win? Pride was in the lead as she asserted her importance as a shop owner. She would not humiliate herself any further and confide in Mr. Harrigan about being accused of a murder of a prostitute and then mauled by the commissioner as if she were a lady of the night.

"We'll have tea soon, in my store," she said quickly. "Mam makes the best soda bread in Five Points, and I've a small table we can sit at. I have China cups and a lovely teapot. The table is for Mary and me when we need to take a break from our all our sewing and…" She hesitated before continuing, "surely, we need to take a break from our difficult labor and staying up most nights sewing and…." Norah's words tumbled out uncontrollably as her pride broke into tiny particles of fear, both emotions unable to detach from one another in order for one to dominate.

"Of course, I'll get you a buggy, Miss McCabe. No need to walk any farther…," Mr. Harrigan said, nervously looking down the street for one.

Norah bowed her head and used the sleeve of her dress to dab at the tears stinging her eyes. Mr. Harrigan turned from her to hail a cart or buggy. She was keenly aware of losing her aplomb and tried to gird herself so she could take charge of all that had happened to her in the last few hours. She looked up to see a buggy had parked near them and imagined numerous onlookers staring at her and Harrigan. Gathering up her skirts, she pushed through the crowd to get to the buggy. Mr. Harrigan followed, handed the driver some money, and opened the door for Norah to get in. She tried not to look at him as she climbed in, tears brimming over. She pulled in her skirts, and a piece of her petticoat trailed out the door when it was shut. She looked out the window toward Mr. Harrigan, but didn't meet his eyes, "Thanks be to God for your kindness. Please come to tea soon in my shop, and we'll have a chat when I'm in better charge of myself."

She was gone from him just like that! Gone before he could ask her what had happened, and before he could attempt to console her. Mr. Harrigan felt chagrined for not recognizing Norah was in some kind of trouble, but he hadn't wanted to specifically ask and violate her privacy. If he stepped over the line with this proud young Irish woman, he could risk losing a new friendship that he very much desired. He didn't have a lot of intimate friends, only many acquaintances, and he was quite alone in the world. His parents had emigrated from Ireland before he had been born, and although he was proud to be an Irish-American, he understood that he was different from the Irish who had come from Ireland. The new ones had come during the Famine where rotting spuds were spewed from the belly of the land as if they were doing the evil bidding of the English. His understanding, however, was minimized and reduced to romantic idealism about the suffering of his people. He responded to the Celtic blood that coursed through his veins, but this blood had not boiled, seethed, and been shed amongst brothers and sisters in the old country.

As he watched the buggy jerk forward and clip clop away with Norah's hand hanging limply out the window after waving at him, he was puzzled and struck by anxiety for her plight, whatever it might be. His feelings were akin to wanting to care for a little hurt bird that had fallen out of its nest, this nest such an unnatural one for the rural Irish who came here. It made him more aware of Ireland's native young being in danger of losing all hope, like the skinballs, the lowliest Irish orphans who became stunted in every aspect of their growth, and who lived worse than wild dogs on the streets. He could clearly see that Norah McCabe was hanging onto a thread of hope for assimilation and success.

Mr. Harrigan suddenly remembered the news item he had to attend to. Why, the enchanting Norah McCabe had caused him to forget about his mission and work! Perhaps he would will himself to care more for this poor mab who had been murdered, he thought, righteous feelings filling him. He couldn't allow himself to become insensitive, for even someone as sweet and unknowing as Norah McCabe could be in grave danger on the sinister New York streets. He walked quickly toward his destination, resolving to do better and bear the burden for the Irish as owner and editor of his Irish-American newspaper.

By the time the buggy pulled up to the tenement building where the McCabes lived, Norah had regained some composure. She was anxious to be inside her home with Mam and Da, especially her da, for he understood the streets better than her mother. How could any woman understand them the way a man could? Mam always acted quite sure and smug about her life, but Norah thought she was unnervingly naive in her assumptions. She quickly climbed up the steps and stepped on a homemade doll, ignoring the children playing there. The door was ajar! She called out a greeting and no one answered. Norah hesitated to go inside, wondering if her parents had quickly left the apartment to look for her. It was unwise to leave the door open, for the dresser, their few pieces of china, and feather bed could be stolen in a flash, even in the middle of the day. She walked through all three rooms, but no one was there and nothing had been touched. Her heart was beating rapidly, her breathing was labored, and her eyes were darting around the apartment. How would she tell them what happened? Would they believe her? Mam would misconstrue the events of the morning and consider her rude for running away from the Irish police officer. She wouldn't understand her horrid plight that nearly took away her virginity, a virginity her mother worried over. Norah wandered from room to room trying to process everything that had recently happened to her. And what about Mary? Would Mary survive in a jail cell another night? Oh God, Mary couldn't have committed the murder or deliberately stolen the bracelet! Would the commissioner go after Mary the way he had come after her? Norah sat down at the table and placed her head on her arms, not knowing what to do. Then she felt something sticking to her arm and saw it was a note from her mother, "Norah, gone for Da and to the police station. Mam."

She put her head back down and closed her eyes. If she left the apartment to look for them, she would be in danger of missing them and possibly risk running into the commissioner. She didn't know if she was still being charged with murder and would have to go to jail as the commissioner had threatened, or if it had been a perverted ploy he had used in order to have his way with her. He couldn't have planned it out beforehand, she thought, and so it must have occurred to him after Mary had confessed she purchased the dress and inadvertently found the expensive bracelet. She couldn't fathom the motives of this Commissioner, except that he had wanted to overpower her and force her to have sex with him. Had she so aroused the man in the short time she had been in his presence? Would there be other men who would react to her the same way? It was as if she had been stripped and exposed; and what had she done to cause him to do this to her? To think she had paraded around the city with Mary in all her fineries amongst men like the commissioner! Stupid girleen, she was! How could she ever be comfortable amongst men now, not knowing if their uncontrollable desires would cause them to become violent and forceful toward her?

Oblivious of her solitary striking beauty surfacing in her young womanhood, Norah never walked, but marched through the streets confidently. She had recently been enjoying mild flirtations from certain men on the street, in spite of having the lovely and buxom Mary by her side. Norah assumed they were interested in a mere frivolous interchange and considered it only entertaining and innocent. One class of men was the Anglo-Saxon gentleman who was scholarly and dressed modestly, and the other was the rough and bawdy transgressor of social protocol and grace, whose kind she mostly encountered. The small sparks from the kindling within her maturating femininity had never ignited into flames. She had clearly seen the struggle for women to maintain a family, and although she believed Da was loyal to her mother, she had learned that many men felt it was their right to visit prostitutes. She was steadfast in her feelings that she never wanted to be roped into and tied up in domestic drudgery, and especially to suffer from a man's domineering presence. She loved her da, but he was the one who had the freedom to explore the world and play his fiddle in the saloons, unlike her mam who scrubbed floors on her hands and knees and sipped tea and gossiped with the Irish neighbor women on the stoops. The admiration she had been enjoying from young men had not been significant enough to change her mind about involvement and marriage. Yes, it had all been so new to her, the flirtations and attention, but now after the commissioner's breath and hands had been all over her, her innocence was sullied. She had obviously been blind and now understood that beneath all male behavior was a more primal and animalistic nature ready to spring forth to devour her.

Norah rested at the table, trying to determine what she should do next. How would she ever be able to walk the streets again? She thought of Mr. Harrigan and blushed. Certainly he wouldn't suggest sex with her one day, too, would he? And to think she had walked alongside Leary, and although a policeman, he could do the same, too. The commissioner, a man of the law had done this to her! She wept quietly, unconsciously moving her arms on the rough pine table.

Time passed and she stood up to pull down the shades in the two windows facing the street and to go to the water closet to tidy up. Water in a tin basin sat in the corner of the tiny, dismal room, dirty from being heated and used in the morning, but she didn't care. She used the necessary and splashed water on her face, neck, and arms, and then pulled off her dress, letting it fall onto the floor. Small splinters of wood from the table had lodged in her forearms and stung, but this discomfort was overshadowed by the sore bruises the commissioner had left. Norah looked down at her petticoats and shivered. Underneath her undergarments was nothing covering and protecting her innocence. She went to the kitchen intending to boil water for tea, but was too tired for this simple routine and decided against it. She got down on her knees next to the dresser and opened up the cupboard to inhale her memories. This was an act of melancholic compulsion she ritualistically performed to exorcise doubt and to glean hope.

Norah pulled out her mother's old shawl from the cupboard and placed it over her shoulders. The texture was rough, but the touch of it always brought comfort mixed with intense sadness. Many years before, Mam had placed this worn-out wrap over her small body when she had hid in the dresser ready to depart for America. She had clung to it while crossing the tumultuous sea, inhaling her mother's scent of strength and toil that reminded her to dry up her tears and bear her burdens. She feared it was now to become her mantle, and she would have to soon place it around her shoulders and become a woman and leave her childish ways behind.

Chaotic thoughts marched around her head and she wished for sleep to escape them. America was no Ireland, to be sure! America was a country that preferred the perfect lines of order, cleanliness, and faith. Although she lived in Five Points, mostly amongst Irish Catholics, the Protestant Anglo-Saxon winds blew into her neighborhood that increasingly made her feel foolish believing in the unseen, and the rigors and superstitions of her Catholic faith. Their hearth at home in Ireland had been a place of learning which had imbued her with ancient stories and music, but here next to their coal stove, there was only silence. It seemed out of place and odd to sit on the one sofa they possessed to try and do what they had once done in Ireland around the hearth, and so it was only in the saloons away from his family that Da played the strains of Irish melodies. Here in America, but not in Five Points, pianofortes were played next to hearths by soft hands that never scrubbed floors. There were no fiddles plucked by calloused and roughened fingers playing along with the dancing flames in American stoves.

Norah laid her sore and exhausted body on the sofa. Sleep was trying to come, but first she had to shove these thoughts into the safe corners of her dresser across from her. This had become her method of letting go of her worries each night before sleep would come. It was worse this day, for her worries had grown into monstrous fears.

She finally slept and her childhood friend, Sean, came to her in a vivid dream. He was awkward and gangly in his blue woolen trousers held together by a thin rope around his waist, but covered up by an old coarse tweed jacket three sizes too large. His plaid woolen cap was too big for a head topped with thick and coarse ginger hair that crowned a face gentle and resolute. In the dream, he was exactly as he had always been. A lad thrust into the future, forgetting his past. His work boots were worn and without their laces, but he stepped lively and sure in them. The skies were gently dropping blue tinted snowflakes as they walked together, and his hand held hers inside her coat pocket. Soon, the snow crowned their heads in lace and they pointed and laughed at one another. As the dream continued, she could see that a royal blue scarf had been tied around her neck, and it sparkled in the moonlight that was sliding between buildings. In this dream, Norah was sixteen and Sean was nineteen, and it was a winter evening in New York.

Norah suddenly woke and sat up with a start, surprised she was not walking down a winter street but instead was on her sofa, a woman, not a child. If only she could return to the dream, for it had been real once. As she reoriented herself out of sleep and the dream, a painful memory materialized into one dark thought. Sean had been alive in her dream and she had felt his breath on her face and his hand in hers. But Sean was dead, not alive. It was believed that he died at sea after becoming a captain's mate and traveling on cargo ships transporting travelers and goods back and forth across the Atlantic. He had promised he would accompany her home to Ireland one day, but then he had gone away as her sister Kate had gone away from her—dead and buried in the sea. Home not on land, but forever in the sea without her, unless she would go there someday, too.

Chapter Six

Norah sat on the sofa and recalled nearly every word and detail of the last winter with Sean.

"There you are Norah, but where is your cart of dreams?" Sean asked her when she was sixteen. He had been a wizened rag tag Irish boy-man of the streets and they had been best friends. He always teased her about her scrappy idealism since meeting when she was thirteen and had just come to America. Sean came from Dublin two years before Norah had arrived. He became her fierce guide, leading her through the mean streets of New York, and sniffing out the imminent dangers a vulnerable young girl from the old country would not understand. He had proudly stated that he could have easily become a Bowery boy, a rook, or a runner welcoming immigrants at the docks with their fragile and broken lives. He could have pandered, but he had become a newsie instead, hawking exaggerated stories to titillate and entertain. When they met, she was a charming, yet hungry, peasant girl, her ivory skin pulled tight over bones that nearly protruded through her shoulders, sharp, and warning everyone to keep their distance. It was Sean who told her that her eyes were sea-green from so long on the boat, a prism of colors that depended upon her mood. She had never known that her eyes were more than green. He said they had softened him and prevented him from becoming a product of the evil streets. Norah would only laugh at his compliments as they both matured, but he was adamant that it was she who had changed him. He told her that he could no longer steal, lie, or cheat after meeting her. They sold papers together, squabbled about right and wrong, and no matter how much time passed before they would see each other again, they felt bound with the strong and dark Celtic knots of their country. The two young people had been a tightly woven team of survival on the streets of New York.

Norah heard his voice as she sat on the sofa. It was so clear and real, as if he were in the room asking her about her cart of dreams.

"There's no cart, just burdens heavy on me shoulders," Norah had responded to him. She recalled placing her head upon Sean's chest and folding her hands together behind her back. He had taken off his cap and placed it upon her head to shield her hair from the large snowflakes falling upon them.

"How many icy winters have we've been together?" Sean asked her. She had encouraged him to take time to notice the snow falling between the tall buildings, claiming that the sparkling flakes danced with the fairies and turned their icy shapes into silver-bluish lace she could wear on her coat as a collar. She had sworn the lacy snow was more beautiful than the ermine collars rich ladies wore, although it always melted away. How foolish she had been then! She sighed and then held her breath in, trying to listen. Sean's presence in the apartment was almost palpable.

Norah continued to reflect on Sean and that particular winter spent together. At the time, Da had announced he was going to leave the family in New York and go to California to dig for gold. She thought he had already gotten over the ridiculous fever to strike it rich. She feared for his life and felt it was inevitable that after traveling miles in a wagon, on horses or even donkeys, crossing plains, rivers, and mountains, he would be slain and buried where gold flecks sparkled like a deceitful seductress.

Norah had said to Sean, "If Da leaves for California and Mam goes to live with Aunt Bridget in western New York to begin another new life, I'll be staying here, but I won't be staying with Meg and her snotty nosed children. She'll have me as their nursemaid day and night and I'll never be wearing the designs of Paris and traveling back to Ireland and going to other parts of the world. I'll be stuck here wearing moth-eaten woolens in every season!"

Sean then lifted his cap off Norah's head and with his right hand he had gently cupped her chin and lifted it toward his face.

"I've become a ship's mate, Norah. I'm not just some paddy cleaning the brigs no more." He let go of her and they stared at one another for a few moments, the snow suddenly making her feel cold and alone. And then he got down on one knee and looked up at her as she gazed down at him bemused and blushing, not knowing whether to laugh or pity him.

"Will you marry me, Norah McCabe, and let me fill your cart with dreams that can become real?"

Although Sean's presence was keenly felt in the apartment, the stark reality that she would never see him again gripped her with desolation. She desired to sleep again and perhaps she could return to him in another dream. She couldn't remember how she had answered him on that day! Had she laughed at his preposterous proposal? She had only been sixteen years old, with big notions about creating new high fashion and traveling to Ireland, to all of Europe, and again returning to America. She had no thoughts of marriage then, as she didn't now. She looked at the dresser next to the stove and wondered about its place in their tenement home, just as she wondered about her place in New York. She had thought herself a high and mighty businesswoman. Sean would laugh at her now, for her dreams hadn't become as grand as she once expressed to him. But the saints be praised, wasn't she still intact and strong? She had told him she would always be her own person, her own woman. She wasn't doing so bad, was she now? Surely, she could have become a schoolteacher like her teacher had encouraged her to do. She'd heard that Margaret O'Brien, from the ward, had become a teacher, but it was hard going for her, with her brogue and all.

Norah didn't want to teach. She wanted to learn. To learn to be more than a ragged colleen, another Bridget who cleaned up after the rich, but more importantly, to learn how to gather the treasures the sky and her dreams had taught her to believe in, loftier and more transcendent than the dirt she walked on. These things to wrap around her, promises of something bigger than the hard insufferable earth! She never wanted to go upstate and toil on a farm as her family desired to do, but likewise, she wasn't at home in the crowded city, either.

Norah rose from the sofa and prepared to light the stove, picking up some pieces of coal that Mam had brought in that morning. It was then she heard herself answering Sean, the only young man to ever ask for her hand in marriage. She looked far back in her mind to where they had been on that cold winter day and heard clearly her answer to him.

"Get up off the frozen ground and be gone with ye, Sean O'Connolly! I'll have none of this talk now! You have seas to cross and I have to keep my cart of dreams from going into the river!"

She had laughed at him. It pained her now to think of how careless her words had been. She had only ever thought of Sean as the most precious of friends, someone during those years who had been neither male or female to her, someone part heaven and part earth, as if he were the comforting treasured toy she had never had as a child. But to marry and put away childish ways, to know Sean as a real man and to become a real woman, would have been the death of herself. She recalled then that it was his proposal which had jolted her from her hopeless state over Da planning a trip to California. She had suddenly felt strong and sure that she had to leave off being tied in her heart to Da, as well as to Sean, or else her dreams would never materialize. But if Sean were alive now, she thought, would he also desire her the vulgar way the commissioner had? Where would the line be drawn between love and passion, or was there no line, no separation?

Norah watched the sparks from the fire in the coal stove and shuddered. It was August. No need for the fire in the middle of the day, but she was cold, as cold as when she stood shivering on that winter street with Sean. Heaviness filled her entire body and she sat down on the sofa to think about this day that had altered her so much to send her back to Sean. A light and fairy-like prayer for the hearth, words silk-like and worn smooth in the Irish language came humming into her mind and upon her lips. It was a prayer invoking St. Brighid that poured out of her in one powerful exhalation:

> Brighid of the mantle encompass us,
> Lady of the Lambs protect us,
> Keeper of the Hearth, kindle us,
> Beneath your mantle, gather us
> And restore us to memory,
> The mantle of Brighid about us,
> The memory of Brighid within us,
> The protection of Brighid keeping us
> From harm, from ignorance, from heartlessness,
> This day and night,
> From dawn till dark
> From dark to dawn.

Norah dropped her head into her hands and wept, rolling her torso close to her lap, her mother's shawl draped over her. The contour and silhouette of the old woman she could grow into became visible before the small flames in the stove. It was too late to pray for Brighid's protection from injury and stupidity. She wept for Sean, for the hearth in her home in Ireland, for the loss of St. Brighid who was only Mother Mary of Sorrows here in New York; but mostly she wept over ambitions that had become mired, and for the peeling back of the skin of her innocence, exposing her to the quagmires of herself. She cried until she felt nothing, and just as she decided to make herself a cup of tea, the wind blew the door open and the flames in the stove leapt into a vibrant dance with hissing and popping. Fear gripped her as she got up from the sofa to shut the door, but when she looked down the stairs, there stood Mam, Da, Mary, and Mr. Harrigan. Her friend, Mary, was not in jail! She immediately flew down the steps and flung herself onto her da as if she were a child again.

"*A Chuisle,* what is this now?" he asked. "You're safe, girl. Mary told us of your battle with the demons of this city!" He gently pushed her away.

Norah looked around nervously and became self-conscious before the few neighbors on the street.

"I'll make some tea," Mam said, eager to bring normalcy back into their lives. Mam's hair fell out of her scarf and her eyes were red-rimmed and tired. Guilt seized Norah for causing her mam so much grief. They all walked up the steps and into the apartment.

"Pull the kitchen chairs over to the stove and we'll have our tea there," Da said. He, too, looked exhausted and worn out to Norah's discerning eyes. She peered at the faces of each person carrying the chairs over to the stove. Mr. Harrigan, normally chipper and talkative, was quiet and morose. Mary's face was as white as clouds and there were long streaks of eye make-up that had dried on her cheeks. She was trembling and reminded Norah of an animal that had put up the fight of its life, only to be cornered, cowering and frozen in fright. It wasn't like Mary to be beaten down by life, and if she had endured a heinous attack against her person or character, she'd still be baring her teeth and lunging at her opponent. Defeat, not victory, permeated the room, and as Norah glanced at the small fire in the stove, she thought what was needed was a real fire that burned with vigor, not one that was tamed and hissing like a garden snake as it was doing now. She and her family, Mary, with an exception to Harrigan, were merely inconsequential tenement dwellers stuck in this city, and the fire in this stove would only ever be meager. She tried to shake these thoughts from her mind, for if they lingered, she would feel imprisoned and defeated forever. She had to battle against the feelings that they were all encamped in a prison for immigrants. Their masters surrounded them with all the wealth and riches of the world that they could only salivate over, perhaps taking small tastes, but never would they be able to fully savor them.

No one said a word, but mindlessly stared into the fire while Mam and Norah placed comforting cups of tea in each of their hands. Then Mr. Harrigan's voice thundered in the awkward silence, as he turned toward Norah, who had taken a seat next to him.

"I must inform you what happened since I met you earlier on the street. You didn't know I was on my way to interview the commissioner about the murder of the renowned Bridie of Motley Street. Apparently, she had been a maid at the Astor House hotel during the day and a prostitute at night, working for a Rabbit pimp. The pimp had her stealing right and left from the till at the Astor place. If a dress went missing, the guest would think she had forgotten to pack it, but this time Bridie and her pimp got more than they could have dreamed of, a dress and bracelet together worth thousands. They didn't care about the dress, but the bracelet they understood was worth more than they could ever get at a popshop. Bridie kept it hidden in the dress where it had been found while they waited for time to pass before they'd have it appraised, not wanting to bring undue attention to themselves so soon after its disappearance.

The night of her murder, Bridie thought she might attract a higher fee from a gentleman customer if she wore the dress; so she paraded the streets forgetting about the bracelet. The mab was intoxicated with some anti-fogmatic and got herself all possessed-like, having been nipping at the bottle with her old madam she used to work for, before going out on the street. Although her pimp had told her to keep her mouth shut about the bracelet inside the dress, in her drunkenness, she told the madam, who swore to protect her and somehow help her keep the bracelet. Later, Bridie was on the street trying to entice a customer and sold the dress to our Mary here, and practically stripped down to her bare body right there on the street. Later, when the Rabbit found her passed out drunk without the dress and bracelet, he murdered her in a rage. The madam saw the gruesome murder and heard the pimp whimpering about the bracelet.

She had also seen Mary buy the dress from Bridie, but out of spite, decided not to tell the pimp she knew where the bracelet was. She planned on discreetly procuring the bracelet from Mary later, and then working out a deal with the pimp. But then the pimp visited the madam, suspecting that she knew what had happened and that she might have the bracelet. He threatened to cut her throat if she talked to anyone about murdering Bridie, and told her she had twenty-four hours to tell him where the bracelet was. She knew well that his sporting men would do the job on her if he went to prison. When the police came sniffing around, she was afraid and lied to the police about Mary murdering Bridie for the dress. Neighbors had already informed the police they had seen you and Mary together that night and she had to do something to save her skin. When the police found Mary with the dress and the bracelet sewn up in it, our dear madam felt she had been given a second chance in life. She even thought of quitting the profession!"

Mr. Harrigan explained that he visited the madam who confessed everything. Everything but the name of the pimp, whose name she conveniently didn't remember. This pimp, now at large, had murdered a mab, but the investigation would be closed. The dress and bracelet had been found, and that was most important.

It wasn't the first time Mr. Harrigan had gotten a story out of this madam, for she trusted him not to expose her and put her life in danger.

Norah was relieved, for she was no longer a suspect and the truth about the murder had been exposed. She looked at Mary's head hanging heavily to her chest, her body shaking the entire time Mr. Harrigan told the story. Whatever could have happened to Mary in the jail cell, Norah wondered, feeling their friendship and life together in New York had now been changed forever.

"What about the commissioner?" Norah asked Mr. Harrigan.

"The good for nothing paddy hater, he is!" Da exclaimed.

Mr. Harrigan didn't say anything and stared blankly out the window.

"He took the bracelet and tried to steal it for himself!" Norah exclaimed. Everyone looked at her and waited for her to say more.

Mr. Harrigan turned to her again, "There's more! The commissioner was fuming over how there were so many reporters converging on his office to get the low-down on the bracelet, but not on the woman murdered. As if he cared about the woman! He told us a young woman had been taken into custody for the murder, but that she wasn't offering the whereabouts of the bracelet, but tactics would be employed to ensure the bracelet would be found. I was leaving with the rest of the reporters, and up the steps come your mam and da, who were asking if we knew where you were. I didn't know you'd been involved in this, Norah," Mr. Harrigan reached out to touch Norah's hand lightly, "or I would have been more understanding when I met you on the street." He gazed at her, his starched cravat uneven and sticking into his handsome chin. Norah smiled back.

"I didn't know if you made it home, or your carriage had been intercepted by the commissioner's men. I wanted to interview the suspect the commissioner was holding and so I suggested your mam and da wait outside. When I went back inside, two policemen were standing outside the door of the commissioner's office. I asked them what was going on, and an officer, Leary's the name, told me that the suspect was being interrogated by the commissioner in his office."

Mary suddenly stood up and yelled, "His grimy fat hands were all over me!" She picked up Norah's shawl and wrapped it around her, covering her chest as she spoke. "He said no one had to know I took the bracelet if I let him have his way with me. He said I owed him some hide, and I might wear the bracelet while he took some. When he began fondling me and pushing me into the closet, I clawed at him and screamed as loud as I could." Mary sank down on the sofa, turning her face away from everyone. Norah looked at Mam's face that had turned pale. Every woman in New York feared being attacked this way, but Norah had never actually felt it could happen to her or Mary. She had always kept herself wrapped up not only in her fancy clothes, but in bold confidence that she would be able to get herself out of a situation such as this one. Now she knew better.

"As I stood outside the door, this Leary, another policeman standing there, and I heard screaming," Mr. Harrigan said. "The cop told me to mind my own business, but this Leary fellow punched him in the face and then opened the door so we could see what was going on."

"Stop!" Mary cried, covering her face with her hands. "I want to forget the whole ordeal! Don't say anything more!" She got up from the sofa and started for the door, but Norah stopped her and lead her back.

"I think there's been enough said about this," Norah said to Mr. Harrigan. "Please tell me the pimp has been charged with murder and the commissioner is in jail for attacking Mary...and me!"

"You? *A Chuisle,* no...not you!" Da exclaimed, standing up and staring at her.

"No, Da, he tried to, but I ran out. That's when I saw Mr. Harrigan here on the street."

Mam sat next to Mary, and wiped Mary's face with a handkerchief, and tidied up her hair. She stared at Norah while she consoled Mary.

"I've told you not to run the streets like strumpets!"

Norah ignored her mother's comment and poured more tea for everyone.

"He's not in jail," Mr. Harrigan answered, "When Mary accused him of attacking her, he denied it and said he was trying to get the bracelet off of her. Leary came to her defense and accused the commissioner of criminal behavior. The commissioner told him he was fired and no one in the city would hire him. Then he told me to take Mary home and that he wouldn't charge her with the murder if I shut my mouth about everything. He said to tell the other reporters the murderer had been found and the bracelet would be returned to the Astor tomorrow."

"Officer Leary lost his job then?" Norah asked.

"He's probably headed back to Ireland if he knows what's good for him. The commissioner will put a price on his head, to be sure. He hates the Irish coming to the department looking for work. Leary got on by a bribe, but he's dead meat now if he stays."

"This is the land of the free and the brave, is it now?" Mam asked, "If Ireland under English rule was the devil's face, America run by thugs is the devil's arse!" Mam stood up to collect the teacups.

"Can't you write the truth about what happened in your paper?" Norah asked Mr. Harrigan.

"He can, Norah, but it'll cost him," Da said.

"Ye don't understand how we Irish are hated," Da continued, staring at Mr. Harrigan. "Your Mr. Harrigan here, now, is a special one, Norah, but at least he doesn't align himself with the Nativists. For the time being, he's full of honeyed ideas about right and wrong, but I don't think he'd want to risk his neck writing about the commissioner."

M r. Harrigan stood up and rubbed his hands over the creases in his pant legs. He felt untidy, as if someone had taken a loose thread in his mind and was unraveling it. He was surprised at the accusation that he was afraid to stand up for the truth. Why, one of the reasons he owned a newspaper such as the *Irish-American* was to make things right for the Irish! He didn't pretend to possess passionate and altruistic motives in running his newspaper. His paper had afforded him the opportunity to fight neatly with words, but of course not to engage in matters too costly. He had the luxury of not having to entangle himself in businesses that would require him to get his hands dirty, such as saloon keeping or owning a store. And, of significant consequence, owning the newspaper had given him the opportunity to wear the clothing he was zealous about. Mr. Harrigan's parents were proud that he had been able to study and better himself beyond their own experience. If he liked fancy clothing, it was something they turned a blind eye to. Many of the aristocratic men liked the same clothing and why not their son?

"I'll do what I can, Mr. McCabe, to bring about fairness and justice for the Irish, but I can't—"

"You can't what, Mr. Harrigan?" Norah interrupted, "You can't get your white-gloved hands smeared with the dirty immigrant, only taking their money for your paper, but never writing anything that goes beyond what saloonkeeper lost his money or who bought a saloon? Sure, you're able to speak quite highly about the ditches the Irish are digging, but you never write about the ditches they're buried in, do you now?"

"Watch your tongue, girl!" Mam said.

Norah stood up to face Mr. Harrigan, her hands on her hips, "If you're after speaking truth in your paper, you'll be writing about what happened today!"

"Are you threatening me, Norah?" Mr. Harrigan looked perturbed and fidgeted with his jacket.

"I'm threatening you with your own conscience, Mr. Harrigan."

Mr. Harrigan looked down at his shoes for a long moment and then moved closer to Norah.

"Then you won't mind coming into the newspaper business yourself and writing about the events of this day, will you?"

No one, including Norah, responded at first.

"Would you be teasing my Norah, now, Harrigan?" Da asked.

"I am utterly sincere, Mr. McCabe," Harrigan smiled and looked at Norah, waiting for her response.

Da turned to Norah, "You might not be able to use your own name, but it'd be grand if you could write...," Da said excitedly.

He turned to Mr. Harrigan, "Would you consider having her write in the Irish language?"

"Da, I don't remember how to write or speak the Irish language," Norah said.

"God help you, girl, if you've lost the language!" Mam exclaimed. "And who would be minding your shop?"

"What is your answer, Miss McCabe? I'm offering you a position as a staff writer at the *Irish-American*, the best newspaper in the city."

"I'll manage your store, Norah," Mary said, lifting her head for the first time since sitting down on the sofa.

"You will?" Norah asked, excitedly.

Mary nodded and Norah rushed to her friend to hug and kiss her cheek. Then she asked Mr. Harrigan, "Did you say how much you'll be paying me for this position, Mr. Harrigan?"

Chapter Seven

Norah strode along East Houston Street with her head held high as she anticipated her future as a newspaper woman for the *Irish-American*. Newspaper*woman!* She would still own her shop as a businesswoman, but she would write words for everyone in the city to read. She hadn't slept much since Mr. Harrigan asked her to become a staff writer for his paper weeks ago. She had made the necessary arrangements with Mary to run her shop, including installing a new padlock on the front and back door. Both girls had become hyper-vigilant as they walked to and from the shop and around the city. Mary was especially jumpy and irritable since the incident with the commissioner, and although Norah was concerned over her friend's loss of security and would do anything to help her feel safe, her mind had been elsewhere. In fact, Norah's mind had risen to heights unimagined! Although she wore her hair tightly pulled back and her clothing was protectively layered over her body, she felt confident in having recovered from the attack. She didn't have time for frivolity of any sort, and flirting with men on the street or in her shop was dispensed with. Mary had become more serious and lost her playfulness with Norah and others, but Norah hardly noticed. She was preoccupied with thoughts about her new job and wasn't fully present when she worked in her store with Mary. She watched her back more closely, but felt certain that God wouldn't allow anything to happen to her now. No, not when she was going to be working as a newspaperwoman, certainly a step up from being a mere businesswoman.

Norah walked briskly, pulling out the memories of her school days to assure herself about her abilities. She recalled her childhood teacher, Mrs. Drake, who had invested extra time in her and wished she could find her to tell her about her job as a newspaperwoman. And what about Mr. Walt Whitman! She met him as a child and had challenged him about the comments he had made in a newspaper article about the Irish being troublemakers. Wouldn't he think it grand now that this Irish troublemaker was going to be writing words for the public, too!

These thoughts and many others flew around her head like morning sparrows flitting to and fro in the springtime. Why, she had grown in stature as a woman in a matter of days. She was also reading every newspaper in the city to learn what the competition was going to be like. Although she was disappointed to learn that the *Irish-American* newspaper wasn't that well known, she vowed it would become so after she worked there. As she walked quickly through the streets, she felt tension in her shoulders and took in a deep breath as she looked up into the brisk, clear autumn sky. Suddenly, she felt something touch her foot that was thick and moist.

No one should walk through the streets of New York with their heads held up so high that they don't watch their feet! Norah had stepped into a pile of steaming manure that had fallen from the rear of a horse. Where was the street cleaner to clean it up? She was annoyed that this could happen to her on her first day at the office. The putrid odor got caught up in her nose as she tried to kick off the excrement that clung to her boot. "Pride goes before a fall," Mam's chastising words resounded in her head. So lofty were the thoughts about herself that Norah didn't think she would stumble onto the despair of the city, including horse shit, of all things! She walked to the side of the street, took off her boot, and tried to clean it with her handkerchief. Mam would be angry at her for ruining her dainty handkerchief, but she didn't care because more handkerchiefs were going to come her way soon enough. She did the best she could in removing the stinking mess, and threw the handkerchief into a gutter. It floated on the purplish red water that was running thick and ready to spill out onto the street. Bile caught in her throat as she watched animal entrails and pigs' ears floating next to the handkerchief.

She would never get used to this city! Never! New York was a bloody past and present always fighting with its dreams for the future, and sometimes it turned to just this. It was a city with streets filled with death marching triumphantly underfoot of life trying to go forward. She would help show this city how to live differently. She would write about the necessity of cleaning up Five Points and making it as grand as Broadway. Perhaps a park could be created for everyone of any class or race to stroll and have picnics in. A place where people could play music together out in the open and not just in the saloons. Her expectations rose headily as she walked away from the gutter filled with blood and waste. She glanced once more at the handkerchief floating in the blood from a slaughterhouse, and smiled. It was just this, alright, she thought self-assuredly. This was what was needed in Five Points—the fine, delicate, and lovely things of life, like a handkerchief, to soak up the filth and hopelessness. Hundreds of handkerchiefs were needed, she mused confidently.

She walked down the street and gradually became certain she could become one of the city's important writers who could make a difference in Five Points. She would not only encourage the women to properly dress in finery, but clean up the city with her words. Before, it had only been her shop. Now it would be beautiful and life changing words. Let Mr. Whitman and Mr. George Templeton Strong go on about the wicked deeds of the Irish and Five Points in their newspapers. She would make a difference. She almost began skipping, but feared her skirts would get caught in her smelly boots. Soon Norah, full of grand vision, was at the address for the *Irish-American* newspaper.

Norah climbed up the crumbling steps of an old brick building with paint-chipped window shutters that hung askew. A pane in the beveled glass door was shattered, and the glass lay just below it on the first step. Two small empty whiskey bottles and a jimmy were lying on the steps. She wondered if she was at the right address.

"You'd best be going on your way, Miss...the place was broken into in the wee hours of the mornin'. They caught the rogues, but I ain't seen the owner come round yet. You'll be cutting yerself on all the glass, Miss."

The woman stood on the sidewalk in front of the building in an over-sized ragged flower printed dress. Over her bulging stomach, she wore an apron that was dusted with flour and a few remnants of pastry clung to it. Norah recognized a Cork accent, very similar to her own. What was wrong with this woman? Her own Mam wouldn't be out on the street with a dirty apron prying into other people's business.

"Is the owner a Mr. Harrigan?" she asked the woman.

"Aye, Harrigan's the name. Do ye know him, then?

"I've come to write for his paper," Norah responded, straightening her shoulders.

"There won't be a paper today, I can assure you, Miss. I don't know if all the presses were broken up, but Harrigan will make sure he gets more so he can print his news."

The woman wiped her nubbly knuckled hands on the apron with small bits of pastry stuck to her fingers.

"You've got the map of Ireland on yer own face, Miss," she said, squinting her eyes.

Norah ignored the woman and stood on her toes to try and see inside a window.

"Where does your family come from?" the woman asked, her head jutted forward to scrutinize Norah.

"I'll be waiting right here for Mr. Harrigan. I'm supposed to meet him at nine o'clock, but maybe I'm early."

Norah pushed aside the broken glass with her foot and picked up the bottles and set them to the side of the steps. Looking up into the sky, she was disappointed about the state of the building she was going to be working in. Had she thought it would be a palatial mansion with a fountain in the front and swans floating in a pond?

"We're from Cork and Kerry…O'Connor's the name. Ye didn't say where you're from, Miss," the woman walked closer to the steps, putting one boot up on it as if she was about to come up and join Norah.

"Dublin… We're from Dublin…"

"Ye don't sound a wee bit like a Dubliner, Miss…excepting your clothing might be as fancy as a Dubliner's."

"Mam's from Dublin…"

"But ye weren't born there, Miss. Me name's Bridie. What's yer name?"

Norah nearly laughed aloud. Of course her name is Bridie! She didn't want to give her name to the old hag, for she would never go away. She would be asking about every cousin, aunt, and uncle in Ireland…and then she would be claiming she was related to her just because they were both from Cork.

"It doesn't matter where I was born. I'm here now, like we all are, just trying to make a living."

"Well, well… So, Mr. Harrigan got a fancy one like himself to help raise us above the sewers we're living in. Never mind telling me yer name, Miss. You're an uppity one, but I'll find out about you before the sun sets!"

The woman stood up straight, wiped at her apron furiously, and walked away. Norah watched her yank the apron off as she climbed up the steps to the building next door.

Shame floated to the surface of Norah's mind like the debris she had just seen in the gutter. Never had she spoken to a fellow Irish woman, especially an older woman, in the way she had today, but then she remembered that this wasn't true, for she had treated the woman with the Cockney accent and her two sniveling children the same way. Tears welled up in her eyes as she looked down the street to see if Mr. Harrigan was coming. Maybe she was mistaken about the day she was supposed to meet him, or maybe he was hurt from the thieves who had broken into his building. She opened her purse for her handkerchief but remembered she had thrown it in the gutter. She puckered her lips, saying the mantra, "peas, prunes, and persimmons," something she and Mary had read in Lady Godey's book that was supposed to keep a woman's lips full and sensuous.

Norah walked back down the steps and stood next to the ornate wrought iron gate. It contained an ornamental medallion of flowers, fruits and foliage, reflecting a neighborhood that was once gentile and wealthy. The painted houses near the brick house wore faded fashionable colors of Chinese red, lavender, and pink. Norah stepped back from the gate and pondered the present state of the homes and how it had come to be that the inhabitants fled from there to a better life. The colorful houses were peeling and fading, and reminded Norah of old prostitutes in Five Points who strutted around in their faded gowns after years of turning tricks. Norah began devising an article for the paper about restoration of the painted ladies in the neighborhoods abandoned by the wealthy. She would write about people—Irish and German, even Italian, coming together to paint the houses and plant flowers to overflow in boxes hung from the sad-looking windows. Her disappointment in arriving too early, and the chagrin and shame she had felt in speaking to the old Irish woman, diminished as she wrote the piece in her head, her heart skipping excitedly through the sentences. She was so engrossed in these writing plans that she hadn't noticed Mr. Harrigan approach her.

"Miss McCabe, you're early! What do they say about Irish time? An hour late is the correct hour for the Irish?" he teased as he reached her and touched her elbow to direct her through the gate and up the steps. He was dressed in his usual expensive looking clothing, this time wearing a black frock coat, a white vest, and a pair of black pantaloons which came down to the ankle.

"I've no way to count the minutes of the days except by the position of the sun in the sky and the chiming of the church bells, Mr. Harrigan, but it was Mam who woke me early and insisted I come here the hour I did. And don't you know, my mam has a clock wound up inside of her ticking away the hours. I'd never question her on it." Norah responded, feeling free and at ease with Mr. Harrigan.

They climbed the steps and Norah saw that Mr. Harrigan appeared unconcerned over the shattered window in his door and the obvious attempt at a break in. He opened the door and walked right in, moving to the side in the foyer for Norah to enter. The two of them stood in the close stale air for a moment.

"I believe there's been a break in, Miss McCabe. Therefore, I shall not be the gentleman and allow you to go before me, but I will go up first and leave you waiting here until I tell you it is clear and safe." Norah watched Harrigan climb the stairs as if it was just another day at the office, humming as he went.

"Mr. Harrigan," Norah called up to him, "I met a woman next door who told me that the police have already caught the thieves."

Norah hoped he wouldn't talk to the woman and learn that Norah had been rude.

Mr. Harrigan turned around and smiled, "No doubt the thugs have done their work in the early morning hours and are behind bars for a couple of days. They'll be back. I'm afraid that the same ones keep coming back to try and thwart me from printing my news, apparently thinking I don't say enough about the plight of their kind. I'm always being criticized, as any newspaperman is these days. And you know this already, for both you and your da surely put me in my place. But not all is lost with these disturbances, never you mind, Norah! I have some friends on the police force who never tire of catching these same rascals, finding the money on them that they have been bribed with to destroy this place. I'm a fortunate one, Miss McCabe. I am Irish and American, Irish-American, a native of this land with the blood of the ancient warriors coursing through my veins. I do not give up easily, my young friend. And I hope you'll be of the same ilk, and for some marvelous reason, I do believe you are. So, come on up and we'll take a look at how they tried to trash the words that cry out to be expressed."

Norah had read a few of the papers and none of them appeared to be too radical or in danger of inciting others to want to destroy the newspaper office, but maybe the thugs were Irish gangs who wanted him to be more aligned with Tammany. In fact, didn't he say himself that he kept his hands clean? She hoped to be able to challenge his mellow and bite-less words to become more colorful, honest, and able to expose all the injustices against her people. Nevertheless, she didn't know enough of politics and newspapers to fathom his position and why thugs were hired to destroy his newspaper office.

Norah's doubts dissipated and she felt buoyant once again. She held her skirts and hurried up the steps to begin her new career as a newspaperwoman. A dangerous position it was going to be, too, she now imagined. She had just learned that the paper and its purpose were so important that there were men in the city trying to destroy it. There would be intrigue and mystery involved in her new work, not just the daily grind of buying dresses off the prostitutes and sewing until her fingers were numb, and only able to talk to her kind at her store. Now she would have Mr. Harrigan to talk to about life, about evil and good, and about justice and peace.

When Mr. Harrigan and Norah walked into the large room that had once been the master bedroom of the house now turned into an office, she saw cabinets turned over, newspapers strewn throughout the room, but the steam press was still standing upright. Harrigan never stopped humming and led her through this room to another room that was much smaller. There was a desk, an oil lamp, and shelves with many books, as well as boxes that were labeled. Inside the boxes, there were newspapers, but they were not filled with the *Irish-American.* The labels read, *The Tribune, The Herald, The Citizen, The Irish Nation* and some other papers Norah had never head of.

"You can settle yourself here, Miss McCabe. The typesetters and others should be along soon to help restore this place to order. Go ahead and catch yourself up on reading some of the newspapers printed in the last week. You'll find just how coarse and biased they are, except for ours—"

Norah interrupted, "I've been reading the papers ever since you asked me to come to work for you. I wanted to learn about the competition and to know all about the *Irish-American.* You're not one of the big ones and you aren't part of the Associated Press. What is your circulation and how many people work for you?"

Norah fired off questions, her good feelings waning as she looked at the mess before her. She was disappointed that Mr. Harrigan hadn't instructed her to sit down and begin writing a piece for the paper, or more importantly, assigning her to cover something in the city. She had on her good walking boots and she was ready to carry a pad and pen to wherever the news might be.

Norah had kept a journal since arriving in America, although now she only possessed rough and grainy paper bound up with leather ties that had been given to her by her teacher when she finished her last year of school. Norah and her teacher had become friends throughout her school years. The words of the old poets from her country and even this country had resonated within her and she knew someday she would have time for them. Now was the time, she thought excitedly, and her words wouldn't just be written down in a musty journal that would someday become mildewed, burned in a fire, or lost.

"I'm ready to roll up my sleeves and help you clean, Mr. Harrigan. Then I'd like to begin working on something for your next issue. Do you get news off the telegraph?"

"You're a girl after my own heart! And you have certainly done your homework. I'm very impressed. We'll be having a meeting after everyone gets here," Harrigan said, looking at his watch and toward the stairs to see if any of his employees might be coming. He took off his coat and hung it on a wooden peg, rolled up his sleeves very carefully and adjusted his belt.

"We'll be deciding at the meeting what needs to be covered, and then giving out assignments. Yes, of course, we use news off the telegraph. I'll probably have you going for it tomorrow. I don't want you to go out alone on your first piece. I promised your da—"

"You promised Da?" Norah was embarrassed that her father would instruct her employer about her, as if she were a child.

"'Tis only sound judgment in a city such as this one that a newspaperwoman should be accompanied by strong muscle when she is out amongst men on her job. Sorry to say it won't be me. My muscles are in need of building and I would be of no use, I'm afraid. But there's Mr. Collins who has been working with me for a few months now. He seems to be in fine shape—"

"I'll only need someone to accompany me once, and then I'll be able to do it alone. I know this city quite well."

As Norah and Mr. Harrigan cleaned up the office, they found that outside of everything being in disarray and a few papers torn and destroyed, the press had not been destroyed, the desks hadn't been broken, and only one lamp had been taken. Mr. Harrigan explained that the thugs understood that if there had been exorbitant cost accrued in the damage of the office, they'd be in jail for much longer than an overnight stay. They were paid to threaten, not destroy, with the hope that it would cause him to use his words for their benefit. It was the third time his office had been attacked in two years, and although each time there was more glass broken and lamps stolen, the press and other equipment hadn't been damaged. Norah wanted to ask him what it was that had been printed or not printed to cause the vandalism, but she kept quiet, not wanting him to think her ignorant. She would have to try and find out tonight when she went home. She had a few papers stacked away in her dresser that she had been studying.

The morning passed uneventfully as Norah and Mr. Harrigan brought order to the office. None of the other employees showed up, and Mr. Harrigan said it was probably because they had heard that there had been another break in and there wouldn't be real work to do until the afternoon. Norah questioned him about when the paper was to go to print and wondered how he could lose so much time because of deadlines.

"I'm afraid we'll be making up for lost time by working throughout the wee hours of the morning, Miss McCabe," he answered.

Norah's stomach growled loudly around twelve thirty, and when Mr. Harrigan heard it, he suggested they go somewhere for lunch. Mam had packed her some food to take with her, just like she did sometimes when Norah went to work at the store for many hours. Norah hadn't taken the lunch with her because she was embarrassed in front of Harrigan. She knew that real businessmen and even some women who worked in the shops frequented some of the eateries for lunch. It was the chic and important thing to do, but she didn't want to spend the money, nor seem so common by bringing a lunch with her like a schoolgirl.

"Will you be giving me some time off before I have to work throughout the night? I'd like to go home to have dinner with Mam and Da. Meg and her family might be coming over tonight, too."

Mr. Harrigan rolled down his sleeves, looked in a mirror that really seemed much too large to be in a newspaper office, and fussed with his appearance.

"It is office policy that lunch, no matter what the time, must be taken. And new employees are treated to free lunches during their first week on the job," he said, smiling, never turning from the mirror.

"Oh no, Mr. Harrigan, I don't want charity. I can pay my own way."

"You're a proud one, Miss McCabe. Of course, it isn't charity. It's part of becoming an employee of the *Irish-American*." He turned from the mirror, retrieved his coat, put it over his arm and gave his other arm for Norah to take so he could lead her down the stairs and out for her first lunch as an employee of the *Irish-American*.

Chapter Eight

Norah was pleasantly surprised when the carriage stopped in front of the Astor House hotel. She had been so busy telling Mr. Harrigan about the magazines and books she had read that she never looked out the window to see where they were going. The Astor! It was only a few years ago that she had been bold enough to walk into the lobby to breathe in the magnificence of the hotel, but then was asked to leave because she didn't have any business there. Maybe Mr. Harrigan would give her an assignment to write about the hotel and she would be able to explore this luxurious building. She wondered what she might wear if she did such an interview, and then she looked down at her dress. Oh, she wished she had worn something grand and colorful. If only she had known she might be going to the Astor! She had worn an elegant, but old, dress because she had been concerned about spilling ink on it. The dress was a wine and green plaid, no longer soft and beginning to look worn. It was trimmed with a narrow, matching green silk passé-menterie, and sherrings of silk.

Mr. Harrigan guided her to the entrance of the hotel where a doorman nodded and smiled while holding the door open for them to enter. Norah tried not to appear inexperienced, but her face flushed with excitement. She was quite curious how Mr. Harrigan could afford to dine at the expensive and splendid Astor House hotel. He certainly wasn't as important as the owners and editors of the *Tribune* or *Herald*, both of which had offices located on Printing House Square.

Worry came over her; it might not be proper for her to be dining at the Astor. It had become acceptable in the past few years for women of refinement to enter public eating houses, but only when accompanied by gentlemen. There were just a few restaurants that allowed mixed dining, other eateries arranged special accommodations, and some had separate entrances for female diners. Hotels had only recently opened eateries attached to their lobbies, but they were highly particular about who dined at them. This was Norah's first dining experience at a fancy restaurant and she wondered if she would be thrown out if she was too unpolished. Would she be recognized as a resident of Five Points?

As a child she had worn rags over her hands in the winter. This memory caused her to quickly clasp them behind her back. She should have worn gloves! Her cheeks blazed as she gazed at the chandelier lights and wallpapered walls. Norah moved her shoulders back and down and ambulated with her head held high to assure any onlookers she was experienced. She hoped Mr. Harrigan would not notice her discomfort. She had spent enough of her hard-earned money on *Godey's Lady's Book* over the years, and it must show in her speech and conduct.

"I come here often, but I've never come with such a lovely woman," Mr. Harrigan said, gripping her elbow more tightly.

Norah glanced at Mr. Harrigan and smiled nervously, but he looked straight ahead. She didn't know how to respond to his compliment.

The host recognized the newspaperman and ushered them to a table in the corner next to a window facing the street. The room felt airless and stuffy, but swanky and elaborately decorated in mauve and blue; the tables were covered with white linen, and fresh flowers and candles adorned each one. As soon as Norah was seated, she looked out the window. Two dirty little faces peered in at her.

"Please excuse the intrusion, Miss," the host said, drawing the heavy paisley brocaded drapes together. The needy faces disappeared and the candle flickered and went out, but the host quickly struck a match and lit the candle that cast a golden hue across the table. Norah remembered her childhood days on the winter streets combing for matches so her family could light their stove in the evening. Even matches had been too expensive to buy in those days, she mused. A waiter came to the table. He couldn't have been much older than the two boys who stood outside the restaurant window. He handed menus to them, bowed slightly, then poured water into their glasses onto slices of lemon. He stated politely he would return to take their orders in a few minutes.

Norah opened the menu. "What would you suggest, Mr. Harrigan?" she asked, nervous laughter erupting at the end of her question. "I've never been to such a fancy place before." She reddened but tried to regain her composure by taking a few sips of water. Yet a lemon slice struck her mouth and splashed water onto her face. She immediately wiped her mouth with the starched linen napkin with a monogrammed *A,* and placed it back on the table.

"I would suggest that you first unfold your napkin and place it on your lap, Miss McCabe. And then I would encourage you to relax and enjoy perusing the menu at your leisure…well, perhaps not too long at your leisure," he smiled warmly at her. "If you would like, I can choose something for you, but I do think that an independent and fiery mind such as yours needs to learn to order food at the finest of establishments."

Norah retrieved the napkin from the table and her water glass tipped slightly, but she caught it before it tumbled to the floor. Rather than feeling entirely awkward, she laughed at herself and her situation. Why should she feel ill at ease! She had plenty of time to learn how to conduct herself in fine restaurants such as the Astor House hotel.

"I have become what is known as the lace curtain Irish, Miss Mc-Cabe, thanks to my ingenious parents who knew how to bury their brogue and assimilate into an Anglo Saxon world. They taught me to deny the negative aspects of being Irish in this country and in so doing, I have marched to every tune a good white male marches to in this city, except to the tune of the Orange parade," he laughed and adjusted his collar, turning his head to and fro as he spoke. Norah was amused by his Adam's apple vibrating through his collar.

"However, I also have something of what the Irish are accused of. It has been said that they are the most obstinate white men of the world, and so with my good fortune in being tenacious and stubborn, along with the hard-earned inheritance of my parents, I'm hopeful that I might be obtaining some worthiness as editor of the *Irish-American*."

"Da says the *Irish-American* newspaper caters to the Irish who have gotten out of Five Points, not the poor, desperate ones who still live there. We still live in Five Points, but as you know, we live on a much better street than most. Maybe you're following your parents' footsteps into Irish obscurity, Mr. Harrigan, and not living up to being as obstinate as some say we Irish are.

"Were you born in New York City, then? Da says you're a moderate, whatever that might mean exactly. He says that at least you don't condone the activities of the political exiles raising money to shed blood for home rule."

Norah was rambling and in danger of saying really stupid things, but she couldn't keep herself quiet. And she didn't want to be silent, for she had so many observations and questions.

The waiter arrived to take their order before Mr. Harrigan could respond. He didn't appear uncomfortable with her pronouncements about his stance on Irish politics. Her ideas weren't new, nor were they her own, and she feared she might not have anything original to offer in conversation. She listened to Mr. Harrigan order the corn and oyster casserole, then ordered the same, although she was certain she would choke on the squiggly things that reminded her of gritty slime. How did the people of this city come to adore such delicacies that turned her stomach?

After their orders came, she took small forkfuls with plenty of sips of water, and when nearly all of her dish was eaten, she was pleased she hadn't shown any revulsion and, as a matter of fact, she could almost admit to liking it. She assumed this was exactly what must happen to girls raised on an abundant diet, although oysters in New York were sold everywhere, and every class of people seemed to like them.

"Fried oysters bought from a vendor and eaten on the street aren't nearly as delicious as this preparation. Do you agree?" Mr. Harrigan asked with a sly smile and a wink at her.

"I've never eaten them—"

"Exactly!" he interrupted, putting down his napkin and leaning over to whisper to her. People were coming and going, and restaurant employees stood nearby listening and watching.

"You must never, I mean never, agree to eat something that is so unappetizing and unappealing, disavowing your own unique dietary preferences."

Norah leaned toward Mr. Harrigan who was grinning at her with his elbows on the table, "So, right...I'm not cut out to be an actress then, Mr. Harrigan."

"I'm most certain you'll be excellent at anything you set your mind to, however, pretending to be someone else or to like something you don't really like does not become you at all, my friend. Not at all! You'll be in danger of losing the many colorful fibers of your soul, and if you do that, you'll be unable to write anything for my paper more than what I am able to write myself. I've a sense that when the pen is in your hand, the girl who lost some of herself on the journey across the Atlantic will be resurrected with all her spirit. And that will be a good thing for my newspaper, Miss McCabe."

He leaned back in his chair, yawning toward the ceiling. It was occurring to Norah that she had never given a thought as to whether he knew of her ability to write prose, report on news, or even if she was literate. Why had he hired her not knowing if she was really capable of contributing to his newspaper?

Mr. Harrigan put his elbows back on the table and leaned toward her again. "Do you know much about the dirty politics of this city?"

"And what other kind of politics might there be?" she asked.

"Ahh, you're a quick one alright. Not just another pretty girl dressing up in fineries to parade down Fifth Avenue. Not that I would ever fault anyone for donning fine silks and weaves, but there has to be more. Do you agree, Miss McCabe?"

"It's for this reason I've agreed to work for your paper, Mr. Harrigan," she said excitedly, hoping he would believe her to be sincere.

Her new employer lifted his hands in the air and sat back in his chair with a wide grin on his face.

"Isn't it time we address one another with our first names, or is it presumptuous of me to ask? We do want to maintain a professional relationship. The other employees and I use our first names in conversation, and I don't want to treat you any differently, but I also want to respect your gender."

"You can call me Norah. Should I call you James?"

"Certainly," he said and leaned in to whisper to her again. "If you look sharp, you'll see one Mr. Murray sitting at the table on the opposite side of the room. Go ahead and take a peek. He won't even notice you, for he's too engrossed in some diabolical scheme or another, but he's altogether forgiven because it's most likely in favor of us Irish."

Norah turned her head slightly to the left to see a man older than her, maybe as much as ten years. Although he sat at the table, he appeared tall and dignified. His hair was dark brown, nearly black, and Norah saw a few blonde strands throughout. Was it the sunlight striking his head or did he indeed have such a blend? His face was countenanced with bookish seriousness. She glimpsed tight restraint in the contours of his face, especially where the corners of his mouth were forcing a smile while he listened to his companion, a man in sharp contrast to himself in appearance.

This man possessed a broad red face and was stocky and bull doggish with bushy whiskers going in all directions on his chin. He was wearing white jean pants of a favorable cut and an elegant blue coat, but Norah surmised that he was a common laborer squeezed into fine clothing that he was obviously uncomfortable in. He looked as if his mother had forced him into wearing this outfit before he left the house in the morning. And now, away from his mother, he had taken out his circus beard and tacked it on to his face. Norah laughed, covering her mouth with her napkin. *American city life is comical with its sundry characters,* she thought, suddenly feeling happy to be where she was and a part of it all.

"Which one is Mr. Murray?" she asked.

"The good-looking fellow is your Mr. Murray, born in the Sixth Ward. He's the son of an Irish patriot who fought against England on a few bloody fields. He's actually one of the fortunate ones in this city. Most Five Pointers leave school to help support their families, but not him. Did you leave school to open your store?" he asked her, changing the subject of Mr. Murray.

"No, I didn't leave school. I stayed and sold newspapers, flowers, and anything I could. I had a teacher who thought me grand, and Da made me finish school."

Norah fidgeted with her napkin and dropped it on the floor. She was agitated with these questions, for she was curious to hear more about this Mr. Murray.

"Tell me more about the Murray fellow," she said, placing both arms on the table and smiling eagerly at Mr. Harrigan.

"Murray was a foreman for Engine Company No. 28..." Mr. Harrigan cupped his hands around his mouth and finished his sentence, "and he was an essayist for a spell in Georgia. An essayist! Can you fathom that, Norah! Someone reared on rebel juice in Five Points becoming an essayist! And he knows his Irish language because his family dragged him back to the ole country from time to time."

Mr. Harrigan sat back in his chair, gave a little snort, and quietly continued his story. "After the Georgia stint, Mr. Murray moved back to the Sixth Ward to study law. He eventually worked his way up and was elected to one of the ward's seats on the board of councilmen. He may have been unspoiled and promising in his ideals at one time, but not now. He writes occasionally for *The New York Leader,* which used to be moderate, but now has ties to Tammany."

Before Norah asked any further questions, the waiter arrived to see if there was anything more they would like. Mr. Harrigan handed him money and stated it was time to return to the office. Norah stood up and felt the eyes of everyone in the room on her. She self-consciously stepped in front of Mr. Harrigan, and he graciously touched her elbow to guide her out of the restaurant. She eased into his touch and wondered if people might think he was her beau, her lover, or whatever it was a young woman might be who dined with a man at the Astor House hotel. She had never considered the possibility that Mr. Harrigan might have a romantic interest in her, but now was immediately warmed by the idea. Their initial relationship had been instant, without flirtation, and Norah felt that friendship was more desired than anything else. She touched the back of her curls that were tightly arranged in a coiffure and relaxed into the gentle pressure of Harrigan's hand on the small of her back. Their exit required them to walk by Mr. Murray's table, and as they did she kept her eyes looking forward, although she keenly listened for any snatches of conversation she might hear. She was more than curious about this Mr. Murray who had climbed out of the muck and mire of Five Points, a son of an Irish patriot, no less. She was thrilled to learn that it really might be possible to rise above the sordid poverty of Five Points!

"Harrigan! You're still here in this wretched city!" The ridiculous looking chubby man Mr. Murray was dining with had jumped to his feet to shake hands with Mr. Harrigan.

"I thought you would have gone on to greener pastures by now. I heard you were going out west to cover the gold fever, dragging along your press and grand ideas with you." He glanced at Norah and back at Mr. Harrigan, lowering his voice. "And perhaps dragging a little inspiration with you, too. A Muse of sorts," he said, winking at them. His red cheeks ballooned and filled with laughter, and then farted out of his fleshy lips. Norah stifled a giggle because the man looked and acted like a stereotypical b'hoy with his whiskers and silly clothing.

"May I introduce you to my colleague at the *Irish-American*, Mr. Cooper?" Mr. Harrigan said, stepping back and motioning for Norah to come closer to be introduced. She sensed Mr. Harrigan recoiling from this man, but he was gracious to introduce her to satisfy the man's rude curiosity and to set him straight on their relationship.

"This is Miss Norah McCabe—"

"McCabe? I know a McCabe...a fiddler, one of the finest fiddlers in Five Points I'd say, even if he was born in the ole country," Mr. Cooper said in a low, gravely voice. His bulging blue eyes looked her up and down, sizing her up.

"It's a pleasure to see you again, Mr. Harrigan," Mr. Murray said, standing up and interrupting Cooper.

He turned to Norah, "So you're a fiddler's daughter from Five Points. I'm certain your identity is worthy of a much more expanded title."

Mr. Murray made a slight bow to her, and she didn't know if she should do a small curtsy, something she had never done before, or ever had to consider if she needed to do. Sure, it was something you did in Ireland when meeting up with the landlord and his family, but this was America and there was no bowing down to landlords here. He reached for her hand. "I'm Thomas Murray, but you can call me Murray."

"I don't mind being called the fiddler McCabe's daughter," Norah responded. "There could be much worse names for women living in Five Points," she continued. "In fact, I've been referred to as 'wench, guttersnipe, and a scalawag, just to name a few special ones."

Knowing that Mr. Murray was also from Five Points had given her courage to confidently state that she, too, was from there. However, after she spoke, she felt demeaned by her acknowledgment that she still lived in such a rough place. She furtively glanced at Mr. Murray's eyes, which were the color of smooth jade, beautiful, and pooling with enigmatic depth. She was tempted to stare, like when she was a child and gawked at the sun when it would finally decide to shine on Ireland. She blushed with embarrassment and hoped he didn't notice her fascination with his eyes. Quickly, she found a grease spot on the wall above his head to focus on. Mr. Harrigan and Mr. Cooper laughed at her response, and Mr. Cooper's booming laughter filled the restaurant. Diners halted in their conversation to look over at them.

"I'd think that an Irish woman working for a newspaper is a rarity. You're to be congratulated already," Mr. Murray said.

So it was that Mr. Murray was as interested in her as she was in him, and a subterranean kinship surfaced in their interchange.

"No congratulations yet! I've not written a single word, and I might be working as a domestic if I don't cut it in the newspaper business, for today is my first day," Norah looked at Mr. Harrigan and smiled, eager for him to take her arm and leave.

"You have the look of a wild warrior, Miss McCabe. I'm sure you'll give the *Irish-American* a run for its money," Mr. Murray said, his eyes darting at Mr. Harrigan and back again to Norah, "In fact, I'm envious of you, Harrigan, for having gotten to her before I did."

The *Leader*'s antipathy towards an Irish newspaper that did not blend in with the current Tammany agenda was typical, but there had never been ill spoken words between Mr. Harrigan and Mr. Murray. Casual relationships normally existed between fellow editors, regardless of competition. Norah saw tension rise between the two men, however, like vapor off a summer earth when the sun shone after a downpour.

"And I'm not about to let her out of my sight, Murray. She's a rare one, alright. A needle in a haystack," Mr. Harrigan responded.

Murray was tall for an Irishman, about six foot, and his build was solid and muscular. He was not spindly and carrying about knotted joints that jutted from small and taut muscles, as seen in many tall and thin men.

"I have no intention of stealing her from you, Harrigan, but I'll be eager to see how your paper prospers having her onboard." Murray cocked his head and gave a wry smile to Norah and then looked over at Cooper who was fumbling with his suspenders and coughing to indicate he was ready to pay their bill and leave.

Mr. Harrigan finally motioned to Norah that they should leave. She tried to look at both Mr. Murray and Mr. Cooper to properly acknowledge them in her departure, but instead gazed at Murray's penetrating eyes for too long. Her face warmed again, and she was reminded of the romance serials she had read when eyes met and beheld one another. Here she was now becoming a silly character like she had read about in a ridiculous story!

"Always a pleasure to see you Murray," Mr. Harrigan said, and then looking at Cooper. "Cooper," he said, with a quick nod.

Back at the office, another employee, Mr. Delaney, arrived, and he was as spiffed up in attire as Mr. Harrigan. He announced he was going to hear Miss Jenny Lind perform at the Barnum Museum that very evening. He had tickets for all of them. Mr. Harrigan turned to Norah with eagerness in his face.

"You will accompany us this evening, will you not, Norah?"

Norah's heart had beat in staccato rhythm all day, and she was tired and ready to go home to sit before the stove with a cup of tea. The last thing she wanted to do was go out that evening, even if it would be with two well dressed gentlemen.

"I'm all for staying at home this evening, Mr. Harrigan."

"You're forgetting to call me James!"

"I've lived a month all in one day, Mr. James, and I'm nearly mad with trying to sort it all out."

Mr. Delaney and James both laughed at her response.

"Tomorrow then. Tomorrow we'll place a pen in your hand and see what you can do. We're moderate, as your father says, but not so moderate that we aren't stirring up some controversy over the slavery issue… and getting our office torn up for this and that. I want you to interview a priest tomorrow and then write what he says. He's a good strong Irish Catholic priest taking a stand against slavery, and that is an anomaly amongst the Irish Catholic community."

Norah yawned and covered her mouth quickly. She couldn't take one more ounce of something new, controversial, or thrilling. All day long, between cleaning up the office and teaching her how to conduct herself at the Astor, James Harrigan had filled her head with facts about the abolitionist movement. She hadn't had time to process all she had learned about this issue, although she had decided long ago that if the Negroes and the Irish could dance together, they were similar in nature. Oh, it was all so thrilling, this new life of a newspaperwoman! It was more than enough to have experienced all of the day's learning, but then meeting the intriguing Mr. Murray was too much for her senses. Tonight she would rest and put away this day in her memory, locking some of it in a tight corner of her mind. She also had to prepare for tomorrow because it would undoubtedly bring her the experience she needed to become a real newspaperwoman.

Tomorrow did not come for Norah to take pen in hand, for again the office was broken into and had to be cleaned; typesetting machines had to be repaired this time, but fortunately, the press had not been damaged. It waylaid Mr. Harrigan's plans to become more outspoken about slavery, but during this time, Norah began to absorb the passionate fire of some of the disenfranchised souls living in Five Points. She gained as much knowledge as she could about strong issues of the day to prepare herself to eventually write powerful articles for the *Irish-American.*

Chapter Nine

Norah was lying on the sofa feeling quite undone and woeful. The embers crackled in the stove as she tried to sleep. She should have washed off the grime of the streets, but had been too exhausted to go through the tedious process of drawing water for a bath. Da sat at the kitchen table with a cup of tea after returning home from a long day of work. If it hadn't been for the ward council-man he met a few months ago, he would still be cleaning the same street over and again in front of the bank and bringing home only half of what he was making now. He had given his vote reluctantly to the councilman, who was a dishonorable man with just enough Irish whiskey in his veins to give him the sanguine spirit needed to warm others to him.

Norah, finally, gave up trying to sleep and sat up on the sofa. She looked lovingly at her da, and the secure warmth of his presence filled her. There was nothing more soothing than to be with him in the evenings sitting next to the stove drinking tea. Mam always went to bed early and Norah was relieved when she did, for Norah recoiled from Mam's constant pestering criticism and questions about her shop,

Mary, Harrigan, and her safety. Her love for Mam was like the familiar cup of tea that was necessary in her life, but her love for Da was full of admiration and adoration. His love for her made her feel there were possibilities beyond a life in Five Points.

D a looked at Norah as she sighed and turned on the sofa, and a fierce desire to protect her came over him. *She has become such a high-minded one,* he thought, remembering his own idealism he had left behind in Ireland. He had none of that now and could never have it again, for there was nothing left but his family and his fiddle. He looked over at the marred and anguished looking instrument that seemed to always take on a life of its own whenever he played it, as if it defied the memories it had carried from Ireland.

He got up from the table and quietly carried his chair next to the sofa. What could he say to Norah to convince her to not waste her youth on a country that was not her own, and on a city that had become a garbage heap for the pathetic races from around the world? Sure, he had been proud she had been hired to work at a newspaper, an Irish newspaper at that, but he had also been proud of her to have saved enough money to open her own used-clothing store. How many Irish born women have shops like his Norah's? How many wore such fine clothes and were as lovely? She didn't have the pampered and flawless complexion of some of the American girls, nor did she have hair that could be tamed, but her coarse, tangled hair was like her free spirit. He was glad she resembled a jewel that had just been mined, and had not yet been polished and appraised. At least for her life now, she might remain free from domestic troubles.

Norah was unlike his daughter, Meg, who had married too quickly and now struggled with a husband never at home and who was always going off to make his fortune working on the rails or in some other venture. As if she knew he was watching her, Norah suddenly sat up and looked at him, anguish in her face. Neither of them said anything for a few moments.

"What's wrong, *A Chuisle?*" he asked as she sat on her treasured sofa, the beat-up piece of junk she had transformed into a comfortable and lovely piece of furniture. That was his Norah, the saints be praised, creating treasure from trash.

"Please don't use those Irish words to address me, Da, especially as I'm grown now." She closed her eyes for they were swollen from crying.

Da smiled and looked at his daughter's hands where ink outlined her fingertips, revealing the patterns of her skin. She had her own special print and she was her own person, his girleen was. Her stained fingers were a badge of belonging to the world of words that marched triumphantly up every street in New York. News! News! The story of life in the words that paraded the streets and pounded on the minds of every literate New Yorker! Two months had passed since his daughter began working for the *Irish-American.* Her hopes had been dashed numerous times because she had only helped with typesetting, cleaned, tromped down the streets to the telegraph office, taken notes for James Harrigan, but hadn't yet done any real writing. The pen had been placed in her hand alright, but it hadn't written her words to be sent out into the world. Only Harrigan's words! Da had tried to tell her that just working alongside an experienced newspaperman such as James Harrigan was teaching her invaluable lessons of the trade. Harrigan's experienced words were coursing through her ink-stained fingers like tiny rivers of knowledge that were carried upstream through her veins and into her heart and mind.

He was worried for her, however, for there had been too many times that he had found her crying at the end of a work day. The two of them had also been having strong arguments about how she was trying to convince Harrigan to give up on the Irish poetry and language that he included in the paper. She was embarrassed over the Irish language and he was unhappy with her for it, but she told him she had her reasons. She wasn't against Irish language and poetry, per se, but felt they all needed to become modern and in tune with Amer-

ican life. It was an American paper and James Harrigan needed to become progressive and publish more like the *Sun* and the *Tribune*, she
had defiantly told him. No matter what Norah believed, however, Da
could not veer from the strong belief that their Irish culture and language needed to be preserved. Many had forsaken the language and
would likely forget they ever came from Ireland.

"I'll not stop calling you *A Chuisle*," he responded, cupping the
teacup with his large roughened hands.

"Promise me, Da, that you'll only be using that endearment when
we're home, then."

"I can't make a promise I can't keep," he said, putting his cup
down on the worn wooden floor, uneven and marred by the feet of
many immigrants who had resided in the apartment before the Mc-
Cabes.

Norah took in a deep breath, let it out quickly, and looked intensely at him. "Mr. Whitman said Five Points is a native grand opera
in America."

"And this makes you unhappy?"

"I don't know what he means by his fancy words. It sounds lovely,
these words of his. Just like when I was a child and we met at Barnum's
and had a puzzling conversation. There's something wonderful, but
odd, about him, and some of the big wigs of this city are taken with
him. I've a feeling about his words. Underneath all his pomp, there's
dirt clinging to those flowery words of his, Da. Not in his poetry, for
that's lovely, of sorts, him a fine lover of the people who dwell in this
city. I imagine he's quite the lover of this world when he can choose
where to walk and where to eat. He speaks of the grand opera when he
speaks of Five Points, but most of them that dwell here aren't going to
any grand opera, now, are they? They'll be going to a blood and thunder play, not a grand opera that he goes to on Broadway. He also makes
light of what is said about the curious and unnatural in Five Points."

"And what is this unnatural thing?" Da asked, throwing his head
back and yawning.

"It's in the saloons and dance halls! Maybe you see it, but it's so familiar that you don't know what the tourists and Mr. Charles Dickens are talking about. And what Mr. Whitman thinks is so grand."

"I don't know what's grand and unnatural you're going on about. You should be going to sleep now. Mam is already sleeping and we both should be doing the same." He got up from his chair as Norah hurled her words at his back.

"The salt and pepper of Five Points! That's what's unnatural! The odd mixing of black and white blood! And don't ye know, Da, that this in itself is causing a mighty stir? And Mr. James Harrigan has taken the most unusual stand on the whole darn thing."

"*A Chuisle*, if this work of yours is going to make you sick…," Da said, sitting back down.

"It's said that an Irishman is only a 'nigger turned inside out'!"

"This is causing you to lose sleep?" Da shook his head and looked toward the window as if his answer might come from outside. "If that is so, then we wear our hearts on the outside of us, and that's grand. So there it is then—a grand opera in Pete Williams' Dance Hall."

He smiled broadly and felt certain of his answer to his daughter. He himself played music with the dark ones, dark as molasses and as smooth, too, in their musical abilities. He could not truly find fault with them like others, excepting they might vie for his jobs.

"Good hearts?" Norah's sarcasm was obvious. "There's many of them with hearts as dark as their skin," she said. She was quiet for a few minutes, and Da, too, was still and somber. He was surprised by her statement. She had danced with the Africans at the dance halls when she was a young girl. What was she going on about? Oh, she was puzzling, his Norah. She was terribly puzzling at times.

"I admit I've known some lovely ones. And then there's plenty of them whose hearts live only in the soles of their spry dancing feet," Norah added.

"And what shade of mankind has your Mr. Harrigan written about?"

"Not the pale Tammany shade. Maybe he should if he wants to get ahead. I've told him that he needs to do an article or two about some of the ward councilmen."

"Listen to what I have to say, Norah. Ye can't be worrying over pleasing the ward bosses who kiss the arses of Tammany Hall."

"You've had to do it! You did it to get your sorry job, Da." Norah turned away from him, looking into the stove.

"And I don't need my own daughter reminding me of it! I had to do it for my family. How else could I put food on the table? You all conspired against me to keep me from going out west."

"I'm frightened you'll be losing your job if I write about Father Driscoll and his abolitionist ideas. That's James for you. Keeping the peace, I suppose. He's against slavery but not supportive of the Republicans who tirelessly work to free the black man. He wants Bishop Hughes' blessing, so he doesn't get too involved with Tammany. I suppose this is why the paper is called moderate."

"I'm not afraid of losing my job with whatever you have to write. I'd be glad for you to finally get to write something. The paper has been standing up for us Irish in some ways, but it certainly hasn't taken a position on this freedom for the slaves everyone's talking about. I know the Irish don't like the idea of them being freed. I'm not against the blacks getting their freedom," Da laughed, "as long as we Irish get our freedom, too!"

"It's nothing to be laughing over. I'll quit the paper if your job is threatened because I write about the priest and his superior ideas for the black man. After all you've been through, Da, it wouldn't be right."

"I don't think justice metes out evenly anywhere in the world. You have to grab for it when it comes your way. It comes and goes. I'll always work with me hands. There's plenty of laboring on the docks and railroads; there's the carting business, too. I'm not so pleased in my work. I'm humbled by it. I'm still strong enough to be carrying bricks and building the tall edifices they want to mount in honor of themselves. Print the truth, Norah, and if you do and I get fired, it'll be an opportunity to make something more of my sorry life."

"I'm proud of you, Da, no matter what kind of work you do," Norah said with tenderness. "But if I write too powerfully about this priest, someone at Tammany might make sure all doors close for you. Look what happened to Office O'Leary."

"Our Officer Leary who lost his '0' soon enough off the boat, is not to be pitied. The scoundrel commissioner wasn't approved by Tammany, you know that, don't you? When he fired Leary for interrupting his evil intentions with our Mary, Leary could no longer be the grand policeman alright, but he got himself another job through his Irish connections. I sometimes think that the young sot should have stayed back in the ole country. But now he's got himself a fleet already, three or four of them, I've heard. Fancy looking horses, carts, harnesses, the works! He's got day laborers begging him for work. Much better than patrolling the streets with a club and not being able to wield it against an Irish brother. He did have a softness about him."

Norah couldn't believe Leary's good fortune. In spite of his stupid peasant ways; he had something curious in him that would aspire to a greater life, but she never would have thought it could happen so soon. Not a bad looking fellow either, but could she ever forgive him for his apathy when he stood outside the room while the commissioner was attacking her?

"That's grand, Da. He protected Mary from that lecherous Commissioner and can't be such a bad fellow."

"He's doing grand alright. I suppose you've been too busy to spend any time with Mary these days and you don't know the latest news about her and Leary."

As sleepy as Norah was, she became fully awake. "What's this about Mary?"

"I'm afraid Leary has been stolen by your fairy queen, Mary, alright. He's pathetically in love with the girleen. He's been spending all his hard-earned money on flowers, food, and clothing for her." Da laughed. "He's had his hired men in the horse carts purchase gifts for her, and she's more fancied up than ever."

Sparks from the stove flew out into the room. Norah jumped up to put out the ones that had fallen onto the floor.

"I need a word with that girl! Mary has been waiting for the right man, an American-born man, so why should she suddenly throw away her good future for an Irishman! She'll be in danger of marrying the greenhorn, having a slew of hungry babies, and ruining our clothing business.

"I'm getting a carriage," Norah said as she looked around the room for her shawl.

"You'll not be going out on a dark rainy night! The carriage will be expensive!" Da said. He was sorry that he had told Norah about Mary and Leary.

"I need to talk to her, Da. I can't go to work tomorrow and think straight until I have a talk with her. And I won't have time tomorrow."

Norah found her shawl and placed it over her shoulders, but then she plopped heavily onto the sofa and slammed her fists down on each side of her, punching them into the tapestry as hard as she could.

"What is wrong with that stupid girl!"

D a stood by the door, thinking he might go with her. She was head-strong, his Norah! Mam would set her straight if she would wake up and learn what her stubborn daughter was up to. But Marion was dead to the world after cleaning and doing laundry all day in a mansion lived in by only a few people. How he hated her washing and ironing other people's expensive and extravagant clothing. It would be a sure thing for him to go to the ward councilman again and ask for her to get a position at Union Hall in the garment district. She wanted to do sewing here at home, and maybe he should encourage her now, but she would be taken advantage of by the middlemen who would take most of her earnings. It would be better for her to work in the huge building at Nassau and Fulton. She was his wife and older now and he worried the seams of her life were fraying. He looked at Norah getting ready to go out into the night. He wanted to wake up Marion to con-front Norah, but his wife was worn out and needed sleep.

"I'll go with ye, *A Chuisle*," he said.

He couldn't ever remember being this wild in his emotions as his daughter was. They were so much alike and yet so different. She looked at him with endearment that he had come to expect.

"I've everything in my life that is most important and why should I be so unhappy sometimes, Da? Look at you! You've planted and dug potatoes, planted and harvested grain, and worked on the roads half-starved. The evil spirit, the *taise,* tried to capture your mind while your body was attacked by gnawing hunger that left you with bones that resembled the strength of oak. But you can't be destroyed! You've sheltered us with your strength. Here in this country we've been together and filled our bellies with all kinds of food. Here in America it's possible to take the invisible dreams that float behind our toil and turn them into gold coins. Let Mary ruin her life if she chooses! I'll keep bettering myself without her!"

Norah got off the sofa and embraced Da, holding on to him for a moment before releasing him from her grasp. His shoulders stiffened under Norah's touch, as they did the day she ran from the apartment and jumped into his arms. It had been difficult for him to let the child go in her because he still viewed her as his young daughter who required his care, albeit she was surviving the streets of New York quite well. She was not like Meg and wouldn't be content as a wife of a railroad worker and dreamer, but he still wished for her to be loved by someone who could protect her and become as enthralled with her qualities as he was.

"I'll not go to Mary tonight. I shouldn't be so impulsive. Mary will have to learn the hard way. Let's both go to bed. Sleep is a great eraser, and in the morning my feelings will be lighter."

Chapter Ten

"The Republicans are sending out a rallying cry not only against popery, but they're also against rum and slavery, Miss McCabe. The popery they rail against, however, is not a religion, philosophy, or scheme. It's a derogatory expression they use to discriminate against Catholics. In regards to their stance against slavery, the Republicans are passionate and correct. The rum issue is debatable, but I am not so compelled to take a stand for or against it," Father Theobald Driscoll said.

Norah and Father Driscoll were sitting in the back pew of The Transfiguration Church on Mott Street. Norah was nervous interviewing the priest, although he was soft spoken and kind. She hadn't been attending Mass regularly because pew rental was expensive. Most Catholic churches were only able to keep their doors open because of the revenue from pew rental, but the McCabes and many of the Irish-born were unfamiliar with pew renting, let alone for the fact that it was impossible for most of them to afford it. Norah and her family were part of a folk Catholicism in Ireland that was a way of life interweaving superstition, myth, and Christianity; and in America, the myth and superstition were going by the wayside. Close observers might have taken note how the vibrant cultural colors of immigrant lives faded by the time they reached the shores of America, as if washed out by the sea's passage. The McCabes' dedication to Catholicism wasn't represented in America in a form they were really comfortable with, and they hadn't found a place for ritual or solace in any church in New York. Most recently, Norah had noticed the placards and signs plastered on buildings inviting Catholics to rent pews to come to listen to the best choirs in America. She read in the papers that Catholic Mass was fast becoming an entertainment of sorts, with concerts and speeches designed to bring in flagging Catholics. She had no desire to be brought in, for it had been enough that Mam's monotone prayers, morning and evening, never ceased. They consoled as well as irritated her.

Norah's hand trembled as she took copious notes. She ignored the tiny rivulet of ink from the steel nib pen that was sliding down her finger leaving a dot on the page. Her letters wouldn't smear if she kept her eye on where the ink spilled. She was madly trying to write every word that came from Father Driscoll, abbreviating words and ignoring punctuation. Adrenalin pumped her brain with startling bursts of energy, as if she was being introduced to an exotic food, unfamiliar but tantalizing. She willed her hand to keep steady while perspiration dripped down her back. The scent of pungent incense and burned candles took up residence in her nose. How much of the pew money went to buy candles, she wondered. To her, burning candles in church was like using up the light, rather than providing light to see by. She didn't look at the priest as these thoughts came to her; but after he finished speaking, she finally set her pen in the inkwell, wiped her fingers on a handkerchief from her pocket, and massaged her wrist. Her notes were a mess, and she pushed out any thoughts in the present time to edit or theorize about his ideas. She sat up straight and looked into the eyes of Father Driscoll to indicate she was ready for more.

"Slavery is our society's plague, Miss McCabe. It will be the ruin of this country. The demolition of its system will no doubt cause economic repercussions that reverberate across the country. It's my moral obligation, rather, our moral obligation, whether Protestant or Catholic, to stand against its evil system and bring freedom to human beings who have come to us disguised as the Christ."

Father Driscoll finished speaking and looked at the altar with Jesus Christ hanging limply and defeated, not powerful and resurrected. As much as he adored the cross with his savior on it, it sometimes bothered him. But mostly, these feelings caused him to feel a kinship with the disciples because they, too, had wanted a strong king, not a crucified one. They eventually had some understanding as to why, and he himself was always trying to learn through them. He sighed, for his understanding could only go so deep. He believed that the core meaning of Christ's resurrection symbolized suffering that brought forth triumph. Strength revealed in weakness. Father Driscoll also believed that as tribal and savage a Negro slave could be, his position was Christ's position because he was continually stripped, whipped, beaten and hung, just as Christ had been. He had agreed to this interview with Norah McCabe because he believed that truth in the printed word was powerful. He had to make sure Norah McCabe knew the truth. There was something transcendent and significant about the young woman, but he also fathomed turbulence stirring in her that wasn't revealed on her radiant face.

"And where do you stand on the issue of slavery, Miss McCabe?" Father Driscoll asked.

"I'm doing very little standing these days, Father," Norah responded, gathering her things and preparing to leave. She didn't want to sort out her feelings about slavery with the priest right now. Where had she been all these years not to fathom how volatile an issue slavery was, her living right in the midst of so many Negroes and dancing with them at Pete Williams' Saloon! She knew that there was great prejudice, but she had never paid much attention to it, for weren't they all hated, the immigrants and the Negro? It was all about survival in Five Points, no matter what your color; prejudice seemed to be aimed at everyone.

"The paper is taking an unusual position for an Irish paper." The priest ignored Norah's hasty preparations to leave.

"To be honest, Father, I haven't thought much about slavery since coming to America. I've been too busy feeling like a slave myself."

Norah held her notes to her chest and looked intently at the priest, waiting for him to dismiss her with a proper blessing and goodbye. Her face was flushed and she didn't want him to know how she had feared taking his words down, wondering whether she knew enough about the subject to write an intelligent article for the paper. And, of course, she wanted to be respectful, for he was a priest, for God's sake!

"We're finished, Miss McCabe, but before you go, I'd like to ask…"

Was this priest not going to give up? Norah thought. She had an aversion to being rude to a priest, for it would be akin to being rude to God.

"Yes, Father?"

"Does your family rent a pew at The Transfiguration?"

"No, Father. You must know it's costly for many families."

"I'm not in favor of it, Miss McCabe, but the Bishop insists." The priest sighed and clasped his hands together.

"I've not seen you at my church. If pew rental prevents you and your family from worshipping at The Transfiguration, I invite you and your family to come and sit in the pew to the right of the altar," he said, pointing toward the front of the church.

"As a young writer for the newspaper, you are in a position to write about truth and liberation, and thus it's paramount for you to partake of the Body of Christ and find peace for your own soul. There is much difficulty and temptation living in America, especially for a young Irish woman."

"Thanks be to God for you, Father. It's very kind of you. I'll speak to my family about it."

"Do you not attend a church at all, then?"

"We go to Mass sometimes, especially during Holy Week."

Norah desired to get away from the priest so she could return to the office to work on the article. James said he wanted the article before she left for the day. Drops of sweat careened down her neck and were soaking into her clothing. She hadn't bathed in a couple of days and she worried she would smell up the office if she didn't find her rose oil to dab on herself.

"You are doing good work, Miss McCabe, but don't neglect your spirit. A lively and passionate spirit a young woman as yourself possesses can become a detriment if you don't channel it properly. It can be plucked and destroyed by dirty and foul beings who only pretend to possess wisdom. I sincerely and seriously caution you, young lady."

The priest stood up and gathered his crumpled black robes from behind him. Norah's heart was beating rapidly like the hooves of a wild horse fleeing captivity.

"I will, Father." She smiled warmly at him as he gave a blessing on her forehead. She walked back to the office feeling the priest's touch of holiness. When she glanced in a shop window, she imagined an imprint of his finger on her forehead.

She walked quietly into the newspaper office and then into the small room filled with books. She didn't want James to come after her and ask a myriad of questions she wasn't ready or able to answer. She needed to read over her notes and find some way to put the priest's words and her thoughts into article form that would be acceptable to James. She was aware he was nervous about her writing this important article, maybe any article, and this eroded her confidence. It was nearing dusk and Norah stumbled into boxes James had set in her office. She dropped her bag and note pad, and some of her notes scattered on the floor. A few minutes later, James walked in with one of the three kerosene lamps they used to light the office in the evening. He placed one on the table in the cramped room and moved the boxes into a corner. Norah picked up her notepad and papers and positioned herself at her desk to indicate she was going to work.

"I can see you are quite eager to write your article," James said, moving the lamp to the desk.

Without turning toward him, she said, "I want to sort out everything Father Driscoll told me. And there's little time left of the day. I'd like to go home sometime tonight." Norah touched her notes repetitively with her ink-stained fingers.

"I'll get you some good writing implements," James said. He returned with an inkwell and pen to find Norah dabbing her eyes with a handkerchief.

"This is my very favorite pen! I give it to you as a sacrament for our holy article about the priest," he said, laying it down beside her papers and then stepping back, reluctant to leave.

"Are you upset about something?" he asked.

Norah turned away from James to look out the window near her desk. She had all the material she needed to write an article about the priest and his abolitionist ideas. The time had finally arrived for her to write printable material that would have her byline on it. To become a real newspaperwoman after all the months running errands and being Mr. James Harrigan's gopher! What was wrong with her! She was eager to rid her brain of the thumping, condemning words of the priest, but it wasn't only the words he spoke about concerning slavery; it was his words about the danger her soul might be in that was bothering her. She wanted to erase and edit them right out of her mind, but they seared into her conscience and made her fearful and confused. The priest would have known that she, a Catholic immigrant, would be putty in his hands. She couldn't extirpate his words from God's words, and what if God Almighty Himself had warned her?

"I'm only tired, is all," she lied to James.

"Is the article too much for you to write? I can do it myself if you give me the interview notes you took today," he said, walking close to her desk. She looked up and his face was lit with eagerness.

"No! I mean to be writing this article, James!" She struck the desk with her fist.

"That's my girl!" James said, backing away again. Norah thought she saw disappointment in his face.

"You do know, Norah, that as editor of the paper, I will read the article and make any necessary changes before it goes to print."

Norah replied with a nod, clearly reading James that he must be having grave reservations about her aptitude and ability. She was having them, too.

"Of course! I'm your apprentice," Norah said, picking up his pen and dipping it into the inkwell. She poised it over a clean page, looked at him and smiled.

"I know when I'm not wanted," he said, laughing. "I'm staying the night, so take your time. I'll make sure you get home safely no matter what the hour."

"Thank you," Norah replied and, after James left, a rush of excitement flooded her. She felt ready to write.

Her first sentences flowed out on the tablet, "Father Theobold Driscoll, parish priest at the Church of the Transfiguration, is to be commended for his abolitionist efforts to rid the country of the evil institution of slavery. He lives and works in Five Points, a melting pot of the disenfranchised African and immigrant alike. Unlike the rest of the country, Five Points is engaged in a radical experiment the world should take note of. The well-heeled and fine-gloved Republicans who write and speak eloquently about abolition, who couldn't live without former slaves doing all their dirty work in their lavish mansions, should come and live in Five Points to see how their high ideals are put into practice. In Five Points, Irish, Germans, Italians, and Africans revel in dance, song, and friendship. They sell their food on the street corners together and fill the air with poignant cries and songs. It is to Five Points that these lily white aristocrats who feel the stirrings of humanitarian concern for slaves need to come."

Norah wrote the article in just under two hours, surprised at her alacrity and the immersion in something that took her out of time and place.

"I've finished, James," she said, her face flushed with satisfaction as she stood in the doorway of his office clutching the article to her chest. He was sitting with his head down on his desk when she walked in. He sat up quickly and turned to her, "That's great! Let's have a look." She handed it to him and sat down in a chair to wait for him to read her first article for the *Irish-American*. Norah watched James nervously for some hint of acknowledgement that it was worthy to be printed. She was sorely disappointed when he began marking up her words! He hummed as he made marks and notes on her article. She almost interrupted him, but kept quiet while he worked. She was exhausted and wanted to go home and forget about the damn article until the morning.

As James worked, she made plans to stop at the shop to see Mary before going home. She hoped to learn more about the relationship between Officer Leary and Mary, and if possible, to talk some sense into her silly friend's head. Suddenly, she could no longer refrain from speaking.

"Is it inferior? It must be if you're attacking it with your pen like you're wielding a knife!"

James put the pen down, folded his hands on her tablet where she could see he was smearing the marks he had just made. He looked at her with a puzzled expression.

"I'm merely doing the job of an editor. You need to grow tough skin and not be so sensitive to the editing process. This is a fine article, Norah. A fine article, indeed."

Norah, relieved, sat back in her chair, her lips slightly twitching. She tried not to smile so he wouldn't notice how thrilled she was. When he leaned back in his chair, she jumped up to stand over his desk and look at the marks he had made on her words.

"It's a fine article indeed…however, it needs some revision," James said, sitting up straight in his chair.

Norah picked up the tablet and tried to read the marks he had placed over her words; her hard-earned words, her inspired, and meaningful words. The priest himself had inspired her. How could James twist and mangle these dear and important thoughts!

"What's wrong with it?" she asked, throwing it down in front of him and immediately feeling chagrin for her indignation. "I'm sorry, James. Go ahead and edit my words…do as you please and must, I suppose. I'll wait." She smiled wanly and marched solemnly into her office.

James wasn't really alarmed at Norah's response, for he had already assumed her controlled spirit would eventually erupt when challenged. And she was young, tender, and too unsophisticated to with-stand criticism. He had originally been drawn to her for this very spirit, and was now prepared to chisel and hone it for the publishing world. She was unskilled and rough, but there was great potential in her. The Protestants had their great women working in the public eye, why not the Irish Catholics? There was the well known Margaret Fuller who had worked for Greeley at the *Tribune* five years before. There was Lydia Maria Child who edited and wrote for the *National Standard* about the abolitionist movement. A female correspondent would be a feature, an allurement, a pretty allurement at that...she would help him sell more papers. And he had felt the flame turned up higher un-derneath his mission as a newspaperman when she had challenged him about writing about the commissioner. The newspaper industry was fast becoming New York's brain—the command center to keep the beaten down immigrants in line, the Knickerbockers comforted, and the revolutionaries inflamed and connected. He had thought he would just tell the news, mostly the Irish news, and maybe give the poor image of the Irish some dignity. And, along with his small inher-itance from his father, he could make a decent enough living.

He might have wished to turn up the flame on issues, but Bishop Hughes kept him in line about voicing anything too radical. Harrigan wanted to write more than news from Europe, domestic servant ads, and shipping news, with an occasional article about some Irishman made good, like John McKeon, a popular district attorney. How many times had it been printed in his paper about McKeon: "What he was, you are...what he is, any of you may become. Be honest, faithful, in-dustrious, and energetic, and the highest honors of the land are open to you."

He was sorry to have to be this blunt and honest with Norah, for her spirit needed as much soldiering and succoring as any Irish person in this crazy city. But dammit, she needed work! In fact, she needed a lot of work. How angry she had looked when she stood in front of him waiting for him to tell her what was wrong. But those eyes! They made his heart digress at times, but now wasn't the time to succumb to them and lose his discretion in correcting and teaching her how to write. He had to be stern and tell her straight, or she would never learn. He turned in his chair and called her to come into his office. She came in quickly and stood resolutely before him.

"Sit down, Norah," he said, and she flung herself down in the chair, her face flushed and her eyes bright and demanding.

"First of all, you have run-on sentences. Your passion about this subject seems to take you over, but it is unbridled, and the sentences become tangled branches with thorns that have captured the priest's heart and mind; but they are clearly adulterated and embellished with fury and grandiosity. These words aren't the priest's; they are your own and, thus, out of balance. I didn't know you cared so much about this issue, but clearly, your words have shown me that you do. That is good, however, you are to report the news, not give your opinions, especially when you are quoting someone as important as the priest of the Church of Transfiguration. This is journalism, Norah..." He hesitated and then continued, "but you are perfect for this work...and you clearly write well—"

"Please, James, no more! I'm not feeling well. I have to go!"

She got up and sprinted out of his office.

Norah retrieved her shawl and belongings, and ran down the creaky steps in great flight away from James Harrigan and the damn *Irish-American* newspaper. She opened the front door, walked out, and slammed it as hard as she could. My God! Didn't she already know that she was young and had much to learn? What had gotten into her silly head to think she was ready to write her own article, especially one as important as this one? Why had James given her the assignment knowing she would fail? Did he want her to fail so he could ridicule her and make her feel belittled? Maybe she wasn't cut out for journalism. If she wasn't allowed to write her own thoughts and feelings about issues, she would quit!

Norah was trembling when she walked out of the building into the night with raucous and threatening noise permeating the city in the distance. She was far from home, but decided to walk the long way to sort out her feelings. She needed to think through everything that had happened. Walking would help, for it always did. She had forgotten, however, that she was going to go to her shop to visit Mary and, after walking a few minutes, she remembered and changed her direction. She walked a while, but decided she wouldn't go to Mary and tell her she had quit her new post at the newspaper. The very thought of returning to the shop to work full time with Mary who was besotted with feelings of love for a boy from Ireland was unbearable. Norah turned around again and briskly walked toward what she believed was the direction of home, but when she turned a corner, she was aghast at what she saw in front of her. She froze on the spot, and then the wind noisily swished the crinoline underneath her skirts. A man was moving rhythmically against something or someone near an old wall of a dilapidated building. It was dark, but Norah caught a glimpse of a young girl, a mere child, holding up her skirts; her thin, ivory legs glowing in the night. The girl cried out and quickly dropped her skirts when the man turned to look at Norah.

Norah emitted a startled cry, turned around, and wandered out into the dusty street, her hand clasped over her mouth. A buggy driver yelled at her to get out of his way and suddenly a crowd arrived, sweeping her along. She heard someone comment that the show at Barnum's had been superb and that it was the best entertainment in town. The crowd traveled slowly down various streets, and she moved along with them, hardly noticing where she was going. There were parties amongst the crowd, but there were many like her who were walking home from somewhere else and had gotten caught up with the movement of people taking up the street. As she walked along, a few people left the crowd and walked in different directions. There were laughing couples intimately clutching one another. She was certain they were on their way to do what she had just seen. In all her years living in Five Points, she had never actually seen people copulating out in the open, although Mary had and told her about it.

Norah watched a giggling couple embrace, kiss, and murmur to one another, caring not about their public display. *Let them have a warm bed to go to,* she thought, *for at least they would not be acting like animals rutting together out underneath the stars. Stars! How could the perfect and mysterious glittering lights in the sky look down upon such a thing!*

She continued to move with the group, as if in a trance, oblivious to her surroundings. Most of the Barnum crowd disbanded, and a couple of men in front of her meandered, engrossed in quiet conversation. Norah followed behind them and soon recognized some buildings that were situated near her tenement building. She quickened her steps as she thought of her sofa and dresser, a warm cup of tea, and the possibility that Da would be up to talk, thus wiping out the day's events with his wisdom. The two men walked to the right and then she was alone.

Norah stumbled on to some garbage lying next to an abandoned building. She hadn't noticed how dark it had become, for there weren't as many gaslights on the street now. She stopped walking to get her bearings. She shivered in the cold and wrapped her shawl more tightly around her, looking to the right and left. It was then she felt the presence of hostility and smelled a warm, sour, yeasty scent mingled with horse sweat. She looked straight ahead, her heart beating wildly as she walked briskly away from the presence of evil. She refused to look back or to the sides, for she knew if she did, she would weaken with anxiety. *Where were all the party goers?* she wondered with mounting apprehension. She wished she hadn't impulsively left the office in a fury, not thinking of the danger she might have been placing herself in. *Not thinking! Impetuous and foolish,* a voice in her head said. Her steps quickened, as did the pounding in her heart and head that covered the sound of a presence behind her. But within minutes she heard footsteps, shuffles, snickers, and grunts that rose above the noise of her heartbeats. Gang members…maybe little boys, but nevertheless, gang members!

She picked up speed and began to run, holding up her skirts. She had to outrun the noise of fear within her and the evil behind her. She still refused to look behind her, for if she did, she would not have the courage to keep going. But within minutes, her chest felt as if it were made of brick and she found it difficult to breathe. Nevertheless, she kept running, grasping her skirts up to her knees.

"'Tis an angel who runs ahead of us!" a man cried out. Norah stopped running and walked a slow pace now, fear choking her as if hands already clasped her neck. She gasped for air, and suddenly felt hot breath on her neck that caused her skin to prickle. She had no choice but to turn around. When she did, she looked beyond the man so close to her and saw five or more young ruffians behind him, the whites of their eyes glowing like cats' eyes underneath their caps. They all appeared the same. *Irish?* A flash of hope swept over her because if they were from Cork, maybe…but then they circled her and a faint came over her that caused her legs to buckle. She prayed silently to God for help, and then her knees straightened as a surge of supernatural strength came over her. She threw her arms up and punched the air, closing her eyes and praying loudly in the Irish language.

"*A Dhia dean trocaire!*"

In the same language she had just uttered, a familiar voice responded that penetrated through her fog of fear. "*Beidh trocaire orm, a duirt,* Norah McCabe!"

She stopped fighting and dared to open her eyes to look at the shameful man who had become a wild animal, a predator of the night. He had to be a deranged Irishman who would drag her into an alleyway to take advantage of her in some way she couldn't comprehend.

"'Tis the young Irish warrior from the *Irish-American,*" he said.

"Cursed is the mother who birthed you!" Norah screamed, and turned quickly to flee.

He gripped her arm, "You'll not be leaving yet, wild one."

The other men came in close to watch the scene, and Norah saw that one man was swinging something in his hand. When Norah noticed that it was an eye gouger, she screamed and a man in the distance came running. When he saw the menacing gang, however, he fled as fast as he had arrived.

"Police!" Norah cried out, but to no avail. The dark street emptied except for the gang members who circled like hungry wolves, hulking and haunted.

"Put it away!" ordered Norah's apprehender to the man swinging the eye gouger. All the men took a few steps back and the gouger was hidden away in the man's clothing.

"Go on, all of you, go on home now. I'll take care of this. The young woman and I know one another."

There was no objection or insubordination amongst the five men who had been ordered to go home. They scampered into alleyways and down streets, as if on all fours. Norah shivered and felt that her life was taking a sharp turn around a corner she had never intended for it to take. Her abductor held on to her arm, which was clothed with an ornate puffed sleeve she had been proud of sewing. Now it appeared ridiculous in the grip of a gang leader. Her blue woolen shawl had fallen from her shoulders and lay on the street; she was shaking, but slightly relieved that the rest of the pack had left. She finally looked into the eyes of this man whose voice sounded almost friendly to her and was shocked to see it was Mr. Murray whom she had met in the Astor House hotel restaurant! And to think she had been so taken by him that she had been unable to get him out of her mind for days! Now she knew her heart had terribly deceived her.

"You're a gangleader!" Norah cried in dismay, casting her eyes down from his after he let go of her arm. She picked up her shawl from the street and shook it out, her fear subsiding. She was unsure why she was suddenly unafraid of him, this one with such power as a gang leader. How did she appear to him? She knew right well that any woman alone on the street so late at night is a woman seeking whoring. Was it her good fortune that it was Mr. Murray and not one of the Dead Rabbits she had met on this flight of vanity and foolishness away from James Harrigan? Here she was ensnared by the great Mr. Murray, the essayist himself, and gang leader extraordinaire. And what gang was this that he was leader of, for she had seen no flamboyant markings to identify them.

Her da had described the gangs, their clothing, and their activities to her, but never in Mam's presence. The violence and chaos they heaved on the city was incomprehensible to her, and she had felt immune from ever encountering it. How many warnings had Da given her about being alone on the streets at night! And what would he think of her now standing before a powerful gang leader whose presence caused her heart to beat as heavy and dark as raven's wings?

Mr. Murray didn't answer Norah, but watched her retrieve her shawl and arrange it around her shoulders. He imagined that she trembled with defiance, as well as fear. How could he explain himself to her? How could he describe to her the condition of her country she had fled from as a child, the ponderous and mournful Eire? And how could he persuade her that her country warranted saving with measures that shook the very core of his moral upbringing, as well as his own integrity?

"If you will listen to me, *Mo Chara,* I'll try to explain my intentions in leading around a wild pack of hoodlums with weapons that should never have been invented."

Norah was stunned that this strange man had called her a friend in the Irish language. No one but Da had ever used the Irish language to affectionately address her.

She backed away, ready to flee again, but he didn't prevent her from leaving. Her few steps were hesitant and delicate, as if she were in some kind of slow dance. When she stopped, it was in a graceful posture that suggested an invitation. He was abhorrent to her, but she couldn't help herself in feeling ready for some kind of wild dalliance.

"You can leave, Norah McCabe," Murray said. "And you can tell your Mr. James Harrigan that Mr. Thomas Murray, born humbly in the muck of the Sixth Ward, who climbed upward with grandiose ideas, has now sunk deep into the mire of gang life. Go ahead and tell him! It'll make a sensational story for his paper, if he dares to print it!"

He paced before her with his hands in his pockets and Norah saw that his breath hovered before him, smoky and ghostly. He reminded her of a dark horse who snorted and pawed the ground. He was bigger than life, bigger than an ordinary Irishman's life, anyway. Norah became self-conscious about the way she stood poised; her head cocked to the right, her left arm swept behind her back, and her right hand on her hip. At once, she released the tension in her body and her arms fell to her sides. She quickly clasped her shawl close around her neck and moved away from him.

"Maybe it would be more suited for the *Sun,* not the *Irish-American* with all its Irish poetry and gleeful ads," she replied.

"And maybe the *Sun* newspaper will hire you, an Irish girl, who has come upon a story more interesting than a blood and thunder play."

He smiled at her and she saw how well groomed he was for a gang leader. His teeth were straight and his face was clean shaven, and of a good color, too, almost radiant in the dark. One dim lamplight was burning and shone on them as if to highlight their odd exchange. Norah was eerily transfixed, as if she were acting in a scene in a play. Maybe a Shakespeare play. She liked his height and built, but his features were not what her friend Mary would consider handsome. His mouth was too full and his nose was too prominent on his face. She could hear Mam say that only a woman should have lips like his. Her Mam would think he was too mysterious, "like those devilish Hitalian men with the greasy skin," she had said about the Italian men selling their wares in the market. But his skin was not dark and swarthy, but the pale fragile porcelain-looking kind, just like her own. His eyes appeared to her like pools of murky, impenetrable liquid. They looked sharply into hers, as if he was trying to find the depth in his own.

"The *Sun* probably wouldn't be interested in a story only half told, Norah McCabe. Up to now, nothing noteworthy has happened. That is, nothing that would interest the *Sun*. They care little to write about an Irishman gone bad, for all Irishmen are inherently so in their estimation, even one who was born and educated here in America. But if you're really interested in a good story, we can sit somewhere and I can tell you why I've been out this night leading around a pack of wild animals."

"I'm not after a good story, Mr. Murray. I'm after getting home safe."

"If you were after getting home safe, you'd not be walking on the street at this hour."

"I've come from the office," Norah looked around her again to see how she might get home.

"I'll walk you home safely and tell you a good story that you can use however you please."

"I'm close to home... I think I'm close to home," she said, frantically looking around her.

He offered her his arm, "Show me the way, then, Miss McCabe."

Norah hesitated but then gently touched his arm, as if she was asked to dance and was being led onto the dance floor. She immediately felt safe holding his arm and listening to him talk as they walked, and at once she forgot that she was being escorted home by a dangerous Five Points gang leader.

Chapter Eleven

A few months later, Norah and Mary were sitting at Taylor's Ice Cream Parlour indulging in bowls of ice cream covered with lingonberry sauce. A few other women were seated nearby and Norah surmised they were more interested in her conversation with Mary than in their own.

"You've nearly become the backbone of the Friendly Sons of St. Patrick's!" Norah exclaimed to Mary.

"Do you need to be telling the whole neighborhood?" Mary responded, "I'll be having every Irish Benevolent Society woman at the door of my shop!"

"Whose shop, Mary?" Norah retorted angrily.

The relationship between the two women had become tenuous; the warmth developed in their childhood friendship was frayed and diminishing. Mary had been tithing some of the proceeds of the sales from the shop to help feed some needy Five Point residents without discussing it with Norah. It was true, Norah was forced to admit, that she hadn't been available to discuss such things with Mary. Her friend had been acting as the sole proprietor of her store, and Norah sensed it was going straight to Mary's head.

"I'm spending the days in the upkeep of the high and mighty Miss Norah McCabe's shop while she's sneaking in and out of alleyways with her Mr. Murray and his notions about Ireland."

"And whose money established the shop, Mary? Where would you be without it?" Norah hissed at her friend. The other two women in the parlour stopped talking and looked over at them.

"Me and Mr. Leary aren't obligated to care for your business now, Norah? It doesn't really make me a sound profit. You, on the other hand, are filling your pockets to squirrel off to the Irish Emigrant Bank. If I went into the carting business with Leary, your shop would be abandoned for the ruffians to steal from!"

"Mr. Leary? Your Mr. O'Leary? Who asked him to step into my store? *My* store, Mary...don't forget, it's *my* store!" Norah whispered.

She could smell the expensive perfume the girleen was wearing. Maybe she had taken extra money out of the sales to buy it. Why, Norah wouldn't be surprised at all! Mary's ice cream had melted in her bowl, but Norah had finished every drop of hers and haughtily wiped her mouth with a handkerchief she pulled from her purse.

"As a matter-of-fact, the reason I asked you to meet me today was to talk about the future of *my* shop." Norah said, looking sadly at her friend. For a brief moment, she saw Mary as the young girl who had come alongside her after school one day so many years before. What merriment and wit Mary had in those days! How innocent had been their dreams in spite of poverty and hunger. But now Mary had turned into a vain and empty headed girl. She reminded Norah of a lovely vase that sat in a department store, perfectly designed and waiting for someone to purchase it to give it real worth. And now she had chosen this Leary to be her vase filler and her all in all. This O'Leary! Norah looked at her friend and was sorry it had come to this.

"I'm selling the shop, Mary."

"And will the proceeds be going to your Mr. Murray to fund his murderous schemes?" Mary blurted out loudly.

"I'm not involved with anyone's schemes, let alone murderous schemes. Hold your foolish tongue, girl!" she said, as loud as she dared.

Mary smiled smugly at Norah, "Is that so?"

"I'll post a sign in front of the store tomorrow morning. I'll give you a quarter of the sale—"

"A quarter? I should be getting at least half! With all the work I've done for you day in and day out while you've been cavorting with newspapermen and rebels with grandiose ideas!"

Mary removed her bonnet. It was adorned with tiny silk pink posies and violets, much too ornate and fancy for an ice cream parlour. She laid it down on the table and adjusted her hair, removing some pins and redoing the coils.

"I'm also giving you some of the clothing in the shop. You can choose a few dresses, but only after an inventory has been taken."

Norah leaned back, eyeing the women who were fidgeting uneasily in their chairs. She grimaced at them and turned again to Mary to wait for her response.

"Will you let me choose, or will it be the rags not yet embellished with my own fine sewing?" Mary asked, a tear slipping out of her eye that she quickly wiped away.

"You'll have first choice at the duds," Norah said coldly. She felt as if she were sliding down a hill and couldn't stop. She recalled the first and only time she went sledding years ago with her friend, Sean. He had insisted she do these very American things such as eat ice cream and hot dogs, as well as play in the snow, which was like bathing in ice water to her. He dragged her outside of the city, and hidden behind some trees had been a wooden plank set atop shining steel blades that glistened in the sunlight. After convincing her it'd be grand to be flying down the hill on something that looked like two knives, she sat behind him, and a minute later she left solid ground and became caught somewhere between heaven and earth. Halfway down the hill, she shouted to him that she wanted to get off, but he shouted back that it was too late and she'd have to go for the full ride. This was how she felt now about her life and her relationship with Mary, selling her shop, and making the decision to help Murray raise funds for John Mitchel and his movement. It was too late to turn back. She listened to her own sharp words slice through her friendship with Mary and saw her life propelled beyond the life she had known since coming to America.

"Thanks be to God for your wee bit of kindness then, Norah," Mary said, her words biting back. She slammed down her spoon and reached for her purse to pull out some coins to pay for the ice cream.

"I suppose you'll be asking me to tend the store until there's a buyer. I'll be requiring an hourly wage then and not just your little hand-out at the end of the week," she said, standing to leave.

"You were the one who insisted I not pay you an hourly wage, Mary. Do you remember?"

"That was only when we had but two or three dresses to sell at a time! You'd think you would have offered me the hourly wage after we became so successful!"

Norah looked out the window and saw the sun setting over the city's horizon. There was an autumn chill creeping into the evening hours already. It would be dark soon and she needed to get a buggy and go home to Da. He had been feeling ill on and off for a month, and had been coming home from work and immediately falling asleep on her sofa. Mam was working long hours and didn't get home until nine o'clock, and she was so tired that she hardly noticed Da wasn't himself. Norah pulled out some coins and placed them on the table, refusing to look at her friend. She had to end this unpleasant conversation with Mary and hurry to pick up a ham bone from the butcher before his shop closed. She wanted to make a nourishing soup for Da before he got home and fell asleep without dinner.

"I'd be grateful, Mary, if you'd be willing to keep the shop up and running until there's a buyer," Norah said.

She stood up from the table, wrapped her shawl around her shoulders, and picked up her things, including the book she had been reading before Mary had arrived at the parlour. Gone were the days of reading Lady Godey's book on how to become a fashionable young woman in America. And forget Sadlier's novels, and the popular pulp fiction she had once read, which was mostly against the Irish anyway. She had just finished reading *Uncle Tom's Cabin* and was aghast and disturbed over its contents. But she had to forget her Negro friends she used to dance with at Pete Williams, for it was her own people she needed to assist. She wanted to help liberate them in Ireland from the poverty imposed upon them by the British. How could she ever have shared any of her reading with Mary? The girleen never showed interest in any of the books Norah had read, and she certainly wouldn't be interested in her reading material now.

Before Norah turned to leave, she saw that Mary was quietly weeping. It upset her to see her friend sorrowful and she reached out to touch her shoulder. When she did, all her belongings dropped to the floor. Mary quickly reached down and picked them up for her, setting everything on the table, including Norah's book.

"So 'tis true then, Norah McCabe, 'tis true what they've been saying about ye and your ways now!" Mary said sarcastically, pointing at the book. Her voice trembled and snot dripped from her nose. She unconsciously wiped her nose with the back of her sleeve.

Norah had hidden the book under some newspapers when Mary walked in to meet her. Mary, as well as her family, didn't know what she had become involved in. As far as they knew, she still worked for the *Irish-American* and for Harrigan, of course. Harrigan, her fearless leader, who had taken her alongside him into the publishing world, believing in her and then doubting her! He was just another spineless Irish-American dandy! It had been a whole year under his tutelage, and the only thing she had learned was how to properly put together articles about news that wouldn't raise too much ardor. Mary would never be able to understand her frustration, nor why she now was so passionate about the cause for Ireland.

"John Mitchel's book you're reading? John Mitchel himself, the criminal who escaped from Van Dieman's Land, come to New York to take hard-earned money away from the Irish for his murderous plots? Are you mad? Do you not remember your da making his promise that he'd never fight for Ireland with guns and knives? What about Daniel O'Connell, the Liberator, who said that human blood was no cement for freedom?"

Mary cupped her hand to the side of her mouth so the other women in the parlour couldn't hear. She hurled her questions at Norah, who stared defiantly at her. For a few seconds, the love for Mary returned, but it quickly dissipated, for it was the love she had possessed when they had been children. No more. And since when did the girleen care about Daniel O'Connell and Ireland? Mary was probably only repeating Leary's words. Honestly, the truth be told, Norah couldn't tolerate her friend's emptiness and apathy any longer. Their days of strolling along the streets and dreaming together were over, for Mary had Leary and she had Murray. And Norah had a higher purpose than flighty Mary!

"Maybe I'm only mad in your eyes," Norah responded.

The women in the parlour were leaving and she was certain they had heard Mary. She could tell by the way they huddled together as they walked out the door. The hell with all of them! She didn't care what Mary thought of her, or for that matter, what her neighbors in Five Points' neighborhood thought of her, either. It was Da she was concerned about. He didn't know that she was reading Mitchel's book. He also didn't know that she was attending meetings in the evening to hear Mitchel and others talk about Ireland's freedom. John Mitchel had been the brave and eloquent leader of the Young Ireland movement. Her da would know of him. But most importantly, her da didn't know about her relationship with Murray, other than learning she had a new friend who, like Harrigan, worked in the newspaper business.

"I'm going now, Mary," Norah said, gathering everything from the table. She felt Mary's sad disappointment follow her out the door, and it did just that—follow. She wouldn't allow it to drape heavily over her as it sought to do, like a cloak of despair and restraint. Norah had passion that pulled on her like the moon's pull on the sea, tide in and tide out, and she was willingly caught in its powerful flow, unwilling to be freed from it. As natural as the waves were in striking and caressing the shore, so was her response to Murray and the cause to free Ireland.

Later, Norah walked into the apartment feeling slightly defeated. The scent of the ham bone tied up in brown paper caused her stomach to cry out for its sustenance. The only food she had eaten all day was the ice cream that had tasted like pure heaven, creamy and sweet, something she could live on forever. Maybe it would be possible to subsist on this luscious treat, like nectar from the fairies. Ha! Fairies! Her mind rejected any thoughts of fairies but occasionally they came prancing into her mind, inviting her to play. No time for fairies, to eat properly, to be owning a shop with the likes of Mary!

Norah dropped the ham bone on the table and fussed with her hair. She was becoming somewhat neglectful in personal upkeep day after day because she had to rush to the office to help Harrigan and the other employees with the paper, and there was no time to care for her grooming as she once had. After work, she would dash home to fix something for Da to eat, but only take a few sips of soup and a few nibbles from the soda bread Mam made each morning before leaving for work. No one had time to notice that Norah was becoming very slim; her heart-shaped face that was usually full was now wan and so thin that her chin appeared pointed and sharp.

She shivered in the cold apartment, for there was no fire lit in the stove. She had stumbled inside feeling her way in the dark for the kitchen table to place her belongings on. After dropping the ham bone on the table, her cat jumped up and immediately started sniffing and clawing at it. She realized she had forgotten to feed him before leaving that morning. She was forgetting to empty the chamber pot, to buy coal, and to care for her personal health.

"Scat!" she yelled, gently pushing the cat away. She found the matches on top of the stove and lit a candle. Her eyes began to adjust to the dark, and in the corner next to the stove she saw something propped up against the wall. What was it? The McCabes' small quarters were sparsely furnished, and this caused the spaces to appear ghostlike. She took a step forward and her right foot struck the object, forcing it fall to the floor. A hollow sound echoed into the apartment, and Norah knew what it was before she could make out the familiar form with her eyes. It was Da's fiddle. She picked up the worn old instrument and held it near to her face and imagined the lilts of wild moon-lit music nights in Ireland as a child. The musical strains had made patterns on her soul that she had sought to cover up and smooth over with her new life in America, but now they were surfacing. The mixture of wood and rosin she inhaled was pungent and rich, and she also smelled the scent of her father, for his presence had also gotten into the wood and it would be there long after they'd all be gone from the earth. She pressed the fiddle to her cheek and felt the wood's armor, warrior armor that had endured famines, storms, and an ocean that had demanded sacrifice for survival. This instrument had ushered them through wakes, funerals, blessings of the parish priest, a dab at the praties for their evening meal, and through many mournful nights in Ireland. Now it was played infrequently in their home and only in dance halls, and not where there was an Irish hearth. But still the fiddle music caused bodies to give off warmth in the fierce and powerful dancing that stupefied the understated temperaments of the gawking slumming parties. How the Protestants and European tourists loved to visit Five Points' dance halls for their curious and sordid entertainment!

Norah looked for the bow, but it wasn't where she had found the fiddle. She walked around the room looking underneath the sofa and inside her dresser. Why was the fiddle left carelessly in the corner and without the bow? Da usually kept it in his bedroom, or else sitting on the shelf of the dresser if Mam hadn't placed too many things there. The fiddle and bow were never separated, as if there was a magnetic pull that kept them together, but now she couldn't find the bow. She traversed the small room a few times and then walked into her parents' bedroom carrying the candle from the table. The bow was lying on the small feather bed covered with the old gray woolen blanket where her parents slept. It appeared in a lamented state, its horsehair loosened and hanging from its alert readiness to bring lively sound into quiet or raucous places. She picked up the bow and the horsehair stayed on the bed, detached from the bow. She carefully picked up the horsehair and carried it and the bow into the other room. She set the candle down and picked up the fiddle. Then she opened the bottom of her cupboard and gently placed the fiddle, bow, and horsehair inside on top of the shawl she kept in the dresser.

Norah quickly scribbled a note to say she had gone out with Mary and Leary, and would be home around midnight or later. Da especially would be disappointed in her that she had become involved with this volatile and covert group, but oh, wouldn't Da be proud, too! He would want to have a cup of tea with the likes of these men who were educated in Europe! Men who held on to truths about history and Ireland's freedom that she knew Da still held in his own heart, though wearily set aside since coming to America. Maybe she could slowly introduce him to some of the writings of the movement, or at least she might be able to quote from some of the material when they sat together in the evenings having their tea in front of the stove. Tonight she would come home all fired up with some interesting facts to share with him. If he was sleeping on her sofa, she would rouse him for some tea and conversation. He had never denied her his listening ear no matter the lateness of the hour. Yes! She decided that this night she would begin to gently persuade him that the work of John Mitchel was worthwhile.

Norah changed her skirt and tried to arrange it over her petticoats that seemed too stiff and cumbersome for a serious political meeting, but she was also meeting Mr. Murray and wanted to be as enticing as possible. She was surprised to find that after hooking the snaps of the skirt, it fell down slightly and revealed the top part of her petticoats. She had lost too much weight to be able to wear her best skirt! She stepped out of it and looked in the trunk next to the bed for something else to wear. She found a blue velvet dress that had delicate black netting covering the top half of it, and decided it was perfect for the evening. It was one of the first dresses she had purchased a few years ago before her body had developed and overcome some of the effects of being half starved. It fit just right now, but she also hoped it wouldn't be too out of fashion. She blushed as this thought entered her mind, for it seemed utterly foolish to be concerned about fashion now that she and Murray, Mr. Thomas D. Murray, were saving their coins to save lives in Ireland. She stood before her mirror, pleased at how she looked, almost as if she had returned to the girl she had been when she first arrived in this country. She was back to that place again, even in her body, she thought, as she noticed her thinness. She took down her hair, re-coiled it and placed a black shawl around her shoulders. Norah skipped to the door, blowing out the candle before leaving, and when she opened the door to the hallway in the building, a breeze at once gripped her with melancholy; it also entered the apartment, and the note Norah had left on the table blew into one of those bare ghostly corners where it wouldn't be found when Mam and Da returned home.

Chapter Twelve

Norah walked the four blocks to Finn McCool's, a semi-respectable snug of a watering hole. Da's cautionary pleading to take public transportation at night no matter what the cost went unheeded, although his reprimands played out in her mind. She walked with forthright purpose down the street amongst a mélange of darkened forms creeping along or swiftly rushing to their destinations. The pullulating streets were mostly filled with a boisterous crowd of workies who were out looking for some fun and entertainment No one strolled arm in arm in leisure, and police whistles were blowing at full alarm in the distance. Norah inhaled burning animal flesh and quickly clenched her handkerchief over her nose. Most likely someone had piled up the dead carcasses of cats, dogs, or maybe even a horse, to get them out of the way in this city that was always on the go, leaving its refuse everywhere. As her eyes adjusted in the purplish starry night, she looked up in the sky for a moment wondering what phase the moon might be in. She was disappointed to see it slacking off low in the sky, looking as if it was a chewed down thumb nail unable to illuminate the earth. She was disappointed it wasn't full and promising, as was her heart this night.

"You're all hell-fired up, Miss," a man said behind her. "You must be one of those big wigs the way you're carrying yourself down the street in such a hurry," he continued.

Norah kept walking. She wasn't frightened because there were too many people on the street for him to try anything. He merely wanted to get the attention of someone like herself, a real lady, which was certainly a rarity to be found on these streets. She lifted her chin and walked more assuredly, swishing her skirts as she did. She was learning that most men never hesitated to woo a woman beyond their class or station in life. She could tell by this man's speech that he was probably a b'hoy, fire laddie, or just a runner. If he was a gang member, he would have approached her differently – more surreptitiously, threatening-like. She shook her head and sighed. She had hoped for a quiet walk before meeting Murray, to listen to her own words forming in her head—a sentence, paragraph, or story about her future that was just beginning to come into focus, like the sun rising on a crisp early morning when she left the house to go to work and believed nothing but good could happen. Suddenly, she felt the man's arm go through hers but she didn't pull away as her mind told her to, but turned toward this bold man who had dared to claim her arm.

"Ye should not be walking the streets like a harlot, Miss Norah McCabe," Murray said, laughing loudly.

How had she not known his voice even if he had altered it to tease her? She was certain she had taken every nuance of his voice and lodged it within the cavity of her heart. It had echoed from that place and into her mind for months now. Her heart had become cave-like with his voice there, a place to be safe from the outside world, as they gradually planned their future in becoming a force for change. How had she been fooled?

"You've nearly frightened the knickers off of me, Murray!" she said.

"I hope so," he said, squeezing her arm. She blushed and was glad for the darkness on the street so he couldn't see her face.

"It appears we're always destined to meet on the streets of New York," he said. "I figured you would be taking a carriage to Finn's. Didn't you learn from your last encounter alone on the streets?"

"Indeed I did! And it was such a magical one, I've been unafraid since," she responded, leaning onto his arm.

"How's our Mr. Harrigan doing these days?" he asked, changing the subject.

"He's back to printing poems in the Irish language, which is good, but since my article was published, entirely rewritten by him, he's backed off from printing anything too bold. I don't think the *Irish-American* is going to be a strong voice for the abolitionist movement. Or any movement, really."

"Did you speak to him about writing an article about Ireland's desperate need for independence?"

"He doesn't like Mitchel."

"But his paper has fifty thousand readers—"

"The *Times* will print up something about Mitchel. Their newspapermen are around every corner looking for news," she said, peering over her shoulder. "They're probably watching us right now to see if we're going to collect arms at the meeting."

"That's what I'm afraid of. They'll be printing we're collecting ammunition to blow up half of Europe!"

As they approached Finn McCool's, Norah's mood changed and she fluctuated between buoyant cheerfulness and the heaviness of a clandestine dark affair. The hairs on the back of her neck prickled, and this sensation ran down her arms and over her chest. Murray let go of her arm and touched the small of her back to gently escort her into the snug. She heard the music at Finn's reverberating through the clapboards and onto the street, strong and warrior-like, the bodhran drumming out a rhythm familiar to her. It was a man's world and a man's pub, but when it came to the Irish revolutionaries, lines were crossed, and male and female became one. Idealism was what she had unconsciously hungered for all her young life, but she hadn't realized it until meeting Murray. The passion for country and her transformation had been stirred and roused through this movement Murray had introduced her to. She had come home to herself even before she had come home to Ireland.

"Top of the evening, Murray… and Norah!" Thomas, the owner and bartender cried out in a greeting when they entered. A spray of street light splashed through the door when they walked into the dark and smoky pub. Most of the streets were not well lit, but some do-gooder city official had thought it important for a gaslight to be placed directly in front of Finn McCool's to keep a keen eye on its activities. The pub appeared small from the outside, with a small entry on a corner lot that was housed in an old, gray, wooden building. Each time Norah entered, she would make the sign of the cross, but her worries would cease after she drank a couple of pints and listened to Murray talk to others about Ireland's freedom.

Murray ushered Norah through the pub. It was packed to the rafters; pungent tobacco smelled like burnt molasses and there were reeking odors from sweat that attacked her senses. Many of the men had come directly to Finn's from laboring on the streets and in the ports all day. These men didn't relish going home to squalor and crying babes in their tenement homes. She was proud to be with Murray who seemed to know everyone. Her Murray! How relieved she felt when she learned he wasn't a real gang leader. The night she met him precariously on the street, he had been at a meeting with John Mitchel. When he was leaving, a gang associated with Tammany Hall informed him that a group of Orangemen had organized a mob to attack St. Mary's Church with the intention of burning it down. They asked him to go with them to help quell the riot, but when he arrived with the gang, it was nearly too late. The church had been attacked, but the police had prevented it from being burned to the ground. The Orangemen who were responsible for the attack were nowhere to be found. Tammany had said they would apply new tactics and there was talk of retaliation for the next day. Murray declined helping them any further, for he was hesitant to get involved in the fighting between Nativists, Orangemen, and Irish gangs.

"Go easy on the pints tonight, Norah," Murray said, helping her onto a stool.

If Da and Mam could see her in this hideaway, this drinking establishment, they would be furious and sick at heart, she thought sadly. Murray ordered them both drinks, and the first few swallows of the ale warmed her and brought color into her pale face. She shifted on the bar stool and turned to look over the crowd to see if there were any familiar faces. She was relieved not to see anyone she knew.

"I'm not into drinking the pints so much," she responded with a warm smile, tossing her head to the side. Some of her hair had fallen out of her neatly coiled bun. She reached back and took the pins out, letting her hair fall naturally down her back. She shook her head back and forth a few times and felt liberated.

"It's a bit early for you to be coming undone, Norah," Murray said, winking at the bartender. Thomas, the bartender, leaned over the counter and whispered something in Murray's ear.

"Don't be gossiping in front of me own face!" she said, giggling.

Murray pressed on Norah's arm to indicate she needed to be still so he could listen to Thomas. This wasn't about her. By the sudden serious look on Murray's face, she understood that Thomas was telling him about the real reason they were at Finn McCool's. She reached back to tuck her hair underneath her shawl, feeling foolish for being carefree and frivolous, forgetting why they had come out together. It had become difficult for her to separate the dedication to the movement from her feelings for Murray. She was also indulging in speaking her heart and mind to this man, and it satiated her need for companionship. She missed the conversations she once had with Mary, but it was her da whom she sorely ached to tell of this new purpose and friend in her life. She leaned into Murray's side to try and hear some of the conversation. Murray was saying something back to Thomas, looking anxiously toward the door as he spoke.

"It won't work… he shouldn't be coming here. He'll be recognized. We need to go somewhere where there's no Irish around," Norah heard Murray whisper to Thomas.

"And where can he go in this city where there's no Irish!" Thomas said back, turning away to wait on a customer who was pounding his empty glass repeatedly on the bar.

Murray jumped off his stool and then cupped his hands around Norah's ear and told her that he would be back in a few minutes. Before she could tell him that she didn't want to be left alone sitting at a bar, he was gone. Just like that, he was out the door and gone from her! Her heart beat rapidly, and she looked at Thomas to ascertain some idea as to what was going on, but he was busy. The only other women in the place had to be street women looking for work, and, without Murray next to her, she might be mistaken for one, too. Did she look like one, she wondered? She didn't know what to do with herself now that Murray had left. Would he be right back, she wondered nervously. Her pint was half full, and the other half she had already drank was causing her head to spin into imaginary tales of seduction and sin.

"And why is a girleen as yerself sitting alone at Finn McCool's?" asked a ruddy, potato-faced, short man wearing a top hat and a tweed jacket.

"I'm not alone. My friend, Murray, is with me," Norah replied, her eyes darting to the door and around the room.

"I'd be obliged to set next to ye then to watch out for you until your friend returns," the man insisted, hopping up on the stool next to her.

Norah clasped her shaking hand around the glass of ale and gulped the rest down. She carefully got off the stool, clutched her purse to her side, pulled her shawl over her shoulders, and prepared to leave, avoiding the man next to her. She took a few steps toward the door and felt a firm grip upon her left shoulder, fingers tightening through her shawl and clothing. She turned to look into the face of the stocky brute who had sat next to her.

"Let go of me!" she yelled.

The man's other hand grasped her right shoulder and then he pulled her close to his bulky body. He leaned his face into hers and Norah was horrified that he was about to kiss her. She pulled away and he reached for her again, yanking her towards him. Where is Murray! And why wasn't Thomas coming to her rescue! She squirmed and tried to get away, and before she screamed, the rogue spoke loudly into her ear.

"You're staying with me, Miss. Your Mr. Murray would be sorely troubled if I let you out of me sight." His breath smelled foul, like rotten fruit, causing her stomach to constrict with nausea.

He winked at her, "He paid me well to care for ye, now, Miss."

So it was Murray who had sent this man to watch over her at Finn's. She let out a slow breath as she got back on the stool. Eventually, she caught Thomas's eye and asked him to bring her another pint.

Norah's lack of sustenance and the two pints she gulped down eventually made her sleepy. The man sent by Murray watched over her and kept the men at bay who were curious about the young woman with the mass of curly hair sitting at the bar. They noted that her clothing was fairly expensive and proper; she wasn't wearing the low-cut lacy bodice the two or three other women in the place wore. As she tried to keep herself awake, the pub atmosphere became agitated; men were talking loudly and their voices rose into a crescendo preparing for a fight. Norah listened to snatches of conversation and ignored the man Murray had sent to care for her. She didn't know if she was angry at Murray for sending this fool, or just angry at him for leaving her and not including her in whatever he was doing.

"We'll not be supportin' the EMA," she heard a man say as her eyes closed. Another man pounded his fists on the bar, "Thomas, you shouldn't be serving any of the bastards!"

Her eyes opened, she sat up straight, and forced herself to listen. Eventually, she laid her shawl on the bar and put her head down on it. Before she fell asleep, she thought of all she had learned in the past few weeks. This EMA was the Emmet Memorial Association that purported to be meeting to raise money for the tombstone of the long since dead patriot, Robert Emmet, as well as to keep alive the cause for Ireland's freedom and help the poor immigrants coming to America. What most people didn't know was that on his deathbed, Robert Emmet declared that his tombstone should *not* be raised until Ireland was liberated from England. And that wasn't even close to taking place. Monies were being raised for the cause, not for the tombstone, but who would know this but insiders?

It hadn't really registered in Norah's mind that real weapons to destroy lives were being smuggled and hoarded, and that the inscription on Robert Emmet's tombstone had to be written in nothing less than English blood. There was a mass EMA meeting coming up, and she and Murray were going to go, but she didn't know if the meeting was today, tomorrow or next week. All she knew was that she had to be able to hiss and boo at the meeting, but she wasn't convinced it was what she wanted to do. Of course, Murray would be taking notes. She wanted to take notes, too, and show Harrigan a thing or two about what he should be writing about in the *Irish-American.* What she didn't understand was why John Mitchel, the EMA, and other organizations like the United Irishmen, couldn't unite and be of the same mind. Murray said that the EMA and other groups were taking good Irishmen away from the cause of liberating Ireland, and these groups had a short-sighted vision about Ireland's freedom. Members of the Irish Emigrant Aid Association were also against the EMA because the EMA wasn't raising enough money to help the Irish immigrant in New York, this being the Irish Emigrant Aid's primary mission. John Mitchel and his men were powerful and educated, men who had suffered at the hands of the British and been imprisoned for their ideals to make Ireland free. They possessed an ideology that was cultural and political, and Norah was proud to be involved with John Mitchel and the members of this group. She had heard about gun smuggling and murder on the lips of the revolutionaries at EMA meetings as well as at John Mitchel's meetings, and this made her uncomfortable, even ashamed for them. But wasn't she already full of shame for her people? The young prostitutes, the ignorant masses of impoverished tenant dwellers who didn't try to help themselves out of their misery! At least the gang members were doing something, although it was misguided power they were wielding. At least they were active and not sitting in the corner of a rat infested dwelling dying of consumption and typhus. John Mitchel's revolutionaries wanted to do so much more. They would fight for Ireland's freedom and this would mean freedom for the Irish in America, too. Norah wouldn't give up on the *Irish American* newspaper for the time being, but she needed more, so much more, than what Harrigan's saintly newspaper had to offer her. Soon, she became so overwhelmed with sleep that she was quietly snoring. The man Murray had sent to watch her was drinking his fourth pint while he talked with some men come to sniff out the young woman sleeping at the bar, surely a woman of the streets, but a high-class one, no doubt.

Less than an hour later, Norah's guard dog was pulling out coins from his pockets to buy drinks for everyone, forgetting his sleeping charge and incapable of watching out for her. He was stone drunk and the men weren't just receiving his generosity in ale, but pocketing his coins that were falling onto the floor. Soon, his head was down on the bar next to Norah. Thomas was disconcerted that Murray hadn't returned, and the thug paid to watch over Norah was sleeping next to her at his bar. He couldn't possibly keep his eye on her, for his place was packed with people. There was hardly any elbow room for the mostly Irish dockworkers and the few whores thronging his establishment. He wanted more than anything to get out of this squalid business, no matter how profitable it had been and still was. It wouldn't be long before the police would find out about the meetings upstairs and the two rooms where the whores took their customers. The police didn't care about the whores, including those murdered, but they did care about insurgents meeting and piling up money and arms. He got a cut from the whores, albeit a small one, but the meetings were becoming notorious for rough behavior and occasional brawls. The famous John Mitchel was supposed to show up tonight, coming in the back alleyway and climbing through the window. He was known in the city because of his *Jail Journal* he had published while incarcerated in Tasmania, and for his lectures from a radical position on liberating Ireland from the British.

Thomas didn't want to miss this meeting upstairs, but his employee, Michael, hadn't come in to cover for him yet and the place was getting out of hand with demands for ale and some shouting and pushing going on. He didn't know if Mitchel had made it inside or not, for Murray had run out to try and stop him from coming. Too many other representatives from rival groups were in the pub, and it might cause a stir that could erupt into a riot.

The musicians had taken a break for the last hour. *If they would just come back and play again,* Thomas thought, *it would soothe the untamed Irish beast that was permeating the room.* He placed two frothy pints down for some customers and then leapt over the bar to look out the door and down the street to see if Murray, Mitchel, or the others might be nearby. It was a Saturday and the streets were packed with revelers and carriages, and the air was thick with fog and rain, just like the ole sod, he thought. It suddenly reminded him of Dublin and he wished he was there. He turned back inside his pub and saw two men scramble from behind the bar with bottles in their hands. It happened all the time, but it really pissed him off tonight. He just couldn't work this place on his own. *Where was that damn Michael!* He hurried outside to look again and walked down the street a bit, sighing with anger. When he walked back inside the pub, he pushed his way through to the end of the bar where Norah and her rogue guard had been sleeping. Her man was still asleep at the bar, but Norah McCabe was nowhere to be seen! He shook the drunk at the bar and looked down to see if Norah had fallen to the floor, the beats of his heart pounding in his ears making him deaf to the protests of a prostitute who was being dragged out the door at the same time. Someone punched him in the back and when he turned around to look, he saw what was happening and shoved his way to the door. He and a couple of other men beat the man off the haggard prostitute.

"Al!" he shouted, "Al!" he pointed toward Norah's empty seat. "Look for her...look for the woman who was here!"

Al was a regular customer and could be trusted. Thomas had to get back behind the bar, for the place was going crazy. His hands shook while pouring pints for a few men who threatened to beat him if he didn't wait on them. He was trying to take the money the men were setting down on the bar before someone grabbed it for themselves. He was too good, too damn good, for this kind of life! These dank, dark moldy drinking establishments grew insidious men like fungi, the poisonous kind. He was being robbed and stolen from all the time, at least a few times a week. Thomas looked around to see if Al had found Norah, and in walked Michael, grinning from ear to ear.

"It's Fernando himself outside your pub, Thomas!" He's coming in for a few swills, I'd say. Maybe he'll be suggesting we move right on out of here and onto Fifth Avenue, the saints be praised!"

Michael, the incurable romantic, had been late because he had arranged for the mayor himself to visit Finn McCool's to hear a bit of the Irish music and enjoy an evening out in Five Points.

"The mayor! Mayor Wood is coming into Finn's!" some of the men shouted, and within a few minutes the place quieted and tables and chairs were turned right side up, men were slapping each other on the back, the prostitutes disappeared, and the musicians began playing a lively jig. A couple of the men began dancing and Thomas laughed to himself. *The god damn Irish were capable of anything,* he thought proudly. He quickly wiped down the bar with a rag, poured a shot of his best whiskey and set it at the end of the bar, waiting for Mayor Fernando Wood to walk through the wooden lopsided door of his pub.

Just before the door opened to let in one of the most corrupt and mean spirited mayors of New York, Thomas remembered Norah. He looked for Al, and when he caught his eye, Al shook his head to indicate that he didn't know what had happened to her. Norah McCabe had completely disappeared from Finn McCool's and Thomas was responsible. Murray wouldn't let him off for this, but he didn't have time to think about it right now. In walked Wood in all his dark glory and power. In walked the mayor to his pub, Thomas's own little watering hole in Five Points.

Chapter Thirteen

"It's the ould same serpent again and again, Miss, the same ould fangs cuttin' and abusing each other. So don't ye be tellin' me what is and isn't right. Do ye think you're a cut above the rest of us?" a filthy young man spat his words at Norah.

Norah was bound with ropes and sitting on a chair in a dark room with one meager candle whose flame quivered, as her own body was doing. Her captor had gotten on his knees to talk to her, but she refused to look at him and kept her head down and her eyes closed. She had awakened horrified to have been abducted by a strange man who yelled and spewed forth obscenities at her. At first, she tried to reason with him, but gave up and closed her eyes, thinking only of Murray, her da, mam, Mary, even Sean who always floated on the periphery of her mind. And just maybe she was still sleeping at Finn's and this was only a dream, a nightmare, and soon she would wake to find Murray next to her. All would be right and then they would make their way to the mass meeting, her arm in his, and afterward, he would buy her tea and take her home. Maybe he would kiss her sweetly as he had done a week ago for the first time. His kiss had been a seal upon her heart and she felt marked for life, and felt as silly, too, like the romance dime novels she had read. Since that time, she had been unable to let an hour go by without reliving the moments up to the kiss, the kiss itself, and the fluttering of small wings within the cavity of her chest that coursed desire farther downward.

She was surprised she could so easily love Murray, for she had loved no one with a woman's love before. It was as natural as loving Da and Mam, and as if she had always loved Murray and carried within her the knowledge of his presence. Had this love been buried within her all of her life, like a nascent flower bulb in the earth waiting for springtime?

"What do you want from me?" Norah asked, lifting her head and looking at the mangy, ugly man. She could see his face because it was close to hers. It was contorted with anger and mud was caked on his forehead. A monster of the streets he was, and she clenched her teeth so they wouldn't clatter and reveal to him her fear. But then she couldn't bear to look at him and put her head down and closed her eyes again to shut out the sight of him. She had to try and calm her pounding heart and think of a way of escape.

Ivan O'Riley peered into Norah's eyes when she opened them and thought of stained glass windows in a church, but it was only the candle flickering before her that caused those eyes to appear so unnatural-like. They were a sea-green color that emitted ominous strength, but something in them was strangely familiar to him. He saw in her eyes that he should be gentle with her, and since gentleness wasn't familiar to him, he didn't know what to do with her. He had been instructed to bring Norah McCabe to the upstairs room of the pub and keep watch over her. His pockets were still empty and until they were filled, he was forced to stay with her. She refused to look at him now, and this infuriated him, making him feel like he was some kind of demon. He kicked her chair and watched her shudder under his power, but still she kept those beautiful eyes closed. He stood up and walked to the door to listen for footsteps, as if in doing so, it would hurry along this uncomfortable work he had been given to do. By God, soon he would be able to eat and drink! This is what he had to think of right now—feeding himself and his Mam.

He leapt toward Norah and she startled and jumped in the chair, but still kept her head down. It angered him that she wouldn't look at him, cry, shout at him again, and acknowledge him in some form. He was so lonely and never had anyone to talk to and for a moment, he thought he might confide in this girleen. Something about those eyes got to him. He hovered over her, breathing heavily, and thought about grabbing her shoulders to force her head up to make her look at him. But the music started up downstairs and the strains of a fiddle playing a slow air calmed his anxiety and smoothed over the rough edges of his thoughts that were dark and disturbing.

He had to be careful with this one, he thought. She was strange and a different kind than most women, and it bothered him what might happen to her after… He tugged at his beard and ran his hand through his greasy hair. What did he care for the bitch! Look at her sitting there not looking at him, he who had control over her now! She should know he was out for the money. She should be able to tell that he was only a middleman, a transporter, doing a job only to feed himself and his old mammy.

"I've nothing to do with it, Miss. Nothing!" Ivan shouted.

Norah jerked her head up, startled by his voice. He watched her forcefully plant her feet on the floor to still her body.

"I don't know what he wants with ye. I've nothing to do with it… nothing, the truth be told," Ivan said, rubbing his hands together.

It was cold in the room and he could see his breath in the air before the candle and it made him feel like the wee boy again when he first saw his breath in the winter outdoors. The experience made him feel that he was real, for he had seen the warm feelings of himself floating outside of himself. Even then, he had been a young boy hardened by life's troubles, but his breath before him had confirmed to him that he was a breathing human being and therefore worthy. It had been a simple apparition come to assuage his burgeoning hate of himself.

You've everything to do with it!" Norah shouted.

She looked fearlessly at him now and sensed a weakness in his countenance and voice, and this made her feel that she could have some command over her plight. He looked to be much younger than her da, but the streets had obviously aged him beyond his years. He was merely a filthy rogue like so many and she wouldn't allow him to ruin her happiness. His clothing was ragged and full of holes and his boots were tied with strips of cloth to hold them together. He was scum! She dared to look straight into his eyes, but was immediately astonished to see they hadn't become the lifeless pools of muck that she saw in so many immigrants on the streets of Five Points. There was a spark of something still there! Maybe she could appeal to whatever it was she saw.

"If you've brought me here and bound me, spoken to me as you have, cursed me, me, a stranger to you… me, having done nothing to harm you, then, yes, you have everything to do with it!" she yelled, her voice cracking.

He stood dumbly before her. He had been instructed to go into Finn's where she was sleeping at the bar and to carefully carry her upstairs to this room, telling anyone who asked that the bartender had told him to take her where she could sleep in safety. The man who had approached him outside Finn's said that he would be paid later and not to ask any questions or say anything to anyone. It was just a job, just another meaningless job. He always hung around Finn's and a few of the other pubs in the area so he would be given jobs as a runner. Sure, nothing quite like this one had ever come his way, but this was still just work he had been hired to do. He had never done any work that really harmed anyone, not yet, and he wasn't going to hurt this one, either. He had a job being a middleman, and he thought of himself like a carriage, a train, or omnibus just taking something, and now someone, from one place to another place.

This woman had been asleep from the drink, and she had been so light that it had been easy work, but he hoped it would soon be over and he would get his damn money, leave, and forget about the bitch. The man in the tweeds said he would be paid well and that might mean enough to buy food for a week. His mouth filled with saliva thinking about food.

"I see by the likes of yer dress that ye have plenty and don't know what I suffer. It's this, and only this, Miss, that I'm guilty of—this need for bread and meat. Just bread sometimes, not even the praties, for I'll never eat praties again!" he said, spitting on the floor and wiping his mouth with the back of his hand.

Ivan was dizzy for he hadn't eaten in a couple of days, except for stale bread thrown out by a bakery that he found in an alley dumpster. Before gobbling it down, he had delicately picked out the green mold rippling through it, as if it was a pattern put there by the baker. Any food he was able to buy had to be given to his Mam, and oftentimes he was left rifling through garbage for something to eat.

Ivan turned from Norah and opened the door slightly to look out, but shut it quietly when he saw that no one was there. The music had gotten louder and he heard stomping downstairs, cheering, and clapping, a real party going on, he thought sadly.

"'Tis the Hunger you've come from," Norah said, her heart softening towards him.

"'Tis the Hunger come upon us all in Ireland as if it was the mark of Satan, Miss. It never goes from us, this hunger, this mark of the beast," he said, his eyes like a tiger's, burnt amber shining in the dark next to the candle.

"You look to have enough bread, though you're a thin one," he said to Norah. "There's color enough in your face, and you're wearing the fancy clothes. You've bread and live differently now, I know it by the looks of ye. But you still have the mark, even if it's not in your body like in me own. But you and me, we're related. I see it in your eyes."

"You're to be shamed for this—shame! 'Tis true that we're of Ireland, you and me!" Norah yelled.

She stomped her feet on the floor and screamed loudly over the music. She wasn't afraid of him now, knowing that he had come from the Hunger as she had. But she was surprised when he leapt across the room and placed his hand over her mouth and held her legs to prevent them from moving. She breathed in the scent of him, and underneath the stench of his filth she breathed in the earth from his hands. She closed her eyes and remembered again the soil she had put in her pocket before she climbed into her dresser that was thrown onto the ship to take her to America. She had wanted to have it with her to always remember, a foolish thing for she could never forget. And this is what she smelled on him—the hungry earth that he could never wash off himself.

Fury rose within Norah! She had come so far in her life and had everything to lose now because she was loved as a woman for the first time. She hated him for his failure, his inability to shake off the dirt of Ireland, and his desperate animal hunger. She had been able to overcome her past and she wouldn't allow this man from the same country she had come from ruin her life now! She dreamed of their country as the *Sean Bhean Bhocht*, as Yeats had viewed Ireland. Murray had taught her of Yeat's vision of Ireland, and told her that it would be resurrected as a heavenly and supernatural being.

She bit hard into Ivan's middle finger that was bent in such a way that she was able to take it between her teeth and bite with all her strength. Ivan cried out in pain and yanked his hand away from Norah's mouth, clutching it to his chest as he waved his other hand in her face.

"Curse ye! You're a right fuckin' bitch, ye are!"

He had to quell the overwhelming urge to pick up the chair with her in it and hurl her through the window. She no longer pounded her feet or made a sound, but stared at him with rage in those devilish eyes. He turned to open the door a crack to see if anyone was coming. When he did, the man in the tweeds pushed open the door and knocked him aside, closing the door behind him.

Norah's eyes opened wide in terror to see a man dressed in fine clothes, a bulky figure whose face wore a bushy gray beard. When he tore off his hat, she saw that it was the commissioner. The commissioner had come for her, although it had taken over a year's time.

"Dear Miss Norah McCabe who likes to pretend she's only sellin' the rags of the rich in her shop. Norah McCabe who didn't mind a prostitute being dead if she could have the jewels off her. Now isn't it interesting that since the mayor no longer has any power over the police force, and a new force has come from Albany, I've been thrown out to find that, like you, Miss McCabe, breaking the law is a little more profitable than keeping the law."

Norah hadn't forgotten how the Commisioner nearly had his way with her, and then Mary's silence after he had also assaulted her; the two of them watching their backs fearing that he would come after them. She looked over at Ivan and pleaded with him with her eyes. If the deranged and hungry derelict from Ireland didn't help her now, she feared she would lose not just her virginity but her soul to this reprobate.

"You, over there…you… help your own or you'll rot in hell!" she yelled in desperation.

The commissioner spat on the floor and then slowly brought his cane up to strike Norah, hesitating before hitting her hard atop of the head. In the moment before she was struck, she prayed silently to live and be loved by Murray and her family. She, Norah McCabe, who had walked the streets of New York confidently and boldly, was struck unconscious by a viscous man who had been removed from a high position, but who could still wield power on the streets through brute force. And he never forgot a wrong done to him. He had never forgotten Norah McCabe.

Ivan didn't wait around to see if the man in the tweeds was going to pay him. When he saw him strike Norah, he opened the door and slithered down the stairs, walking through the crowded pub, and out the door. He crouched behind some barrels and garbage next to Finn's and waited.

The commissioner didn't know Mayor Wood was downstairs in the pub making a speech condemning the government boys in Albany for partisanship and tyranny, oppressing the rights of the Irish and every immigrant. There were shouts after his speech, "Murder! Murder the damn metro police sons of bitches!" Thomas was pouring so much whiskey that he couldn't keep track of the money being placed on the bar. He was being taken advantage of and the last thing on his mind was what had happened to Norah McCabe. He was also preoccupied with keeping up his business, for if his pub failed, he wouldn't eat. The mayor having come to his pub this evening might become his demise.

Five Points was growing restless and agitated over the do-gooder Republicans who wanted more rights for the blacks than the immigrants, mostly the Irish immigrants. Thomas had bought this business and his life was saved by a thread, but many of his people swelled the taverns with brick bats and knives under their coats, ready to fight. Not only England had been against them, but America was against them, too. The two countries had become one in their minds as they raised fists, emitted cries for justice, and brandished weapons to destroy the depravity they felt in their own hearts, as well as it being forced upon them in their new land. Thomas was worried that having Mayor Wood come into his pub might bring the new Metropolitan police to close him down for good. Finn's would be boarded up and he would be unable to obtain a license to run another pub. It was happening all over the city.

Thomas and Michael shoved drinks in front of customers who were bellowing for their rights and ale, and the more these men drank the more rights they needed. Thomas looked up to see a bulky man carrying a woman through his open door and down the street. It occurred to him that it might be Norah McCabe being carried away. As he tried to get outside to follow the man, he spilled a mug of ale on the bar and some of it splashed onto the mayor. By the time Thomas made his way through the compacted and agitated crowd and out the door, he saw the man with the woman climb into a black carriage, which then slowly made its way down the street.

He turned to go back into the pub and despair sloshed over him. Norah McCabe was a good-hearted woman, albeit somewhat proud; there was something about her that was right and pure, something that should not be destroyed, he thought wearily. He walked back into the pub with the weight of guilt on him, and someone grabbed his shoulder to pull him back outside. There stood Murray in all his handsome finery and aplomb, looking like an important gentleman. Thomas had always respected the like-minded patriotic spirit within Murray, but at the moment he despised him for having left Norah McCabe alone at his pub.

"I walked in and out again, Thomas. Norah's not here! Where is she?" Murray asked, his eyes wide, flashing anger.

"I don't know. I saw a man carrying a woman into a carriage. It went that way," he said, pointing down the street. "I'm sorry. The place got busy and the mayor—"

Murray shoved Thomas away and looked down the street, but he didn't see just one carriage. He saw three of them vying for a place on the dusty street. He had to find Norah McCabe and forget about Mitchel and the meeting. He ran down the street, pushing people out of the way, trying to keep his eye on every carriage that turned or kept straight.

Moments later, Murray felt someone behind him grabbing at his coat. He turned to strike at the thief, and when he did, he saw a pathetic-looking man in rags whimpering and pleading with him that he could help him find the Irish woman from Finn's.

"I know where the green-eyed girleen went, now…I saw her taken…," Ivan was saying, breathing hard and doubling over, foam from his mouth forming a stream that he spat out onto the ground. Murray was repulsed by the hapless creature and turned away to look at the carriages going down the street. *The creep is just another desperate street creature after my coins,* he thought. He ran toward the corner where he saw the carriage Thomas had pointed out to him, but the son of a bitch came running up behind him.

"It's the man who was the police commissioner who took her. He takes the fancy ones to Corlear's Hook…," Ivan said.

The foul man's words felt like a knife in Murray's back. Murray faced the dirty no-gooder whose eyes were red-rimmed and wild, darting here and there.

"Go on ahead of me then! If you don't find her, you'll be wishing you hadn't followed me," Murray yelled, pulling on the man's collar and shaking him. Ivan didn't resist Murray's throttle.

"Me name's Ivan O'Riley. I'll find your woman!" Ivan said when Murray let go of him. Ivan took off running, as if his legs weren't his own, amazed that they still carried him as well as they did. It felt good to be doing something right for a change, and as he pushed and shoved his way through the throngs of people, his hunger pains began to abate.

Murray ran behind Ivan and tried to keep up with the deranged lunatic, and if anyone jostled him, he pushed at them as hard as he could. It was his fault, all his god damn fault that Norah had been taken. He should have never left her sitting at the pub, even if it was Finn's! He didn't know if he should believe this derelict, Ivan, but if it was true that Norah had been taken to Corlear's Hook, it would be difficult to find her before she'd be drugged and wake up to some man having his way with her.

High-priced prostitutes in the bordellos in Corlear's Hook were sought after by city officials and visiting European men with large amounts of cash in their pockets. Murray ran, barely able to breathe, his head pounding with facts about impoverished young women—kidnapped and drugged, waking up to rich tapestry filled bedrooms and luxuries they never knew existed. Throughout the years, he had heard stories about how these women would become aware of the ache between their legs and then realize they were no longer virgins. If they became hysterical, they were given just enough opium to calm their emotions. Loss of innocence or otherwise, they were seduced into a lifestyle they could never have back in the poor tenements. It wasn't until the victims were manipulated into believing there was no way out of their predicament that they began to desire the food, opium, and clothing of a lavish lifestyle of a high-class prostitute.

Some women, as impoverished as they had been, couldn't cut this new life and would fight like wild cats and were finally let go. Murray knew the horrific details and had helped some of these women in finding new positions in their lives. The editor of a newspaper he had once worked for had a daughter merely fourteen who was kidnapped for prostitution. The father had murdered the man who took his daughter and was in prison for many years, his daughter never fully recovering from the ordeal. Corlear's Hook was an anathema in a country filled with young women underpaid in their diverse work, forcing them into prostitution. This was just one of the many issues Murray had once written about in the *Citizen*—the problem of immigrant women not being paid adequately for their sewing and cleaning jobs, and being forced into prostitution. The irony was that he had to save Norah from this nightmare, a woman he was falling in love with. He tripped on some stones in the street and fell to his knees. He momentarily thought of how weak he really was, then jumped up and yelled for Ivan to wait.

Murray flagged down a carriage and instructed the driver to take them to Corlear's Hook, ignoring how the driver looked askance at him and the filthy man climbing in after him. Well-dressed gentlemen visited at night, creeping clandestinely into Corlear's Hook. If they took a carriage, they asked to be let off a few blocks away from the bordellos. Murray asked to be driven right up to the main buildings that housed the most expensive houses of prostitution. These houses were multi-purposed brothels, disguised as dance halls, theaters, hotels, and saloons, all under one roof. He had never been a customer, although his uncle, without his father's consent, had brought him to one when he was sixteen, thinking it would make him a man. He had been curious and even aroused, but when he was actually alone with a young girl just a few years older than himself, he bolted from the room and hid in the alley waiting for his uncle. A word wasn't spoken by either of them as they took a carriage home. He never ventured there again, nor did he desire to. His early experiences would never include visiting houses of prostitution, regardless of how hungry he would become for the touch of a woman.

Murray and Ivan climbed out of the carriage in front of a large and well lit building. Murray paid the driver and the two men walked up the steps and looked into the lace-curtained windows.

Murray walked back and forth on the top step, not knowing what to do. The carriage would have come and gone by now, and Norah could be drugged in some back room. He turned to face Ivan, who had gone back down the steps and was standing on the street.

"What good are you, man? You're just standing there! Do something!" Murray said, rage burning in his eyes.

Ivan sprinted up the steps to the bordello, rang the doorbell, and didn't wait for someone to answer. He opened the door and ran down the perfumed hall hollering that he was there to break up the prostitution ring and that everyone should gather together in one room for questioning. Who would believe the rag man was an official arm of the police force that was in major transition anyway? Murray was dismayed at Ivan's behavior, but followed him inside the building. Women, half clad, fully dressed, and of all ages were running back and forth, and in and out of rooms. A few male customers clutched their jackets and were leaving as fast as they were able. No one thought to question Ivan's authority, but now that Murray stood next to him, this intrusion looked like an official one. Murray scanned the place looking for Norah.

"Everyone in here!" Murray shouted. "Everyone in this room!" Murray pointed to a room that was used as a parlor. There were bookshelves, over-stuffed chairs, and Victorian couches scattered haphazardly throughout the room. Heavy scented and powdered women entered the parlor, falling onto chairs or standing in corners. There were fifteen women packed into the small room. It reeked of lust, Murray thought; not the coil of snake-like, tranquilizing lust he knew of, but the lust for money.

"You'll not be spending the night in a jail cell if you cooperate," he said.

An exquisitely dressed woman, about forty years old with dark features and hair, obviously the madam, approached him.

"Who are you coming here to frighten and interrogate us?" she asked, eyeing Ivan with disgust, a Mediterranean accent heavy in her speech.

"There's a young woman who's been kidnapped and taken away against her will. I believe she's been brought here." He breathed in a pungent warm scent as the madam stood near him.

"There are brothels elsewhere, sir. We're a boarding house for young women and many of us work late in the garment business."

"I don't give a damn if you're a nunnery. I want your help in finding a woman named Norah McCabe!" Murray demanded.

The women huddled together and Murray announced that they would be compensated for their time in helping him find Norah. They murmured and whispered to one another while Murray described Norah in detail and gave them his address, as well as the address of Finn's, insisting they begin looking immediately. There were protests, and the madam stated that only some of them would be able to help. The rest had to go to work. Tension in the room lessened when the women realized they weren't going to be taken away in a paddy wagon, a common experience for the mabs when some city official decided to do a little clean-up of Five Points.

"We'll need to know the specifics of the compensation," the madam said to Murray, her eyes downcast as she swished her thick layered petticoats.

"That won't be a problem," Murray said. He pulled out a wad of bills and placed them in her hands. "This will be a down payment. The rest will depend on how well you perform."

Murray immediately felt chagrined for the double entendre. This would actually be the first time he ever paid a prostitute to perform. He hoped he would come away satisfied, and within the hour have Norah at his side again.

The madam smiled at his wit, took the money and shoved three girls toward him.

"You instruct them what to do. They're used to being asked to perform," she said with a smirk.

Ivan stood behind Murray waiting to be told what to do. The girls looked at him, scowled, and turned to Murray, asking him how they could please him, tittering and pushing one another out of the way. Ivan was ready to bolt as soon as he saw Norah or heard that she was going to be fine. A feeling of murky contempt for his life churned within him; his self-loathing was mirrored in the eyes of the girls who glanced at him.

Murray told the girls to look for Norah in all the buildings in Corlear's Hook, and then meet him back in the parlor in an hour. He turned to Ivan and wanted to be rid of the man.

"I don't know if you expect a handful of bills yourself. You've been no real use to me. Let's walk around to the back of the buildings and see what we can see and hear. If I don't find her…"

Murray couldn't finish his sentence because the possibility that Norah had been sexually transgressed struck him with stark reality. He turned away from Ivan, walked out the door and down the steps, trying to hide a sob. He watched groups of men standing in front of the buildings and smelled lust in their alluring colognes. Bergamot, sandalwood, and citrus scents permeated the atmosphere and he choked in repulsion, tears stinging his eyes as he stood on the street.

"Have you heard of John Mitchel and the Young Ireland revolt back in '48?" Murray asked Ivan who had followed him down the steps.

Ivan's already chalky and gaunt face drained of all color underneath a gaslight. He walked close to Murray and held up a fist to his face. Murray was startled by the man's behavior.

"Me father was killed at the Widow McCormick's in the uprising in '48. He was with Meagher himself, one of the grand ones who got away alive. The man's here in this city, I've heard it rumored! Me father was dying from the Hunger, he was, but still willin' to die for his country. Don't ye be asking me about John Mitchel! Curse the Young Irelanders! Curse Meagher! Curse ye, too, if you're part of it!" He stepped back from Murray and put his head down, wobbling and nearly falling to the street.

"Then I must be redeemed in your eyes, man. And maybe you'll be redeemed as well in your good father's eyes, and join the movement that can redeem us all in Ireland!" Murray responded, distracted momentarily from the pain and mire of losing Norah.

Ivan hadn't wept since he had been hurt running through the fields or working on his parents' small farm when he was a boy Tears stung his eyes and he wasn't sure if they were for his dead father, hungry mother, dead dreams, or the deadening hunger still with him. Maybe it was for Norah McCabe, as well, for he had a premonition that she had already crossed over to the side of despair and it would be a long journey back.

Chapter Fourteen

When Murray was first introduced to Norah, he saw reflected in her eyes what his father had taught him about many of Ireland's arriving immigrants—that hunger for food had been replaced with hunger for worth. And then there would be the ravenous pursuit to return to Ireland, which lay as a jewel beyond their reach, in order to get something back that they never had. It was unusual for an Irish immigrant to explore the soul's contours to understand this desperation within him. Stature was sought after rigorously, and often through complex vengeance. Esteem and success were more precious because of it having been denied them. The Irish immigrants possessed a potato madness that never left them, for this tuber that had become everything had become nothing, and it had come to represent more than sustenance for the body. Murray perceived that Norah had no real comprehension of this yet, but there was a drowsy awakening within her for justice and a place to live within it. And then she had utterly surprised him when she agreed to have him guide and teach her about Irish freedom.

After first meeting Norah at the Astor House hotel, Murray hadn't been in any hurry to see her again. It had been enough to let his imagination of her play out in his head. He also didn't want to interfere with the rare path she had taken in working for a newspaper that paid her a salary. Murray had followed his father to and from Ireland throughout his young years to know that timing was everything, especially for revolution, as well as for love. He had learned there could be something unseen and powerful, moving in darkness or in light, that brought men and women together; the same also brought about battles and victory in those battles, cities being founded, countries being destroyed, and revelations that unrolled as scrolls from the depths of time. Murray had long ago given up following the god of his fathers, the rigid god who hung on the cross confined to a church that felt more like a tomb. If this god had risen from the dead, Murray could not believe he was in these sterile structures that men built. But still he kept watch over his shoulder for this god to come after him, for good or for evil. He had to be sure, and he would never be quite sure, even if he had given up the practice of believing. Presently, he was desperate to find Norah, and if he believed in any god at all, he believed this god had sent her to him.

"Keep watch of the buildings. Walk to the front and back and keep vigil," Murray said to Ivan who stood before him, confused. If you see her and even if she's with someone, don't let her go. Don't let her disappear again. I'm counting on you, man!"

Murray sprinted down the street, but this time it wasn't to chase a carriage, but to seek out the god of his childhood. He was running to the Church of the Transfiguration that would be open to welcome him. If only for a dab at the holy water to bolster him! And for the miracle he needed to find Norah and take them both to England with the money to help liberate Ireland. He would say a prayer for Ivan, too, for there was brotherhood in the man, as conniving and grotesque the scamp was.

Murray slowed down to a fast-paced walk, suddenly aware of his dead mother's presence, as well as his dignified father's, telling him to always behave as a gentleman. The words of his father never left him—

to have passion, and loyalty to that passion, and to never believe it was wrong to give up one's life for the freedom and justice of a country that had been denied it for hundreds of years. He walked, aware of the people around him, curious as to what drove them to get out of bed every morning to strive for food and for all the hungers of the body. He could only remember trying to live up to the dreams of his father and his father's father. After his first journey to Ireland, he understood this blazing idealism that had smoldered and burned in his father. Murray believed that his father had ultimately laid himself on a funeral pyre for Ireland. There had been no other life for Murray after his father's flame caught fire of him, even after going to Georgia to study law and learn the ways of the aristocratic class, not the revolutionary class. He had come back to New York when his father was dying, and then his mother's death had soon followed. After losing his parents, the New York newspapers honed his rebel spirit, focused his drive, but all the while the teaching of his father and his father's muse, Ireland, remained.

Murray entered the Church of the Transfiguration, and the familiar fragrance of incense greeted him at the door. Each time he entered a church, as rare as it had become, his decision to not become a priest played out before him. To serve a god of mercy, love, and justice would only have been possible if he hadn't learned that this god often withheld these principles and required others to become gods who could bring them forth. He couldn't be a priest and a rebel at the same time, not in his understanding of theology and the church. And as the years marched on, he became less a believer and more of a revolutionary. And yet there were times that he was compelled to enter the church in which he no longer believed.

The church was empty and he stood in its stillness. The rough hewn pews were in sharp contrast to the ornate and vibrant stories in the stained glass windows. In one of the windows, Mother Mary assured him that she, too, was a sufferer for good. He turned away from this window, forcing himself to gaze at the cross. The small blood spots on Christ's hands and feet deceived him into believing suffering for righteousness was meaningful with little pain.

He kneeled and rested his elbows on the back of a pew. He bowed his head, shut his eyes, and pressed his fists into his forehead. There was no peace he so ardently desired.

Murray felt the stiff coldness of the black robes before he felt the gentle touch of the priest's hand upon his shoulder. He waited, recoiling from having to answer questions and meet the priest's penetrating gaze. He wished he had rosary beads in his hands, for then he would be left to this formal act. The touch came again, not as gentle as the first time. He looked up and immediately felt compelled to tell the priest about Norah.

"What causes such agony at this hour?" the priest asked Murray, searching his face for clues. Father Driscoll had become observant and perceptive in discerning the countenances of the people who entered his church. It was his special calling, more than his calling to fathom the mysteries of the faith. The priest had begun to think that they were one and the same, the gift of discernment and faith.

Murray surrendered to the priest and stood before him; his broad and handsome shoulders drooped while he clenched and unfolded his fists repeatedly.

"And what person in this city is not in agony, Father?" he asked, turning to stare again at the stained glass window that contained the sorrowful Christ's head in the lap of his all knowing Mother. He wished he could place his own head in the lap of the Mother of God.

"Agony is part of the human condition, but we don't have to carry it without relief. As you can see all around you, here in this church, there is representation for our agony. A place to take our agony," Father Driscoll said.

"Father, I don't want to be disrespectful, but I need to leave...," Murray said, suddenly deciding not to ask for help. There would be too many questions and it might bring more shame on Norah. And, of course, he didn't want the priest to find out about his involvement with John Mitchel.

"But you have come here for help, no doubt, and perhaps I can, to some extent, become an answer to your prayers. I'm a master at listening."

His hand swept toward the pew Murray stood in, inviting him to sit down.

"Father, forgive me, but there's someone who's been kidnapped and I have to…" He took a step to leave, but the priest moved in front of him, cajoling him with a warm, all knowing smile. *He has the Virgin's smile,* Murray thought. *This priest has the Virgin's smile!* It was almost comical to him, although he wasn't in the mood for humor.

"I can help."

"No, Father, I'm sorry, but I can't take time to explain." He turned to leave.

"I have some influence in this city. Please let me assist you." The priest turned and walked quickly down the aisle.

"I've an appointment early in the morning, but I'll get my cloak and accompany you," he called back to Murray, his voice filled with excitement.

Murray released a tense breath and reluctantly followed Father Driscoll down the aisle. He might as well take advantage of the priest's holy robes to bring fear and trembling into Corlear's Hook so he could find Norah.

Father Driscoll quickly got his cloak and the two men left the Church of the Transfiguration and walked down the midnight street, creating a haunting effect with the priest's robes billowing in the darkened breezes.

"A young woman has been kidnapped and taken to Corlear's. I fear she's being forced into prostitution." Murray leaned into the priest and whispered.

They walked at a steady and determined pace, and late-night people tipsy and guilt-ridden, nodded to the priest in greeting or bowed their heads and quickly stepped out of the way. For the first time since he had learned Norah had been kidnapped, Murray felt hope. God would intervene through this priest! The respect for the robes of the church was enabling them to move quickly through some crowds of people.

"Who is this young woman to you?" Father Driscoll asked.

"She's a friend," Murray said, not wanting to divulge anything further.

"Tell me what happened…from the beginning."

Murray delicately told the story of how he and Norah were at Finn's to wait for the Mayor to come and give a speech, and when he left her to meet someone outside of the pub, he returned to find that she had been kidnapped.

Father Driscoll hadn't prepared for his meeting with Bishop Hughes scheduled for the next day. The Bishop didn't endorse the strong position he had taken on abolitionism. However, Father Driscoll was optimistic he could change the Bishop's mind about his endeavors. As he walked, however, he realized he could ruin his chance of persuading him of his good intentions all because he was responding in a spirit of compassion toward this young man. If he was honest with himself, he also felt a sense of adventure. Surely, this desperate and passionate man was at a major crossroad in his young life; and this, of course, constituted an ecclesiastical responsibility within him as a priest. There was another spirit about Murray, however, that the priest recognized— one of kinship and like-mindedness. This young man hadn't come into his church because he had an addiction to the high-priced prostitutes or couldn't get off the drink. Father Driscoll speculated it was something more lofty and risky, something more soul changing and dangerous, and he was determined to find out.

Finn's, Father Driscoll knew, was a meeting place for rebels. It certainly had to be God himself who brought this man into his church, his Church of the Transfiguration. Transfiguration…the word itself was not lost on him, for he believed that the souls he found bent before the bleeding and lifted-up Christ spoke of major change churning within them. In addition to being involved in the movement to free Africans and return to them the dignity they had lost in slavery, it was this that he treasured—the touch of his life upon these men and women who dared to come to God alone, informally and bereft, in the hope of transfiguration.

The large and impressive brick building in Corlear's the madam claimed was a boarding house was lit with so many gas lamps that when Father Driscoll and Murray arrived, it appeared as if a large fire was blazing from within. They climbed the steps, knocked on the door, and quickly walked in. A fragrant scent of jasmine and roses permeated the premises, a seductive ploy arranged to entice men whose loins were the weakest part of them. No one was there to greet potential customers and the two men walked down a hallway lined with doors that had "Do Not Disturb" signs on them. Father Driscoll raised his fist to pound on one of them in righteous rage, but Murray gently pushed his arm down. They stood a few moments listening to loud street noises, including an Italian violinist playing mournfully.

"What now, Father?"

"Perhaps prayer?" he said, placing his hand on Murray's shoulder and bowing his head. Murray sighed heavily, but acquiesced to the priest's authority.

"And how can I help you two boys?" the madam's voice interrupted them. She came sauntering down the hall, an interesting mixture of playfulness and business in her demeanor.

Father Driscoll made the sign of the cross and forgave the woman for addressing him as "boy" and not with the usual reverential greeting, but then he recognized her from the confession booth. He knew her voice, as well as her scent. She came once a week for confession, repenting over the same sin of lust, but he felt there was more than lust that was de-railing her life. It was a lust to live beyond poverty and mediocrity, and for this she broke the commandments. He didn't think she attended Mass anywhere in the city, and it was only to his confession booth she came for help. With each visit, he comforted her with words of God's love, although he spoke strongly about her need for repentance. He gave her enough penances that required her to sit in the church for at least an hour, but he was discouraged by her refusal to alter her life. And now here he was, face-to-face with her on her turf, not his. He girded his mind with conviction that he would not let on that he knew her. He would not break the holy confidence the confession booth held for her, for both of them.

"Father, it's you!" exclaimed the madam. He felt the blood drain from his face. Oh, why was he in such a place! He was embarrassed for her and for himself as he watched her aplomb and brazenness fade after recognizing him. He had to be very delicate with her in this improbable situation. She dropped her head to hide the embarrassment that crept into her face and this gave him confidence in his priestly power over her.

"Follow me," the madam said, turning quickly to walk down the hall, her skirts flouncing with each exaggerated movement. She had just been to confession the day before and hadn't done anything to feel ashamed of yet. It was alright the priest was here. Maybe she might engender more of God's blessings. She was glad she could turn away from the priest for a moment, for she needed time to collect herself. Mr. Murray, the man the priest was with, had fascinated her when she met him earlier. How rare was authentic love and fleshly passion woven intricately together in men, but in him, she recognized it was very alive for this young woman he desperately wanted to find. He surely would not be putty in her hands, for good men did not relish her power. As intrigued as they might be with her sexual mystique, if they surrendered themselves to her, they would despise her later. No matter how wealthy she had been in her native country of Spain, men like Mr. Murray would never be tempted by her.

"There are suites in my boardinghouse, gentlemen," she said over her shoulder. "I'll take you to the third floor, for it is there, I believe, you will find your young woman."

She stopped walking and waited for the two men to catch up with her. *Why was her priest here?* She turned to face them and spoke as if she was taking the men on a casual tour of the premises.

"They are expensive rooms for elite tastes, for women who have enough money to pay for some time away from the mainstream of life," she said, avoiding looking at the priest.

She couldn't possibly acknowledge this was her brothel, for it would be boldly unmasking her sin before the priest without the protection of the confession booth. When pangs of guilt didn't engulf her, she was proud of her success and didn't think it ill-fitting for women to live in style, especially women who would otherwise be destitute. Other houses across the city were merely whorehouses for women who called themselves prostitutes and lifted their skirts for a few moments and a few coins. She made certain that the women who lived in her boardinghouse were exquisite and artful in the practice of their profession. And they would never solicit on the street. An album of fine charcoal sketches of her girls was kept in the parlor for customers to make their choice for an evening. The girls experienced no coercion to this lifestyle, and could also participate in the selection of a gentleman. Her women in training, so to speak, were always placed in the first-floor rooms. They were a little rough around the edges after living hand-to-mouth for most of their young lives, but with her patient guidance, they would become sublime experts in pleasing in every way, including price.

The madam guided the men down the hall and shook her keys as if they were castanets. *Yes, my girls always became enchantresses possessing sangfroid and beauty,* she thought.

Murray was mildly affected by the madam's regal presence and stunning aura, recognizing she was a well-bred woman from Europe. He knew her kind because he had written about crimes associated with bordellos. She had apparently gained independence and power in this depraved, but profitable, business that city officials often turned their backs on. The police did not ignore the kidnapping of young women into the trade, however, and once this madam learned that Norah had been taken against her will, he was certain she would want Norah removed from her premises as quickly and quietly as possible.

Murray and Father Driscoll followed the madam down the hall and turned right at the end of the corridor. Before opening the door to the stairs, she lit a candle that set on a small table and opened a drawer to take out another set of keys. Unlocking the door, they then climbed the very narrow and darkened stairs to the third floor. They walked down another long hallway that only had three doors, one of which was at the very end. The madam stopped in front of this door and waited.

A large window was at the end of the corridor and Murray pulled back the lace curtain to look down into an alleyway, too far down for escape. He feared Norah might lay altered and changed forever behind this door. The rage within him since he first learned she had been kidnapped began to slowly uncoil and creep up to his throat. He had faced danger in small amounts on the streets, as well as in his involvement with John Mitchel, but this situation was taxing his resolve. He had only known Norah McCabe in innocence, and thought of her as a spring flower in first bloom; a woman he was tenderly beginning to love. He turned toward the courtesan who reigned as queen in this place of stifling ill repute to spew forth his fury, but he couldn't speak. Father Driscoll touched his shoulder firmly, but he shook it off. Murray took a step toward the madam and grasped her shoulders.

"Is Norah inside? Is she?" he yelled.

The madam brought up her arms and pushed him away. "If your woman is here, it is because I said yes to her young life. I said yes to her being saved from a drooling idiot who once had power, but toppled from his high position. This man who brought the woman here is the worst kind, a man without his claws! If this is your young goddess, she was brought here drunk and unconscious and could have been left for dead in an alleyway, but she has been safe in the very best of rooms in this city. I have saved her life! My boardinghouse is only for the choicest of women! My business is not so unlike the Astor House hotel, Senōr Murray! And you dare to accost me?"

She shook her keys in front of Murray's face, stomped her foot, and shouted, "I do not have to let you in. The young woman has not indicated to me she wished to see you or anyone!"

The madam stomped her foot again and swiveled around, as if she was about to dance a flamenco. She wouldn't acquiesce to the demands of a mad lover or to the power of the church. There were other churches and confession booths she could visit. No one would deny her entry into a church, but she could deny anyone entry into her bordello!

Father Driscoll pulled Murray close.

"Please calm yourself for your friend. She'll need your help, help that isn't besought with anger and confusion."

The madam moved down the corridor and her footsteps resounded in Murray's head as if it was being pummeled. He sprinted after her and touched her arm gently. She turned sharply and faced him.

"I will listen and try to help, but only if I'm respected. And never touch me again," she said, pulling her arm away from him, "unless, of course, I ask you to!"

"I apologize," Murray said.

He needed this tough woman to help him bring Norah back to life. The candle flickered in the darkness and Murray glimpsed a softening in the madam's face. For a moment, he saw the Virgin's expression. He was seeing the Virgin everywhere, it seemed. Father Driscoll came closer and his presence gave him strength. With the help of the priest and the madam, and yes, perhaps even the Virgin, in this peculiar dance of darkness and light, he might again have Norah McCabe in his life.

Chapter Fifteen

The wooden ship was like a bitter old woman who doesn't want life to dwell in her any longer, but she can't quit. She didn't ride the waves like she used to; her prow stabbed the sea as if attacking an enemy rather than trusting a loyal friend who would carry her on her journeys. Filled with declining, she had once carried strong timber to be used to build ships like her. On this last journey, however, she carried only yearning Irish immigrants. She was the ship called *The Star* and would return to Ireland nearly empty, except for a few stowaways and sailors who lost their saltiness to want to sail again. Many Irish famine immigrants died and were buried in the sea while journeying on *The Star*. Norah McCabe, clinging to the frayed threads of life, was one of the survivors who made it to America, hidden in a dresser, ill near to death. When her friend, Maggie, opened the doors of the dresser and exclaimed they had arrived in America, Norah crawled out amidst stunned and weak immigrants, and dragged herself to the shore. She didn't stand up at first, but sat and listened to the dismal thunder of the waves striking the coastline of her new country.

She picked up a rock with black and pink streaks running through it. Its sharp edges cut her hand when she squeezed it tightly while staring at the sea that separated her from her homeland. She vowed never to be taken as a prisoner of an old mean ship and the volatile sea again. She would begin her journey with the rock, a piece of America she would carry in her pocket. The soil she had put in her dresser before leaving Ireland was nearly gone, having spilled out like useless fairy dust while climbing in and out of the dresser, sick and dream-like, hopeful and despairing.

"You'll be killin' yerself, Norah McCabe!" Maggie had yelled at her. "The saints be praised for keeping you alive, but don't ye be crawling around half naked in Amerikay!"

Norah crawled back into the dresser then, pulling her over-sized tattered dress in with her. She glanced at her feet that were bare and was surprised at how long her toenails had grown, a source of discomfort as she lay in the fetal position to sleep, the nails digging into her skin. She ran her hand across the bottom of the cupboard of the dresser that had been her hiding place, a womb-like sanctuary, and found scattered bits of the soil still there. She swept it up into her right hand and climbed out of the dresser and stood for the first time in America. Lifting her hand toward the sky, she let go of the soil. It blew away in the wind as she gripped the new rock that she held tightly in her left hand. She was merely thirteen years old, but had undergone a dramatic change like Jonah in the belly of the whale, and now she had been spewed out on shore in a form she didn't recognize. But when she looked down at herself, even at her feet with the strange toes, she was relieved it was still herself, even if she had been altered. This was how Norah McCabe began her life in America over ten years ago.

Norah woke slowly from her dream, her eyes heavy as they tried to adjust to pale light filtering through a laced-curtained window that resembled an intricate spider's web. She held her head still, but her eyes moved around the room to take in her surroundings. Eye movement was painful and, when she gazed upon the red velvet gathered together on one of the bedposts, she thought there was a tall woman wearing a gorgeous cape standing before her. She sat up to speak to the woman, but realized her mistake and lay back down. And then she remembered the dream and could nearly feel the rock in her hand, but in moving her fingers, it was not there. Her eyelids felt like someone was pressing upon them and she slept again and returned to the dream. Norah was on the shore again, but this time she was lying on rocks that were smooth and soft, not hard and sharp, and as the tide came in, the waves touched her tentatively at first, but then lapped at her with immense force. When they reached her face and thundered loudly in her ears, she couldn't breathe.

Norah woke, sobbing like a banshee, her face wet with tears. Her head throbbed with pain, but she willed herself to stop weeping. The lower half of her body was underneath a heavy coverlet and she raised herself up to look underneath it. She was surprised to see that she wore a sheer lavender gown with ribbons, unlike any bedclothes she had ever worn. Her head and eyes hurt so unbearably that she had to lie down again for immediate relief. Unknown to Norah, the effect of the laudanum the madam had administered to her was wearing off. The pain in her head from the blow the commissioner had given her was severe, but she couldn't remember what had happened. A sudden paroxysm attacked her and she moaned loudly, turned on her side, and brought her knees up to her chest. She wrapped her arms around herself as if to prevent her insides from falling out. She clutched her waist and prayed, but soon drifted into sleep.

After a few minutes, Norah heard the sound of waves again and feared she would drown if she didn't wake up. She slowly turned onto her back, kicked the heavy covers off, and searing jabs of pain attacked her lower extremities. She forced her swollen eyes open to gaze at the tin ceiling. If she could focus her mind on the designs in the ceiling, perhaps it would help lessen the overwhelming pain she felt throughout her body. After a few minutes, there was a slight lessening of her discomfort and she decided to explore her body to ascertain what had happened. She needed to touch her body first before she would have the courage to look at it.

Norah tried hard to think of how she might have gotten to this mysterious room, but it hurt her head too much. She breathed in and out slowly to calm herself and stared at the shiny ceiling as she touched her neck with her right hand. Then she placed both her hands gently atop her breasts and felt her nipples harden. A twinge of pain passed through her and she placed her hands on her stomach, a place that was always flat and oftentimes sloped like an empty bowl. It was hollow and empty, but she was not hungry. She then separated the gown she was wearing to place her hands on the part of herself her mother had taught her to respect as a place of sacred creation. She remembered how she had imagined herself as holy as the Virgin Mother when she was a young girl. She would lie on her bed and pretend an angel like Gabriel would come to tell her she was special like the Holy Mother. When she was older, she felt foolish to have wanted an ethereal being to love her. It was the dark angel she then had to do battle with, reciting prayers so she wouldn't think about anyone loving her. Sometimes she would dream strange dreams and wake in a sweat to feel dampness between her legs.

Norah tenderly placed both hands over the curly, soft mound of hair that lay over her opening, this place that had to be saved for God's holiness. With her index finger, she touched the inside of herself and cried out in pain, feeling terror. What if the dark angel had won over her? Could she have been in a carriage accident or fallen? Nausea swept over her and her abdomen cramped; she forced her knees up to her chest and clutched her arms around them. Her chest tightened as she kept herself from sobbing. She stayed this way for a few minutes and then released her legs and forced herself to sit up to look at herself. When she did, she saw blood on the sheet. Dizzy and confused, questions fired off in her head one after another. How could she be bleeding without the rags to place there and the undergarments to hold them in place? She was never unprepared when her bleeding time came because her mother made sure she had clean rags for her monthlies even before she needed them. Norah feared accidents that would ruin her lovely clothing or to ever be seen with blood stains on the back of her.

Her friend, Mary, had worn a dress an entire day with a blood stain on her backside. Mary, of course, had laughed it off, but Norah had been humiliated for her friend as well as for herself in having to accompany her with the stain. She was becoming more conscious now, remembering her mother and Mary, but she couldn't seem to go any further in her mind about anyone else or what had happened to her. Certainly, other things had happened in her life, especially recently, to have brought her to this mysterious and lovely room.

Norah thrust her legs over the side of the bed and touched her feet to the floor. She gradually brought herself up to a standing position while leaning against the bed. Dizziness overcame her, however, and she collapsed slowly onto the thick carpet. She pulled herself up to the bed and flopped down, face first, her feet dangling over the side.

She felt blood trickling down between her legs and prayed to God that she had not been violated, but also that she might live and not die. She feared she had done something to invite this transgression. She sobbed fiercely and tried to think what could have happened.

"I want to go home, please God," Norah cried. She desired to return to sleep, and especially to her dream. The return of the dream would give her a place in her dresser, a place to be small and innocent, and a place to escape. By the time the madam entered the room, Norah was in a deep state of sleep.

It was the effusive odor of cloves and rose water that woke Norah. She opened her eyes to see a beautiful, mystifying woman standing next to the bed. The woman's skin was silky and glowed behind the candle she held. She was of no discernable age to Norah, but appeared vibrant and youthful; her eyes were large, a soft brown, and shaped like almonds seen in the market. It was very odd to wake and peer into such a face, but she felt no real alarm. Her throbbing pain had lessened and before she had time to recall her thoughts prior to falling asleep, the woman kissed her cheek.

"Little gem, are you awake? Has the medicine worn off?" the madam asked as she stroked Norah's hair.

"I don't know where I am, Miss."

"You are safe now," the madam smiled and her teeth, though uneven, were white as clouds.

"Friends of yours are outside the door waiting to come in to see you. Are you ready for them, my little flower?" She stroked Norah's forehead, "If you are too tired, I can send them away until later."

Norah could only think of Mary.

"Is it Mary come to see me, Miss?"

"No, there is no Mary. There are two gentlemen. One is young and the other is a priest."

Norah then remembered the blood between her legs and pain attacked her stomach. A priest must have been called so she might confess her sins! She imagined Mam's face before her instead of this lovely woman's. The woman did not appear alarmed by her state at all, but her mam, no doubt, would soon be peering over her full of worry and accusation. She was to be shamed! An issue of blood, just like in the Bible. The woman in the Bible had been a freak until she touched the hem of the garment of Jesus. Then she was healed and could be taken home again. But it wasn't Jesus outside the door now, but a priest who had come to condemn her!

"No….I don't want to see the priest! I want to go home!"

The madam placed her hand gently over Norah's eyes, cooing to her that all would be well. Norah didn't resist, but was surprised when the woman climbed into bed and wrapped her arm around Norah's waist, whispering sweetly to her. The woman didn't scream at her that she should be ashamed or tell her she was unclean, but gently spoke words of solace. Heaviness overcame Norah again and she fell into a trance-like sleep, forgetting everything.

Chapter Sixteen

"The authorities need to be solicited," Father Driscoll whispered to Murray as they stood in the stifling, dark hallway. The madam had sternly instructed them to wait quietly, but they were becoming agitated and impatient. The candle trembled in Murray's hand and dripped wax onto his newly polished boots. Boots ready for travel with Norah to England and Ireland.

"With all respect, Father, contacting the police will make things worse. There's been nothing but chaos since Albany took away the mayor's right to oversee the police department. They don't know if they're coming or going and I don't want them involved."

Murray was really worried that his plans with John Mitchel would be found out. He was taking a hell of a lot of money out of the country and if the police found out, it wouldn't fair too well.

"Are you certain the young woman was taken against her will?" Father Driscoll asked, feeling uneasy about his role in all of this. Sure, he was going to miss an important meeting with the Bishop, but he also wanted to conserve his energy for other issues, other parishioners.

Maybe this was pure folly, he thought, maybe he had been foolish for being high-spirited and taken in by this charismatic young man. He had insisted on helping him and insinuated himself into the man's mysterious problems just because he found him kneeling in his church.

"She wouldn't have left Finn's without me." Murray swallowed, the sound filling the hallway.

"I don't believe you've told me the name of this young woman you're looking for."

Murray looked at the priest and felt the old submissive feelings toward the holy robes rattling his nerves.

"Norah McCabe. Her name is Norah McCabe." She's righteous, Father; she's not a loose woman. She works for the *Irish-American*—"

"Slow down, son. I'm wearing the robes of compassion, not judgment. I leave that to Him." The wax from the candle Murray held dripped onto the priest's hands that were clasped together and held against his chest. Father Driscoll was startled by the hot wax and shook his arms. Murray immediately reached out to help him, but dropped the candle, and the flame was diminished. Sinister darkness overcame Murray as he listened to the heavy breathing of the priest and the rustling of his robes. A wave of despair came over him, rendering him immobile. They stood in the hallway, their eyes trying to adjust to the darkness when the door opened and the madam came out, quickly shutting the door behind her. She held a candle and nodded toward the end of the hall as her left hand reached back to make sure the door had locked behind her.

"Our young woman is sound asleep and cannot be awakened at the moment. We'll wait in the parlor."

The madam strutted down the hall, expecting the men to follow her.

"I'm not leaving until I see her! I'll go to the police. She's been taken against her will."

The madam's head swiveled sharply to look at Murray.

"I suggest you not threaten me. If you took the young woman from her bed, you'd be the one taking her against her will. She doesn't want to leave and she's made it clear that she doesn't want to see you or the priest!"

"You can wait in the parlor or go home until she wishes to see you...if she ever does again!"

Murray turned to the priest for help, but the priest had walked over to the window. He pulled his watch from his pocket, realizing he was too late to meet Mitchel and his men. He was supposed to give the stats on their funds and set the date they would be setting sail for England.

"I have to leave for an hour or so," Murray said, walking up behind Father Driscoll. "I don't want to keep you from your parish work, but would you consider waiting in the parlor until I return...just in case she wakes up?"

The priest turned from the window, sighed, and touched Murray's shoulder again.

"Of course...of course. I had a meeting, but it can wait."

The two men walked behind the madam who paraded triumphantly before them, leading them down the stairs and into the parlor.

Murray's stomach lurched when he walked into the dimly lit parlor. The rich red velvet and satin upholstered sofa and chairs were blatantly alluring, and a stab of disgust welled up within him. It felt like he was waiting for a parade of ladies to come waltzing in for him to choose from. What was he thinking to ask the priest to stay in this place? He glanced at Father Driscoll, but he didn't look disturbed at all as he sat down and assembled his robes. Murray breathed in the scent of the girls before he heard them prancing down the hall toward the parlor, laughing and tittering. He turned and nodded goodbye to the madam and priest and walked out the door. Let the priest deal with these ladies of the night, for certainly his flesh had surely died to sensuality in order to serve his Christ.

Clouds covered the moon and rendered the night sinister when Murray walked out of the bordello. The air was thick with the stench of horse manure and rancid smoke from the glue factories. He didn't see Ivan and jaunted around to the back of the building to look for him. He noticed the well dressed men in top hats who sported canes and umbrellas; they were making their way into some of the buildings that housed the discreet bagnios that replicated the atmosphere of private residences. He didn't find Ivan and went to the front of the building again, but Ivan was nowhere to be seen. Murray ran down a narrow alleyway and his foot struck a wooden barrel. It fell over and odorous garbage tumbled out in the dark before him. He kicked at the refuse to get it out of his pathway and suddenly saw the dark outline of someone sitting up against the building next to some of the other barrels. It wasn't unusual for a drunk to be sleeping in an alleyway, and on impulse he went to see if it was Ivan.

"Ivan, is it you there, man? Ivan?"

"It's me, sir, I'm sorry for yer troubles, but I'm in no way able to help you with your woman—"

"Get up!" yelled Murray. "Come with me and I'll get you cleaned up, fed, and you can sleep at my place. I've found Norah, but she's sleeping. I have to meet someone first before coming back to get her."

"I won't be going to no rebel meeting. I won't end up like me father—"

"Get up and have some self-respect," Murray responded, offering Ivan his hand.

"I have an old mother, sir, I don't know if I told ye already, but I have an old mother…," Ivan said, giving his hand to Murray.

There was commotion in the alleywayand when Murray looked up, he saw a gang of men, boys really, hardly men. He knew who they were. They had asked him for his help one night…the night he met Norah on the street. He pulled Ivan up and he was so light, he practically carried him down the alley and away from the gang who were assembling at the other end. He kept close to the wall as he scurried them both away from danger and the noise of human bones crunching, and then there was the horrific sound of moaning, of pain. There was no sound of the blood that spilled, for blood didn't possess tone or timbre, Murray knew well. It would be much later after it had been shed that it would become loud and demand restitution and recompense. It would sing mournfully throughout places on the earth where it had been shed, and for those who heard it, they would be deafened by it unless they responded. This is what Ireland was like for Murray—a landscape full of old blood shed hundreds of years before that had never been recompensed. New blood in this city was being spilled all the time, but he would be out of here someday for good and not have to hear its cries for justice and vengeance. Instead he heard the cries of the poet, James Mangan, "Alas! Alas! Why pine I a thousand miles away, From the fair hills of Eire," a lament that ran through his head time and time again.

"Come on, man, come on!' Murray yelled to Ivan as they reached the street and saw that life, such as it was in this city, went on as usual; all the while murder was being committed just a few feet away. Murray pulled Ivan along with him without any resistance. As they made their way down the street, he saw a buggy and motioned for it to stop. It would cost him more than he wanted to pay, but it would be worth it to flee from the violence…and then a fear came over him that the gang was right outside the bordello where his Norah lay, innocent and foolish, Norah. Was he responsible for jeopardizing her life, sullying her with teachings of insurrection, and seducing her into believing that their plans to liberate Ireland was a worthy mission for her to give her life to? Was it? He shook these thoughts from his head as the carriage jaunted along the disconsolate streets of New York.

*N*orah McCabe…Norah McCabe. This name sounded familiar to the priest ever since Murray had told him it was the name of the young woman abducted and taken to this bordello.

Father Driscoll sat alone on the sofa in the parlor after the women and the madam had left him in peace. The madam promised him a hot cup of tea and she was off to make it. He was glad for the time alone, but he kept rolling the name, Norah McCabe, over in his mind and could almost remember who she was. He stood up and walked around the dimly lit room and then it dawned on him who this Norah McCabe was. She was the young correspondent for the *Irish-American* he had met months ago in his church! He felt his heart quicken and took in a faltering breath and adjusted his robes. It was true then! It was true what the Bishop had told him many years ago in Rome. He did have the gift of one of the mysteries—the gift of prophecy.

Norah McCabe wasn't the first person that he had prophesized would encounter danger. Before he moved to New York from the mission in Latin America, he was always seeing visions or auroras for the men and women whose lives were desperate and on the edge of violence. But since coming to America, he hadn't had any premonitions and had begun thinking that it had been only his sensitivity to the natural distress that thronged Latin America. Anyone could see that the lives of the people in Peru were in danger. Norah McCabe was the first person in this country for whom he had been privy to see that a volcanic future was in store for her life. He had sensed the Spirit of God moving over both of them as the earnest young woman, full of confidence and self-importance, interviewed him for the newspaper. He surmised she only pretended to be interested in the abolitionist movement. Her questions were well thought out and intelligent, but her heart had been far away from the interview. She had indeed possessed something he couldn't quite comprehend. Something poignant and warm had been stirring in her. When she was preparing to leave, he glimpsed a foreboding future for her and could see that if she didn't make a concerted effort to change, there would be devastation. All he could do at the time was give her a strong warning to be cautious about the steps in her life she was presently taking. He didn't know anything about her life. But he felt it was a warning sent from God Himself! He was certain that the Holy Spirit had hounded him during the last moments he had with her before she left his church. The rest of that day and during the next few days he kept thinking about Norah McCabe and praying for her, even lighting a candle one evening when he had been alone in the church.

The madam walked into the parlor with a tray and all the implements for a fine tea, something he didn't think she did too often. He was thankful for her willingness to oblige a man of the cloth. She sat down next to him and served him graciously. After taking a few sips that calmed his nerves, he turned to her.

"Do you have someone here who can deliver a message to Bishop Hughes?"

Everyone knew Bishop Hughes's influence, including his work to prevent young orphaned girls from going into the bordellos.

"We have messengers, but rarely have they taken a message to the Bishop," she retorted with a laugh. "But for you, Father Driscoll, yes, I can arrange for a message to be sent."

"I'll write it now, if you'll give me some paper."

"You may tell me the message and I'll pass it on, Father." He could see in her face worry that he was going to bring the Bishop and police here to her bordello, including the newspapermen who would show up on the heels of the police. Her place would be closed down. *Not such a bad idea at that,* he thought.

"Tell the Bishop that I am sincerely apologetic for missing our meeting due to being involved in a new ministry for misguided young women," he said, smiling at the madam who immediately left him to find a messenger.

Father Driscoll was alone again in the parlor and prayed no one would come in. *Oh God,* he thought, *don't let any of the madam's customers find a priest sitting in this place!* They would be caught off guard to encounter a holy man sitting in a bordello and might feel they were being forced into some kind of confession. He was surprised that Murray had left him so suddenly, but right now he had to think only of Norah McCabe and her plight. Just below the surface of his conscience, however, were the exhilarating feelings of renewal. He had the gift! He wasn't just a mere man taking on the mantle of God like so many men did in the church. Norah McCabe had indeed brought him hope in himself and his calling. Yes, he had the gift! It was beginning to sink in and he felt like shouting praises to God. Imagine! An epiphany in a bordello! He would miss the meeting with the Bishop because he was sitting on scarlet pillows of seduction in this room instead. Surely, he would suffer the consequences of this act. Rumors would undoubtedly fly around his parish. He might even be cast out of his parish. But what did it matter? He had already taken an unusual position as an Irish-Catholic priest on abolitionism, and if he was accused of visiting a house of prostitution, what would it matter now that he had been assured of his gift? Father Driscoll's face was dark and finely lined from the many years he had spent in South America's hot sun, but as he sat in the parlor with the soft pink reflected from the lamps and red cushions, his face softened into attractive youthfulness. He smoothed his robes and bowed his head in prayer, ignoring the women in the hallway and the two men who had walked in and then out of the parlor once they saw that there was a priest sitting there praying.

"Father," the madam whispered, coming into the room a few minutes later and tapping him on the shoulder. She had no shame in interrupting his prayers. He was in her territory, she was not in his, the church, and so she felt in command of herself and even of receiving his grace and forgiveness. But she had to get him out of her parlor, for it had been foolish to suggest that he wait there. None of the established customers, let alone new customers, would be comfortable coming into the parlor to wait for their appointments with a priest sitting with them. Why hadn't she thought more clearly about this? Then it came to her why she wouldn't allow her practical mind to rule in this instance. Father Driscoll's presence in her home felt like a luxurious cushion for her soul, even if it wasn't right for her business. She sat down quietly next to the priest who hadn't looked up when she walked into the room. She had to get herself together, nevertheless, and put her nonsensical feelings behind her, for her business came first and foremost.

Father Driscoll opened his eyes and looked into the madam's face. She knew he was curiously matching her voice with her face. He had never seen her up close, only the back of her quickly leaving the confessional.

"Is the young woman now awake for me to see?" he asked.

"No, Father. I think she'll be sleeping for awhile." He was so sincere and just, she thought warmly.

"I need you to please come back in the morning. She will sleep through the night and you can come back in the morning to see her."

"I promised Mr. Murray I would wait here. He's quite distraught over her. She has been taken against her will. You must understand that waiting throughout the night for someone you love who has been abducted—"

"Please, Father, trust me. I will take extra good care of her."

The madam noted a sudden change in the priest's face. It clouded with anger as he abruptly stood to his feet, the bottom of his robe catching on the toe of his shoe.

"How can I trust a woman who runs a whorehouse?" he whispered accusingly.

"Father, I'm not...my young women aren't.... Let me start again, the young woman sleeping upstairs was not brought here by my volition or for my purposes. I am only caring for her because she has been injured."

She was disappointed in his distrust of her, as she watched him pull his robe from underneath his shoe, preparing to leave.

"I'll leave, then, and return in the morning. Just as you suggest," he smiled feebly. There was commotion outside in the hall as two men began arguing. She watched shame paint Father Driscoll's face a deep pink, his demeanor hardening into one of the holy statutes of the saints in his church.

"You must turn from this kind of life—," he grimly stated, but the madam interrupted him. She couldn't help herself.

"Before you leave, Father...," she hesitated, her cheeks enflamed. She had planned on asking him for a blessing now that he was here, but he was telling her she must change her life. It didn't work that way with her! She would not be told to flee from sin, for she was the master of choosing to sin and choosing to confess.

"Yes?"

"Never mind...I'll see you in the morning."

Chapter Seventeen

"Ye must lie down, Eoin....ye must not worry yourself now," Mam said, following her husband into the room where they lay down together night after night into the familiar repose of nestling, fitting like spoons in a drawer. This plain small room was their private sanctuary.

"Come lie with me then, A Stór," he murmured feebly, carefully lowering himself onto their feather-filled mattress that took up all the space in the room. She turned to re-arrange things on a trunk that was positioned between the door and their bed. Eoin stared at her faded golden hair that had once been the ginger color he found irresistible. A powerful urge came over him to reach out and touch her hair. It had been a long time since he had taken her hair down from the tightly coiled chignon she had worn nearly every day of their marriage, but life was too rushed in America, too desperate for anything more than putting meat on their table. In Ireland, they hadn't the proper sustenance and were oftentimes too tired to couple together, but there had always been time to touch her lovely hair. But here in this country, plenty of what they desired was always just around the corner and almost possible if only they worked hard enough. There was no time for leisure or taking down his wife's hair.

Eoin had been asking her all day to lie down with him but he knew she wouldn't until her usual bedtime. She had never laid down in the middle of the day in her life, except for the coming of their babies. Not even when she was sick with hunger or illness had she taken to her straw bed in Ireland or this old feather mattress here in America. He always encouraged her to rest, but these days she never rested for she was too busy working and caring for him since he had become so ill that he hadn't been able to work as many hours or play his fiddle in the saloons. It was his wife's income at the sewing factory, as well as Norah's pay working for the newspaper, that kept them from starving and being turned out from their tenement apartment. His dear Norah had called for a doctor to come to their home a week ago, but when he arrived, Eoin had turned him away. He thought the sum too exorbitant and was angry that Norah had to pay half the doctor's fees regardless of not being examined. The doctor had some compassion, perhaps guilt in taking Norah's money, and he gave them a cough and fever medicine free of charge. For consumption, the doctor said.

They didn't know what this diagnosis meant, or how serious it was, but he knew that his friend had died from it, and that Five Points was plagued with it. He thought of the fever in Ireland and how they had almost perished. *What could kill them in America after surviving Ireland and the Famine fever! They had to be immune now,* he thought. Norah had pronounced the word, consumption, slowly after the doctor left, and Eoin thought about its definition. How ironic, to have a disease called consumption after he had nearly been consumed and devoured by the hunger in Ireland!

This consumption was a seductive thing, with the beginning symptoms merely a need to sleep and then he had to rest from the congestion building up in his lungs. Mam made poultices for his chest and kindly whispered to him that she didn't mind caring for him, her dear husband. He had been surprised by her sudden sensuous affection and when, through her tears, she announced that he always healed in the past and he would heal again, he wept quietly, too. She said that she loved rubbing his chest and applying the heated herbs to bring back the glow of love to his face. He gazed into her face as she cared for him so fiercely and gently. But the poultices were only a salve to soothe the discomfort they both felt, as his symptoms grew worse and in just a day he wasn't able to get up from bed, breathe properly, or eat even the best cut of meat cooked in a stew to strengthen him.

Eoin was overcome with coughing that wracked his entire body with spasms that didn't stop for five long minutes. It was a dry and hollow cough that brought nothing up but the flailing of his arms, as if he was trying to extract the oxygen in the room to bring into his tightened chest.

Mam stood back from the bed and tried not to imagine the worst. This disease demon was claiming her husband, her dear and precious husband, and there was nothing she could do about it. She poured him a cup of water from the water jug and tried to put it into his hand.

"Take it, Eoin, take it…ye must drink to open up your lungs. Ye must…," her voice weak and trembling. He stopped coughing and then she held the cup to his mouth. He grabbed it with both hands and swallowed a few gulps before erupting again into a spasm of coughs. He handed her back the cup and stood up quickly, bending over and coughing while clutching his waist. He was embarrassed to be this weak in front of her. Even during the Hunger when he worked on the road works for a month and returned home to her a thin man she barely recognized, he had maintained a proud countenance. Always her hero, a Celtic warrior farmer ready to fight for her and their family, for Ireland, for what was good and right. He did this without bearing arms, for his strength was in his love for his family and his love of justice and mercy. But now here he was in America, the country he had taken them to in order to save them from starvation, a country that they sometimes thought about fleeing from, for instead of famine, there was hunger for place, for home, for dignity, and so much more. And now, her beloved was languishing between death and life. He was in danger of perishing, and if she didn't sustain herself with hope and see Norah come home soon, she would become like Eoin. The two of them would soon be lying next to one another and journeying home alright, but home to their God. If this God was here with them in America, that is, she thought with a cynicism she wasn't normally prone to.

Eoin sat back down on the bed continuing to cough while Mam stood behind him rubbing his back and praying for mercy. She was immediately sorry she had allowed such a thought about God come over her. She had far too many battles to fight and was terribly weary. Where was Norah? Why hadn't she come home? It wasn't like her daughter to not come home or leave a note. Would she be with Mary now? Maybe she was with the Harrigan fellow because of extra work, or maybe he had taken a fancy to her. No, she re-considered, her Norah wouldn't be spending all night with a man, even if he was a gentleman and editor of a fine Irish paper!

"Where's our Norah?" Eoin asked, as if he had been reading her thoughts. He slid down on the bed and turned on his side. They knew each other so well after all these years of struggle and devotion that nothing could be secretive between them.

"She must be with Mary." Mam lay down beside him and gave in to overwhelming exhaustion. His breathing was labored and loud in the still room. Where was the street noise that had lulled them into troubled dreams every night since moving here? If ever she had wanted noise from the streets, it was now. She didn't want to listen to her husband's noisy lungs that reminded her he was desperately ill.

"She's not with Mary. She's with that newspaper man who's going to bring her trouble, A Stór," he said, closing his eyes.

"No, no, Eoin, 'tis not true what ye say. Plenty of young men have come knocking on our door for Norah, but she isn't so taken with young men. She's of a different mind, our Norah. A different mind altogether, Norah is. Don't worry yourself. Ye must sleep now. Please sleep now…," Mam responded, folding herself into his presence and bowing her head into his poor heaving chest as it went in and out accordion-like.

"Go for her, Marion, go for Norah…," he said, his voice reverberating through the top of her head and down into her heart. She knew then that he had some knowledge about Norah that he had been withholding from her. Something was wrong, very wrong, or he wouldn't be speaking to her like this. *But maybe it's his sickness,* she thought. She sat up on the bed and looked at her husband. He was right. She had to find their daughter, but how could she leave her ill husband alone?

"I'll go for Meg. She'll find Norah for us. Sleep now. I'll be back."

God would not do this to her, she thought, her body trembling as she got herself together to go for Meg. No, not after all they had been through. A dark dread began to creep up into her thoughts that made her heart feel so heavy that she wanted to lie down with her husband and sleep. Eoin could not be taken from her without her saying goodbye. So she would not say goodbye to ensure he would still be here when she returned. She found her shawl and started out the door, but stopped. It would take her too long to walk to Meg's home and it would be dangerous to be out on the streets. She would have to spend money on a carriage, something she never did. She could never pay the price for a carriage when her two good legs could take her where she needed to go. But tonight it was different. She would have spent all her money on a carriage to get to her daughters to bring them home to their dying father. She pulled out coins from a jar in the cupboard and went out the door, shutting it firmly.

Murray took Ivan home to clean him up and feed him. As soon as he brought him into the house, he was sorry he had become diverted from his purpose. He had been finished with proselytizing and inducting people into the movement to free Ireland. Norah McCabe had been his last recruit and look what had happened because he allowed his heart to rule over his head! What had gotten into him to bring an angry rapscallion into his life! This man was too destitute and weak to be of any real good right now, but because Ivan's poor father had died in Ireland for the cause, this in itself had appealed to him.

"Set yourself into the water room, man, and wash yourself. There's some lye soap that's good for the bugs if you have any," he told him. Ivan had begun ranting about how there was lots of food in America but given only sparingly and bird-like to the poor immigrants living in dilapidated buildings like magpies in nests made of twigs, string, and garbage.

"Ye are all the same!"

"What are you accusing me of? I've brought you into my home to help you!" Murray responded.

"And what is it that you'll be taking from me, then?" he asked.

"Nothing but your friendship...and maybe your strength when you gain it...," Murray answered, not wishing to divulge anymore than he already had when he had talked to him on the street about Ireland. It would be wasted on him now, but soon perhaps he would be able to convince him to live for something purposeful than pick-pocketing old ladies and waiting outside of saloons to do the dirty business for men like the commissioner.

"The friendship you speak of will be at a cost," Ivan said, his eyes greedily darting around the rooms. "You're well off, then," he said, "not like the Irish in this city...or the other immigrants."

"Ivan, listen to me! I'm Irish, too," Murray stated, knowing that he was forever up against the impossible task of convincing another Irish-born person that he was just as Irish as anyone born there. He had an advantage being in the middle as he was. Middle of what? To the Protestant upper class, he was born here in this country and although Catholic, his position in their eyes was one of moderate esteem. His family had worked hard at assimilation, as well as taking a stand on an acceptable Irish podium in their new country. His parents had taken what was most respectful in coming from the old country, in the eyes of the natives as well as in their own eyes. It was a matter of political pride and religious fervor that his father had been committed to the movement to free Ireland from England. The trips back and forth to Ireland and England had imbued Murray with the passionate pursuit of finishing what his father had been unable to do.

"Ye are more American than Irish, I'd say. You'll be doing yerself a favor to join the Society of the Friendly Sons of Saint Patrick. Ye can then be loyal to the old country as well as give praise to the Queen," Ivan retorted.

The organization that met at Waldorf's on Fifth Avenue was for the well-to-do Irish gentlemen. Surprisingly, there were quite a few. His father had become good at handling the money that came his way, but he had refused to kiss the asses of the Irish and the British who valued their cultural ties with England.

"I wouldn't dirty my hands with such hypocritical trash…most of them are the privileged Scots who came here after a short trip through Ireland…a generation or two. Why are you so against me, Ivan? I can open the door for you right now and you're free to leave."

Murray opened his front door inlaid with beveled glass that sparkled in the light from the street lamp. The neighborhood he lived in was well lit, for the homes were worth more than all the tenement buildings in Five Points combined. There were policemen who patrolled his well-lit neighborhood all the time. He was glad for it, but it also made him nervous because of the clandestine activity he was involved in.

Ivan shuffled over to the Victorian sofa whose upholstery was a rich blue paisley material covering a mahogany frame. It had been one of Murray's mother's favorite pieces of furniture. Ivan hesitated before sitting down. When he sat down, he slumped to his side, sighed, and closed his eyes.

Murray slammed the door and Ivan's eyes opened. He didn't move, but stared at Murray without blinking.

"When I come back in a couple of hours, it'll be morning. I want you to be washed and cleaned up. Later, you and I are going to retrieve Norah McCabe. You've come too far in this situation to get yourself out now."

Ivan shut his eyes.

"Did you hear me?" Murray shouted, walking over to him and shaking his shoulders. When he did so, Ivan shuddered and began crying. Murray was incredulous.

"What's wrong?"

Ivan's eyes opened again. "I'm here for two reasons only," he said between sobs. "One is that I helped your woman fall into despair. I didn't know she was Irish! How'd I know what country she was from!"

"Go on, man, tell me the second reason then," Murray said as he stood over him, irritation and anger flooding him.

Ivan sat up, "I want to meet the man, Meagher, who killed my father!"

"My God, man, you're disturbed! Meagher didn't kill your father. He could have been a dead man himself! They bore arms together to fight the British bastards and one was killed and the other wasn't. They were on the same side!"

"Me father had five wee ones to feed and it was Meagher who convinced him to join the cause. A hopeless cause!"

"You should be honoring your father, Ivan. He joined the cause for you and your family. How can you...?"

Ivan jumped to his feet, weak and wobbly, and when he did, Murray saw strength in the man, as if a bolt of lightening had surged through him. Then he felt this current sending a shock wave through him when Ivan put both his hands around his neck and squeezed.

"Four of the wee ones died from starvation! If me da had brought food home to us instead of fighting at a widow's farm, they'd be alive!" Ivan shouted, his boney hands clasping Murray's neck.

Ivan kept squeezing until Murray's Adam's apple slackened and all resistance escaped him. When there was no more fight in either of the two men, Ivan fell back onto the sofa. Murray fell to the floor with a thud. Ivan nestled into the thick comfort of the sofa. He wanted to sleep and forget everything.

"I won't end up like me da...I won't...," he whimpered, but when Ivan said this, he felt worse off than his father had ever been and even worse off than his father being dead. His da had died for a cause, a good cause, a hopeless one, at that, but he himself, his father's son, was here in America without any cause, just a cause to feed his belly. At least he cared for his mother. He had to care and feed her before she died. And then he'd be free, wouldn't he? His father had thought it more of a cause to save Ireland than save his wife and his own children, and he wouldn't become like him. Dark thoughts devilishly circled within his pounding feverish head. What good was he if he couldn't feed his mam? He looked down at the floor where Murray was lying. Maybe the man was trustworthy and could help him and his mam. But they both needed their sleep, and then he would work it out with him and then go home to his Mam.

Chapter Eighteen

ather Driscoll left the bordello and walked down the street, spicy incense and acrid swine odor filling his nostrils. His senses were unusually heightened after spending a few hours in the bordello. He tried to shake off this irritation and bask in the renewal of his spiritual gift that had come through his contact with Norah McCabe. He was a serious man, not prone to hilarity, but he erupted into schoolboy laughter when he thought of his peers and the bishop learning that he had been renewed in a house of prostitution. His robes moved heavily around his legs as he walked, the sound reminding him of his calling to be handpicked and set apart by God. Walking swiftly, he lifted his head above the crowd so he wouldn't have to greet anyone and lose this inspiring reverie. The muted acknowledgements and curious looks of the people he passed ensured him that the Holy Spirit was surrounding and blessing him. At first, it didn't worry him when he heard glass shattering and angry yelps coming from a distance. Piercing the night air were men's bullish barks and shouts mingling with the seductive laughter of women's voices.

The lively melodies of a fiddle came from a nearby saloon, incongruent with the hostile mien that was beginning to prevail over the evening. He nearly turned toward the music, desiring to be in a place of celebration rather than returning to a musty and dank room where he would feel compelled to be on his knees in praise. This music, although heard many times before, was inviting and reflective of his joy and he wanted to praise differently tonight. A giddy and liberating feeling took hold of him and he laughed aloud. His next sermon should be titled, "Finding God in a Bordello!"

Father Driscoll strode along and hummed a few lines from a hymn that he especially liked, but minutes later, he heard more glass breaking and shrieks coming from the direction he was going in. Two more blocks and he would be home at the Church of the Transfiguration. As the noise increased, he recognized the unique cacophony of a gang. There wasn't a street or neighborhood exempt from the gangs that reminded him of destructive locusts who devoured any harmony or hope of peace. They were barbaric and determined to make their territorial mark in blood brotherhood to avenge having been born into destitution and poverty. Father Driscoll was convinced that they were too eager to defend a political stance with a motive to kill and destroy. It was an excuse for them to have power, but in reality they had none. He had counseled many that the only power they were using in their lives was to live in darkness when they could live in the light. He had beseeched Bishop Hughes to provide him with the means to help the young boys and even women, to get off the street and into dock work or good jobs. But usually before he could organize work or charity for them, the Tammany bosses and ward heelers would offer jobs in exchange for their bloodthirsty ways.

Father Driscoll walked onto a crowded street and his joy quickly dissipated. Panic overtook him as a heightened expectation for violence circled the neighborhood ready to attack. He smelled it, that sharp odor of men's sweat emanating from them just before they went into battle. Smoke was also in the air. Something was on fire! Sensing acute danger, he clutched at his rosary in the pocket of his robe and made his way through the crowd, hoping his robes and collar would enable him to get through. The people in his neighborhood, usually respectful, didn't pay heed to him now and tried to push him back before he could get to where his church loomed over the neighborhood. Using his elbows, he plunged through the mass of people and saw plumes of dark smoke rising above the steeple of his church.

"Holy Mary, Mother of God!" he cried out, forcing his way to where two policemen were trying to control a mob striking one another with bottles. Firemen were on ladders hosing down his church. He didn't see any flames, just smoke rising high in the sky and forming a pattern of a hulking giant. A dark hulking giant had come to destroy his church.

"I'm the priest of this church, this parish…," he shouted at a policeman who was handcuffing a short stocky man whose clothes were bloodied and dirty.

"You should get to safety, Father," the officer answered him, dragging the man to a wagon.

Father Driscoll's pulse was rapid and pounding in his ears, his chest felt heavy, and his eyes tried to focus on the scene before him. He rushed to the steps of his church, but was pushed back.

"Disrobe the priest! Disrobe the priest!" shouted a man in the crowd.

An officer was beating people away and Father Driscoll shouted that he wanted to be let into his own church, his own home. The altar, the communion bread, his Bible…he thought, sadly. The Christ on the cross! He couldn't let Jesus burn! He climbed up the steps and reached the front door when suddenly his robes were being tugged and he had to cling to someone in front of him to keep from falling backwards.

Someone yelled, "'Tis the Know Nothings! Kill the God damned nigger metro police sons of bitches! They've come to kill our priest!"

"I'm here, Father… It's me, Patrick!" called out a young man's familiar voice. Patrick came alongside him and grabbed his arm, pulling him down the steps and away from the violent crowd. It was Patrick who had saved him! He was thrilled to see the young man again. He had met Patrick O'Leary after he had come from Ireland and gotten himself involved in Sixth Ward politics. The greenhorn had come to his church a couple of times a month for Mass and communion and was soon patrolling the streets with his club as an officer of the law, determined to bring justice to his new country because he couldn't find it in his own. Father Driscoll thought him a pleasant fellow, a young man with a lot of pain from his past, not unlike so many who had come from that hard scrabble and destitute country. He often saw O'Leary parade around the streets of Five Points wielding his proud position like a peacock in the barnyard pluming out his colors. Patrick was a handsome lad with a strong physique and a head topped with brilliant red hair. He had come to him for counsel when he had learned that his strength and good looks were no match for the dirty dealings of his new land. He was one of the few Irish immigrant men whose hearts hadn't turned into stone because of it, however, and this made the priest like him all the more.

"Father, come with me. I've got the cart down the street. I was going by on my way home and saw the commotion and smoke."

Father Driscoll allowed himself to be led away from his church and into Patrick's cart. As the young O'Leary directed his horses down the street, the priest looked out at the destruction and hopeless pangs of dread waved over him.

"The Lord giveth and the Lord taketh away," he whispered in a prayer of resignation. His gift, after all, had been returned to him and it could not be burned by an angry mob of Orangemen come to exact retribution for some crime an Irish Catholic gang member had done. He turned from looking at his church that was growing smaller in the distance as Patrick led them away from the chaos.

Patrick O'Leary, the boy from Ireland whom he counseled to live right, had now saved his life. Certainly God was with him and all of them, he thought, trying to encourage himself as his church smoldered behind him.

The young man had come to him after being fired as a police officer and having a death threat made against him because he turned in the police commissioner who had been trying to seduce a young woman brought into the station for questioning. He had no choice, Patrick had told him, but to return to Ireland. But then Patrick said he would die of hunger there, but would perish of knife wounds here, so he came to the priest for solace, direction, forgiveness, and for much more than the priest was able to give him. He had counseled the boy and in just two meetings, had grown extremely fond of his character. He hid him in the church until the commissioner was fired from his position and was wandering the streets like a wounded animal. He then helped Patrick to secure a fleet of wagons to begin his own business and to his astonishment, the young man had flourished in his work, even remembering to come to Mass once in awhile and shake the priest's hand, hope restored in his countenance.

Leary drove his horses as fast as they could possibly go through the streets of Five Points. It was close to dawn and the streets were nearly as busy as during the day. It was a puzzling city that never slept, this New York, and Leary promised himself that he would capture some of this high energy and use it to his advantage. Many people of the night desired to hire him to take them to hotels, brothels, and saloons. He worked mostly at night, his prices higher than in the daytime because it was more difficult to carry around the drunken rich men of the city than when they were sober and conducting proper business during the day. And they were typically too drunk to care how much he charged and gave him tips that were sometimes more than the fare. Only once had a man realized his folly as Leary was driving away, coming after him cursing and throwing rocks at him. Leary had stopped and given the money back to the man, but most of the time, his night customers didn't realize how much they had given him once they climbed out of his cart.

Right now, he was immensely proud for being in the right place at the right time to save Father Driscoll. He was more than a priest in the Roman Catholic Church to Patrick Leary, although he couldn't acknowledge this to him. Father Driscoll had become a treasured counselor, unlike the priests in Ireland who usually made him feel guilty and sin-ridden. Leary had become close to the priest since leaving the police force in humiliating circumstances. Once, he encountered the former commissioner on the street, but the man hadn't recognized him. He even dared to speak to him, but the commissioner looked right through him and walked away. Afterward, Leary ran all the way to the church to tell Father Driscoll that he was free and wouldn't be having to move back to Ireland. Father Driscoll arranged for him to find new work in the carting business and his whole life changed. It was then he possessed the courage to go calling at *A Bee in Your Bonnet* to ask Mary to go walking with him one evening. And then he and Mary were together nearly every night. His immense struggles were over for the time being, and for the first time in a long time, he felt close to God. But then, just a few nights ago on one of their walks, Mary became solemn and said they needed to have a serious talk. It had been a sweltering summer evening, his shirt soaked with sweat which made him uneasy with the scent of himself, especially near Mary.

"I'm not well, Patrick," she said to him, her face wan and chalky in the light of a full moon. He took her hand and it was clammy and cold.

"Your blood has gone cold, me love," he said to her affectionately. "We need to go back to the store for tea." She was breathing heavily and he couldn't help becoming excited by the mere sight of her. She was a temptress and his flesh had taken on a life of its own since meeting her. His hands, his face, and even the parts of himself forbidden to be spoken of, had birthed into newness, as if surfacing for the first time from somewhere deep within himself. He had never known that a woman's hands could mold him into a different shape altogether!

"Patrick," she said, clutching his arms tightly and laying her head on his chest. She sobbed quietly into his sweaty shirt. He was surprised by her outburst, but the roundness of her breasts moving against him aroused him even more. He was chagrined that in her despair, he couldn't keep from being enticed by her flesh. People walked by, jostled them, and stared with derision. For a moment he was fearful she was going to tell him she didn't want him in her life. His love had blossomed for her in a few months and he treasured her more than his own life. He let her cry and his shirt became drenched, the night wrapping them in a cocoon of heat and intensity. After a few minutes, he stepped gently away from her and she looked up at him, her face as full and round as the moon, and as white as that orb in the sky.

"I'll be going to Madame Restall's tomorrow, Patrick. I'm going to get rid of this…." She crumpled to the ground, the life going out of her and only the flounces of silk and ribbons that had adorned her were visible. It was as if she had disappeared in front of him and all that was left were her clothing. He gently pulled her up to him, kissing her mouth, and tried to breathe life back into her. She was no longer weeping and her breathing was nearly stilled.

"We'll go to the priest, Mary. We'll go to Father Driscoll," he said to her. His heart and mind had turned to stone, however. Stone mad, he'd become. He had nearly been driven from the country a few months ago and now this would be his ruin. He would talk to the priest, but not about their baby they had made together. He would talk to the priest about getting married right away, no mention of the life growing inside of Mary that had formed from the newness of his own life. No, he would not tell the priest and no one had to ever know the timing of the baby being born. Why should he feel guilty here in America? In America, prostitutes and their clients did the dirty deed on the streets in front of anyone! He thought about his father back in Ireland and shame came upon him. He had come to understand that his mother had been kept from shame, for she had become pregnant with him before marrying. Patrick would never know his biological father and now he had inherited his mother's shame by impregnating Mary. No, he would never let his father know, nor would he let his priest know.

"Whoa there, boys!" Leary said, bringing his thoughts into the present and his horses to a halt in front of *A Bee in Your Bonnet*. He was concerned about Father Driscoll's plight, but eager to see Mary. It was nearly morning, but she would probably be sitting in a straight back chair with a few candles giving her enough light to work on the gowns she would sell tomorrow, Saturday, the busiest day in the shop. She often sat rigidly in her chair so as not to fall asleep and be endangered by a candle toppling over and burning the store down. She had convinced the orphanage to let her work three days a week and to allow her to sleep at the store. The headmistress, at first, hadn't agreed until she came to inspect the store to learn whether Mary was telling the truth. Before she came, Leary helped Mary clean up the store and hide his clothes that he kept there. The mistress knew about their promenading around the city and going to blood-and-thunder plays. She didn't approve for she wanted Mary to remain at the orphanage so they could instill their Protestant ways into her, but mostly to keep her as a slave to low wages. They had never been happy with her friendship with Norah McCabe, either. *Norah!* Leary, thought angrily. *Where was she now when her friend needed her so desperately?* They hadn't seen Norah McCabe in two weeks. She wasn't stopping by the store to see how her business was being conducted, nor had she followed up with selling the place and giving Mary some of the money from the sale.

When Leary pulled his horses up to the store, the door of the shop was open and the darkness inside was ominous. He jumped from the cart and ran inside calling out for Mary, but there was no answer. He stumbled around until he placed his hand on a candle and matches. Father Driscoll came in behind him and they searched the room for a note or any hint of why Mary had left her shop so suddenly, leaving it open for thieves to come in. Leary became frantic with concern, his chest burning and his head pounding. When the thought came to him that Mary could have gone to Madame Restall for the abortion, he sat down and put his head in his hands, defeat overcoming him. The priest put his hand on his shoulder and Leary jumped up and marched around the room tugging at his hair.

"Patrick...tell me about this shop and this woman. I didn't know you were attached to someone who owned a used-clothing store." Father Driscoll's own troubles about his church dissipated into the heavy atmosphere of Patrick's presence.

"I was going to come to you...we were going to come to you, Father, to ask you to marry us. She's from Ireland, too, but she's been here for ten years. She still lives in an orphanage, working for her keep. She also works here at this shop with her friend, Norah McCabe."

"You know Norah McCabe?"

"Norah McCabe owns this shop."

"Norah McCabe is in serious trouble."

The priest turned toward the door. "I have to leave, Patrick. I'll be staying at the Astor tonight. I'm going to be staying there on church business, as a matter of fact, but first you have to take me to Norah McCabe. My church is smoldering and burning, and I can't return there. Bring Mary to the Astor tomorrow and I'll marry you in my hotel room."

Father Driscoll gripped Leary's shoulders firmly and then hurried out the door to Patrick's cart. Patrick numbly followed the priest and they both climbed into the cart. *Mary had to be with Norah and they must both be in trouble,* he thought.

"Father, I have to see Norah McCabe."

"I'm not certain I can see her myself."

"Mary'll be with her. I know it!"

"Go to Corlear's Hook."

"Why Corlear's?" Patrick asked, astounded.

"Just go!" the priest answered and Patrick took the reigns with trembling hands, and the cart moved quickly down the street.

Chapter Nineteen

Some nights in Five Points take siege of its inhabitants to such an extent that the atmosphere trembles and wavers when it is time to give up its ravaging secrets to the light of the sun. This night had been one of them, as Norah McCabe slowly awakened from sleep. She had dreamed of being a child in Ireland, picking bluebells and berries; she had dreamed of being in the dank hold of a ship hoarding bread in her dresser. Throughout her night of dreaming, she would partially awaken to feel the heavy quilts over her body and the soft slippery silk nightgown cocooning her, and then remember she was somewhere in America, somewhere hidden away from her mam and da. And she would sleep again and go into another dream that told the stories of her young life up until the present. Her waking moments were saturated with agony, as if someone had come in the night to pour hot liquid through her body that brought immense sorrow and physical ache. She felt full and round with the warmth of pain, if pain could be felt that way.

She was rocking in a ship with sea water spilling over the sides and onto her, when she awoke and tasted the salt and smelled the sea. She sat up and pushed the covers from her sweaty body and when she touched her face, it was wet with tears. She rolled over and fell out of the high-poster bed onto the floor. She cried out for her da, but as soon as she heard her tremulous voice, she remembered that she had been trying to avoid him and Mam, but especially him. She didn't get up from the floor, but stayed there so she wouldn't forget what was now rapidly coming to her. She remembered worrying that Da wouldn't be pleased with her friendship with Murray.

Murray! Where was Murray? He had left her at Finn's. It was all coming back to her now. She had been taken against her will, tied up in a room above the saloon with some disgusting guard dog of a man watching over her. And then the commissioner had come into the room. That's all she could remember. She slowly got on her knees and looked down at herself in the strange nightgown. She groaned and collapsed onto the floor when she saw patterned on the nightgown hideous dried brick-red blood. In the end, the commissioner must have come to take what she was unable to protect—that part of herself that had only recently been aroused out of its protective cradled incubation.

She had become aware of desire when Murray paraded her about the city, his body close to hers, and especially when he had kissed her, just once, but that one time had brought passion cracking through her hard shell. She was a fledgling in this part of her life–unable to fly, to open herself up to the possibilities, but the newness she had wanted to protect and savor, leave it as it was, and not take any further. Norah had been ready to give her life to Murray's vision—all because he had made her come alive as a woman. Soon after meeting him, she had quit sleeping with Mam's shawl because it reminded her of becoming like her mother. She wanted nothing to do with her mam's life. She was afraid it would make her narrow like her mam and suffocate the desires she had to be more like her da. She thought of the ragged shawl lying in the bottom of the cupboard of her dresser. When she returned home, she would rip it into shreds! She had never wanted any of it! Not her mother's life, nor a life with Murray. And to think she had once felt she could choose!

Norah lay on the floor for a long time. The pain in her body lessened, as if it flowed out of her and attached itself to the carpeted floor. During this time, she quietly declared that she would be true to that girl of herself and never try to exorcise her or think she had to give her up. She would never give that girl away to any man or cause on the earth. That girl she would preserve in the well and center of her being. She would still have her stationed solidly inside her soul, for no one could take her away from herself. The commissioner might have taken something from her, but only from her body, not her soul.

She grasped the sides of the bed and pulled herself up to stand. When she did, the door opened and the striking, mysterious woman walked in. The woman was dressed in layers of red and black lace and there was a braided gold belt around her waist. Norah wondered if it was a rope to tie her up with.

"Are you feeling better?" the strange woman asked. An accent cadenced her question and Norah was intrigued. When the woman shut the door and came towards her, Norah's vision blurred and she felt a sudden pounding in the back of her head. She fell forward onto the bed before she could answer.

"You've got quite a large lump on the back of your head," the woman said in a faraway voice. Norah tried to push herself up to look at the woman again, but she was unable. She stopped struggling and lay still.

"I bought a small block of ice from the vendor yesterday to put on your head, but it melted too quickly before it did any good," the woman's voice was still distant, but Norah felt her hands gently caressing the back of her head. She emitted a loud moan, for the touch to her head was tender.

"I'm sorry to further your pain, sweet one. You awoke briefly and I told you there were two men here looking for you. You said you wanted nothing to do with them and I sent them away. They'll return and unless you tell them yourself to go away for good, they will keep returning, I'm afraid. One of the men is very appealing, quite the lady's man, I'd presume. The other one is a priest. My priest, in fact… Do you remember me telling you they were here to see you?"

Norah's eyes opened and she struggled to lift herself up. The woman helped her turn around and settle back onto the bed, her head cradled by the pillows she doubled for her. Norah moved her eyes around the room and it began to swirl in red and gold colors. One window with velvet drapes had been opened, the curtains tied back. She centered her vision on the window to gain equilibrium and a new color floated before her. A deep cobalt blue made its way through the red and gold delirium and brought her serenity to compliment the strength that had begun to well up within her. She was amazed to see sky. Looking into the sky would always bring her back to a proper assessment of herself.

"Do you wish me to close the drapes?" the woman asked.

"No, please no…open them wide! I'd like to see the entire sky! Do you notice how blue it is? Can you see the deep, deep blue of the sky, Miss?"

Norah looked at the woman and something in her face revealed that she did not wish for Norah to see this color, to be this hopeful. She became acutely aware that her abduction hadn't ended. Although the commissioner was not in the room, she was still a prisoner, maybe his prisoner and this woman's! This bewitching woman was a seductress of young women! She had heard about them. They had been pointed out to her on the streets of New York by Mary. She was always curious to learn more about these women who had their independence and a business that sold soft and silky flesh of the young! Now that she was alone with one of them, it was as if her desire to learn more of their mystery had come to be, but in a horrid and destructive way. Norah turned to look at the window again, but it was only the dark sky she saw, not the beautiful blue that had aroused her out of her turmoil and pain.

"Who are you? Where am I?" Norah's mind was becoming her own again, lucid thoughts lining up in order, memories of Murray, Finn's, and the abduction. There was a gaping hole that couldn't be accounted for that sat darkly in a corner of her mind, but it was only that, in a corner of her, in a piece of her, and not in all of her. She

knew, however, that it was like a sink hole, a black hole that could easily pull the rest of her mind and herself into. It was this place that had
to be sealed up, but not until she understood what had happened. Her
left hand lying underneath the covers, touched that part of herself that
may have been violated. Only a part of her had been violated, she
thought, her heart pounding. She laid her hand atop of herself to feel
if there was injury, a mark left on the outside of her to indicate the violence done within. Would his poison crawl up through her and come
into her mind?

"What is wrong?" asked the madam.

Norah ignored the woman and as her hand lay atop of herself, she
felt nothing. She pressed harder wondering about bruising, but there
was none she could feel. She moved her hands down to touch the inside of her thighs, but she felt nothing. No pain, no sign of having been
violated. There was no memory of exploring herself and experiencing
pain when she had awakened earlier.

"Are you in pain?"

Norah was discreet in touching herself underneath the covers. She
really knew nothing about these things. She knew nothing about sex.
She could hardly say the word. She had been raised to pretend it didn't
exist and yet it had been sashaying and dancing erotically all around
her ever since arriving in America.

"No," she stated firmly, pushing the covers off and sitting up in
bed ready to flee this place and find Murray again. *How long could she
have been in this room?* She turned to the opposite side of the bed and
away from the woman. Strength was returning to her, and she slid off
the bed to stand up. She was dizzy, but walked carefully towards the
window.

"Oh my dear, you've soiled your nightgown with your bleeding
time!" the woman said.

Norah turned to look at her captor.

"How do you know? How do you know what it is? Do you know?"
she shouted. How would she ever really know what had happened.

"You must stay in bed until you are stronger," the woman said, leading her back to bed, but Norah refused to lie down. She sat on the bed, her feet dangling. She looked at her pale, dirty feet. She was a mess.

"I'll have some water brought in so you can bathe and then we'll change this soiled nightgown and bed sheets."

"Ye can't take away the filth!" Norah said, pushing the woman as hard as she could backward onto the carpet, luxurious flounces of clothing flying up around the madam's head. Norah was emboldened by the rage within her, and before the woman could get off the floor, Norah was upon her, ripping her clothing and screaming that she would kill her.

Chapter Twenty

It was four in the morning and Thomas, the congenial bartender of Finn's, was sitting in the upper room of his saloon with one candle burning. He had closed up his pub around two and was pleased that there hadn't been much brawling and raucous activity. It would have sent him over the edge if some b'hoy had been murdered in his establishment this night, or even if a murder had taken place on the street in front of his business. Once he had learned that Norah McCabe had been carried off, hidden in his saloon, and then taken away to who knows where, he had made a serious decision. He already had to live with the truth that six men over a five-year period had been murdered in his establishment, but if a woman such as Norah McCabe was abused or murdered, it was time for him to shut up shop and go into another line of work.

He rolled a cigarette, curled his lips around it, lit it, inhaled deeply, and coughed. Shit! How could he live without the god damn pay-offs! How could he survive without them? And didn't he know that fighting the British through powerful words like John Mitchel's and others who met in his saloon was an honor? Money was being raised to buy arms to kill the god damn British sons of bitches! Who would have believed big business would be happening in his drinking hole and he would be blind to it? Did he think the Irish rebels who escaped from Van Dien's Land would come to this country to fight with white kid gloves and be asking West Point for help? God, how ignorant and idealistic he could be even after all he had lived through.

Thomas lifted himself up to reach into his pocket and pull out the wad of money Mitchel had given him. He counted it. It was more money than he had made in the last year operating his saloon. Money for running messages and arranging for the secret meetings in his pub, Mitchel had told him. Meetings he thought were about starting newspapers and fighting evil in the world with words, potent and condemning words. Let them drink ale and the whiskey that burned guts and caused early deaths, as long as they were doing something else in his place that mattered. And here he had been proud of not having the riotous and bloodthirsty O'Connell Guards meeting in his saloon like the Bowery saloons were notorious for. He stood up and threw the money on the floor and kicked it about the room.

"The Liberator said himself that human blood was no cement for freedom!"

He was free. Mitchel was gone. Murray was gone. No more meetings for *The Citizen*, for *The Leader*, or any supposed newspaper in his saloon. No more meetings for Mitchel. Thomas was closing up his business.

He threw his fag on the floor, stomped on it, and sat down and cried. Thomas cried mournfully and quietly, like he used to do as a boy in his bed. He hadn't cried in years. He looked at his hands as he cried and saw one deep creviced line going from his forefinger down to a big vein in his wrist. A fortuneteller had told him that this meant long life and success, but never did she tell him how that success would come to be in his life. And at what price.

"Five thousand dollars for your troubles, Thomas," Thomas mimicked Mitchel, remembering how he had placed the cash in his hands. And because Murray hadn't come back with Norah McCabe, he told

Mitchel to go to Murray's to look for him. And then Mitchel turned to him and said, "It's over now, Thomas. It's bloody well over now. We've raised the money to buy enough arms to blow the English out of our country! You've been a good man to open your business to us."

Thomas would sell the place soon enough and then he would take the money and buy a decent business, one that didn't require him to cover up lies and feed the dragon that lived inside men's guts for the drink. He would open up a shop on Broadway and sell men's clothing. Fancy duds they would be, and he would be wearing them himself, he would. He would meet moral people and maybe come up in the world and get the respect he longed for. He was due it! He had never been one for the drink himself and so why should he sell it to others and live like he had been living? Thomas gathered the money from the floor and stuffed it back into his pocket. He blew out the candle, left the room, and climbed the stairs to the side of the saloon to go to bed, resolved to pursue good work with the money Mitchel had placed in his hands.

Father Driscoll was silent as Leary drove his cart through the dusky, sober streets. He clutched his rosary while they traveled and this gave him strength for the task ahead. He liked to touch and caress the familiar beads that warmed his fingers and gave comfort. Eventually, the slow-rising sun on the city horizon ballooned with eager rays to shed light on the darkness that had prevailed.

"Father," Leary said, turning to look over his shoulder as he guided the horses through the streets, "Father, ye must be tired now. We're almost in Corlear's. Are you alright, Father?"

"Let's get on with our business, son. I'll be fine."

Father Driscoll leaned back and relaxed into the seat, looking out the window to see a young woman waving frantically at them. Her mouth was wide open, but there was no sound. Leary yelled for the horses to halt, jumped out of the carriage, and fell to his knees.

"Mary! Mary!" he cried, crawling to the woman who had also fallen to her knees on the street. *It had to be this Mary who worked at the shop, Norah McCabe's friend,* Father Driscoll thought.

The horses snorted and pawed the ground. The few people on the street quickly walked away from the scene and the priest slowly climbed out of the carriage, hesitant to confront another new situation that was full of pain and emotion. He grabbed the reins of the horses and held them tightly in his hand along with his rosary. He was dirty, exhausted, and he could hardly stand up. All he could manage to do was stand with the horses. He and the horses were only there for support, that's all. Just support, and like the horses, he couldn't utter a word or offer any comfort. He watched the woman put her head down in the dirt as she sprawled on the street in front of Leary. His dear parishioner, Leary, was whimpering and stroking the woman's head over and over, repeating, "Did you kill our baby?"

When Father Driscoll registered the full meaning of what Leary was saying, he was anguished that yet another young woman had been desperate enough to put herself in the hands of Madam Restell and her murderous deeds. He had counseled only a very few of these women who had survived abortions, but mostly he had sat with families who had lost daughters to her instruments of torture and death. He watched the two young people in the pitiful and shameful aftermath of their sins and wanted to turn away, get in the carriage, and go to the Astor. Forget Norah McCabe, forget the whole sorry state of things, but as soon as he thought this, he knew he couldn't. It had been Norah McCabe who had brought him back to who he really was in God. He had to go through with this, no matter what befell him on the way.

Father Driscoll saw blood seeping out onto the dirt from underneath the woman. It was coming like a fast moving stream that couldn't be stopped. It came as quickly and as bright as the sun on the horizon. The woman's blood and the sun's rays were similar, he thought, for they had no choice in the natural flow of their creation.

Father Driscoll let go of the reins and walked near the two lovers, unable to speak or know what to do. Leary's head was down on top of the woman's mass of hair the very hue of the blood she shed; they both wept, but she was barely moving.

"Leary..." he whispered, his voice barely audible to his own ears. He walked closer and was going to speak again, but hesitated when he saw how strange it was that the woman's blood was circling them as they lay on the street. He clutched his rosary beads and swung them above the couple lying on the street in the pool of the woman's blood.

"Help!" he shouted, his voice returning and booming out into the early morning.

Crows responded, slapping the cool morning air with shrill calls as if to wake up the neighborhood to the doom below them. He looked around to see if there was anyone who could help, but everyone who had been on the streets had finally gone to bed. He watched Leary lift his head and stare incredulously at the blood that was seeping into the earth. The priest's heart was pounding as he watched him shake the woman who had gone limp. When Leary jumped to his feet, Father Driscoll reached out for him and his rosary fell onto the blood-soaked ground. Leary wept and screamed, circling the priest like a wounded animal.

"She's dying! My God, Mary is dying!"

Father Driscoll wanted to retrieve his rosary, but just then two policemen walked onto the street and were soon standing over the young woman, checking her pulse, and telling Leary to calm down and tell them what happened. And when the priest heard the brassy notes of the policeman's voice pronounce that the woman was dead, he walked away, leaving his rosary, Leary, and the woman on the street. There was nothing more he could do, but conduct a funeral later.

He walked numbly in a befuddled daze down the street away from death and grief that had occurred as rapidly as gunfire in a battle. One of the policemen followed and asked him specific questions about what had happened. Father Driscoll spoke plainly, "Mr. Leary's girlfriend had an abortion and bled to death."

The priest had a reputation for compassion and empathy, and shame overcame him momentarily before he continued down the street. He had to set his face toward saving Norah McCabe and the only way to do so was to be resolute and leave behind his suffering friend. After walking a few minutes, he felt the light from on high compel him to keep going, and he felt like the angel sent by God to warn Sodom and Gomorrah of the destruction to follow. Norah McCabe had to be guided out of danger and the judgment of God that would come upon her if she stayed in the house of prostitution. Destruction would eventually come to the madam's business and bring her down, too, and perhaps he could save her. She could become his Lot who reluctantly left Sodom.

He walked quickly, but soon was out of breath, panting and feeling he might collapse. He hadn't given a thought about his lack of sleep and food for nearly two days now. He was sixty years old with gout and rheumatism, and the reality of this nearly struck him down. *No,* he thought. *I can't listen to what my body is telling me! Only what God is telling me.* "Please, Holy Spirit, imbue me with strength to carry out the Father's will," he uttered as he walked at a much slower pace, clenching and unclenching his hand, missing his rosary beads.

Norah McCabe had escaped the bordello like a doe elusively bounding through a field away from a hunter. She was being lifted by something other than her own legs, legs that were especially weak from lying unconscious for nearly two days. She looked up in the sky to try and ascertain the hour, but was confused. The sky's black-and-blue palette, studded with stars, had lightened and there were finger-like streaks of an azure hue that seemed to reach out to her as she found a patch of dew drenched grass to sit on when fatigue overtook her. She was very cold, but was relieved she had grabbed her dress and shawl before leaving. She had been nearly naked when she ran into an alley to dress herself after she had fled. She closed her eyes and breathed rhythmically and deeply to try and gather the pieces of her life back together. She touched the back of her head and it was so tender, she gasped and wondered how she must look to anyone walking by. But was anyone walking by?

A shadow fell over her when a large hand covered her face. It was the worst time of the day for crime—four in the morning—when even the most vile of criminals had to finally sleep, but the smartest ones knew it to be the best time to operate. Norah was eerily silent when the large soap-scented hand covered not just her mouth, but her nose and eyes. She was being attacked again and would she be raped? The irony of being raped again, if she had already been raped, filled her with odd feelings. What more could she lose? Her life? And how many times would her life be lost and be given back? If this was the last time and she would be dead like her sister, Kate, and her friend, Sean, wouldn't it be a relief to finally be free?

And then she knew she wanted to live! She became enraged and kicked and screamed as a bag was placed over her head and she was dragged onto a wagon whose horses clipped clopped down the early morning street, adding rhythm to Norah's stifled cries and pleas. No one heard and if they did, they didn't care.

The madam was stunned by the ferocity of the attack. The long, red scratch on her cheek reminded her of the stray cat she had taken in one time. She had given it food and water and when she went to pet it, it had given her a nasty scratch. Norah McCabe was of no concern of hers now.

The commissioner's hand had been shaking violently when he had taken the wad of bills in exchange for the girl he had brought to her unconscious and bleeding. He said the stupid Irish girl had been calling out to men on the street offering herself up for ten dollars. Another man had been interested in the girl the same time he came upon her and then clobbered her over the head when she chose to go with the commissioner. The madam never asked too many questions, especially if a young and potentially sensuous woman was brought to her. She could tell the girl was a virgin just by looking at her. Her virgins cost twenty-five dollars! The commissioner was a lowly son of a bitch, having fallen from his throne in city politics and she figured he wasn't really telling the truth, but if the girl woke up and wanted to stay in her surroundings, so what if he had lied? A poor street girl waking up in a lavish room would more than likely want to stay. But the little slut had spurned her and attacked her! And now she had to get treatment for the scratch.

Some of her girls had heard the commotion and came running after the girl fled. They had been genuinely concerned for her safety and wanted to help. There had never been a violent incident in her bordello. Never! She had conducted her business with finesse and class, and then this little Irish bitch had sullied not just her, but her reputation. She might even end up with a scar on her face!

One of her girls went for a nurse in the neighborhood who'd care for her wound and didn't require her to fill out a report, a report that could ultimately end up at the police station. After the incident and first-aid treatment, she sat in the parlour with a bandage on her face, sipping whiskey and lemon. She hadn't slept a wink and was just beginning to drift into slumber when there was a loud knock on her door. *The police! No, it couldn't be, she surmised. They left her alone unless there was a raid. Customers?* All customers had to be out by two in the morning. It was nearly five in the morning and there wouldn't be any new customers now. Her sign read: "Exquisite Rooms for Rent. Inquiries Can Be Made After Twelve Noon." *Who could it be?*

She set her drink on the large glass-topped table with carved lion claws on its pedestal, thinking of the claw mark on her own skin. Should she answer it? It could be a gang member or even a gang of boys who had been raising hell and drinking all night. Her friend and bodyguard was asleep in the back room, but did she have time to go for him? She got up and peered out the window, and to her astonishment, there was Father Driscoll standing on the steps, ghostly pale, especially in contrast to his black robe. The gaslight hadn't been extinguished and the glow from the light put a halo around his head. The madam smiled at him and relief spread through her, for she would be fine now. Her priest would console and bless her.

"Father, what are you doing here at this hour?" she asked, opening the door.

"May I come in?" Father Driscoll nervously looked around.

"Of course…always you are invited."

The priest walked in and she quickly shut and locked the door behind him. They went into the parlour and a couple of the girls came in to ask how she was feeling, but saw the priest and quickly left the room. The madam had wanted to ask them to make tea, as if this was a pleasant visit. She sat down on the sofa, fluffed the pillows, and then tapped the place next to her to indicate to Father Driscoll to sit down. He was shaking and grabbed the back of the sofa to stabilize himself.

"I need to see Norah McCabe right away. A friend of hers—"

"Father, she attacked me and fled my home." The madam wondered why he hadn't asked about her wound.

"Where did she go? Do you know?" He sat down next to her, put his head back on the pillow, and sighed. Then he sat up straight. Empathy and affection for her priest rose within the madam and she desired to console him, but the only way she knew how to do so was by touch; and she knew better than to touch the priest.

"Her friend just died from an abortion. I should have stayed to comfort him, Leary...the father...but I have to help Norah McCabe. I promised I'd return for her. And now you tell me she's gone?"

"The wench is gone... and I paid—," she abruptly stopped herself from finishing her sentence.

"You *paid* for her?" The priest looked at her sorrowfully.

"She was brought to me by the old commissioner. She had been hit on the head and I was letting her rest. I cleaned her up and she slept in my room. When she came to, she fought me like a wild animal and did this to my face," the madam said as she touched the bandage.

"I met Norah McCabe awhile ago and there was much agony in my soul over her. I sensed that she was headed for trouble." The priest clutched his chest and sat back again. "My prophetic gift returned to me when I met her."

"Prophetic gift, indeed! Anyone could prophesize that young women are headed down the road of destruction in this city! Few young women don't head down that road, Father!"

The priest stood up and nearly lost his balance, reaching for the side of the couch to steady himself.

"My church...my church was attacked tonight. Or yesterday. I don't even know the time of day or if tomorrow ever came." He placed his hands together and closed his eyes, as if in prayer.

"Father, you have nowhere to lay your head...just like Jesus. He was ministered to by a woman. He was ministered to by a prostitute, Father. Please..." The madam stood up and put her arm around the priest. "Please let me minister to you likewise. You may sleep in my own private room."

The priest didn't pull away from her, but looked into her face solemnly.

"No, Father…I haven't…I do not…I do not take customers there. I do not take customers myself. It perhaps isn't as holy a place as where you sleep, but it is clean and restful. Come with me, Father."

Father Driscoll surrendered to the madam's touch and allowed her to lead him down the hallway and up the stairs to her private quarters. The two girls who had seen him come into the bordello opened their doors to sneak a look as the madam led the priest up the stairs. They glanced at one another in astonishment, snickered, and closed their doors.

Chapter Twenty-One

The faithful carriage horses clipped noisily down the near empty streets with perfect rhythmic steps carrying Mam and Meg to *A Bee in Your Bonnet*. Both women were weary and infuriated at Norah for this disruption in their already harsh lives where sleep was oftentimes their only comfort. As the carriage came near the dark store, they were confident that Norah and Mary would be sleeping inside on cots, as they often did after working a long day into the evening. However, when they saw the door left ajar, they quickly climbed out of the carriage and rushed inside. Mam walked in first and frantic thoughts enveloped her that she might just find her daughter injured or dead. It happened all the time in Five Points and why should she be spared losing someone in this violent city? She fumbled and groped in the dark until she found a candle that she lit and carried with both hands, walking slowly to the table near the front window. She bumped into a clothing rack that toppled to the floor, the sound of crinoline and velvet landing softly next to her. Perhaps her daughter's dreams were collapsing, too, because they were too large and heavy for a young woman living in Five Points. Oh, where was her Norah!

Soon after, a policeman walked in ready to handcuff and haul them to jail. He had already written up the report about the girl who had bled to death, the girl who had worked at this little store. The officer had a few more hours to complete his beat and thought it best to check the place out. He was surprised to find the two women, but soon learned they were looking for Norah McCabe, owner of the shop. His beat never ended that night because the Irish policeman accompanied the women around Five Points to look for the young woman who was not to be found. The mother was not to be comforted, and he took her and her daughter back to the mother's apartment where her husband was lying ill. He thought Norah McCabe's father looked like he might be on his last legs and when the officer volunteered to go for a doctor, the ill man ranted in both Irish and English that they would all be late for the ship. The policeman left. What was there for him to do? He would make a report about the missing woman, this Norah McCabe, but he couldn't force a doctor on the father. He left their apartment with the mother quietly weeping, the daughter trying to comfort her, and the father yelling about getting a dresser on a ship before it departed. Ireland wasn't that far away from these people, the policeman darkly considered; never far were the sorrows of that land from them all.

Ivan thought about tying up Murray before he left, but didn't do it. He had never been a criminal, by God. Maybe he had become one since coming to America, but he wasn't a criminal in the old country and the only reason he had been involved in questionable activity here was to keep his Mammy alive. He didn't even know anymore if he wanted to keep himself alive, but to be sure, he wanted his Mammy to stay alive in America. Every time he was certain he would lie down in an alley and welcome a gang of boys to put an end to his life, he thought about his Mammy and how he wanted her to live long enough to dress in some fancy clothes and have lunch at the Astor, maybe go for a carriage ride and have an evening at Barnum's. He also wanted to live frivolously just once and be free from worry over the next meal. His mother was probably sitting in their one-room apartment right now worrying about him and wondering why he wasn't home. She would have already finished stitching up people's clothing for the day, and would be covered in black dye. He joked with her that she was nearly black now, like one of the Negroes in Five Points dancing for eels on the docks. He wasn't sure if her skin could be completely washed clean of the black dye. It had been too long that she had been up to her neck in sewing men's pants and changing the color of her skin.

So he rifled through Murray's pockets, the thought crossing his mind that maybe his Mam had sewn the very pants he was now stealing from. He found a wad of bills, but it was a pittance for all his trouble. Murray moaned, his eyes still closed, and Ivan was worried he would come to before he found anything substantial. He went into the bedroom and thought he saw a shadow pass by the window. He ducked and jumped, doing some kind of nervous dance as if he was outside his own body. He liked the feeling—being outside of his own body. He went to the window, daring himself to face the next challenge, but it was only the wind moving the branches of a tree. A tree! The man had a tree next to his house. Ivan had forgotten about trees since leaving Ireland. Hadn't he even eaten the leaves off a bitter-tasting tree before he left? He had been that hungry! Was he that hungry now? His thoughts were going to get him in trouble yet…he didn't have time to indulge in them as he was wont to do. He turned from the window, scanned the room, and hurried to a dresser, pulling open drawers. Nothing but clothing. The man had so much clothing! Should he take some of his clothing and sell it on the streets? No, he needed cash. He didn't want to prance about the streets like an old-clothes man selling duds. Then Ivan caught sight of something wrapped up in newspaper sticking out of the corner of the bed beneath the mattress. He pulled it out and tucked it inside his coat pocket, intuition telling him that he had found something important. He ran from the bedroom into the living room and before he opened the front door to leave, he looked at Murray who had sat up dazed. Their eyes met and a puzzling understanding passed between them.

Come back!" Murray's words came out in a croak. He stood to his feet, held on to a chair, and the room swirled around him. He was too weak to chase after Ivan and as much as he knew he should hate the man, he respected him for the survival skills that were animal-like, the skills he himself did not possess. The desperate Irishman had now taken from him what he had worked for most of his life, but he felt strangely relieved. He didn't have time to sort out his feelings because within minutes there was a loud knock on his door. Mitchel opened the door and walked in. He wasn't alone. He was never alone because he was too important to be alone. He always had an entourage of men willing to do his high minded bidding, even if it broke all laws. He once told Murray that he felt he had a higher calling, a calling for his country, and that this was God's calling. Murray admired Mitchel for his eloquent speech, his writing, and his passion for his country, but he thought the man would have gathered much more support for Ireland if only he hadn't started putting in his two cents about the abolitionist movement. Mitchel had glibly declared that if every white man had a plantation with working slaves, it would be a great world. Whether or not Mitchel really believed this, it had been printed in the papers! Murray had helped Mitchel raise more money than any other secret society had ever done and now it was time to leave, and along with Norah, his new protégé who was ripe for the movement, they were ready to go. Only now he realized he shouldn't have allowed himself to love the girl. He had gone slowly in courting her, sensing her fear, her tenderness, and a ferocious desire to transcend the lowly life of most women in Five Points.

"The ship's ready to leave. Where's the money? Where's the girl? What happened?" Mitchel's questions spilled out into the quiet room and he ignored Murray's injury.

"Did you see the skin ball running down the street with the money? Did you see the man? Ivan's his god damn name! He's run off with the money. I don't have it!"

Mitchel and his men left Murray and ran down the street to find Ivan. Murray felt a small lump on the back of his head. He sat down on the couch and was in no hurry to do anything. What would Mitchel do to him if Ivan couldn't be found with the money? And what happened to Norah? Did the priest find her and take her home? Father Driscoll would make sure she was safe until Murray could get to her. The money didn't matter as much as she did. He had other money saved and he would use it to get them both to England and then to Ireland. They would start over somewhere, regardless of what happened. They would start their own damn movement, but would he be able to convince her to board the ship tonight?

"Oh God!" he cried, "Norah!"

He cleaned himself up and retrieved the luggage they had packed together. He walked by the photo of his father and mother and nodded his head to them. They were dead. He was alive and he had to let go of their dreams and live his own, whether or not that included freeing Ireland.

When Murray saw Norah sitting on the wet grass with her eyes closed, he was more concerned that she would not willingly board the ship to go to England than whether she was hurt. It was apparent that she had been in some other world besides the thrilling world of freeing Ireland that he had brought her to over the last few months. Throughout their relationship, Murray had appealed to her desire to live beyond her Irish peasantry, Five Points, poverty, and shame, and had found her at a time in her life when she had already taken steps to do this—extraordinary steps for a young Irish woman. He believed that Harrigan was just using her as his personal secretary, a messenger girl, and he probably wouldn't ever allow her to use a by-line, no matter how big his talk was. Murray had to get her away from him before the man groomed her to be satisfied with the crumbs from his table. Norah McCabe had guts and talent, and although physical attraction was never the driving force in his life as in other men, he was wholly enticed by her spirit and her charms. He looked at her now and realized he had indeed grown to love her - with a steady and easy-going love. And he felt a painful ardor new to him. Passion in his past had been for the movement, the same rebel blood flowing in his father flowed through his own, and there had never been any left over for a woman. His mother had been his father's friend and support, the bearer of his child to continue on the cause, but not someone his father had passion for. He shuddered in the cold and from the pain in his head, but also because of the alarming awareness that he was altering the course of familial blood in order to have Norah in his life.

Before he approached her, Murray saw a crumpled burlap bag sitting next to a grocer's. A bag that had once held potatoes brought in from some farm in upstate. Potatoes! The irony of using a bag that once held spuds did not escape him. He put the bag over Norah's head and at first she was still; there was no struggle in her, but soon she was fighting him. If he got her to Finn's, he could send Thomas to the ship to tell Mitchel to wait for them.

The driver of the carriage had been paid well and instructed to keep quiet about whatever he might see. He was nervous about his involvement until Murray pulled the bag off Norah's head and he watched the couple embrace.

"My God, it's you! Murray!"

"We have to hurry, Norah. The ship is at the docks and we can't miss it."

"Now? It's time to go already?"

"It's now."

"What about our clothing?"

"Everything's ready to go."

"Why did you leave me at Finn's?"

"I was only gone a short time…"

"The commissioner…he…"

"The madam kept you safe."

"The commissioner—"

"He didn't, Norah."

Murray lied, more to himself than to Norah. He was convinced he could love her back to herself and her innocence.

"How do you know?" she asked mournfully.

"Please trust me. I've come for you. I love you…and nothing can destroy it. Please, Norah."

"Da…he's been sick. I can't leave him." Murray heard hysteria in her voice. He knew she possessed strong feelings for her father.

"We'll write. And we'll be returning soon. But we have to leave now!"

Norah wrapped her arms around his waist, "Let's go, then." They made it to Finn's around six in the morning when vendors were preparing for the market.

Chapter Twenty-Two

Norah was a dreamer. She dreamed nearly every night and was able to recall vivid details. A recurrence of one dream was about floating in, not on, the ocean. She would become fish-like and breathe in the water as if it was air; she was at peace and natural in the water of her dreams. She had never bathed in the sea and had only touched the water at the shore with her feet, and so the sea was ever a mystery to her. In these dreams, there were silver streaks of light swirling with indigo that swam past her as she hovered effortlessly in the water. She never knew if these iridescent beings were fish or not, but she assumed they were and that they and her were of the same ilk and of the same purpose. These were the comforting dreams, but over the last few days she had dreamed of falling into the sea. Hands would reach for her and when she would go underneath the surface of the sea, she would wake, gasping for breath. But mostly her dreams about the sea were restful because she was cradled and rocked gently; these dreams never hinted that this same comforting sea could also turn into a sea dragon that tried to devour her. Coincidentally, her memory of coming to America and sitting on the shore as if she had been spit out like Jonah from the whale was never equated with the frightening dreams or the sea lover dreams. Norah ignored the bad dreams, for they hadn't come but twice.

Norah agreed to go with Murray to England and to Ireland, and to finally return to New York. They planned on doing all of this in a few months. She would only be in Ireland for a short time, but it would be enough to savor her homeland again. Most wonderful was that she would be traveling as a woman of some means. These thoughts rose ambitiously in her mind, but she didn't share them with Murray. Nor had she told Murray about the nightmare of falling into the sea because when she and Murray came together on deck, memory of the terrifying dream dissipated in the excitement of her adventure and romance. She wanted to tell Murray about the dream, but didn't know how. She would begin to tell him, but then stop because all she wanted to do was kiss him. Small wings of joy and pleasure would flutter delicately within her abdomen, especially when Murray lightly touched her lips over and over again. She could do this forever, but whenever he pressed his lips over her mouth and thrust his tongue down her throat, she pulled back, horrified by the incongruity of his gentle touched kisses and this kind of ardent devouring. She made it clear to him that she only wanted the soft and tender kisses and not the other ones. He had laughed at her, and in the back of her mind there was worry that if they married he would press himself into her so hard that she would have his imprint on her and no longer be herself. An adhesion of his soul upon hers through her flesh! She wanted her own soul intact and not joined with anyone else's. Although she thought of these things quite logically she was at a loss how to convey them in words, especially to this man, the first man she had ever kissed and loved. Well, she had loved once before, but it certainly hadn't been this kind of love. It had been a mere childhood love without the touch of flesh inside flesh, this kind of exploring she and Murray were doing with their mouths.

Exhilarating feelings filled her in spite of the haranguing fear that lingered from the dreams. Here she was, Norah McCabe, now a passenger on a palatial ship! No sleeping in the hold as before! When kissing Murray in the spray of sea water, she learned about the re-arranging of her insides that happens in love. This love for Murray had grown and her love for Ireland had grown, too. Sometimes, however, she wondered if these loves were inextricably bound together in an unnatural way. The picture of Ireland in her mind had moved beyond the Hunger years as she imagined the family cottage extending itself into something larger than what it had been; like one of the big houses that dotted the land where she had come from. She wasn't unlike many young women who wanted a grandiose and enchanting life, but most of the Irish women who dared to envision and hope for one never looked back over the ocean they had once crossed. And most Irish women didn't travel with a group of rebels across that sea to defend their native land.

"The sea confuses me," Norah said, facing away from Murray as they stood together one evening on the deck.

He was confused, too, about her erratic emotional behavior of late. He watched her intensely as she stared at the moon-shined pewter sea as if it contained an answer. Her arms stretched out and tightly gripped the railing, her elegant head was held high. She continued to speak, but she wasn't really addressing him.

"I was separated from my family when I was last on a ship. A ship alright, but not like this one, but it was a ship all the same." He saw that her thin arms slightly quivered.

"I was so weak and hungry and my friend…my friend, Maggie… Did I tell you about Maggie?" She didn't give him time to answer, but continued on.

"One night, we were marveling at the silver stars that were creating patterns in the sky. And then fish began jumping out of the water like they wanted to entertain us with a dance. Fish! The fish leapt out of the water and their scales were shining and glistening as if the stars had fallen on them. At first we couldn't believe it! There were so many and they kept leaping and diving. My childish mind thought they might be mermaids. Mermaids! Can you imagine, Murray?"

He didn't answer and she didn't turn towards him. The sea was her companion now, he thought sadly.

"We ran out of food. And some of it was my fault. Did I ever tell you why?"

"No, my love, you never told me any of this."

"But that night we caught the starry fish and they tasted sweet and salty, but mostly sweet. Sweet cod and dogfish. To me and Maggie, they were sent from heaven! We were so hungry and they came to feed us. And now here I am again. But this time, I'm not hungry. I'm nearly too full of fine food that I never thought I'd be eating."

She didn't say anything for a few minutes and he was glad she was happy with the food, for maybe she would be happy with him on this journey.

"Some dreams have come true."

She released her hands from the railing and leaned her delicate but surprisingly strong body against him. He cautiously and gently put one arm around her waist. He knew she had never wanted to love like this. They both had this in common and had laughed over it together.

"But here I am again separated from my family," she turned and hid her face against his chest to stifle a cry.

"Please don't think me childish…"

Murray put both his arms around her and held her for a moment. Then he stroked her hair, his fingers becoming entangled in her curls. She didn't like wearing a hat or bonnet on deck, even a shawl when it was cold. She had proclaimed to him that she wished the sea air could touch every part of her. He found her on deck yesterday morning before breakfast, in the afternoon after lunch, and in the evening after dinner staring out at the sea without a coat or shawl. The cool temperatures didn't seem to matter to her. She would have her sleeves rolled up and her shoes and stockings off. She had been acting strangely and he saw an aspect of her personality that he had never noticed prior to this trip. Although jubilant, she cried easily and said she missed her da and mam. The day after their departure, she had wept hard and said she had made a terrible mistake and wanted to return to New York. Murray felt extremely protective of her, but he was also anxious over her odd behavior. The night before, she crept into his bed asking him to hold her. He was cautious in his affections because he didn't want his physical desire to become uncontrollable. When she curled up next to him, her backside pressing into his groin, he feared she would feel him harden.

"Norah, I've been thinking about us—"

"No, Murray. I don't want to go that way. I don't want to be in your bed." She moved away from him to look into his face.

He laughed. She was the one who had wandered into his room wanting to cuddle and kiss him.

"There's a minister on board...He's not a priest. A Protestant minister, but he can marry us. Wouldn't that be one way for a Catholic to get something out of a Protestant? He can marry us. I've already spoken to him about it—"

"Are you mad? Not in the Church! Without Da or Mam knowing? Without Mary at my side!" The sorrow in her eyes disappeared and she put her arms around him.

"I want you to be my wife, Norah. It probably sounds unromantic for me to say that I want you to be my wife. It's the same line that many men say. But how else can I say it?"

She laid her head against him again, but didn't respond. He waited a few moments before continuing.

"We'll take vows on the sea and it will certainly be romantic. It'll be different and unlike tradition. When we return to New York, we'll have a proper ceremony in the Church– "

He moved away to look at her because she wasn't saying anything. Then he kissed her full on the mouth, but she pulled away. He forgot. She didn't like him to kiss her too fervently. She looked at him anxiously.

"I've been having dreams. I've always dreamed a lot. Sometimes about the sea, but one of my dreams is terrifying."

"It's normal to be frightened on a ship," he said, relieved this was all that was bothering her.

"He continued, "Especially during a storm...and that's why you dream, my sweet. It's your fear showing up in your dreams. Believe me, I've been on a few ships in my life traveling with my father…I've been in terrible storms, but here I am now, all in one piece…And in love with you!"

Norah turned toward the sea again. She clutched the rails so hard that her knuckles turned white. He didn't want to force her to do this. There was perhaps too much at stake, but how else could they consummate this desire they both had? After a few moments, she turned to him and her eyes were the same hue as the sea.

"I know it's foolish of me to ask…I feel a wee bit selfish and embarrassed…," she said.

"What, Norah? What? You can ask me anything!" He grasped her hands and they were cold and shaking. A sea mist made her face glisten in the moonlight. She was so rare in her beauty…not a typical pretty face that he had seen plenty of on the streets of New York.

She looked down at her feet while he held her hands. "Do you have a ring?" she asked.

Murray tried to keep from laughing. That was all she was concerned about? He had not only put away cash for their trip, cash separate from the bank notes they had raised at meetings, but he had also taken his mother's wedding ring along with lace and other jewelry belonging to her. His mother had bequeathed it to him and wanted her son to marry someday. He was not concerned that Norah might be vain and desired the little money he possessed and a position as his wife more than she loved him. He knew her well enough to know that as much as she pursued the latest Parisian fashion, she was more in pursuit of something else, something higher and lofty.

"I will not only place a special ring on your finger, I will place other jewels on your neck and wrists…"

Norah stood on her toes and hugged him, burying her face in his neck. Her breath was warm and alluring. He held her and pressed his lips into her hair that smelled like lavender, the brackish sea, and her own earthy scent he had come to desire.

He laughed aloud and it lilted happily out to sea; he felt light-hearted for the first time on their journey.

"We'll marry and live lives of adventure." He was giddy like a schoolboy. Had he ever even felt like a schoolboy, he wondered.

"I know…I know it sounds contrived, doesn't it? Living lives of adventure! But we'll do it, Norah. We'll do it! Look at all we've been through already! We'll grow old together and keep each other warm on cold winter nights. And we'll begin our marriage being rocked to sleep in each other's arms by the sea herself, my Norah. The sea will cradle us and maybe the fish will come again and dance just for us!"

When Norah looked up at him, there was a strange mix of rapture and fear. Maybe even something akin to terror. He had seen something like this surface in her on the way to the ship after she had fled the bordello. And before, when they had first met and she talked about Ireland. He looked at the sea and it was still calm, but clouds covered half of the brilliant moon. Both dark and radiant, just like Norah.

Murray, Mitchel, and some of Mitchel's cohorts surreptitiously congregated at a table in the damp corner of the officer's mess. A bottle of rum sat as a centerpiece atop a yellowed linen table cloth. Men's foul breaths scented the air and made it thick, having nowhere to leave, as if their very spirits were caught and imprisoned there. It wasn't a place for new ideas or inspiration; merely a place for a secret meeting.

"Jack here…," Mitchel said, pointing to the boney-faced man with a weather-worn face. He was probably only thirty, but looked fifty.

"Jack heard the captain speaking to the ship's mate early this morning. He said that someone was going to be brought up to the mast." He looked fixedly into each of the men's faces to ascertain whether their soldiering allegiance was still intact.

"I haven't been able to read the captain well," Murray commented. Is he easy or hard?"

"He put a crew member in the lazarette for some slight grievance," one of the men said, shaking his head nervously.

"But there's no one quarantined with a contagion. Not likely the man suffered much for his crime, being able to lie down for a spell."

"No food or water, I heard."

"Not much difference between him and us, then…," Jack said

laughing, causing the rest of the men to laugh, too.

"Thought we'd have us a bit of fancy dining on this grand ship, not hard tack dressed up in cream sauces and herbs."

"We're going to England for Christ's sake…English citizens on board. You'd think they'd want to impress the mother country—"

"Listen up," Mitchel interrupted, "we haven't got time to sit here complaining. It's time to firm up our plans and we can't stay down here much longer or we'll be suspect…especially if this captain is as rotten as they're saying."

The men put their drinks down and leaned into the table to listen. Their Mitchel was an impressive man, having made an escape from a Tasmanian prison to America. Most banished Irish criminals would have stayed tucked away in upstate New York, done some farming, but not John Mitchel. His courage and loyalty to Ireland was remarkable. His speeches and writing were eloquent, convincing, and revolutionary, but it was Ireland he was trying to save, not America, and his zeal was not fully appreciated in New York. One of his best men, a lawyer and orator, decided to hightail it to Canada and now Mitchel was ensconced with men who had nothing to lose, men he had met at the pubs who were either survivors of the Hunger or children of survivors. Most of his former men were learned men and except for Murray, his head man, the men he had now were merely survivor smart.

"Murray!" he turned to him sharply, "Your man, there, Ivan… where is he?"

"Hasn't eaten so well in years, even if it's only hard biscuits covered in sauce." The men laughed again. Murray thought of Norah and how both she and Ivan were thoroughly enjoying the food, without any complaints.

"Is he to be trusted?"

"His Mam is all he has left. Famine killed out his whole family in Ireland before they came to New York. And then they were starving on the streets and he became a runner and gopher just to stay alive. He's not a sicko, but his animal instincts are heightened and can be brutal, I'd say. You can get to Ivan through his Mammy. That's how it is when there's just one other person and yourself who have survived something. He handed over the money quickly, didn't he? And agreed to work with us because we set up his Mam." He smiled weakly. "No worry there, no worry over Ivan."

Mitchel sighed and ran his hand through his thick, graying hair. "What about the Irish girl?"

Murray squirmed in his chair, took a swig of rum, and stood up. "We're getting married."

The rest of the men, except for Mitchel, got up and pounded his back, wishing him well.

"Righto!" one of them said, laughing.

"You'd best not be beddin' her before we land, then, mate!" Jack said.

"I'll be bedding her on our honeymoon right here on this ship tomorrow," Murray said sheepishly.

"We won't be your straw boys…," Jack laughed.

"Murray, isn't this a bit rash, especially considering this insurgency…this war we're trying to navigate…," Mitchel asked.

"She's dedicated to the cause and to me—"

"She's young—"

"She's young, but she's old. She survived the Hunger."

Mitchel stood up and put out his hand to Murray who shook it excitedly.

"May you and Norah McCabe have a hearth to sit 'round about in a new Ireland, Ireland freed from the British murderers!"

"Here…Here!" the men chimed, shaking Murray's hand.

The approval and affirmation of the men Murray had come to know in the movement buoyed his decision to marry Norah. He had been most concerned about the response from Mitchel who believed that few women were capable of carrying on the mission that he had given his life to. The fervor and devotion for a grandiose cause didn't leave much room for anything else in a man's heart, but not so for Murray. There was a concentration of something more potent that needed to be given. And this was now distilled into an elixir just for Norah.

Norah didn't like Ivan no matter how hard Murray tried to convince her that Ivan was a changed man. On the evening they boarded the ship, Mitchel and his crew sat down to dinner in the dining hall. Norah quickly finished her dinner and left, for she did not relish being in the presence of the snake-like creature, Ivan. Murray found her later on the deck looking out to sea and singing a song. He had pleaded with her to accept Ivan into their band of dedicated revolutionaries.

"Sure, he's changed. Don't we all change for the better when coins are placed in our hands," she said.

"He knows to keep his distance from you, love, but he's a part of our mission. And it'd be best for all if you keep peace with the man."

"He stole me and then he stole from you. He took the movement's money and then you reward him with money to feed his mother to bribe him to be a part of our movement. I thought Mitchel was more selective."

"Trust me, Norah, Ivan has a heart bigger than all of Ireland."

Norah made sure to sit at the end of the dining room table away from Ivan when the group met together for dinner in the evenings. Once she caught him staring at her and she became livid and uneasy. He smiled at her and she set a severe gaze upon him, letting him know that he shouldn't expect forgiveness even if he was part of their group.

One evening, Norah, Murray, and the group were quiet while they ate, talking low and whispering to one another. There was a violinist seated in a corner to entertain the diners to help them forget they were floating on a large wooden ship far out in the sea. When the sea was moody and seemed to want to fling them away as if she herself was a body trying to get something off of her skin, they could hardly pretend they were in some posh restaurant in New York. The enormous gleaming chandelier dangled overhead and clinked in rhythm to the empty crystal goblets that struck each other lightly as they sat on the sideboard. Nothing on the ship was sealed from the wind, and the candles flickered wildly and eventually would go out. Candelabras skated across tables to be apprehended by someone before they caught the dining room on fire.

Norah delighted in the strength of the wind and since agreeing to marry Murray, she had made peace with the nightmares and was sleeping soundly. She would stride throughout the steamer with her head held high, feeling like a full-fledged woman. She reveled in promenading on the deck and going to dinner in her expensive duds she had packed for the trip. She was savoring every moment of her plans to become Murray's wife. There was a mighty rhythm to life, as heard in music, she told herself, and she had finally entered into it. The ship had rhythm as it rocked on the waves, the stars as they flickered, her skirts when they swished, the violin when played, and even Murray's kisses had a cadence to them. Everything became nearly perfect in her present world, and that was all she wanted right now—the present moments. And no matter how much the men complained of the food not being as fine as it should be, it tasted heavenly to her.

This evening, Norah wore a pink and gold silk dupion gown with pearl-edged sleeves while dining. After dinner, she lounged in the saloon with Murray and some of the men. Prior to her marriage plans she had merely tolerated the men, acutely aware they questioned her loyalty to their mission. But now she eagerly wanted them to accept her dedication because of Murray. And she was not disappointed, for after Murray informed them he and Norah were to be married, they congratulated her and tended to her needs during their dining hour. Norah would not allow herself to consider the decision to marry Murray rash, for then everything she had lived through up to this point might come tumbling down in her mind. Before Murray proposed, she had been breathlessly in love one moment and then feeling breathlessly suffocated the next.

"Women weren't made to be free," her mam had told her once. "No woman was meant for it; God made them to want to be dependent on their fathers and husbands." But her da always treated her as if she could be independent, and since coming to America, she believed that even if she couldn't have everything she desired, she could have independence. The women of the suffrage movement believed women should have important rights and many times Norah had been curious about their meetings, but Mary said they weren't meetings for Catholic girls. And now here she was about to lose her independence in marriage! Murray sensed she might be worried over losing her freedom and stated she could be as free as she desired, but that she must always be dependent upon his love. She was still quite young, but she knew better. She wouldn't really be independent if she married Murray or anyone.

Her body changed, too, after saying yes to marriage, and that evening she allowed Murray to kiss her and put his tongue inside of her mouth as long as he was gentle. She also let him kiss her neck and near her bosom. She had never known such sensations existed and the hunger for him to be physically near her was overwhelming. Whatever might have happened with the commissioner seemed to be erased from her memory, but this night she became powerfully aroused and thought Murray's fingers were inside her clothing. She pulled away from him and quickly said goodnight, going to her room and drinking some sherry before falling asleep. And the next day when Murray kissed her, she pictured Da sitting at the kitchen table for one of their many late night conversations. When this vision erupted on the day before they were to be wed, she felt Da was pleading with her to return home. It nearly tore her heart out, but because she was enraptured and in love with Murray, this feeling was short-lived. She had already written two letters to Da and was eager to send them once they arrived in Liverpool. She was confident he would eventually understand why she had become involved in the movement. In a letter, she stated that although they had raised money to purchase weapons, she and Murray wouldn't become soldiers themselves. He would have to be proud. John Mitchel was revered by the Irish, even amongst those like Da who didn't believe in taking up arms. She wasn't certain how he would feel about Murray, however. They had never discussed her involvement with a young man. Thinking about Da, she had pulled away from Murray and talked about the kind of wedding they would have after returning to New York. She said she wanted three weddings. One would be their upcoming wedding on the ship, merely a ceremony; one in Ireland with her cousins; but the grandest of all would be in New York. She wanted it all and Murray seemed to be obliging. Three wedding celebrations!

Norah was basking in the entire luxury liner journey, the ambiance far exceeding anything she had experienced. There were rose, satin, and olive woods throughout the ship, thick exotic carpets, marble-topped tables, and richly upholstered chairs and sofas. There was a smoking room for male passengers at the end of the ship that separated them from the non-smoking passengers. There were musicians who were hired to play for their dining in opulent surroundings. Her life had surely taken a course she only had read about in novels.

There were no sweet smelling flowers in Norah McCabe's hair when she was wed to Thomas D. Murray on the grand steamer, the *Diana*. She asked the staff if she could have some flowers for her hair, but they retorted that the few flowers on board were solely for the dining room. Norah experienced some embarrassment, but immediately went to her room and pulled a blouse out of her trunk. The collar was embroidered with yellow and pink flowers that she cut out and sewed into a long strip to tie into her hair. Of course she didn't have a real wedding gown, but Murray promised he would purchase one in London, not Liverpool, but in London, for the other ceremonies.

Norah didn't need a traditional wedding gown, for she was stunning in the red taffeta gown that had been fashioned for an Austrian Countess who attended a ball at the Astor. According to the newspapers, the Countess never wore the same gown twice and had generously donated it to charity. Norah was first in line at the mission to purchase it with money she had made from the sale of five gowns. She had fallen in love with the plush gown. Red. Passionate. Forbidden. Mary had drooled over it and begged her for it, but Norah was certain it was meant for her to wear someday. The dress had been packed for the journey, but she never imagined it would be worn for her wedding. No one on the ship knew she was getting married, but "the boys," and, of course, the pretentious minister with the pointy nose. Murray and the boys would not be audacious to comment on her choice for a wedding gown, but she saw the minister's face harden against her before he began to officiate. His stiff demeanor and lack of warmth didn't bother her one bit and in an odd way, she was glad for it. It suited her. He was paid handsomely for the task, but she knew he resented it.

The fish didn't jump and entertain them on their wedding night, but Norah declared that God had decorated the sky just for them. It was a clear and serene evening, for the water was placid, the winds quiet, and Norah saw this as a blessing from God. It was the first time on their journey that the sea was this calm. But as staid the sea was, the heavens were the opposite in a luminous show. After their vows, Norah looked up into the sky studded with sparkling, radiant silver-like jewels. They flared, winked, and some fell gracefully from their position in the sky.

"Let's stand in the moonlight, Murray!" she declared, giggling and positioning him next to her so they could stand in the pathway of the moon's glow. It was a novel way to marry! Who else had ever married like this? On a ship with a bunch of Irish rebels and wearing a flamboyant red gown! She felt sensationally unleashed from her painful past, and no longer was she just Norah McCabe, daughter of her mam and da, a resident of Five Points. She was new. Boisterous laughter rolled out of her as she covered her mouth with the black lacquered oriental fan that had been found in a used-clothing shop, a perfect accessory for her dress.

God was with Norah and she would live long and prosperous, in love with a brilliant man, and together they would help free Ireland. She didn't use the word, "blessed," easily and didn't like it when others did. But tonight she felt it and she whispered it to Murray, "I'm blessed." Just before taking their vows, Murray told Norah to look quickly, for Ivan had lit candles around the deck. Starlight, moonlight, and candlelight harmonized in a celebration of their love.

Norah and Murray were quickly and uniquely wed, reciting vows with smiles that appeared permanently placed on their faces. It was only when Murray was hungrily removing the red gown that Norah felt the pang of an old fear come to visit her on her wedding night. She would have to learn how to exorcise it from her life, beginning on her wedding night. She thought it might have come because her wedding night was born of the Holy Spirit and the demons of hell were angry for this perfection. Little did she know that this fear would become as much a part of her life as what was about to befall her.

Chapter Twenty-Three

On their wedding night, the sea was reserved and still, as if its watery world was holding itself back, going within itself; contained and smooth surfaced; unspeaking. Its undulating measures recoiled, lowered its volume, and gave the new lovers a chance at rhythmic-like movement. The sea was tame and Norah became untamed as passion coursed through her, wave-like, and new wings of desire beat strong within her. Overall, she dissolved into oneness with Murray and oneness with herself.

One evening after an afternoon of knowing, they climbed to the deck from their lovemaking nest to breathe in more than themselves, to breathe in the sea air and remember they were a part of a much larger world than their own. Norah commented that the sky was not strewn with stars as it had been for their wedding night.

"Look, Murray, there are no stars tonight."

"They've all fallen on us," Murray said, laughing and pressing against her as she looked at the sea.

They silently wondered if it would last, this incomprehensible fusing of their love. Norah's doubts and her homesickness for Mam and Da disappeared within the sheets of their honeymooning. For Murray, the voices of his father and comrades faded from his mind.

"Sure now, I won't be needing another wedding, Murray. If I have another one like this, I'll die from the pleasure," she said shyly.

"We'll take a break before the next one, my love."

A sharp wind carrying raindrops suddenly swept across the deck and wrapped itself around them as if to whisk them away. The calm seas erupted into a furious dance while they embraced.

At breakfast that day, the captain had commented it was the first time he remembered the weather being so complacent, "neither here nor there," he said to Murray, laughing. The journey to England was usually calm, as compared to the return to New York, but it had never been this tranquil.

"I don't mind it, by God, but I don't trust it. It's ominous and out of character, I'd say. We'll see...we'll see," he said, laughing nervously. Murray and Norah had thought nothing of his comment and barely took it in, for they were only taking each other in. They couldn't wait to be alone again, eating little on their plates, only hungry for one another. But now the weather was no longer silent and the raindrops beat loudly upon the wooden deck. They released one another and were disappointed that the stars were blanketed with clouds and the rain coldly slapped against them. Murray and Norah hurried back down to their cabin, and because they were sore and tired from all their lovemaking, the luxury of sleep drugged them almost immediately.

The flippant remarks the captain made about the weather nagged him much later when he was in his quarters readying for sleep. His ship was not on a maiden voyage, but had been hailed as a queen of the sea and dubbed the most celebrated of the ships in the Smythe line. Run by the Trans-Atlantic U.S. Mail Steamship Company, the *Diana* had made many crossings. On one journey, she had thrashed across the North Atlantic in a record-breaking ten days, in spite of winter conditions and ice drifts. The captain reminded himself of these facts as he was undressing, but he felt uneasy. Putting his wool shirt back on and buckling his belt, he decided he would sleep in his clothing in case his Second Officer needed him. Plopping down on the bunk, he closed his eyes. He had been at the helm for too many hours which had turned into two days. Rather than falling into sleep, however, he went over the conditions of the weather, the state of the ship, and his crew. The weather was odd and although he should have been relieved there had been no stormy conditions, he was more familiar with Mother Nature doing freakish things. *Was this the calm before a storm?* He countered these thoughts with memories of manning ships in disastrous conditions since he was eighteen years of age. His advancing years must be causing him to worry. He had engineers, carpenters, firemen, and more men on this crew than he needed. Everything would be fine. Mulling over the passengers, he was puzzled about the group who dined together with the young woman who was pleasing to the eye. She had suddenly decided to marry the striking gentleman who stood out from the rest of the strange group with Irish accents. Not poor Irish peasants, these men. They had money to buy first-class tickets and thus far, they had been astute in behavior and above reproach, so he had no reason to question them. But he didn't trust them, although their names were recorded and none were on a list of wanted men.

The captain turned over on his side and thought of his wife. She wanted to travel with him this time, and had pleaded with him to take her. In thirty years of marriage, she had only been on two voyages. She always waited for him at home with the children, two whom died while he had been at sea. Now their children were grown and she wanted to go to Liverpool and on to London. She had relatives she hadn't seen in years, she insisted. He was adamant. No, he had said, it wasn't a good time. He had more passengers on this ship than he ever had and he also had an obligation to the U.S. Mail Steamship Company to try and break the ten hour record. He turned over again and the details of his ship crowded his mind. It was the finest ship in the Smythe line and was made to compete with the British-flag competitors. The *Diana* was nearly three thousand tons; a wooden paddle wheeler that required constant attention every time it docked. The engines kept the massive paddle wheels churning the waters, pushing it along at about three hundred miles a day. There was no reason to believe that in the days they had left at sea, anything out of the ordinary would happen. This consoled him, but he still couldn't sleep. He sat up and reached for the flask of whiskey that he kept by his bed. He took a swig and swallowed. It burned going down, but there was immediate relief. *Medicine for men,* he thought, proud of himself that he only used it on occasions like this when he couldn't sleep because he missed his wife's body or worried over his crew or financial problems. He took another swig and the ship rocked like a large cradle. The tension in his shoulders relaxed, for this was what he was used to when he captained ships—an active sea, not a silent sea, with rain and wind to journey through. To think that he couldn't rest on a still and quiet sea, but was only at home on a stormy one! He laughed and lay back down. Now he could sleep.

"Captain? Mr. Foley here, sir…Captain?" Chief Engineer John Foley called to the captain around five the next morning.

He knocked softly on his door, not wanting to anger the main man in charge. He was already in trouble because his estimation in coal consumption required for the journey had been slightly miscalculated. Although they would certainly make it to England, they would be required to purchase more for the return journey. The budget would be altered and not in their favor. He had ordered and bunkered two-thousand tons of coal for the round trip, which at sixty-five tons a day going at fourteen knots would have been adequate, leaving a margin for safety if weather altered and more fuel was burned during a rough return. But now there was something else quirky and worrisome. The ship's engines were not running smoothly and there were grinding noises. He didn't know what was wrong, but was reluctant to ask the captain for help.

Earlier in the evening, Chief Engineer Foley, like the others in the first class saloon, had been in good spirits downing top of the line whiskey and telling tales of sailing experiences that included port romances. They had been sailing for nearly four days without incidence and it looked like the journey would be easy. Foley had his eye on one of the daughters of a wealthy passenger, a millionaire, one of many of the usual assortment who could afford the first-class ticket. She was only twenty and ripe and pretty as a peach. He was thirty-three and was ready to settle down, this excursion being his last before he took a permanent post in an engineering firm that designed bridges in New York State. His new position would be a lot different than toiling with engines on the dangerous seas. Margaret Stevens was responding to his advances and her parents weren't turning him away, either. He wore a badge that said "Chief Engineer" and they were impressed, especially after learning of his new position in an engineering firm in New York. Foley waited a few moments before knocking on the captain's door again.

"Cap..tain…," his voice cracked. He called out much louder, "Captain!"

The door opened and the captain stood before him fully dressed, but disheveled, his eyes blood-shot and a week's growth on his chin. The captain had a serious case of rheumatism and the crew knew to let him rest when he needed it. Everyone had been instructed to not disturb him for eight solid hours. Foley was hesitant to tell him about the noise in the engines. He was already feeling disdain regarding the coal miscalculation and although this was his last hire on the *Diana*, he was worried about the ship's safety, as well as for the loss of his good reputation.

"It'd better be good, Foley…it'd better be good."

Captain Hammond's gruff response made Foley step back. Putting his hands in his pockets, Foley sighed heavily. "There's a problem with the engines, sir."

The captain straightened and tucked his shirt into his trousers, rubbed his chin and squinted at Foley. "Is there a real problem here, Foley?" He exhaled a raspy breath.

"The engines are running, but not as smoothly as they should be doing."

"We never take risks, Foley," the captain stepped closer to him and clasped his belt buckle with both hands. "You know that," he continued. "We don't take risks on ships with inferior structures or inferior maintenance. The only risk we take is going on the sea herself, and that, my son, is where it lies. We do everything humanly possible and then we are in the hands of the sea and the Almighty. But the risk of having faulty engines before departure is a human error and can't be blamed on the sea."

"Yes sir, but—"

"We will discuss your error in judgment after we look at the engines. Not now. Take your leave and inform Second Officer Barstow and Quartermaster Connolly that we are meeting to look at the engines."

Foley didn't move. He was relieved the captain was not exhibiting as much anger as he thought he might.

"It's a command, Foley. Go!"

Gale-force winds had blown the *Diana* off course and the captain, fearing the engines might die, wanted to get to land. Burdened and whale-like, the ship responded to the command of the captain and they turned due south towards the one hundred miles to Halifax. The captain decided they were in serious danger, and they had been blown in that direction anyway. Although putting into Halifax to buy coal was a common experience for ships on the North Atlantic for their return to New York, this was not a typical scenario. He was inordinately angry because he longed to beat the record for crossing and he had hoped that if he did, he might be offered prize money. This prize might be just hearsay talked about amongst his peers, but he didn't want to risk losing money that might be due him. He ran a tight ship and he was tight fisted with his bank account. Now it would be impossible to beat the record. He made a note to himself that when he was back in New York he would write up a complaint about Foley.

The winds swirled into action and whipped the ship from any former restful state; and in a few hours, a gale set in that produced mountainous waves. The captain and his crew were familiar with this kind of weather, but as time went on, this storm proved to be worse than usual. The gale force winds and the thick stormy sea slowed the *Diana* to seven to eight knots. The barometer was dropping and everyone knew this meant more bad weather. The captain stayed all day and into the night on the bridge. He refused to take a break, although every part of his body ached and he longed to rest. And then when the engines seized and stopped, they were at the mercy of the storm and wind. Around midnight, Quartermaster Connelly begged to take the helm from the captain, but Captain Hammond was reluctant to give up trying to steer the ship into Halifax. It was quite impossible, but he was determined and believed occasional miracles happened at sea. But the human body is also under command of exhaustion and if orders for rest aren't followed, there is a breakdown. Captain Hammond was breaking down and while his crew insisted he go to his bunk, he fell to the floor. He refused to go to his own bunk, but retired to a bunk in the chart room just twenty feet away from the bridge and the helm. His crew was instructed to assuage the fears of the passengers and keep them in their rooms, and to wake him as soon as they saw the Canadian coast. The crew was incredulous. Even if they saw the coast, how would they get there? But mercifully and surprisingly, the *Diana* appeared to be nearing the Canadian coast. The captain, unable to resist the rigors placed on his body, finally collapsed into a dreamless, but fitful, sleep.

The passengers had been informed of the change in the course, but not about the engines seizing. The storm was so noisy, the crew hoped they wouldn't notice the engines had stopped; and Second Officer Barstow assured them the change in course was not out of the ordinary. Large luxury liners like the *Diana* often take port in Halifax before continuing on to their destinations, he said, not indicating that it was on the return journey only. It was merely cautionary, he told them, and not only due to the inclement weather. They were mostly seasoned travelers, but they had to be concerned by this type of weather. Nevertheless, Barstow appealed to their desire for all to be right. The weather, he said, was harsh and uncomfortable, but not unmanageable. The passengers had already gotten their sea legs and it was true that most of them had traveled on luxury liners before and were used to some severe weather. None of them were too worried. They stayed in the saloon or smoking room and kept themselves sufficiently inebriated to ride out the rough seas, except for most of the women who kept close to the toilets and their beds. In fact, the whiskey and social interactions enlivened the men's feelings for a little adventure and so they trusted themselves entirely to the captain and to the famed reputation of the *Diana*.

No one questioned altering the ship's course except John Mitchel who had been convicted of treason, insurgency, and disloyalty to the Crown and had sailed on a ship from Ireland to an Australian island and then escaped to America years past. He knew ships and storms, and in his mind there was something precarious and uncanny in this change of course. He sensed the captain and crew were keeping important information from the passengers and he was going to damn sure find out. His escape from a Tasmania prison and sailing on fishing boats, packets, and tankers and anything that would float in order to get him to New York had refined his experience on the sea. He smelled danger and it wasn't just in the inclement weather. He should have listened to his instincts and heeded to his reservations about boarding the *Diana*. He had originally bought tickets for another ship in the Smythe line, one slightly less expensive and with less frills, but Murray insisted he had to save this girleen of his who had been kidnapped or some crazy cockamamie story. Mitchel nearly boarded without Murray, but decided he needed him way too much. Murray was an educated and reasonable man, and Mitchel had known Murray's father and respected him for his life long commitment to free Ireland from British rule. He had confidence in Murray to carry on this mission for he had already proven to be loyal and trustworthy. So Mitchel had cancelled the tickets for the less expensive liner and now they were dangerously sailing on the *Diana*. This grand dame of the Smythe line had glided easily through the North Atlantic with all sails set on her four masts when the weather was kind, but now was trudging along, as if on its knees and sorry to have dressed too elaborately in all its fineries. Before Mitchel pounded on the door of the chart room where he was told the captain was sleeping, he promised himself that he would always rely on his instincts in the future.

When the weather changed from balmy to stormy and Murray and Norah returned to their bunk, they slept undisturbed until late the next morning, ignorant of the foul state of affairs. Thoroughly refreshed when they were awakened by the thrashing of the ship in the storm, Murray left Norah in the cabin to go for tea and breakfast. When the ship swayed, it reminded her of the movement of their arduous lovemaking. Murray returned and told Norah he was surprised that the ship had to take port in Halifax before going to Liverpool. She didn't care, for wouldn't it be lovely, she said, to stay a little longer in this place cradled and rocked in their love? She was also relieved to not have to dress and go to the dining room or saloon. She had had enough of promenading in her Paris fashions, as well as having to dine with Ivan and the others. Murray had not taken notice of the panic rising amongst the ship's crew, for his head was still in the fog of sleep and he was eager to return to Norah. The two lovers laughed at one another when the ship pitched back and forth as they tried to eat. Later, they rolled themselves up in one blanket and slept again. Minutes later, a knock came on the door and Mitchel asked if he could enter their cabin. Norah was embarrassed and before she had time to object, Mitchel walked in and informed them he had reason to believe the Diana could be in danger of not making it to Halifax, let alone Liverpool.

"We're going to miss the meeting in Liverpool. We need the help of the others, god dammit."

"What can be done? We can't just hop on another ship to take us to Liverpool!"

Murray suddenly felt thrust back into the intricate world of his father and this mission.

"We need to devise a plan, an alternative plan…We need to make sure the money we've raised in New York doesn't dwindle…and if we don't get the men and arms we're depending on because we don't show up for this meeting, we'll need to take things in our own hands."

"What do you want me to do?" Murray asked.

"What I'm saying is…" Mitchel hesitated, glancing at Norah who was sitting in bed with the coverlet up to her neck.

"I know you're honeymooning, but we need to watch how much we drink and spend now…we've an account—"

"I have my own money, Mitchel. I never assumed you were putting us on the tab."

"You're my right hand man, Murray…of course you're on my account, as well as the others, but—"

"Rest easy, man. I'm comfortable with it," Murray said, getting out of bed. He leaned close to Mitchel and whispered, "What do you mean we might be in danger?"

"We float and wait for mercy. That's what we do. We wait for mercy. Just like I did getting myself to New York from hell's island."

After Mitchel left the cabin, Murray looked at Norah and saw the fear he had seen before. This time he knew what it was. It had been in his da's eyes and in all the Famine survivors' eyes he ever met. Maybe he unconsciously thought that by marrying Norah, he could eliminate it. He sat on the bed and held her. She felt different—fragile, like a small animal in his arms. As he stroked her hair and hummed a ditty in her ear, he remembered that his da had died with the haunted look in his eyes. It had never left him and Murray hadn't been able to do anything about it.

Chapter Twenty-Four

The great Artic Current that flows southward across the Arctic Sea until it reaches the North Atlantic, mingles with other waters whose descent from the heavens has gathered below. All waters never cease in movement and are unpredictable, at the will of wind and the subtle shifting of the planet. Meeting up with the Gulf Stream, the Artic Current journeys east and north again toward Europe, and carries itself in different form. The waters of the Artic Current have emerged and escaped from under the polar ice cap. They are frigid and formidable, hiding within its flowing freedom menacing things of its past—chunks of ice that have broken off from the Greenland glaciers.

It was one in the morning and Captain Hammond was finally asleep in the bunk wrapped up in blankets that stank of men's sweat and cigars. He had gone to the helm again early in the evening, after sleeping a few hours and listening to his crew try to manage his ship as it floated precariously at the whim of the winds. He was convinced, however, that the winds were on their side and they were headed for Halifax. He insisted he would steer the *Diana* to Canada himself, but after a couple of hours he collapsed and now was asleep in the chart room. And because days had gone by without adequate sleep, he slept like the dead.

Quartermaster Connolly was at the helm and although the wind was fierce and the ship moved slowly against its invisible power, he, like the captain, felt the wind was mercifully guiding them to land. The Canadian coast could be spotted now and he would be honored to steer the luxury liner to safety in spite of the dangerous circumstances. Mitchel, unable to sleep and sensing danger, approached Quartermaster Connolly to ask him if someone was watching out for breakers. Connolly didn't like it that a passenger, this secretive man with the strong accent who had his gang of men, questioned him. He felt challenged and in more ways than one. He was an Irishman himself, with parents who had been born in Cork and come to America. He knew what Mitchel was about and although Connolly would say nothing, he did not want his own authority called into question by the man. He had made good in his young life, a promise to his parents, unlike many of his kind growing up in Five Points. He would not allow this high and mighty Irish rebel to belittle him.

"There's a man in the aft wheelhouse, sir. No need to worry yourself. We're right able to run this ship. We've gone through these waters many times."

Connolly's voice crumbled in the wind and he gripped the wheel that was becoming more difficult to control. He looked away from Mitchel and wished the man would leave.

"We're in icy waters, Mr. Connolly, and breakers are typical. All I'm asking is if any have been spotted. And why is there no power to this ship? Even in this storm, there should be more control. What's wrong with the engines?"

"Men in the wheelhouse and men in the lookout. We're all keen on looking out for icebergs," Connolly quickly answered.

"I'm to bed then."

"Good idea. We'll be on the coast soon enough."

Mitchel turned to go, but Connolly couldn't help himself. He had to ask.

"Are you John Mitchel, the one who escaped from Australia and—"

"Are you an Irishman?"

"My parents were born in Cork and—"

"I asked if you were an Irishman."

"I am."

"Then you'll not say another word about who I am or where I've come from."

Connolly turned toward the sea and was relieved to deal with something he had power over, even if it was a ship without engines, unlike the feelings he had about being Irish and American or whether he could be loyal to someone like John Mitchel.

At three in the morning, Second Officer Barstow went to the aft wheelhouse and found the Third Officer, Morgan, asleep. He was too weary to wake and reprimand the man, so he looked out to sea, forcing himself to stand and not sit and fall asleep himself. After a few minutes, he spied something on the starboard. Breakers! He dashed from the wheelhouse to the bridge and shouted at lookout, asking if any breakers had been seen. It was seconds later that someone in lookout yelled, "Ice, dead ahead!"

Quartermaster Connolly frantically tried to turn the ship, but it was futile without engine power. the *Diana* crashed into something more solid than ice. She crashed full speed into a rock at Mars Head on the tip of Prospect Cape, approximately twenty miles from entering Halifax Harbor.

As if angry for being crippled by her engine loss, re-routed, and inconvenienced in all her finery, this luxury liner didn't strike the rock once, but at least six times. She pounded herself against the rock as if she would sail through it, but destroyed her hull and doomed herself to death instead.

Captain Hammond woke after the third strike against the rock. He knew they hadn't hit an iceberg. They had arrived in Canada, alright, but not the way he had planned. He stood to his feet and when the fifth battering against the rock occurred he was knocked against the wall and slid down to the floor. Adrenalin coursed through his weary body and he became hell bent on saving his ship. He defied his weakness and by the time the sixth and last strike came, he was rushing out the door to take command on deck. The winds were lashing the sea and violent waves were spilling over into the wrecked ship. The captain saw that the ship's hull was destroyed and the life boats on the port side of the vessel had swept out to sea. Second Officer Barstow and the captain began pulling down the rest of the lifeboats. Passengers came out of their cabins and up from the stern, huddling together in shock. A number of them panicked and climbed into three of the lifeboats. The boats toppled and screams could be heard as everyone was carried away. It all happened in minutes. Barstow and Morgan had been in one of the boats and more crew members were in the others. Captain Hammond remained surprisingly calm and ordered women and children first into the other lifeboats. To his horror and dismay, male passengers pushed the women and children aside and jumped into the boats. He screamed commands at them to let the women and children go first, but to no avail was his authority heeded. And then suddenly the *Diana* shifted because of the power of the angry waves, and the lifeboats were smashed, killing all of the men in them. The stern of the liner was swiftly filling with water and hanging on to the rest of the ship with shreds of wood that was creaking and snapping. It would soon break away and sink below the waves. Mass confusion and hysteria ensued and there were no other lifeboats. Rockets were fired by Quartermaster Connolly that lit up the starless night sky before the luxury liner in all its glory lost its stern, rocked, and tried to roll over, giving itself up to the might of the temperamental seas. Wood and flesh became one and moaned in unison. The iceberg that Mitchel feared would be the cause of a disaster was there waiting for them, but the winds chose Mars Rock. No one saw the mighty iceberg thrust up from the sea they just passed on the right. The ship was only twenty miles from Halifax Harbor but had perilously struck the first rock in the peninsular cape that forms the western limit of Pennant Bay.

The dawn of morning light came and the captain spied another large rock that lay ahead of the wrecked liner. Men climbed the rigging to hold on. They knew the rest of the ship was going to go to its demise. Death had already come to most of the passengers, but there was still salvation for some to be found in a rock. Captain Hammond and the survivors stood cautiously in a corner of the deck that was still afloat. The captain shouted for someone to swim to the rock with a rope. He himself was not a confident swimmer. John Mitchel rushed to put on the signal halyards and swim the thirty five yards to the rock. He had been forced to learn to swim or drown when he had escaped Tasmania, and now he courageously swam through freezing waters to rig a rope between the wreck and the rock. This way, survivors could pass over the breaking waves between the rock and the ship, and although dangerous, it was the only means of escape. Those on the rigging would freeze to death in a matter of time, unless they fell first, but the ones who passed through the waters had more of a chance in being saved.

Ivan came alongside Mitchel and they looked at one another knowingly.

"I'll go with each one," Ivan said.

The remainder of Captain Hammond's ship was quickly filling with water; soon the only place above water would be the rigging some people were clinging to. The captain wondered if any were women. It was eerily quiet, no more human wailing, just the sound of the wild waves triumphing over human endeavor.

"How many to cross?" he asked Mitchel.

Mitchel looked up at the rigging and then at Ivan, "Go on up for them! I'll get the rest across."

"Foley!" the captain shouted over the noise. He looked around and there were maybe twenty men, passengers, shivering and crowding around him. Quartermaster Connolly shook his head at the captain to indicate Foley was gone. His crew had disappeared, unless they were the ones clutching the poles above him, like trapeze artists in a circus act.

Over the next hour, Mitchel and the captain took each surviving passenger through the frigid waters to the unsure safety of the rock. The captain became adept in the icy waters by mere survival instinct. And mercifully, the fierce winds ceased and there was some calm in the sea. Quartermaster Connolly went first and stayed on the rock assisting the passengers. Ivan, in the meantime, made his way to each person on the rigging who wanted to be as far away from the terrorizing sea as possible. He convinced four men to come down to escape to the rock, but one man dropped into the water and drowned. Another shouted madly that there was no hope and he would not budge from the rigging no matter what Ivan said to him. Ivan, however, was undeterred, for he had already come through the worst storm of his life and had nearly perished. As long as his mammy was not on this ship and was safe in New York, he was ready to fight man, beast, and nature again. He didn't have anything to lose, he told himself, and thus was buoyed by new strength. If he saved someone's life, he would not have lived in vain; if he died, he would not have to remember the past nor scrape by to make a living. He had made an agreement with God to save his mother's life, not his own. And when Ivan saw the young woman with the eyes that had pierced his heart with loathing and scorn, he knew then where his redemption lay.

Norah was clad only in a cotton nightgown, not far from the railing near the mast. She gripped the rigging, her legs bare and dangling a few feet from the floor. Her ankles and feet were snow white, delicate, and Ivan thought how doll-like she appeared.

"Mother of God, have mercy...Mother of God..." Ivan heard Norah pray. And then he heard a wail he was quite familiar with. It was a sound for the dead; the keening sounds filled him with memory of home.

Ivan understood then what had happened as soon as he heard Norah's grief-stricken cries. It was Murray. He must have succumbed to the sea and Ivan immediately saw this young woman's young life with a shadow cast over it as far back as Ireland, as far back as his own life there. When he approached her to where she was on the rigging, he placed his large hands over her small ones and felt their fierce energy as her thin arms wound like ivy tendrils around the pole.

When Norah turned toward Ivan, he saw in her heartsick eyes the monstrous irony that he had survived and Murray had perished. Or maybe he felt this, too, and was able to immediately detect it in her.

She turned to face the sea and gripped the pole more intensely. When he tried to pry her hands free, she kicked at him and struck him in the face. Her feet felt frozen and he was momentarily blinded by the blow. He didn't give up and put a rope securely around her waist. She flailed against him and then a wave came and washed over them, slapping Norah hard against the pole. She let go and was flung out over the railing and carried into the sea. He watched incredulously the quick and graceful manner by which the tempestuous sea captured her before he could. But then he had to correct his thinking. He had once captured her; perhaps when he was as ominous as the sea, and for his own hungry profit, but now he wanted to save her to tear away the dark shroud that had been cast over both of them.

Chapter Twenty-Five

"The wave came to carry me… to him…to Murray. I wasn't afraid because God himself was coming for me. Something greater than my sorrow was coming for me. My mind was nowhere, but then I remembered this dresser."

Norah looked fondly at it and continued. "I was hidden inside years ago…remember?"

She didn't say anything for a few moments and tense awkwardness wavered in the room. She fidgeted with the buttons on her dress, peering at each face. "You, Da, flung me onto a ship! Remember? …I let go then, too. Death came and I lost Kate…God bless her soul… Our neighbors in Ireland, remember them, Mam?"

Norah looked at her mother whose face was pale and deeply creased. Mam didn't respond, but sat unflinching, waiting for Norah to continue. Mr. Harrigan and Da listened attentively, and pity curled crookedly in the corners of their mouths when they attempted to smile at her. She saw their embarrassment, but it wouldn't stop her from going on. She needed to tell her story. She would always need to tell her stories, no matter how difficult or tragic. Norah was dressed in a long black cotton dress, plain and simple. She thought she looked like a Quaker and this pleased her, for she remembered how the Quakers freely cared for her people during the Hunger.

"I made a new friend on the ship coming to America...he died from the fever...and then Sean never came back from the sea...although he promised me he would. And there's more, but I won't go on about it. Sure, I'm supposed to gird up and be strong!

"I thought God would have mercy and death wouldn't strike me again until I was an old woman. But it never stops. I don't believe there's a hell underneath the earth; it dwells in the depths of the ocean."

Norah looked fully into each face, but no one responded. They looked down onto their laps and Mam got up to pour more tea. Norah closed her eyes before she continued.

"Murray was thrown away and dumped into the sea, this hell, but who knows; maybe it's not really hell, but heaven."

She opened her eyes and watched her mother carefully pour tea into each of their cups.

"Should we ask a priest, Mam? Will he know where heaven and hell are, and where Murray is?"

Her eyes were wide, as green and dark as the sea can appear at times, but there were dark violet circles underneath them, resembling bruises. The rest of her face was ghostly pale.

"I clung to the pole on the ship. I refused to follow him, throwing myself into death as some wives do in faraway countries when their husbands die. Oh no, not me. No funeral pyre or icy grave! My priest's voice was in my head then tellin' me that Murray was in heaven and if I threw my life away, I'd be in hell, for God did take him and he didn't take himself there. If God doesn't take you, you've no right to take your own life. So I stayed above the sea clutching at life. Murray leaving me had already brought death to me anyway and I'd be carrying this dying with me until I went to a real grave. Sure, death circles us all the time. None of the priests in Ireland could protect us from it, could they now?"

Norah closed her eyes again and leaned her head back against the chair.

"Murray now gone..."

"Ye might be needing a rest now, Norah," Mam said after she sat down again.

Norah ignored her mother and continued to talk with her eyes closed.

"Sean's love rolled my child's heart over a few times, making it soft for Murray's love to come to rest upon later. A grown woman I was with Murray."

Norah sat forward and opened her eyes, a stream of tears flowed down her face and into the collar of her dress. She didn't wipe them or make a sound.

It was a few minutes before Norah continued. Sorrow permeated the room.

"I wasn't afraid!" she proclaimed, standing up.

"I felt nothing when the wave came for me and forced me into the sea. I thought God had come for me, too. When my head rose above the water, hands were reaching for me. But then I let myself go under again, to God...to Murray. Maybe the priest would say I was sinning for not fighting to live, but I was too close to Murray then. I went down again, pushed under by another wave that felt angry for nearly losing me. Then I saw colors that had to be what tranquility looks like. Every hue of blue and green with specks of silver swirled in a waltz before me and then wrapped itself around me. Could this be God, these colors I saw? I didn't fight, but I was very alone and Murray wasn't there after all. I wasn't afraid, but I started to feel my chest tighten and my head exploding."

Norah spoke unfettered and animated, pacing the room and looking at her audience as if she was a stage actress.

Then she sat down on the sofa next to Da and looked at her wedding ring, moving it up and down on her finger. It was too extravagant and showy to wear now and she was uncomfortable with its touch upon her skin. When Ivan rescued her and took her to the rock where he and others rubbed her limbs to bring life back into them, the ring was taken off because her fingers were swelling. When she returned to New York, the only possession she carried was the ring tied up in a cloth Ivan had saved for her. She had just put it back on yesterday, but immediately took it off and placed it in her dresser. Mam said it was a memento, a symbol of her love and marriage, and it should comfort her to look at it and remember Murray. No, she had said, it was not a comfort. It only made her heart hurt worse than it did, but she put it back on anyway. Now she wanted to take it off and scrape at her aching heart with it.

"Forgive me, Norah...forgive me a hundred-fold for introducing you to this dangerous man! When I introduced Murray to you at the Astor, I knew. I knew he would draw you into his life, like a spider to his web."

Mr. Harrigan got out of his chair and stood in front of Norah.

Norah looked up at him, but said nothing in response. She had come home to New York only two weeks before and was unpredictable in her mood and behavior. At first, she hadn't remembered being pulled from the sea and who survived or who didn't survive. At times, she didn't know if it had really happened and she had to be told what happened, but then she would ask again what happened after she was rescued. She vividly remembered clinging to life and then wanting death and being in the sea that was full of colors.

The survivors of the *Diana* spent the night on the rock, two of them went mad and Norah had been nearly out of her mind herself. She might be crazy now and was fooling everyone around her. Or maybe they were fooling her and pretending she hadn't become a lunatic. But she had survived, as well as fifteen other passengers, Captain Hammond, Quartermaster Connolly, John Mitchel, and Ivan. The news was all over New York and the country about the wreck of the *Diana*, and Mr. Harrigan, the consummate newspaperman, had asked if he could interview her. Norah agreed only if she was allowed to edit the final draft before it was printed. She pondered how she could have thought so highly of the man and didn't want to say anything further about what had happened, let alone defend her husband and marriage. However, she felt compelled to speak because there was so much misunderstanding about the fight for Ireland's freedom. Sure, a great deal of money had been lost in the wreck, but even she knew it was a trivial amount to pay for an army large enough to fight England. Just the day before, John Mitchel sent a note saying he wanted to visit her, but she had refused. No, she wanted nothing to do with insurrection and Ireland. In regards to Ivan, she didn't know yet whether she was grateful to him for having saved her, for in her confused mourning, she thought of him having abducted her twice. Abducted her from Murray at Finn's and abducted her from Murray in the sea. She took in a large breath and spoke forthrightly to Mr. Harrigan.

"My marriage to an honorable man who sought freedom for Ireland is not to be spoken of as a mistake, nor should Murray be considered a criminal. He should be revered in memory just as the patriots of America who fought for their freedom from Great Britain are remembered."

Norah stood up and walked to the kitchen table to pour another cup of tea. Yes, she must write an article about the *Diana!* What else could she do with all that she had experienced? But it was more than that. Her plunge into the sea and sorrow were one and the same and she had come forth a different person, wearing a heavy mantle of not just grief, but purpose, although she had no understanding what to do with it. It was unfamiliar, unlike her prior conviction to travel with Murray, and it separated her from those who were trying to comfort her. She kept her back to her family and Mr. Harrigan, and sipped the comforting tea. After a few minutes, she faced them and stated that she herself must write about her ordeal, not Mr. Harrigan, and that he had to promise not to censor what she wrote. She was surprised that he agreed to this. They set a time for her to come to his office and then he left. Mam and Da returned to their jobs and Norah lay on her sofa and slept for the rest of the day.

A few days later, Da sat on the sofa with her after coming home from work. He surprised her with the news that he was going to work on a railroad and would be leaving soon. He laughed heartily when he told her that he had received a large sum of money up front and this money would help take care of them while he was gone. He was pleased with this job offer, he said, but Norah detected confusion and restlessness in him. Mam was still at work and wouldn't be home until later. She had quit the sewing factory for conditions were too harsh and now was working at the Astor House hotel. Da had just pulled Norah from a dream, for as always, she dreamed. It was a dream repeated since she had come home and it frightened her because she now understood that the dreams she had prior to the shipwreck had been a premonition. In this new dream, words circled her in the ocean, but soon they turned into sharks who shouted words at her. She didn't understand this dream, nor did she remember the words the sharks screamed at her. But they were words—commanding and authoritative words. Mam would sometimes come to sit with her, putting a cool cloth on her head and making her tea, the Irish remedy for every problem and ill.

Da handed her a cup of tea now and the steam rose into her face, bringing comfort. She was waiting to come to who she was and hoping her da could help her. Her dear father nearly died when she had been away, having been diagnosed with consumption and going into delirium with a high fever. Mam and Meg had cared for him, with Meg moving in with her youngest child.

Mam told Norah what Meg said when they learned Norah had left New York. "She'll see for herself, she will. She'll see Ireland not dressed in anything but rags and she'll come back to America. She will, mind you. She will."

Mam spoke very little when Norah was away, but dutifully carried on tending to her husband, grief carefully stored away for later. Norah learned that it had been Leary who knocked on the door with the news about the *Diana* having wrecked and there being survivors coming home on a ship from Halifax, one of them being their Norah. Mam had whispered in Da's ear that Norah was coming home and he had to be getting out of bed and playing his fiddle for her. A few days later, he was on the mend and was strengthened enough to rise out of bed and survive the consumption. He had been weak, but eventually returned to work although the doctor told him he needed more rest. And here he was now, her father who still bore the marks of hunger but was strong, and going to work on a railroad somewhere in America. Norah sat up straight to begin a conversation she needed to have with him. Of late, she had been feeling a desire to work with her hands and get on her knees to scrub and labor. She would find work as a domestic to help her family and write the article for Harrigan and his silly Irish newspaper, but then get on with reality. Norah's hands shook and she spilled tea onto her lap.

Da took her teacup away and moved close to her.

"You are much stronger now, *A Chuisle*."

Norah regained her composure. She could not allow her sorrow to destroy the rest of her life, for she might as well have drowned, too. Her chest felt tight and constricted, as if the sea water was still in her lungs, but now as tears stored there forever. She had trouble breathing, sleeping without dreaming, and she hadn't been able to eat much of anything since coming home. Tears fell and were hot on her cheeks, rolling into her mouth and tasting like the salty sea. She leaned into her da who held her and whispered, "It will be alright…we are survivors, you and I, we Irish—""

Norah sat back and looked hard at her father, "I don't want to be Irish, Da! I don't want to always have to fight to survive!"

And then she laid her head against his chest. He breathed down on her head, and this warmed her and made her feel safe. For a few moments she felt at peace.

Then Da placed a pillow behind her and retrieved Mam's shawl from the dresser to place over her. Her mother's scent was in the shawl and Norah recalled how she hadn't wanted to take it with her on the trip with Murray. It had been difficult to separate herself from the child she was leaving behind and the woman she was becoming. She was warmed by the shawl, and yes, she thought, perhaps she and Mam could do domestic work together at the Astor. She would force her mind to think only of simple things while she did the chores she had always despised doing. This would be her new cloak of purpose, not anything grandiose or epoch. To think she had wanted to wear furs on her shoulders and not drape this red shawl of her mother's over her. And maybe after the article for the newspaper was written, she would be free from the words coming at her from the mouths of sharks in her dreams. She could, and would, work with her hands. She looked at Da ready to tell him about her plans, but he began speaking solemnly.

"Mary…your friend, Mary, is dead. We can't be holding this news from you any longer…"

Norah could not register the truth of these words.

"She's not dead…Mary's not—"

"Mary died from an abortion. She and Leary's baby died from Madam Restell's work."

Dear Mary, her childhood friend, had faded from her life even before she became involved with Murray. They had been distant from one another, but she had stored away the girleen's friendship for later. What they once had together, she thought could be retrieved someday, like a treasure from an old trunk that could be found. But this was not to be.

Norah had grown into something else that Mary hadn't and it had become too uncomfortable to spend time together. They began having cross words and eventually agreed to go separate ways after Norah's store would be sold. No, Mary could not be dead! She was Irish and a survivor, too.

Norah tried to remember what they had said to one another and how her friend's face looked when they last spoke. Had they been angry then? She crossed her hands over her heart and chest and felt hollow.

"God have mercy on her soul," she whispered and closed her eyes. She pictured Mary walking the streets of Five Points smiling, hopeful, and turning her head coyly this way and that way, catching the eyes of gentlemen, giggling at the power she had. She wondered why Mary couldn't accept a child growing within her, a child who symbolized a new beginning. It wouldn't be like Mary to worry over the Church punishing her for her sins with Leary, would it? Perhaps she didn't know her friend as well as she thought she had. She opened her eyes to see Mam walking into the apartment.

"I've a stew to warm up now. Are ye up for some fine cooking, Norah?" Mam asked.

Norah clutched the shawl tightly around her shoulders and smiled, hunger pangs visiting her for the first time since her last meal with Murray.

"Aye, Mam, I'm ready for some of your fine stew."

After Norah had a simple meal with Mam and Da, she said she wanted to take a walk around the block to digest her food. Norah possessed no fear to be on the streets alone, and the idea of walking appealed to her enormously. After devouring a large bowl of stew and two pieces of bread slathered with butter, she was certain she could walk anywhere in the world—as a woman, as an Irish woman, and also as an American. Was she an American?

Norah wanted to see if she belonged in New York again, for during her waking hours she felt trapped in grief. Her childhood with Mary, her store, working at the newspaper, becoming involved with Mitchel's movement, and even the horrid bordello captivity that her parents knew nothing about, all seemed unreal. Her present desire was to walk and perhaps she would remember that her life wasn't a series of dreams, nightmares, and tragedies, but her own unique story. She had difficulty remembering details, or maybe it was difficulty feeling the memories. Since returning to New York, she felt like a spirit hovering above her life, as if she was reading about it in a work of fiction. She could remember being kidnapped by Ivan, the commissioner's contorted face of evil, the icy waters she fell into, but it was like an imaginary tale of adventure and mystery. What did feel very real, at times, was that she was married, but this incited unimaginable sorrow, and she would press her fist into the hollow of her belly, trying to feel physical pain, not heart pain.

She walked down the street full of her mother's hearty stew, relishing the physical one foot forward at a time, the senses of her body reviving. She had been surprised to feel hunger and then satisfaction with a home-cooked meal. At one time, Norah had loathed her mother's stew for it had been a symbol of limitation, a reminder she came from poor Irish. The streets were dim and full of shadows, gas lamps lit here and there, but most of them pulled down by gangs who felt compelled to smash something, not yet daring to break the glass of stores or homes. Mam had been especially upset when Norah left and tried to convince Da to walk with her.

"Nay! Nay! You're to be givin' us all heartaches and early deaths!" Mam cried, but Norah said she must go alone.

The streets in Five Points, as usual, were strewn with refuse. *Signs they were,* Norah thought, *signs of living like savages, whereas near the Astor House hotel, the garbage was hauled away as if the wealthy ones never made any mess out of their living.* The putrid air mingled with new breezes and her mind was full of strange questions, such as whether the wind alone had a scent without city smells intruding upon it. What was the scent of her childhood? Potatoes clean and potatoes rotted? Bog and hearth and gentians and lilies? Fever? Did she remember what it smelled like? A scent all its own, she remembered. Words. Do words have a scent? Where do they go after they are spoken and are they like the wind and drift invisibly around the earth? Words began filling the air surrounding her, for they were no longer stuck inside her head. They were lively, sparkling silver words hanging in the air wherever she looked. There were Irish words mixed in with English words and as she disbelievingly stared at them, they wavered and pushed against one another until they were all pressed together and no longer appeared as words. She closed her eyes and opened them quickly. The words were gone and stars filled the spaces where the words had been. The words had become stars. So that is what happened to all the words spoken around the world. She stared in wonder as she leaned against a lamp post and slid down onto the street. Striking the ground startled her from these nonsensical thoughts and she shivered and swallowed the sadness creeping into her because there were no more words or stars. There were only people who crowded around her and gawked. She heard murmurings and laughter, but none of their words hung in the air. Their words fell back into their mouths and didn't transform into stars. She felt utter bereavement for the loss of words that weren't significant enough to turn into something as beautiful as stars.

"*A Chuisle,* Norah!" Da's voice broke through her grief as he pulled her up from the ground and put his arm around her waist, walking her through the crowd.

"She's been tippin' the bottle, that one...," Norah heard a man say.

"Come from Cat Hollow, she's a lucky one to be in one piece—"

"No, it ain't so; don't ye know it's the girleen from the wreck? The shipwreck took her husband and hundreds of others. They say her mind's not workin' since she nearly drowned.

Norah walked home with Da and remembered and felt everything. It was her story, alright, not one she had read, not anyone else's story, and she was feeling all of it—hunger pains from the Famine, a sister dying, friends dying, the commissioner, the bordello, Murray—and when she got to this part of her story, she allowed herself to wholly feel the inconsolable pain of loss.

"I'm bruised on the insides, Da...it feels like I've been punched again and again, as if a gang found me on the streets and beat me up."

"It will pass, Norah...it will pass...these sorrows ye will spin into gold."

When they returned to their tenement apartment, Mam led her to the sofa and rocked her like a baby.

"A cup of tea, Norah...do ye want a cup of tea?"

Norah pulled away from her, "Nay, I'll be having meself a wee 'drop of the creatur'..."

Da went to the kitchen and returned with a bottle of whiskey, pouring a glass for Norah. She drank it entirely and lay down on the sofa.

"I'll be grand now. I'm still breathing and the stars still shine...and we're here together." Norah went to sleep and slept late into the next day. It was the first sleep since the accident that she didn't dream.

Chapter Twenty-Six

"Will you reconsider my offer?" Mr. Harrigan asked Norah who was sitting in the room she once used as an office. "I've no desire to write for your dull newspaper!" She answered, laughing boldly. It had been over a month since returning from the shipwreck and she had finally brought him the article for his paper.

"You would deliver the paper from its mediocrity, Norah, and then it would no longer be boring. You could write about tragedies and cause readers to really care, just like you've done with the *Diana* wreck. I'm surprised at your astute eye for detail and how you could write after such loss."

"Say nothing of my loss. I didn't write of my personal loss. And I do not wish to speak of it."

She stood up, yawned and stretched, and walked to the window across the narrow room. She watched children playing stickball in the street and a cart suddenly flew through the middle of them, nearly running over a young boy.

"'Tis tempting…but I'll be working with Mam at the Astor. I'll make more money than being your slave here…and do you remember how I never wrote a single article, but the one you massacred about the priest? Mostly, I ran around the city like your errand girl!" She folded her arms and faced him.

"No, Mr. Harrigan, I'm not interested. This is one article I've written to unleash my heart and it's all I need to do. This piece is a containment of the bigger picture. The *Diana* was a miniature world of what New York is like and I want people to see how ridiculous our differences are because of money… the education, the country we come from, matters not in the end."

She looked out the window again and watched the children playing in the street. It consoled her that they found a way for play even if there was no field or a real ball. They were striking a pumpkin and soon it would be smashed and they would find something else to use in its place for their game. She wondered how many of them would soon become young gang members.

"Well then…," Mr. Harrigan said.

Norah sensed he liked her company and didn't want her to leave. From the beginning of their first encounter in her store, this man had desired a friendship with her that was liberating. She was coming to know this slowly.

"Do you mind if I take a look at some of your books you have here in the office?" she asked, changing the subject.

Norah didn't want to make arrangements for tea or lunch or talk of whether she would ever write another article for him. But she did want to have the opportunity to look at the books that lined his shelves. She never had time to read when she first came to work for him, but now she would have this luxury. She was anticipating working with Mam during the day and reading all night. Just the thought of curling up on her sofa with a book at night, even if she had to read by candlelight, made her feel hopeful. She desired to read about life and not live it too fully for the time being.

"You may borrow as many books as you can carry home. I'd be pleased to have you enjoy my collection." Mr. Harrigan adjusted his waist coat and swiped at his shoulders to remove any hair strands.

"I must give this article to Thomas right away so he can set it to print," he said, waving it in front of her. "Take your time here and when you're ready, I'll hire a carriage to take you home."

He smiled warmly and slightly bowed before he left. Norah warmed to this gesture and smiled in return. Turning to the shelves to read some of the titles, she thought of what she had just written in the article and was pleased. It wasn't just an article about a shipwreck and suffering, but about the misery of the living before they die because of limitations and cruelty placed on them due to class and race.

Mr. Harrigan had been excited about novelty in his paper, but of course, he was concerned her article might cause a stir. It was exactly what she wanted it to do, she told him. To cause his Irish-American readers to see the folly of their clubs and societies, as they mimicked wealthy Protestants and paraded around with acceptable Irish slogans. She had been compelled to write this one piece because she had lived it, not only because she had been full of foolish idealism and youthful zeal. She had written about the wreck of the *Diana*, leaving out any references to John Mitchel and the movement. It would taint the real picture and because their intentions had failed, why speak of them? She had written the article in a fury with potent words marching across her tablet. Factual and eloquent sentences regarding the luxury liner's extravagance that included detailed observations of the dancing, dinners, and music. She described not only the wealthy travelers, but told of the passengers in the hold of the ship who didn't attend the dinners and dances. And she wrote about a group of men who were uneducated but had enough money to purchase first-class tickets. They, she reported, were eyed suspiciously and were distrusted. But when nearly everyone perished in the storm, there was no class distinction and they went to the same end no matter how much money they possessed and who they were. It was pithy and sharp writing and she wrote it as if she was writing a story. She didn't cite names of any of the passengers, but described families and children and what they had said to one another. And she never included Murray in the story of the *Diana*, for he wasn't there in the past but with her in the present, helping her write and see the story behind the story, the story of individuals caught in life's snares and becoming freed at death.

Norah moved around the office lighthearted, thinking how her article might cause eyebrows to raise and whether anyone would guess that she had been a member of the secret group on the ship. A list of the names of the dead had already gone out in the papers, but none were listed as members of a rebel organization. Norah had been listed as Miss Norah McCabe, daughter of Eoin McCabe, of Five Points, New York, survivor. The marriage license had been lost and those who survived never gave a thought to whether she was Norah McCabe or Norah Murray. It was a relief to her father and mother, however, when she showed them the ring and explained they had married on the ship. Of course, Mam was shocked that the marriage had been officiated by a Protestant minister, but the fact this poor minister had died in the wreck lessened her criticism. Mr. Harrigan also knew and felt chastened for introducing her to Murray. This made her feel slightly cheapened as if her marriage was not real because it had not been sanctioned by a Catholic priest and by people like himself. He had never liked Murray, but Norah saw it as jealousy because Murray had become radical in his ideals. Mr. Harrigan merely strode the safe route and his paper was no *Irish Citizen* or *The Nation* full of petulance and angry truths spewed out by Irish political exiles. True, he had finally taken a stand against slavery, which was a very hostile and volatile issue.

Norah and Da had drank many cups of tea while discussing abolitionism, and although he believed the African should be treated as equal as the white man, he surmised it was a difficult concept to make a reality because even the white man wasn't equal to a white man. He concluded that Negroes were different alright, but more in their physical appearance than anything else and that they were mostly alike with the Irish in their struggle to find jobs. Most Irishmen were vying for jobs that the Negroes held and this brought them into conflict. Norah felt it was a much deeper issue, but struggled to define it. She recalled one conversation she had with her da.

"But dear Norah, if we hate them, we hate them for fighting against us in obtaining work, not because their skin is black," he had said.

"No, I think there are some Irish who hate them for their skin, too. These feeble-minded ones are as uneducated as many Negroes, and although we Irish don't come from slavery, we might have felt we were slaves of England. We identify with the Negro and this makes some of us enraged because the Negro is considered a very low class of people, some say even without souls. These Irish are fighting against themselves because they feel inferior."

"We all feel inferior, Norah."

"We all feel inferior? The Irish? Or all human beings? I don't think the Nativists feel inferior. They possess high and mighty feelings of superiority."

"Don't ye know, *A Chuisle,* that their superior feelings are based on falsity? If you take any Negro man or Irish man and give him an education, a job, and some money in his pocket, he'd soon gather respect for himself and begin strutting around as if he had the world by the tail."

Norah ceased wandering around the office thinking about her conversations with Da and the article she had written. And so it all ended the same, she kept thinking again and again. And this simple understanding gave her freedom from strife and to be at ease with herself. She had been seeped in Paris fashion, hiding her Irish speech, and at the same time involving herself in a rebellion. Hypocrite! She felt humbled. But, thank God, she had the good fortune of coming to a new sense of herself. And she had loved someone and had been loved by someone in spite of her false and naïve ways. *But...here it is,* she thought, *here is the dilemma. I feel superior now because I've survived to have these insights!*

Norah laughed aloud and Mr. Harrigan came into the room.

"Let me in on the humor!"

"Nay," she said, "it wouldn't be humorous to you."

He stood there looking like a colorful bird in his fancy duds. The man straddled two cultures—Irish and American, but there was no doubt, he was mostly American. Would her children do the same someday? Children! Why, she would not have any children, to be sure. She would never want them and now that Murray had left her, she would never have any. It suddenly occurred to her that she could be carrying Murray's child. No, she was certain there had been no sign of this in her body. So overcome by these thoughts, she had to sit down. Norah pulled on her wedding ring and tears fell onto her hands, spreading over them as grief did the same within her.

"I'm sorry." Mr. Harrigan quickly gave her his handkerchief.

"Maybe someday I'll have memories without tears, but not now…," she said, dabbing at her eyes and standing up.

"I haven't picked out any books! I need to get home to Mam. She'll be wringing her hands and pullin' out her hair!"

Harrigan went back to his office and Norah randomly pulled books off the shelves, hoping some would interest her.

She carried the books to the Windsor chair by the window because the ending of the day's light was softly streaming in. The sun had gathered the colors of the day and delicately placed them in layers above the earth. They concentrated into thick and dazzling pastels, and she wanted to sit for a few moments in this light that ended a day. Again, she thought of endings and how everyone is given equally of the light at the end of a day. No matter what a person did during the day in this city, she thought, they will receive the same display from the sun. If a person saved someone from jumping off a bridge, if a person murdered someone and was taken to prison, or if a woman scrubbed floors on her knees—all would be given this same light that was warming her through the window. She turned the chair slightly to feel the ardency of light on the back of her neck and through her shoulders that were tense. She settled on borrowing the books she had arbitrarily chosen, even if they would prove to be uninteresting. She felt too relaxed basking in the sun's descending rays to jump up and look for others. As soon as the sun set, she would leave as quietly as a cat that had slept contentedly in a sunbeam and needed to go out. She didn't want Mr. Harrigan to bother with hailing a cart or a carriage for her. She would do it herself!

Before her trip on the *Diana*, Norah had sewn some of her earnings into the hems of skirts from her clothing store. It wasn't much, but it was enough to pay for incidentals and help her family purchase food until she began working again. The used-clothing store had been sold and the money was used to pay for doctor visits, medicine, and rent when Da was ill. Murray had mentioned he held a bank account, but she had no idea how much there was, nor how to prove she had been his wife! But certainly she could pay for her own carriage ride home. She closed her eyes for a few moments to focus on feeling the sun's rays caressing her shoulders and when she opened them, she looked down to read the titles of the books she had placed on her lap. She was both surprised and intimidated by the selection, wondering if she should look for others. They looked to be highbrow books and some-one like herself might not be able to understand them. Her teacher in the Public School Society had stated Norah possessed a gifted mind, but how wrong her teacher had been!

Henry Wadsworth Longfellow's *Voices of the Night, Moby Dick* by Herman Melville, *Walden; or, Life in the Woods* by Henry D. Thoreau, Maria Edgeworth's *Castle Rackrent, The Cause of Ireland Pleaded Before the Civilized World* by Reverend Bernard O'Reilly, and *Woman in the Nineteenth Century* by Margaret Fuller.

Norah clasped her hands together excitedly and decided she wouldn't bother with Thoreau and O'Reilly, but she was intrigued by the others, especially *Woman in the Nineteenth Century.* Her friend, Mr. Harrigan, definitely had a wide interest in reading subjects, she thought fondly. Perhaps in the future, she would re-establish a friendship with him and enter into stimulating conversations about his reading material. But for now, she had to educate herself or she would never be able to hold herself up to his level. Her face went crimson when she thought how flippant she had been with him and how lazy in her communication skills, not realizing that he was more of a man of letters than she knew. She stood up, clasping the books to her bosom, and left quietly from Mr. Harrigan's office.

Chapter Twenty-Seven

In the evening, Norah sat alone on the sofa full of expectation. Mam and Da went to bed early after Mam became slightly hysterical trying to persuade Da not to leave to work on the railroad until spring. Da was making light of his upcoming trip, which was going to be in two weeks. And Mam was becoming more nervous and agitated as the time approached. She had never been without her husband except during the trying time when he worked on the road works in Ireland during the Hunger. Norah and Da assured Mam that it wasn't the same and that they, the McCabes, even their married Meg, were doing grand now, not starving as they had been in Ireland.

Norah lit three candles so she could read more comfortably in the dark apartment. There were no gas lamps outside their building and no moonbeams to help her see. She placed the candles on a kitchen chair and pulled the chair near the sofa. She first decided on Mr. Longfellow because his name was familiar and she hoped a poem would knead her mind and make it pliable so she would be able to read something longer. Maybe. She wasn't certain what she was after, but there was a stirring within her to read voraciously and find something to feed her mind and spirit in the books that lay before her.

"He's the poet!" she whispered after realizing it was Mr. Longfellow who had written *The Village Blacksmith*. At school many years ago, her class of varying ages was required to memorize this eight stanza poem. Norah recalled there were eight stanzas because eight pupils had been chosen to read aloud one stanza by memory. She had been relieved she hadn't been asked, but at the end of the year, each pupil was required to write out the entire poem from memory. She always liked poetry, mostly the poetry she learned in the Irish language that her da and the schoolmaster in Ireland had taught her. But having to memorize this poem had nearly destroyed her love of poetry. She started to lay aside the poetry book, but changed her mind and opened it to take a look at Mr. Longfellow's other poems. Her eyes fastened on a poem titled, *The Light of Stars*.

> *The star of the unconquered will,*
> *He rises in my breast,*
> *Serene, and resolute, and still,*
> *And calm, and self possessed.*
>
> *And thou, too, whosoe'ver thou art,*
> *That readest this brief psalm,*
> *As one by one thy hopes depart,*
> *Be resolute and calm.*
>
> *Oh, fear not in a world like this,*
> *And thou shall know erelong,*
> *Know how sublime a thing it is*
> *To suffer and be strong.*

It was the last stanza that touched Norah deeply. She read the entire poem a few times and decided it was enough for one evening. She had possessed great plans to spend the night warm and happy underneath Mam's shawl reading to her heart's content, but her heart was not cooperating. This poem had made her aware of her anguish. Was she strong? She blew out the candles and curled up on the sofa, pulling the shawl up to her shoulders and immediately fell asleep.

A few hours later, Norah woke in the dark still room with no sounds coming from the streets. Since coming to America, there was little quiet because there were always comings and goings happening outside the McCabes's building. She sat up on the sofa, relishing the silence and these rare, peaceful moments. After a few minutes she remembered the books she had purposed to read and was eager to be alone with them, as if they were friends asking her to come out and play. She wasn't working with Mam yet at the Astor and could sleep in every morning. She shivered in the chilly room and from the excitement she felt in the decision to read until the sun came up. She got up from the sofa to light the stove and heat up water for tea. After she set the kettle to boil, she went to the water closet to relieve herself. There was also a pail of water Da had brought up after dinner, and she splashed the cool water on her face and found a little baking soda and charcoal from the tin can so she could brush her teeth. She tiptoed back into the kitchen and made her tea, bringing it over to the sofa and lighting the candles in preparation to read.

She chose Margaret Fuller's *Woman in the Nineteenth Century* to tackle first, ignoring any doubts about not being able to understand it. That it had been written by a woman piqued her interest. She contemplated the sketch of the author on the cover before opening the book. A doleful countenance altogether, she concluded, with the author's head slightly cocked to the side as if she were trying to convince someone of something. Not a lifting of her chin to reveal haughtiness, but there was something pristine about the woman's appearance nevertheless. Margaret Fuller's eyes intrigued Norah and although they were sad, she perceived intelligence not only of the mind, but of the spirit in them. How does one judge how smart spirits or souls are? She thought that if Mam came out to sit with her now and Norah spoke of these things, she would laugh and say her own daughter's brains were addled and she possessed too many high-and-mighty thoughts. But maybe not...Mam was changing, too. Norah breathed in slowly and exhaled, basking in quietly thinking her own thoughts in the middle of the night; thoughts not as painful as they had been, even if Mr. Longfellow's words had reminded her of her loss. Well then! She wasn't just going to stare at the woman into the wee hours now, but find out what she had to say. She placed the old shawl over her legs and turned sideways on the sofa, flipping to the last page of the book, something she had a habit of doing when she took to reading something new. She read:

> I stand in the sunny noon of life. Objects no longer glitter in the dews of morning, neither are yet softened by the shadows of evening. Every spot is seen, every chasm revealed. Climbing the dusty hill, some fair effigies that once stood for symbols of human destiny have been broken; those I still have with me show defects in this broad light. Yet enough is left, even by experience, to point distinctly to the glories of that destiny; faint, but not to be mistaken streaks of the future day. I can say with the bard, 'Though many have suffered shipwreck, still beat noble hearts.'

One of the candles flickered and went out when Norah dropped the book and picked it up to read again. Her mind pulsed with what she had read, although some of it was too nebulous without having read the first part of the book. She read the last line aloud, "'Though many have suffered shipwreck, still beat noble hearts.'" Norah threw the shawl off because an intense heat surged through her body, up her neck, and into her face. She felt her forehead, wondering if she had a fever and was ill. She picked up Longfellow's book and turned again to his poem to read the last stanza,

> Oh, fear not in a world like this,
> And thou shall know erelong,
> Know how sublime a thing it is
> To suffer and be strong.

And then she read Margaret Fuller's last line one more time, and the beats of her heart could be heard in the stillness of the night.

"I, too, have suffered shipwreck!" she proclaimed quietly. She stared at the two candles that had burned to the same height, their flames dancing in unison.

"Strength and nobility. Do I possess these?"

The regal dresser stood opposite her aglow in the candlelight. She gazed at it and was filled with wonder. Then she blew out the candles and once more nestled into the old comfortable sofa to sleep.

"Strength and nobility be unto me," she whispered as tranquility brought the heaviness of sleep.

A few days later, Norah sat at the New Labor Employment Bureau. She felt ill at ease amongst women who wore fancy skirts, bright shawls, and flowered bonnets. Hushed conversation permeated the room as the women brought their chairs close to each other, glancing nervously here and there as they chatted. Irish speech and some familiar faces from Five Points convinced her that most were Irish women seeking jobs in domestic service. She was there because she decided she didn't want to work with Mam and Meg at the Astor House hotel. Working side-by-side with her sister would become intolerable and the other maids at the hotel knew too much about her life and what she had been through. Meg, always accusatory, said that she didn't believe Norah had actually married anyone, let alone someone of Murray's caliber. Mam scolded Meg for her impudence and insinuation that Norah had lied about being married. After that afternoon with Meg, Norah clearly understood what it would be like to work with the women at the Astor. Women with such dull and laborious work to do day after day, they could not help but wag their tongues about someone who had lived through an adventure as she had. But now she was thinking she had made a mistake in coming to the Bureau. Did she really want to do this? Sullen thoughts pooled in her mind and she felt trapped. But didn't she know the fat purses the domestics had and how they were able to command their own lives by learning the white-gloved ways of the Protestant households?

Norah was especially lonely for Murray just now, but also mourned the loss of Mary whose friendship at one time had been as bright as the moonlight that shone between the tenement buildings. She looked out the window at snowflakes floating in the gray mist and closed her eyes. She remembered Sean's hand in hers and the royal blue scarf he had purchased and tied around her neck. She had been on the verge of crawling out of her child's cocoon then, with Sean coaxing her to shuffle off Irish country ways to enter into New York's newness. But she had been too attached to her mother country and to the old ways, her heart still broken from fever and famine.

Norah sensed someone had come near her and she kept her eyes shut. She didn't want to engage in conversation with anyone at the moment.

"This is for you, Miss. It's about a meeting coming up ye should be attending." There was a scent of acrid soap that mingled with rose oil.

Something was placed underneath Norah's tightly held hands. Fanatics of every religion and political party put up posters, handbills, and handed out pamphlets. Often the city looked like one large bulletin board people plastered their thoughts on, as if they didn't dare speak them aloud.

When she heard the woman walk away, Norah sighed and let the pamphlet fall to the floor. She wasn't interested, but watched the woman work the room handing out pamphlets. Many of the women thrust the pamphlets back at the pamphleteer and waved her away. Some shouted, "Shame on ye!" The young woman's frizzy blonde hair had fallen out of her bun; she wore an apron over a blue dress that didn't have any hoops underneath it. If she felt different, Norah might have been interested in speaking to her, for how she missed Mary. Mary! She felt an ache as she looked down at the floor and read the words printed on the pamphlet. She quickly picked it up, for Margaret Fuller's words had sought her again:

> *It is not woman, but the law of right, the law of growth, that speaks in us, and demands the perfection of each being in its kind, apple as apple, woman as woman.*

The pamphleteer was in the hallway trying to talk to an angry woman who waved a pamphlet in her face. Clutching the pamphlet to her purse, Norah discreetly stepped into the hallway to listen to the red-faced woman's complaints. "Harlot!" the woman cried, and stomped out the door. The young woman looked at Norah and smiled, tucking some strands of her unkempt hair back into her bun. A basket of her pamphlets sat on the floor and Norah realized she hadn't read enough of the pamphlet to understand what it was about. She only knew that this Margaret Fuller seemed to be pursuing her for some reason, but then again, perhaps she was just imagining things. It was the second time she had come upon this writer's words, words profound as if it was known that she, Norah McCabe, had lived through a ship-wreck. God had spared her life, but for what? Suddenly, she heard her name being called inside the waiting room.

"Norah McCabe."

Norah turned to go back inside, but her steps felt leaden and heavy. She stopped and went toward the woman in the hallway.

"Norah McCabe." The man in the employment office called again. It was finally her turn after a long wait and she moved away from the woman, but felt a light tap on her shoulder.

"Did you have a question about the pamphlet?" the woman asked.

"Norah McCabe." The voice called out again.

Some of the women in the waiting room knew who she was and pointed at her. Norah smiled apprehensively at them and shook her head. She would return to the Bureau in a few days, for she still had some savings and a roof over her head. She didn't need to find a job this very day, did she? And wouldn't it be grand to make a new friend who read fine words like Margaret Fuller's? Sunlight broke through the gloomy day and filtered through the cut glass door of the Bureau. Norah noticed it moving in circled patterns on the floor before them. She immediately felt a buoyancy and lightness in her spirit that spread through her entire body, making her want to dance in the flickering light. She looked into the resolute, but warm, face of the pamphleteer.

"Aye…and do ye have time for a cup of tea to answer my questions?" Norah was surprised to hear her voice confidently ask a strange woman to go for tea. She would have to pay for the woman's refreshment just for asking her to go and she hated to part with her money, but the words were out of her mouth without fully willing them to be.

The woman picked up her basket of pamphlets and put it on her arm. Her free arm circled Norah's arm.

"It'd be grand altogether."

They walked cheerfully out of the employment bureau while a couple of women in the waiting room gawked and shook their heads. "The poor thing…," one whispered, "she survived the wreck, but lost her mind."

Chapter Twenty-Eight

It had been raining all morning and New Yorkers were being pelted and stung with sleet as they hurried to scheduled meetings, entered diners and bars, and stood underneath the canopies of buildings. Those with money to spare could climb into a hack or omnibus, rather than walk in the inclement weather. At first, Norah was glad for the rain as she walked, but now she shivered beneath the wool capuchin, a lovely cape that Mam had altered the evening before. The rain and snow that cleansed the streets was heaven's housekeeping chore, for she hated the refuse on the street—entrails of pigs, fowl, and other animals left to rot by butchers and restaurant cooks. Norah had just a few more blocks to walk, but the unfriendly wind felt like a cruel onslaught. She looked around for a town coach or even the sociable she had ridden in once with Murray. She waved at a few, but they were full and she decided to endure the discomfort and continue walking.

Eventually, Norah stopped on the busy street across from the Broadway Tabernacle. She read the directions scribbled on butcher paper that her new friend, Nellie Gorman, had given her. The sleet struck her ungloved hands, for she had forgotten her fancy limerick gloves in the haste to leave the apartment before Mam bombarded her with questions. She told Mam she was meeting a friend and going to the employment bureau. It wasn't likely that Norah would be going to the bureau this day, but Mam would never understand what she had planned. She hardly understood it herself! Mam's biting remarks about her gadabouts with Nellie had hurt her, much like the sleet was doing now. She didn't wish to be impertinent and disrespectful to her parents, but she had already crossed the line for independence.

Norah and Nellie Gorman had been frequenting the Ladies Lunchroom each afternoon to discuss women's rights and the annual convention. Norah liked Nellie and desired to have a friend, but she didn't understand why the girl would involve herself in this movement that was mostly run by a horde of wealthy Protestant women. Nellie's family had come from Northern Ireland in the early 1800s and Nellie couldn't really comprehend Norah's childhood in Ireland. It was mostly due to Margaret Fuller that made Norah walk out of the employment bureau with Nellie to have tea with her one afternoon two weeks ago. Finding Margaret Fuller's words on the pamphlets that Nellie was handing out after reading *Woman in the Nineteenth Century* could not be coincidental and Norah had felt something mysterious moving through her, as if the author was following her, urging her on. For what, she didn't know, and when Nellie began spouting the tenets of women's rights and passionately speaking of marriage being legal prostitution and women having no property rights and no voice in politics, Norah was disappointed. She had her fill of movements and didn't want to be a part of this movement or any movement. And weren't there hundreds of them to get involved in? She had politely told Nellie that she was only interested in learning more about this Margaret Fuller and maybe she could meet her someday, but she didn't want to go to meetings and fight for women's rights. After all, she and her family lived in the Sixth Ward and it was a fight just to stay alive there! Five Points needed their own movement, of a different sort, she told Nellie. Just the day before, twelve gang members had been violently killed when the Bowery Boys and Rabbits had battled yet again.

But here she was now standing on a bustling cold street, women's skirts whishing by and carriages spattering mud on her. The Tabernacle was stately and loomed with great spires over the street. She hesitated, however, before crossing the street to enter a church where she wouldn't be going to Mass. Should she really go inside? She shuddered with fear and from the icy air, and thought back to her conversation with Nellie when Norah told her about reading Margaret Fuller's book. Nellie had pushed her pie away and grasped Norah's hands in hers.

Her eyes sparkling, she said excitedly, "Norah, I do believe that if the esteemed Margaret Fuller were alive today, she'd march right into the Sixth Ward and up to your door to meet you."

So her Margaret Fuller was dead.

Norah readied herself to cross the street, for indeed Margaret Fuller was the real reason why she was attending the Seventh National Woman's Rights Convention. When Nellie explained that Margaret Fuller had died in a shipwreck off Long Island after returning with her husband from fighting in Italy's failed revolution, the words from *Woman in the Nineteenth Century* rose up in Norah's mind. Both she and Margaret Fuller shared significance, although her own heart still beat on this perplexing earth and Margaret Fuller's didn't. But was her heart noble after coming through a shipwreck, like Margaret Fuller had written about? How little the two women had in common—Margaret Fuller, her blood line Anglo-Saxon, born in America into a prominent family, learned; Norah, her blood line Celt, born in Ireland into poverty, her learning sparse. And yet didn't they have grief in common! And in death, Margaret Fuller's words remained alive and had found Norah. Mournful, Norah was still; noble, she felt she wasn't.

Norah stepped across the street, along with other women who walked quickly and purposely. None of them laughed or talked together the way she used to do with Mary when they went to the theater. Oh, she wished she wasn't alone! Nellie hadn't shown up at the coffee shop to meet her as planned, but Norah had decided to go by herself. It didn't feel like a merrymaking event and she almost turned around in the middle of the street, but was thronged by people, mostly women, on every side of her.

When she finally stood in front of the Tabernacle, Norah saw women handing out the same pamphlets Nellie had been handing out at the bureau. There were also young boys and men, heckling and laughing at them, taking their pamphlets, and tearing them up.

"Man haters!" yelled an elderly gentleman walking by, his cane thrust angrily towards the Tabernacle.

"Man Tamers!" a man wearing soaplocks and a top hat said, who then went into a fit of laughter.

The women ignored them and with resolute and unsmiling faces, continued to pass out the pamphlets. An older woman walking by who wore great hoops underneath her skirts yelled out, "You're bringing shame on our sex!"

Norah climbed the steps and stopped, but a woman behind her pushed her and because others around her were rushing to get in out of the nasty weather, she was carried along into the Tabernacle. As soon as she entered, her skin tingled, but not with cold; the beats of her heart quickened and excitement filled her. She felt heroic for just making it inside and decided that whatever happened this day, it would be momentous. She waited for her eyes to adjust to the dim light in the building before finding a seat. She breathed in the musk, honey, and orange blossom toilet soaps of well-groomed ladies, as well as the odor of fried food that clung to the clothing of those having just left eateries for their noon meals. She stood still and watched everyone moving around her. It became clear that much had conspired to bring her to this place, but that it wasn't just the place and event she had been brought to. Revelation came to her that she, Norah McCabe, would live and not just live, but live like she had always wanted to live and hadn't known how. She hadn't just walked into a curious event in a strange building, but had come to the place within herself she knew she would be able to settle into. She wanted to think with other women and talk about thinking and real possibilities, and not keep this part hidden inside of her. She would always want to wear fancy clothing, but she wanted what her Murray had possessed so eloquently and what Mr. Harrigan had with his newspaper, and even temperamental John Mitchel had bounding around in his active mind. She didn't want to save Ireland or save women, but she did want to think about life freely, to mine the spirit, not just practice religion, and she desired to learn and not just learn to become a teacher. It had never occurred to her that she could think like Murray, or Harrigan, and John Mitchel. She looked around at the room full of women, the platform full of women, and a few men scattered throughout, and novel excitement coursed through her. She had once thought the newspaper office, dining at the grand Astor, and even returning to her homeland was enough for her, but she understood that all these experiences had prepared her for this day. As women lit gas lamps in the cathedral and someone played a solemn march on a pump organ, she found a seat in the third row down from the platform. She had made it inside! But she would make sure it wouldn't be the only door she would walk through, but one of many to become a noble woman. She unclasped her cape and shook out her curls that had been confined underneath her hood. As she settled in her seat, she felt a touch on her shoulder and looked up to see Nellie, her blonde hair plastered to her head, wet from the rain and sleet.

"Norah, I'm so sorry I missed you, but I'm pleased you've come anyway!" She gave Norah a quick hug and sat down next to her, squeezing her hand.

The anticipated meeting was soon called to order and when Lucy Stone stood to speak, a reverent silence filled the room. Norah listened through the sound of her heart beats, and although much of what the speaker said was alien to her way of thinking, she opened her mind. Lucy Stone spoke convincingly about women who were treated like chattel and had no self-government; neither did they possess equal control of their children or have a claim to property rightfully due them. She spoke of how women had cast their rights and properties at the feet of their husbands in exchange for affection.

Norah was impressed with Lucy Stone's speech, but was also puzzled. She concluded that any limitation Irish women had felt had not been experienced merely in being women, but as citizens treated unfairly by their government. She looked at the women on the platform and surmised they had not known hunger and deprivation as she had. For women like her mam and other Irish women, a good meal, a warm hearth, and love of family in a free country was great liberation. There hadn't been time to notice the lack of rights as Irish women because there had been no say in governing themselves anyway and they had been equal with their husbands in suffering inequality. Now that they were living in America, she supposed the crumbs of freedom had been enough to sustain them, for even this was hard work. Who had the luxury to consider inequality with men in office, property, marriage, and having a say in government? She nearly laughed aloud thinking how her mam and other Irish women dictated the behavior of their husbands. These women were unafraid to confront their husbands about what they believed was right and just, and they were the ones running the households and ordering them how to live! But it was still a struggle to survive even in America and as Norah peered around the room, she wondered if these women were pampered and had too much time on their hands.

Norah stopped listening to Lucy Stone and was consumed with thoughts about the freedom she needed to give herself. She looked at Nellie and desired to converse with her about these matters. Would her friend believe that she, Norah, had been married for a few days and in that marriage had felt equal and not like a possession? Murray's love had not been beastly lust she had needed to be unbounded from that this speaker ranted on about, but sensuality she had shared in as well. Norah sighed loudly, and Nellie reached for her hand. She regained her composure and sat upright to listen to the next speaker, Mrs. Elizabeth Jones from Ohio. Norah was surprised at the powerful venom in the woman's words.

> *And yet it was strange that in a country, priding itself upon intelligence, hosts of ignorant and filthy Irish and Germans are received upon our shores and all the privileges of citizenship conferred upon them, while the most intelligent woman of the land is permitted neither voice or act in the matter of her own Government.*

Norah was not unaware of how immigrants were viewed, especially the Irish, as well as the African, but the African often had more sympathy and was a prick against the conscience of Americans in this city. As yet, she and her people did not have this empathy, but were reviled and despised. *Oh my, this woman hates the likes of my kind!* What was she doing here listening to this nonsense? How had she allowed herself to be so moved by the honeyed words of American poets and writers? The speakers on the platform were talking about freedom for American women, native born women, not immigrant women! Norah's face flushed and shame coursed through her. Mostly she felt shame for not understanding this movement and thinking she might belong to it. Certainly women should have a say in living their lives, but as goodhearted these Protestant women were, they did not represent her!

Norah looked around for a way to escape without making a scene. She feared she might have to sit through another hour or two of more speeches. She looked over at Nellie and saw her smiling and pleased with the speaking. There were some men in the audience who were yelling out how outlandish these women's claims were. As she watched Nellie, she felt so lonely and misunderstood. No, Nellie could never understand all Norah had lived through in her young life. She hardly understood it herself! But what she did know at the moment was that she needed to get out of this building and home to her mam and da and find a way to be free with herself and her own people, which was enough of a challenge for now. Becoming noble, indeed!

"Nellie, I'm not feeling well. I'm going home," she whispered.

"It'll be over soon, Norah. Please don't leave yet. I thought we could go for tea—"

"Another time…"

Nellie stared at her as she stood to leave. Her new friend was perceptive in sizing up people and situations. But Norah did feel suddenly ill and it would be good to get home and have a hot cup of tea. Her stomach churned and her cheeks blazed as she walked down the aisle toward the door. No one else was leaving, but as she neared the door she saw a few men standing together, their arms folded and their faces grim. She wished she could avoid passing by them and quickly scanned the room to see if there was another exit, but there wasn't.

She straightened her back and girded up her new found confidence and quickly made for the door, not making eye contact with any of the men. One of them leapt to open the door for her, whispering loudly,

"Ye don't have the look of them, Miss, and I'm pleased to open the door for a real lady."

"Thank you kindly, sir," she said, without looking at him. An icy breeze met her full in the face as she stood on the top step. She grasped the railing, a faint coming over her. There was something familiar about the man's voice. His voice and the warm scent of him had touched a faraway place within her. She closed her eyes to keep her head from spinning and listened to vendors hawking their wares, the clip clop of horses, dogs barking, children yelling, and police whistles. It all rolled into one cacophonous disharmony, as if musicians in a band had forgotten their parts and were playing random notes. Norah breathed in the cold air and exhaled slowly, trying to steady herself. And then she heard the wooden door creak open and felt the presence of someone come near her. She was glad that someone was there, someone who might be able to help her sit down. She turned to see if her friend, Nellie, had followed her.

"Wee one! 'Tis you! And what would you be doin' going to a meeting with a bunch of cackling and crowing suffragists?"

"Sean?" He had left her when he was still a boy. He had left her to work as a ship's mate and never returned again to New York. Or maybe it isn't really him, she thought, as she let go of the railing and crumpled into a faint.

Chapter Twenty-Nine

"**N**orah! *A Chuisle!* Norah, wake up...wake up!"

Norah roused and opened her eyes, but Da's face was hazy. She closed her eyes again and remembered Sean standing on the steps of the Tabernacle and then helping her into a carriage. The bouncing and rocking had made her so ill that she had thrown up in her hat.

"The doctor is here...do you hear me?"

"Is Sean here?"

"Sean who?"

Norah looked around to see who was in the room, if Sean was in the room. Mam, Da, and the man who had to be the doctor were the only ones. The doctor came over to the sofa and put his hand on her shoulder.

"I'm Dr. Murphy, Norah. I've brought the usual—castor oil, calomel, but first I'd like to determine if your symptoms might be related to your recent accident."

"He was there...Sean O'Connolly. Sean Connolly...Sean Connolly without the O. He was there at the meeting. Where is he now?" Norah covered her mouth with her hand. "I'm going to be sick!"

Mam held a bowl under her head, but Norah only coughed, for there was nothing more to be brought up.

"She's not been stable, Doctor... My Norah has been through a terrible grief, she has. Her mind is not proper, Doctor. Can ye give her something to calm her nerves?"

Norah leaned back on the sofa and moaned. Maybe she was crazy. She was crazy Irish just like the speakers at the convention said they all were, even her mam was crazy, she thought, as she listened to her babbling to the doctor. Wasn't it said that the Irish were ignorant, lacked common sense, had volatile tempers, and were slaves of the Pope? And maybe she was mad to parade around the streets with Nellie, thinking her mind and spirit were special. Margaret Fuller died and yet the woman still lived through her words! But she, Norah, had lived and yet she had no words like Margaret Fuller's superior ones.

"Who was it then who brought me home?" she asked.

"A stranger saw that you were ill and put you in a carriage. You must have given the driver your address," Da said.

"And what were you doing at that church meeting, Norah? What has gotten into your foolhardy head now?" Mam asked.

"Marion...not now...leave her be. Dr. Murphy needs to tend to her. Leave her be." Da grasped his wife's arm.

Mam turned away to tidy up the kitchen, complaining quietly.

"Don't be worrying over the state of my soul just because I walked into a meeting at a Protestant church. I didn't stay, now, did I?"

It's worse, Norah thought, worse to become a little enlightened and then return to a place where that much light is not understood. *Neither here nor there,* she thought, sadly. *I belong nowhere! And what about Sean? Was it him or just my imagination and the stranger was someone who reminded me of him?*

"Your mam and I will leave while Dr. Murphy examines you," Da said.

Norah's recent experience with doctors after the shipwreck had lessened the self-consciousness she felt about her body, but she was annoyed by the intrusion.

"I'm ready, I suppose, Dr. Murphy, but please no blood-letting."

After the doctor's examination and pronouncement that she was fit as a fiddle and her dyspepsia should not to be treated with bitters, bloodletting, or calomel, Norah was perplexed although relieved. And then he smiled broadly and announced that she, Norah McCabe, was going to have a baby. Mam and Da returned to hear the news and nervously fluttered around her and then left with the doctor so she could sleep. They said they were going to the general store to purchase some fresh fruit and vegetables, if Maguire's had any. After everyone left, Norah looked over at her dresser and said aloud, "Sure now, didn't I know there was life growing in me!"

Over the next two months, Norah suffered with great bouts of agonizing nausea and dyspepsia, and her body required great amounts of sleep. She lived on broth, tea, and moderate amounts of sub nitrate of bismuth. The baby sought so much nourishment from her that her body couldn't keep up with its own needs and she had to have two teeth pulled. Fortunately, they were in the back of her mouth, but no matter how much she brushed, the rest of her teeth dulled; her thick hair became lackluster and lost much of its curl. Her complexion, once creamy and rosy, was pallid. She lost too much weight for a pregnant woman, but her belly grew round and hard and because of her thinness, it boldly thrust out before her, reminding her that life could not be halted in its intention. She endured the whispers and gossip of the neighborhood women who sat on the stoops of the tenement houses eyeing her with sharp eagle eyes.

Da left to work on the rails in Oregon and Mam was melancholy as she toiled at the Astor. And she nearly collapsed under the weight of the gossip over Norah. She was excited about the baby, she told her daughter, but worried over their finances, although Da had left them with some money and promised to send more. Norah's mind was changing as rapidly as her body. At times she feared she would end up as other Irish widows with children—in the poorhouse or even the insane asylum, but she also felt transcending hope that sustained and girded her throughout each difficult day. Oftentimes, she would sit on the sofa and embrace her belly, rocking and cooing to the baby that hadn't yet been born. After three months passed, Norah regained strength and her appetite increased, the nausea having dissipated. Her complexion cleared and by the fourth month, a light peach colored her cheeks.

One morning, she rose from the sofa and looked at the dresser that was now full of baby things and declared to it that she had to get on with her life, baby in tow. She had to find work to sustain herself and her child, as well as contribute to the apartment and alleviate Mam's constant worries. She would be useless as a domestic, for already her belly was extended and soon it would be impossible to bend over to scrub floors. Her shop had been sold, the money spent, and she didn't want to own another one. She momentarily thought about her school-teacher and her suggestion Norah train to become a teacher. Should she try and find out where this teacher lived? She looked down at her belly and realized it was too much for the moment. But…who knows, maybe after the baby was born.

Norah's mind raced with possibilities, although none formulated realistically in her mind. Nevertheless, she was determined and felt light-hearted and positive with Murray's baby growing within her. She walked into the bedroom and opened the trunk of clothing she had saved from her dress shop. She would have to let out the waist of some of the dresses if she was ever going to leave the house in a few months when she would be as large as a whale.

Later, when Norah was struggling at the kitchen table to make soda bread to have it baked and warm for when Mam returned from work, there was a series of knocks on the door. Flour covered her hands and the front of an old dress she had let the seams out of. She hurried to the water closet to wash up, but gave up and rushed to open the door to Mr. Harrigan who took off his velvet stove pipe hat and gave a slow nod in greeting. He was wearing a black chesterfield with a velvet collar that matched his hat. Norah smiled at the sight of him, this Mr. Harrigan always the gentleman.

"And who might you be quoting from in Five Points for your next issue, Mr. Harrigan?" she asked with a sweep of her arm indicating he should enter. He had seen her in so many circumstances she wasn't that uncomfortable now.

"Oh! It's your books! You've come for them!" she exclaimed, remembering the last time she had seen him was at his office when she borrowed books.

"I'm not even slightly worried about my books, Miss McCabe, and that is not why I have come for a visit, although I'm certainly confused by the look of you!"

He laughed heartily, his penetrating eyes looking her over. She looked down and saw that Mam's apron was twisted to the side and her belly stuck out, completely covered in flour.

"I'm not like my mam or sister, Meg, Mr. Harrigan. I don't do this...well...I'm trying...," she said, pointing to the glob of dough on the table.

"I give up then! But I can make tea and I'm all for taking this apron off and making us a strong cup."

Norah laughed and removed the apron, excusing herself.

"I'll make the tea, Norah...by the looks of you, girl, you need my help," he said.

A few minutes later, Norah returned to see that cups had been placed on a chair before the sofa and the water on the stove was set to boil. She dragged another chair from the kitchen table to sit opposite Mr. Harrigan who sat on the sofa with his coat unbuttoned. He wore a white ruffled shirt underneath his woolen gray vest and gold chains were wrapped around his neck and flowed to his breast pocket that gathered to a breast pin holding one large pearl. He was dressed more elaborate than she had ever seen him.

"And why are ye all dressed up as fancy as a peacock this day?" she asked.

"I was hoping to convince you to go to dinner with me at the Astor, but I see..." He cast his eyes down and then abruptly stood up to make the tea.

"I'll wait until after you pour the tea, Mr. Harrigan, before I explain my present situation."

Mr. Harrigan stood at the stove and let the tea steep a few minutes in strained silence, and then poured them both cups. He sat back down and folded his hands in his lap, looking affectionately into Norah's face. She sensed sincere friendship, not judgment, and for this she was relieved. How she needed him as a friend!

"I'm going to have Murray's baby...I think in five or so months... and I'm pleased, but—"

"Are you well? You look a trite too thin. Have you seen a doctor?"

"I'm well now. And yes a doctor has seen me. I couldn't eat for weeks, but now I'm hungry all the time...but as you can see, I'm in grave danger of starving for I'm useless making soda bread!"

"Then put on another dress, pinch your cheeks as Lady Godey's book instructs girls like yourself to do, put on a fine hat and..." Mr. Harrigan stood to his feet and bowed, "we'll celebrate new life in all its varied and interesting forms at dinner!"

Norah jumped up, catching her cup and saucer before it fell onto the floor. No need for bad luck with a broken teacup!

"But there'll be gossip...with my condition I shouldn't be in public. I can't hide—"

"I don't want you hidden, Norah McCabe. I want you proclaimed to the world or at least to our New York world, that you have survived a shipwreck and lived to become a female correspondent for the *Irish-American* newspaper. In fact, don't they all know now what a grand writer you are, Miss McCabe. After your article was published, there was much response and I've been meaning to tell you, but I've been so busy...but dear Norah, I'm rambling on and on...hurry and change so we can celebrate!"

Norah overcame her surprise and changed into a gown that once had been too large. It was an especially elegant and beautiful gown that she had been unable to resist buying. And now, nearly two years later, it was a perfect fit for her body that was round with child. She was being hired to work for a newspaper, and not as an errand girl this time!

Chapter Thirty

"It's worse in Boston! The Irish men there are after keeping women in chains…their own Paddy chains," Norah exclaimed to Mr. Harrigan.

They sat in the office together taking a much needed break after editing and laying out the next issue of the newspaper. Norah was seven months pregnant and radiant; her body having warmly aligned itself to the growing child within. She had gained a healthy weight and her creamy skin with the myriad of freckles had a soft glow, as if the sun had gently brushed its rays over her. Since there had been a positive response to the wreck of the *Diana* article Norah had written, Mr. Harrigan had given her some liberty to express her views about a variety of topics, including the women's movement. Norah's opinions straddled the line between support and antipathy and because she was entombed in an Irish enclave, as well as in her own Irish skin, she was no real feminist. She thought hard about the movement's various positions on issues of the day. For the Negro, she wanted freedom, but Mr. Harrigan was cautious about this subject; for women, Norah believed possessing property rights and being able to vote alongside men seemed evident of basic human rights. She was also reading the words of the Transcendentalists and longed to sit amongst them, although there was a line of separation drawn between these writers and most Irish, regardless how far the Irish had come. The Century Club the Irish might push their way into, but not into the living rooms in Concord. As for abortion, she was against it, but not because she was Catholic. She had lost her best friend to the knife of an abortionist and even if Mary had survived she would have experienced immense guilt. And Norah was fervidly against abortion because she was in love with the growing child within her. When she considered the anti-Irish, anti-immigrant, anti-Catholic message and rhetoric of the women in the movement, she wrote heatedly about these issues.

Norah's pen flowed with ease and passion, but Mr. Harrigan, proud of his moderate newspaper, was ever cautious. He admitted slavery was in conflict with the Declaration of Independence, but believed this dark institution was too ingrained in American society to suddenly abolish it. Norah disagreed, but her hands were tied, or rather, spattered with Mr. Harrigan's ink opposing her radical views. He seemed to be sitting on the fence about a great deal of issues, but at least he was not espousing the extreme position that John Boyle O'Reilly of The Boston Pilot was doing.

"Aye, his paper is a storm center against women voting and he, like most Irish men, feels threatened. You have to understand, Norah… Irish men are still new at pumping up their muscles and screwing up their courage to partake of the powerful machinery of the Democrats, nonetheless, they are finally having a voice in the political climate of major cities, especially New York and Boston. Can you blame them for not wanting women usurping their fragile position?" Harrigan laughed and grabbed his black satin cravat to cover his mouth.

"And what is there to laugh about?" Norah asked, slightly irritated. She was thinking about what she had just written for the issue gone to print. The recent riot on July fourth between the Bowery gang and Mulberry Street Gang had been plaguing her thoughts, especially because Mam, Meg, Meg's children, and herself boarded up their windows and holed themselves up in their apartment until the riot was over. She had written a passionate article about the riot and innocently pleaded for sensible tolerance and peace. She titled the article, 'The History of Irish Fury Knows No Bounds.' She wrote that inter-ethnic strife was not to blame, because in the blood of her people there was a wound from oppression that belied reason and erupted into senseless fury. They would even kill for a place in the custom house or to be a street cleaner. The Metropolitan Police Act was said to be the blame, which had taken away the mayoral power of Fernando Wood and placed it in the hands of Albany. Most Irish believed that it was Black Republicanism, so called by Democrats because of their obsession with freedom for African Americans. They felt there was an outright plan to disenfranchise foreign-born citizens and keep them from political rights. And she had just read that the Know Nothings were shutting down saloons on Sundays and enforcing temperance laws.

Mr. Harrigan didn't have time to read her final draft before it went to print and he might be surprised how she had written about her own people. It was an injustice for the Irish who were denied rights to then deny rights for their own! Was it human nature to always destroy itself? Who was the enemy? Norah had sensed this riot brewing before it gushed forth onto the streets and would write to help her people, but mostly she realized she couldn't change the world all that much, but was willing to change a corner of it for her child.

"I'm laughing because the men know the women have them all honey-fuggled as it is. How many Irish men run their households?" Harrigan asked.

"In my home, there's gentleness between Mam and Da. We are different from other Irish families, I suppose. And I, myself, never had a home with my husband..."

Norah stood up and walked to the window, her mood darkening as she felt her baby move within her, a reminder of her loss as well as her gain in her brief marriage.

"About the article, Norah...I'm a bit concerned...maybe just a trifle worried about..." Mr. Harrigan fumbled to speak and stopped. Norah turned to look at him.

"It's too late…the paper will be sold on the streets tomorrow morning. It's not a good time to wonder whether it should have been printed! You tell me to write what I want and then you whine and wring your hands…just like an old woman!"

She looked out the window again, knowing she had probably hurt his feelings. She was becoming more frustrated with him over his yellow-bellied doubts, and perhaps even with his lack of manliness. What did she believe a man should be? A brutish thug who punched his way into getting what he wanted? A fawning obsequious gentleman who politely served others out of fear? Or was it someone like one of the Tammany men who wielded power without really getting his hands dirty? Mr. Harrigan was strong minded, but his convictions were usually safe and sound ones and he was apt to keep his white gloves on. But once in awhile he took off a glove and took Norah's hand and welcomed her to get at the jugular vein of the issue. She sighed and wrapped her arms around her baby and her self—they were one, and in a puzzling way, she almost wished that the two of them could stay together like this and her babe would not be born into this puzzling world.

Later in the day, Norah sat in the office struggling to write a simple article about the Irish charity organizations in New York, but was unable to keep her mind from straying to other things, including the recent riot. She was also flipping through the pages of old newspapers and saw that most of them contained front page news about consensual sodomy. She was surprised that this particular subject matter dominated a pile of papers that went as far back as 1845. She read an article in the *Herald* printed in 1846 about acts of buggery and sodomy, as well as males in New York who dressed in feminine attire and took on female names. Since arriving in New York, she had listened to Mam and other Irish women sit on the stoops of the tenements and talk about the sexual transgressions of America, but mostly these were the vagrancies of women or about women abused by men. Never had she heard anything spoken about the "other." It was dear Mary, of course, who once told her about male boardinghouses and what went on in them and that women, too, loved one another as husband and wife do.

"You need to go home, Norah…do you not feel safe there since the riot?" Mr. Harrigan swooped through the door, startling her.

"I thought you'd have gone home before dark," he said, carrying in the humidity of a late summer evening.

"Mam is staying with Meg…she's frightened. I told her I'd be staying here the night…if you don't mind."

"You are most welcome to spend the night, Norah!"

Mr. Harrigan had obtained a mahogany circular Victorian sofa a few months back, inviting Norah to recline on it for rest in her condition. She had only sat on the rich upholstered couch, but had never stayed the night. She wanted to be in the office in the early morning when the paper was printed and Mr. Harrigan would read what she had written. It might be the last article she would write for him after this one. She was concerned about being out of work, but was weary of Five Points and working for Mr. Harrigan, anyway. Her friend from the convention, Nellie Gorman, had recently come to visit and they had a lengthy lunch at Taylor's ice cream parlor. Norah told her everything about herself, including her marriage, the shipwreck, and her job at the *Irish-American*. Nellie thought Norah very brave and admired her for her choices. She herself had separated from her family to pursue a teacher's education and was living in the city alone, purposed to make changes in her life as well as in poor children's lives in the city. As they talked, it became clear that they had much in common as women, and their differences were minor compared to the bond of friendship that had grown. Nellie had even suggested they share an apartment to lessen expenses. Norah was frank with Nellie about what she thought of the women's movement, and Nellie had laughed and said she only attended the meetings occasionally because she needed to focus on getting her teaching certification.

"Your babe will be my first student, Norah!" Nellie said, laughing and tenderly patting Norah's bulging stomach.

Yes, she was becoming restless with life in Five Points, but there was apprehension about untying the umbilical cord to her people. Walking amongst them in Five Points was familiar and the rough accents and manners of her people felt like the warmth of her sofa. She often became irritated with them for their stubborn old ways, but she also loved them for it because within the confines of it came the early scents and myths of her childhood. And now there was Nellie's offer and it would be like flying the nest, but hadn't she already done so when she ran off with Murray? Why not do it again, but oh, how much safer it would be.

Mr. Harrigan took off his coat and walked toward her. Then he saw that she had found the newspapers he had meant to take home long ago. He fumbled with his buttons on his vest and looked down, then clapped his hands together, keeping them pressed.

"I see that you've found the newspapers I've collected."

Norah was embarrassed for both of them. She knew he was a dandy, but she didn't actually believe he was…well, she had never seen him with…but one never knew…Oh my, she didn't want to know. She just wanted him to stay her friend.

"I was just reading some of the old—"

"I am not a sodomist, Norah, as you might think I am."

"Oh, I never thought—"

"Let me finish what I have to say…"

Mr. Harrigan's handsome face shed its color and his coal black pupils expanded. He hesitated, stared at her, and then sat down on the sofa, patting the space next to him. She sat down and placed her hands over her belly for comfort.

"I've never had the desire to marry…" He leaned his head against her shoulder which startled her, but she didn't move. "Except when I met you…and even with our differences, I thought it could work, but then you left and came home with Murray's baby. But I would still marry you…"

Norah's heart was thudding so loudly, she was certain he could hear it. Could she marry him? Mr. Harrigan? There would be security for both her and her baby! He was fairly well off, but she felt no real passion for him as she had felt for Murray.

Mr. Harrigan sat up and looked straight ahead as he spoke. "You probably don't know about the rumors that once circulated about my life. But, dear Norah, they ceased circulating in Five Points a couple of years ago. I haven't heard anyone say anything about my single life for awhile now…and that is because…I believe it's because…you've been attached to me through my newspaper and people have conjectured or felt that at last, my odd and peculiar state, is over.

Norah felt bewildered, not fully comprehending him.

"I was going to ask you to marry me when I came to take you to dinner. Of course I wanted you to become a writer for my paper, but there was more to it. When I met you, you were the first woman I'd ever had romantic feelings for. The only one! But then I also came to the sad conclusion that I wasn't being honest with myself. I wanted you in my life to make myself more acceptable to the world. This world can't believe that I am happy being single and wearing my fineries."

"I saved these old newspapers with articles about sodomy because many of them are false! And also my name appeared in one of the articles years ago…in the *Herald.* It was ruinous! It said that my paper never published anything about the evils of sodomy and being that I am one who loves my fashion and was not married, I must, too, be a participant of this sin. I kept these papers to someday write an article about the entire subject, including responding to the charge that I am a homosexual. But then the rumors died down and…I meant to take the papers home with me."

Norah sat silent for a few moments; she was very tired and really didn't know what to say. And then she smiled at him and spoke.

"Mr. James Harrigan, I accept you as you are. I'm very flattered that you considered proposing to me, but we both know that our friendship doesn't warrant more. Right now, I'm so weary that I'm sure I can't even sit up any longer. Might I just lie down as I am and sleep?"

Harrigan went into action and retrieved an old blanket he kept in a closet. He placed it on Norah gently as she curled up on the sofa, her arms around her belly and her eyes closed in exhaustion.

"I'll take care of finishing up the paper, Norah, and maybe I'll sleep here tonight, too."

The blanket warmed and soothed Norah as she listened to Mr. Harrigan sighing and shuffling papers at his desk. Soon, she fell asleep, unable to think any further about his curious pronouncements of love.

Chapter Thirty-One

His cumbersome presses long ago sold, Mr. Harrigan had his newspaper printed on Printing House Row, paying the *Sun* a considerable fee for using their presses. The lad hired for delivery and pick-up pounded on the door around four in the morning. Harrigan had been sleeping with his head on his desk only a couple of hours, for after Norah fell asleep, he wrote an article for his next issue that would be the first one written without fear of contempt or backlash. He had to write more than the mediocre slop he had been dishing out to his readers. Norah had become his inspiration and after confiding in her, he felt liberated. And as he wrote, his heart was inflamed with love for this Irish woman who was unique with all her complexities. Maybe this is how romantic love feels, he thought, as he wrote an article about Tammany Hall.

He opened the door and took two bundles of newspapers from the boy. He looked out at the sun rising and the wavering of red heat between buildings, and felt his spirits also rising for this new day. He paid the boy and shut the door, hurrying to sit at his desk to read the issue. It was his favorite part of newspaper work—seeing all the bits and pieces of an issue finally organized into one body. And each time, he would read every single word all the way through before getting himself washed and ready for breakfast at Jim's Eatery. He unfolded the paper, put his feet on his desk, and looked over at Norah. She stirred, sat up briefly, but lay back down to sleep. He wondered if the newspaper boy had seen her lying on his sofa and the news would be all around town. He might even relish the gossip that a woman such as Norah McCabe had spent the night with him in his office.

Norah slept while Mr. Harrigan read her article with pride. Although his article wasn't printed yet, they were both stepping before the firing squad (so to speak) of the powerful Tammany Hall by addressing their latest maneuverings in Five Point neighborhoods. It was not going to abide well for an Irish newspaper to have scolded the very machine that was enabling the Irish immigrant to gain footage and rights in his or her new country. Even the *Herald* or the *Sun* did not like to print harsh criticism about Tammany, for this strong arm of politics wrapped around all of New York and could squeeze to death whom it wanted. Norah had gone further in her writing than he had, using her pen as a scalpel to dig into the Irish immigrant heart and cut out the sinister disease of shame and pride that thrust them into murderous acts through gangs. His hands shook when he folded the newspaper and laid it on his desk.

He got up and went to Norah who was sleeping on her back, her belly large and round. Her face was pale, which made her freckles prominent and child-like. Her thick brown hair stuck to her neck and forehead because of the humidity of the morning. Her round breasts were hidden underneath a white blouse that had come unbuttoned, revealing an undergarment displaying the shadow line that separated them, like a stream flowing further into something larger. He watched them move in a gentle rhythm as she breathed and he couldn't take his eyes off of them. Desire coursed its way into his already weakened body. He wanted to lay his hands upon them and feel the tempo and cadence of a part of life he had never experienced. He resisted, for he was a gentleman, but he stood watching her for many minutes, finally kneeling before her and opening his mouth slightly as he touched his lips as light as a feather to her own parted ones. A puzzle piece locked in place within him and he stayed this way until the rhythm of her breath accelerated and she closed her lips and moaned, moving them within his own that now gently covered hers. And then she woke and pushed him away.

"What are you doing?" She sat up on the sofa.

He jumped to his feet and turned back to his desk, shocked at himself and unable to face her. The only kiss he had given someone was when he was fifteen years of age. A neighborhood girl had dared him to kiss her, but then taunted and rejected him afterward.

"I thought...it was Murray. I was dreaming of him and then I woke up," Norah said, buttoning her blouse and fixing her hair.

"Why would you do such a thing?"

Mr. Harrigan stood facing his desk, "I'm sorry, Norah, please forgive me. After reading your article—"

"You read it? It's out? Oh no...well, go ahead and fire me if you want, but I don't want to write only what you want me to write!"

Harrigan turned to face her and his face was lit up with eagerness.

"You're wrong! We both have written articles that are bold! Me, for the first time... and you daring to be what you've always been—honest and real. We have something that others don't have, Norah. We have insight and truth about our world right here in New York and in Five Points and together we can change it. Can't we? Harrigan went to Norah and kneeled before her again.

"I'm asking if you'll let me be your husband and father of your child...and together we can make this newspaper stand out and be a voice for change."

"Don't kneel down like that, Harrigan...I'm not someone to adore. Please stand up....I think I liked it better when you disagreed with me." She laughed but then saw in his face that she had hurt his feelings.

He stood and then helped her off the sofa. Norah smiled up at him.

"I said last night that I was flattered. I was, but this morning, I'm greatly flattered—"

"I don't want you to be flattered. I want you to let me love you."

He rushed over to his desk and picked up the article he had written, bringing it to Norah.

"Here, read this. Read my article. We are both one in our thoughts and I believe we can be one in many ways."

She read it and then laughed, clapping her hands together.

"How could you have changed so much and I didn't see it? But just because we see eye-to-eye now on confronting serious issues doesn't mean we're meant to get married. I've already been married for a few nights and it was enough for my whole life…look at me now?"

Oh, why not be loved, she thought. He is quite a handsome man, well established…and she liked him very much. He had seen her through many distressing times, but how awkward it would be for intimacy! She felt a flush of arousal as she remembered waking to his kiss. Maybe…

"I accept your proposal, James Harrigan," and Norah felt her life, that had been on a long hard journey, had finally come to a specific destination. A destination she wasn't sure she wanted to arrive at, but it would be good for both her and her baby.

Mr. Harrigan, as gentle as a lamb, wrapped his arms around her, pressing against her warm baby belly. He had never in his life felt such belonging and rapture. He buried his face in her neck that was moist with the rising heat of the summer morning.

"I love you, Norah McCabe. Indeed, I love you."

M am wrote Da telling him he had to come home because Norah was going to be married, properly now. She had always liked Mr. Harrigan and secretly hoped he would ask her daughter to marry him. And now Norah wouldn't be strapped having a baby to care for as a widow and, of course, she hoped the gossip about her daughter would subside. Their marriage was planned for a day in October, before Norah's due date. Mam thought Norah's life was going to be normal and secure, but fewer papers were selling and nasty letters had been received after Norah's and Mr. Harrigan's articles about Tammany were printed. Mam had pleaded with them to write articles about Ireland, to print Irish poetry, and to write about the Irish in America who were successful.

"I think it's time, James," Norah said a few weeks later as they worked together in the office. "Time for change! We aren't selling papers and it's time to move on to something else. We can start another newspaper that is more widely read and not just by Irish readers. We've said all we can say about Tammany and it isn't being received and we're only making people angry. Maybe we can—"

"Norah, how can you suggest such a thing? My father started this newspaper and made it what it is. And I've recently had hopes that someday my own child would take over the paper—"

"This child?" she asked, patting her big belly. Lately, she had become too tired to walk and she was suffering from painful varicose veins that Mam rubbed with crushed chamomile and lavender in the evenings.

Mr. Harrigan rushed to Norah who was sitting at her desk writing an article about the eateries in Five Points who allowed women to frequent them without the accompaniment of a male. He pulled her to her feet and hugged her, rubbing his hands all over the backside of her and through her hair, kissing her forehead and cheeks and then trying to kiss her lips, but she pulled away.

"Stop…your passion is out of control!" she laughed. He was unable to keep his hands off of her since she had accepted his proposal. Her doctor indicated that although they were going to be married, it was paramount that they not have sexual relations until a month or more after the baby was born. She was relieved. In fact, she was more than relieved, for she possessed no desire. She could not see herself having the same intimacy with James that she had with Murray. She wasn't worried over this, and felt that, in time, after her baby was born, it would become natural for them to come together as man and wife. It was more important now that he consider starting another newspaper.

"Your baby will be my baby, too, Norah dear," Harrigan said, reaching for her again, his hands sliding over her breasts that were nearly as swollen as her belly.

"James Harrigan!" she yelled. She felt too big and uncomfortable to be touched, although she liked him to hold her affectionately when they sat together in the evenings.

"Can't you think of nothing else?" she asked.

He backed away, trying to discreetly cover his arousal. He sat down at his desk and picked up his pen.

"James…"

He looked at her and she had a smirk on her face. The woman was glad for his suffering, he thought.

"Let's start another newspaper. It can be more balanced in views and have a greater readership—"

"No! It's impossible—"

"But we're not selling papers…."

"It's temporary, Norah. I've seen it over the years. Why do you think you know more than me about these things?"

"I don't, but aren't you weary of only writing about Tammany?"

He slammed his pen down and ink splattered on his papers.

"Before, you said I was producing dull material about unimportant events…and then you said I should take a stand in my editorials. Now that I have, you criticize me. What do you want from me? I am not going to close down this newspaper and that is that!" Harrigan sighed and picked up his pen again.

Norah went back to writing the article, but was displeased and unnerved…and she felt trapped. *It's probably because the baby is coming soon, she thought, and after this babe is born, I won't be so irritable. I'll be able to do more, think better, and…* Her thoughts halted and she stared at the tablet in front of her. Had she been under the delusion that she would have more expression, more experience, and more of a say as James Harrigan's wife? It was a given that she would become his possession and although she would have more than she ever had in her life financially, as well as a father for her child, she would be more limited than she was now! What had she gotten herself into? These thoughts rammed up against the somber reality that she could end up being alone with a baby, without work, and living with Mam who would be scraping by until Da returned home to them. She would become a child again with a child. She clasped her head in her hands in turmoil. She couldn't go through with this marriage although she liked James more than any man she knew and he adored her and wanted to care for her and her baby. She thought they would work together equally on the newspaper, but he had declared they would not start another newspaper. She wouldn't be his equal, for it was his newspaper and it would never be her newspaper! But most importantly, she couldn't love him the way a woman should love her husband. She turned in her chair to face him.

"James," she said softly.

He looked over at her and neither of them spoke for a few moments. It was just like the time they both wrote articles about Tammany and had been in sync. It had happened again. He knew she couldn't marry him. And he had come to a place within himself that pooled like clear water about who he was. Yes, he loved Norah, but his feelings were displaced. He had loved his mother fervently and when he was twelve years old, she had died in childbirth. From that time, he had shut down emotionally. It was dear Norah in her pregnancy who had brought him to a place of loving again. But he wasn't ready for marriage and he knew she wasn't either. She loved Murray and it was too soon for her to love someone else.

"I...," they said simultaneously, and laughed.

Norah and James Harrigan would always care for one another. He would keep her working for him even if she needed to flee elsewhere occasionally. But there had to be mutual respect and equality, the only way this special Irish woman would ever have it. She had been beautifully engraving on his mind the need for women to be equal. His experience with Norah would alter and diversify his newspaper as New York expanded into the future.

Chapter Thirty-Two

Norah left James sitting at his desk with his head in his hands. They said all they could manage to say without losing control of their emotions. His last words were that he would remain faithfully her friend for the rest of their lives. He insisted she continue writing for the newspaper, but she said it would be too difficult for both of them if she stayed. His hands were shaking when he placed a month's salary into her hands and told her to ask for his help when she needed it. When he began questioning what she would do for work when her baby was born and whether she and Mam would have enough to eat, she quieted him with a kiss on the cheek saying she would be fine. He hugged her to himself, holding her too tightly and desperately. She felt her belly tighten and the baby move, as if he or she were pushing him away. She left, but nearly turned back to say she had made a mistake. Indeed, perhaps it was a grave error to leave this gentle and caring man who could provide for both her and her baby.

She walked slowly down the street and it became evident to her that she should learn what her financial situation really was. She had received a letter from Murray's bank two days before. The letter only relayed that she, as the deceased's wife, should come to the bank to close out his account. What account, she didn't know, for she assumed Murray had taken all of his money out of the bank when they left New York. She didn't say anything to anyone, but laid the letter aside, thinking it was merely a formality of the bank. Now in the back of her mind, there was real possibility there might be something in this account. Wouldn't that be right and God's blessing upon her sorrows and troubles, she thought. She moved as quickly down the street as she was able, her full skirts ballooning over her belly and her undergarments sticking to her legs because of the humidity. She hailed a buggy and climbed in and sat with her closed eyes in an attempt to relieve the intensity of her situation.

"Your time is near?" asked a woman dressed in a black laced gown and bonnet.

"Near enough…but no worry, it won't be today," she said, looking out the window as the carriage bounced down the street. She didn't really know when the baby would come, but she knew it wasn't going to be soon.

There were two gentlemen in the carriage and they looked away when the woman asked Norah about her baby. She assumed these men had wives who had never left their homes when they began showing, as was considered improper for the upper classes. She felt a stab of embarrassment and smoothed out her skirts, continuing to look out the window.

The carriage came to a stop at Tompkins Square and Norah and the other passengers climbed out just as the skies opened up and poured rain. Puddles pooled beneath her skirts and her clothing was soaked within minutes. She hadn't brought an umbrella and wanted to quickly get underneath an awning of a storefront. As she moved toward the sidewalk, a crowd carrying umbrellas had gathered and she was moved along with them. She was protected from the pelting raindrops, but she didn't know where she was going and wanted to stop to ask someone where the bank was located before she went any further. But she was forced to keep moving forward with the crowd.

Norah looked around and thought it odd that there were mostly men, merchants and gentlemen, their faces filled with consternation. There was a strange silence amongst them and no one said a word. All Norah could hear was the somber pelting of the raindrops striking their umbrellas.

"Excuse me, sir, can you tell me where everyone is going in such a hurry?" she asked, reaching up to clutch a man's arm, fearing she might tumble onto the street and be trampled by the lot of them.

"The banks are closed...the banks are closed...disastrous...," the man said irately, shaking off Norah's arm as if to throw off the truth of the words he spoke. He walked ahead of Norah and she was pushed into another man who steadied her and helped her to where there were buildings with awnings. Saloonkeepers and merchants stood underneath the awnings to watch the crowd and shield themselves from the rain.

"'Tis no place for a woman in your condition... a riot's coming and you need to go home. It's been coming for a long time now. All the city's banks, but one, are closed and businesses will close. I have to get to the bank that isn't closed...there'll be a line. You should go home, Miss!" and he gave her a nod and walked away.

Norah wrapped her arms around her belly and stood underneath the ripped awning of a millinery shop trying to avoid the drips. She turned to look in the window and saw a display of richly textured hats with feathers and flowers adorning them. For a moment, she thought about purchasing one with the money James had given her. How foolish! Here she was with child, without a husband and a job, the streets were becoming riotous, and she was considering buying a new hat. She turned away and then jumped when rapid tapping struck the pane behind her head. She looked and it was her sister, Meg. In the confusion of the crowd and the downpour of rain, she had failed to notice she had ended up at the store her sister worked in part time. Meg's face was screwed up in dismay and worry as she waved for her to come inside. Of course, she would embarrass her sister in her place of employment because of her condition, but she didn't care. She needed her family, and hurried inside. Meg immediately removed Norah's damp shawl and placed it over a heater in the corner of the store to dry, clucking her tongue and muttering about Norah's lack of common sense. One other woman and a man stood at the counter staring at her.

Norah smiled and greeted them and then Meg's concerned face was before her.

"And what might you be doing here instead of being at work?" Meg asked.

"I'm not going to work—"

"Did you know the banks have all closed and we'll all be starving and there'll be no jobs for any of us...Norah, I won't be working much longer and my husband, well, he won't...," Meg said. She dabbed at her eyes with a handkerchief and Norah put her arm around her, but Meg broke away and smoothed out her skirts, glancing at the counter to see if anyone had seen and heard them.

"Why are you here?" she asked sternly.

"I had a letter from the bank that Murray had an account in—"

"What's the name of this bank?"

"The Municipal Savings Bank and Holding Company—"

"My God, Norah...that bank is closed. It closed yesterday before the rest of them that closed today—"

"Oh, well then..."

"Did you suppose Murray left some money in his account and you'd get it?

"I'd hoped—"

"Forget it now, Norah...oh, what will we all do in times like this?"

"What about your Tom, Meg? Isn't he working?"

"Yes, he's still working, but it isn't enough...you are a simpleton about real life, Norah...always dreaming and going off on tangents—"

"Please, Meg, don't start on me now..."

Meg's face softened when she saw how miserable Norah was. She looked at the others at the counter.

"I'll be taking my sister, Norah, for tea down the street for my break now," she stated and then whispered to her, "I'm to be let go, anyways..."

Norah and Meg left and walked through the crowd, mostly of men whom Norah thought looked as if they were in a funeral procession, dressed in black suits and black top hats, their faces grim and hard. Money! The need and desire for it pulsed through their veins and all through their lives. What was she going to do? Mam would not be able to care for them and certainly her Meg couldn't help now. She tried to push these desperate thoughts out of her mind as she and her sister walked to The Eatery. She was what her sister said she was, a fanciful and foolish girl! She, however, was no longer a girl, but a woman pregnant and alone. Meg pulled her to her side in a friendly hug and Norah was warmed by her sister's sudden affection, something she had wished for throughout the years. Maybe they could become friends now and not only be sisters. She desired for her baby and her sister's children to know one another, to grow up together and be close, to keep their ties to Ireland and to one another, never forgetting the past, but still moving on into wonderful things in the future. Her thoughts were suddenly more optimistic now that Meg had shown some sisterly love toward her. She hugged her sister back and they walked into the Eatery.

The diner was teeming with people coming in from the rain who had decided a late lunch or early dinner would be well worth spending their money on to get out of the nasty weather. Norah and Meg pressed themselves against others standing at the door waiting for a table to open up. The scent of frying onions and meat mingling with smoke and wet wool nauseated Norah and she covered her mouth worried she might be ill. For two months now, she had her strong stomach back, although she could only take a little food at a time. She hadn't eaten anything since early morning and hoped they would be given a table soon.

"Excuse us, sir…excuse us…pardon…," Meg said as she made her way ahead of others, pulling Norah behind her. Just like her, Norah thought, embarrassed for her sister who was always plowing her way through life. Small protests and snide remarks were made, but when they noticed Norah's pregnancy, they let the women pass. When the sisters reached the counter where every stool was taken by grimy faced men, Meg positioned herself next to a man shoving spoonfuls of soup into his mouth, impervious to anyone around him. Meg sighed and cleared her throat and the man put his spoon down and reached for his bread. While he buttered it, he stared into Meg's face belligerently and said nothing. He took a big bite and chewed all the while staring at her, daring her to say a word.

"If ye don't mind, sir, but my sister here, needs to sit down…"

Norah was incredulous that Meg would be this bold.

The man stopped chewing, put his piece of bread into his soup and looked at Norah. His face immediately softened and he gave her a large toothless grin.

"Yer most welcome to have my seat here, Miss…," he said gleefully, looking at her up and down.

"Yer most welcome, that is, after I have eaten me soup."

The man turned back to his soup and pulled out the soaked piece of bread, plopping it down on the counter. Then he picked up his soup bowl and slurped it down, taking his time.

Suddenly, before Meg and Norah or anyone in the eatery knew what was happening, hands came down upon the shoulders of the man defiantly slurping his soup.

"You'll not be taking one more mouthful, my good man, but removing yourself so the woman with child here can be seated!" a swashbuckling voice echoed throughout the diner that had suddenly become quiet.

Norah was looking down at the floor, or rather her belly, for she could not see beyond it. Sweat beaded on her forehead and she felt sick. The booming voice instructing the stubborn diner to finish his soup possessed a familiar timbre striking a chord in her memory. She looked up to see Sean O'Connolly, her childhood friend, who had been missing at sea for years. Sean, who had disappeared from her life, was now standing before her. Norah didn't hear the man at the counter argue with Sean, see him spit at Meg, or even notice when he left the diner shouting curses. She had looked down again because the place was closing in on her and she needed to steady herself. She placed her hand on the corner of the counter and her mind reeled back in time. It had been a peculiar time in her life as an immigrant – a time of falling in love with America unawares; snowflakes that cleansed; alien languages from around the world; possibilities, and then meeting Sean. And then he vanished from her life. She had carried him in a place in her memory that was sealed up, like a tomb, and except for dreaming of him occasionally, there was no inclination to open that place ever again. But now as he stood before her, her heart was being excavated and memories were coming into the light. She looked up into his face creased with grime and tales.

"Sean O'Connolly... or might you be Sean without an O?" she asked as he put his arm around her shoulders and led her to the stool that was now unoccupied.

Meg left Norah and walked back to work. Norah sat at the counter for only a few minutes before a few men offered their table to her and Sean. It was the same table they had sat at together many years ago when she had thought 'hot dogs and beans' were pieces of dog meat, believing that just about anything happened in America. She wanted to return to Ireland desperately then, too, but unlike her recent plans to go there, it had been homesickness propelling her to go. She looked into the same face, although now it was weathered and altered, and remembered how he had insisted that only in America could dreams come true. She stared at him without speaking, while mugs of coffee, soup, and bread were placed in front of her. He had ordered food for them and was speaking to a few of the other men at the diner. All the while she watched him curiously, flying in and out of the present and the past, sipping small spoonfuls of celery soup without tasting it. He was not even thirty and yet she saw that his face appeared stone-like, chiseled and fixed in a certain time or event and with only one mien – a storm ravished landscape trying to recover. What had happened to him all these years?

He turned to her, his eyes red rimmed, his food untouched, and she noticed a small piece of caked dirt on the left side of his face that cracked each time he smiled.

"I've been enslaved in hauling human cargo, wee one." Sean looked up to the ceiling and squeezed his eyes shut for a moment, and then returned a sad gaze upon Norah.

"I remember well that I called you 'wee one,' but now I see you've become a grand one, a woman certainly above me now. And you who desperately wanted to return to the ole country, but who sits before me now all gussied up and important…as well as married with child. I see clearly the babe is nearly ready to be born! Did you never go back to Ireland?" He looked down a moment before continuing, "It would have been better for me to have gone back with you than where I've been!"

Sean looked away and his jaw tightened as he wiped at the dirt on his face. His shoulders slumped, but his broad chest rose and fell with a sigh that Norah thought could be heard by everyone around them.

"Ships run by murderers and thugs, manned by fools like me who became the weapons in the bastards' hands. All for the gold, for the greed that was groomed within us because we had hope of prospering in our sorry lives. I ran ships from Africa into the arse of America, those little countries trailing behind the United States of Amerikay! I did it for years and lost my soul, I tell you."

"And now all of that is finished?" Norah asked, startled by the knowledge that this once gentle and idealist boy had become a puppet for slave owners and buyers. She had read about the brutality of the slave trade and she was unable to meld together the Sean she once had known to this one who had become an instrument of darkness.

"Aye, 'tis finished now, but the memories will remain." His voice gave way to the low growl of a sea man.

He reached across the table for her hands and she dropped her spoon and let him hold them while he played with her quivering fingers that were cold.

"Don't be afraid, Norah. I would never hurt you."

"Why didn't you make yourself known to me at the convention? Why did you take me home, but never come back? Did you know who I was then?"

Norah bombarded him with questions and then pulled her hands away, desiring to run out of the diner, to find Meg at the store, and to go home. Home? She had no home of her own! She and her baby were alone in New York City! Ireland was no longer a home she could go to and her da and mam could not give her a home!

"I was ashamed, Norah, me having the devil gone the once over with and no longer the friend you once knew."

Sean pulled coins from his pocket, throwing them on the table.

"I have money enough...blood money though it is. But if you don't object to me using this money for good, I'll hire a hack to return you to your husband and home. You look poorly, Norah, and a woman in your condition, now, shouldn't be out like ye are. And besides, 'tis a sad day today, not just because of the rain trying to wipe away the sins of this city, but because the money hoarded up by the swell heads and even by the poor ones squirreling some away to send home, is now gone. Gone!"

Sean put his head close to Norah and whispered, "And I'm right glad I didn't put the money I made sellin' me soul to the devil into the banks. Like an ole woman, Norah, I sewed up my money in me pants so no one, now, would ever know."

He stood and reached out his hand to help her up, but Norah didn't take it, but looked resolutely in front of her.

"Come now, Norah, yer husband will be worrying over you and the baby, and if I were him, I'd not let you out of me sight because of your condition and beauty—"

"I have no husband...I have no husband, Sean, and no father for this babe...," she said quietly.

Sean sat back down opposite Norah. He felt lightness and hope come into him for the first time in months.

"I'll not ask you to tell me your story, Norah, for my own is dark and sinister and I've no right to judge—"

"My husband and I were going to England and then on to Ireland. We'd been married on the ship and then a storm came and he died, as well as many others. Me...I lived... and the baby lived..."

The baby thrust a small fist into her belly and Norah leaned over the table and took Sean's hands in hers.

"I loved him, Sean. I loved him like I never loved anyone else. And there's no more love in me for anyone, except for this baby."

She didn't know why she felt compelled to say this. Maybe it was Murray's baby reminding her to be true to him.

"Then you and the baby need to be going home where it is warm and safe, now," Sean responded and helped her out of the booth.

He hailed a carriage for Norah and promised to come by to visit her in a few days. He had never become a gentleman, but because he had watched them with a keen eye, he knew someday he would be able to get away with their airs and polished ways. And now he was determined to do so to capture the heart of Norah McCabe. He stood and watched the carriage move down the street with the first girl he had given his heart to. He felt his life being corralled into prime pasture that could only happen in America, a land where freedom rang so loudly, integrity was often drowned out. Nevertheless, the choice for good from here on out, would always be his.

A month after Norah gave birth to her daughter, Katharine Marion Murray McCabe, Mam went for a long visit to Rochester, New York. Da's sister, Bridgit, and her family had lived there for years. Da was doing well enough working on the rails and was sending enough money so Mam could travel upstate and take a long holiday. She promised Norah she would return soon to visit her grandchildren, four altogether now, including Meg's three children. She wrote a letter to Norah and Meg once a week and it was clear that the country air had renewed her strength and enlivened her mind. Mam spoke highly of the country and expressed desire that they all live there someday. She had been to Corning, Ithaca, and the surrounding Finger Lakes, and described it as being as beautiful as Ireland. Norah felt that when Da returned from the west, it wouldn't be to the city, but to the country with Mam. For now, all was well with her soul concerning her family, and although she missed Da immensely, their letter exchanges were enough to stay close to him.

Katharine Marion Murray McCabe! The child was named Katharine after her sister, Kate; Marion after her mam; and Murray after the babe's own father. The McCabe name was a reminder that her daughter would always be betrothed to Ireland. Norah was wont to whisper, "Katie Marion, dear Katie Marion," as she cuddled and nursed the child, sitting in a well-cushioned rocker Da had bought for her. He had mailed money requesting specifically that it be spent for the rocking chair.

"My daughter will be rockin' me grandbabe in style," he said in his letter, a letter she did not share with Meg, who had never had a rocking chair for her babies. But Meg never nursed for long and the cuddling was sparse, for she was back at the shop selling hats and working at the Astor as soon as her children were of school age.

Norah and Nellie Gorman shared a two bedroom apartment and for Norah, it was a luxury to have her own bedroom with little Katie Marion. Not since she was a child in Ireland when she would climb into the bottom of her dresser, had she felt so at home. Home! The struggle to be at home with herself had been the real battle she had engaged in for many years and although there would be plenty more opportunities to settle into herself, for now, there was serenity. And her dresser, her Irish dresser, was still with her after all these years, sitting regally and charming in the corner of her bedroom. One day she placed sleeping Katie Marion on the bottom of the cupboard and carefully shut the doors. Norah lay down beside the dresser, closed her eyes, and prayed for her daughter. This gesture became a baptism and anointing of her history and her people's history over her child's spirit. She never told anyone she had done this, but felt assured this symbolic act was known by her God whom she still invoked in her own unique way.

Norah returned to sewing, but not to altering expensive used gowns this time. She designed and sewed her own hats, selling them to milliners in New York. And after James Harrigan got over his heartache, he hired her occasionally to write for his newspaper. She wasn't without her demons—memories of the Hunger, the abduction, the shipwreck and the loss of Murray came bearing great sorrow at times. She also fiercely saved her earnings for she wanted Katie Marion to have an education and a life that was as grand as any well-born American woman.

New York and America were rapidly changing and Irish Catholics were still despised, but they were a spirited and complex ethnic group that would grow and become a people to be seriously reckoned with. There were now many gifted Irish Catholic luminaries dwelling in New York City, Boston, and all the major cities. Time was marching on and Norah vowed to dance to the beats of change in her new country.

On a September day a year after Katie Marion was born, Norah was sitting in her living room sketching a new design for a hat. It was going to be sold to a factory that would reproduce as many hats as the milliners in New York could sell. If this design did well, it would be bought by other factories in other states, even in the South. Katie Marion was with her Aunt Meg and cousins for the day and Norah expected them to come walking into the apartment any minute. She had promised to make them an excellent dinner, and the roast in the oven was probably going to be tough and not up to Meg's liking, but at least there would be enough food for all of them, she thought, contentedly. Enough food—how wonderful it was to have enough food. She didn't like to cook, but between Nellie and herself, they managed quite well. It had been a real feat this day to make a large dinner for Meg, her three children, herself, and Katie Marion, especially in the suffocating heat.

Norah put down her charcoal pencil and pushed away the pattern she had drawn. It was nearly finished for tomorrow's deadline, but she still wanted to add some delicate details to the hat—small cheerful morning glory flowers swirling around the back and side. She took in a deep breath and sighed happily but nervously. Would she forever doubt herself, worrying that this good fortune that had come from diligent and persistent work would not last?

There was a knock on the door and Norah hurried to answer it. Meg wouldn't knock on the door and neither would Nellie. Who could it be? She rushed to open it and there stood Sean, dressed in a fine suit of clothing, his hat in his hand, and a broad smile on his face.

"I'm thinking I might be inhaling a fine roast, turnips, carrots, and…," he hesitated, closing his eyes and taking in a long breath, "… and yes, I do smell some spuds!"

"Come in, Sean…you're invited, although you've not been properly asked. I'd think a gentleman, and I do believe you might be thinking you are one the way you're dressed in all your fancy duds, would not just show up at someone's door sniffing the good food being prepared."

Norah laughed and reached for Sean's arm to pull him inside. He stumbled in, quickly shutting the door with his foot, and then dropped his hat onto the floor. Norah closed her eyes and opened her arms for him to enter into her embrace. When Sean's strong and muscled body pressed onto Norah's, it became malleable; like clay that had been formed into one thing, but now was softening and molding into something else. It was like that for Sean every time they came together. But it was never just once, this making…and it wasn't just for him. Norah, too, was surrendering to love's way that was not so much changing the shape of her, but stamping her with more patterns of beauty and texture that matched what was already present.

They released one another and Sean pulled a royal blue scarf patterned with Celtic knots and circles out of his coat pocket. He wrapped it around Norah's neck and then placed his hands on her shoulders. He was slightly taller than she was, but his body fit well with hers. His sandy colored hair possessed traces of the original red, his freckles had lightened and many of them had merged and flowed into the creases underneath his large brown eyes that still shone with liveliness and youth. His spirit and enthusiasm for life hadn't faltered, in spite of his many struggles and travails over the years. He had been hungry, married and divorced, imprisoned slaves and carried them across the seas, and now he had come home to Norah McCabe.

"You'll be going out on the town with me tonight, my queen, my Irish queen. I've already talked to Nellie about watching Katie Marion so we can step out to Pete Williams place and do a little dancing, just like the ole days when you were the wee one and I was your Irish lad with American stars in me eyes."

Norah McCabe stood back from Sean and with her arms to her sides and her green eyes sparkling, danced a lively jig to the music in her head and heart.

Epilogue

Norah McCabe never returned to Ireland. She designed ladies' fashionable hats that eventually were factory made and sold throughout major cities in the country. Her label was patented and in vogue for ten years, mostly in New York City. She and her Katie Marion were comfortably provided for during this time and later, Norah took up the pen to occasionally write for *Lady Godey's Magazine* as well as for the *Irish-American*. Sean remained in her life until he died in a construction accident eight years later. She was at peace with the love she had experienced in her marriage to Murray and then in her relationship with Sean. The loss of Sean followed with the loss of her father and it was a few years before she was able to feel sound in mind and spirit again. Mam continued to live in the country in New York State and there were many visits, back and forth, throughout the years. Two years after Norah gave birth to Katie Marion, an orphan baby girl was placed on the door-step of Nellie's and Norah's apartment. Nellie adopted the child and the two children grew up together. Nellie and Norah remained friends and bought a home together, living full and productive lives right into their seventies. Norah never gave up going to dance halls on occasion and doing Irish dancing, as well as other dances of the day. When Norah was dying, she asked Katie Marion to promise she would always keep the Irish dresser and make certain that it stayed in the family. In her grief, the day after Norah died, Katie Marion opened the dresser and found her grandmother's red shawl, her mother's royal blue scarf, and an inscription:

> *"Hope dances in the darkness and believes in the Lover*
> *who casts light at our feet."*

Cynthia G. Neale

Cynthia G. Neale is a native of the Finger Lakes region of New York and now resides in an antique house in New Hampshire with her husband and a few pets. She has long possessed a deep interest in the tragedies and triumphs of the Irish during The Great Hunger. She enjoys Irish set dancing; traveling, especially to Ireland; reading; art classes and painting; baking fanciful desserts; hiking; kayaking; creating events for food, dance, and fund raising; laughing until it hurts; and dreaming about possibilities. *Norah* is her first historical novel for adult readers. She is also the author of *the young adult novels, The Irish Dresser, A Story of Hope during The Great Hunger (An Gorta Mor, 1845–1850)* and *Hope in New York City, The Continuing Story of The Irish Dresser.* Ms. Neale also writes plays, short stories, and essays, and holds a B.A. in Writing and Literature from Vermont College.

♣ ♣ ♣

Author's Website: www.cynthianeale.com
Author's Blog: cynthianeale.wordpress.com

Publisher's Website:
www.luckypress.com/cynthianeale.html

View the book trailer for *Norah*:
www.youtube.com/user/LuckyPressLLC

Breinigsville, PA USA
18 February 2011
255849BV00001B/6/P